Orphan Dinah

by

Eden Phillpotts

Double 9
BOOKS

Orphan Dinah
by Eden Phillpotts

ISBN: 978-93-64281-23-2

Published by

DOUBLE 9 BOOKS

2/13-B, Ansari Road
Daryaganj, New Delhi – 110002
info@double9books.com
www.double9books.com
Tel. 011-40042856

ABOUT THE AUTHOR

Eden Phillpotts (1862–1960) was a prolific English author, poet, and dramatist known for his diverse literary output, which spanned novels, plays, poetry, and short stories. Born in Mount Abu, India, Phillpotts spent much of his childhood in Devon, England, a region that would later influence his writing significantly. Phillpotts' literary career began with poetry, but he soon gained recognition for his novels and plays, which often depicted rural life in Devon and the complexities of human relationships. His works are noted for their vivid portrayal of characters, rich descriptive prose, and exploration of psychological depth. One of Phillpotts' notable achievements was the creation of the "Dartmoor cycle" of novels, which captured the rugged beauty and folklore of Dartmoor, a region he knew intimately. These novels, such as "The Three Brothers" (1914) and "Widecombe Fair" (1913), are celebrated for their atmospheric depiction of Dartmoor's landscape and its influence on the lives of its inhabitants. In addition to his regional novels, Phillpotts wrote in various genres, including historical fiction, mystery, and supernatural tales. His versatility as a writer allowed him to explore a wide range of themes, from social issues to the supernatural, often with a keen eye for detail and a deep understanding of human nature. Throughout his long career, Phillpotts remained dedicated to his craft, producing a body of work that continues to be appreciated for its literary merit and its insight into the human condition. His contributions to English literature have left a lasting impact, cementing his place among the notable writers of his time.

CONTENTS

CHAPTER I
THE HILLTOP

The spectacle of a free horizon from Buckland Beacon, at the southern rampart of Dartmoor, challenges the least discerning eye by the accident of its immensity, and attracts an understanding vision for weightier reasons. Beheld from this high place, Dart Vale and the land beyond it afford a great composition of nature, orbicular and complete. Its obvious grandeur none can question, but there is much more to be said for it, and from beneath the conspicuous and rhetorical qualities there emerge enduring distinctions. The scene belongs to an order of beauty that does not grow old. Its sensitiveness to light and the operations of the sky; its gracious, yet austere, composition and its far flung arena for the masques and interludes of the dancing hours render it a centre of sleepless variation. Its native fabrics, now gay, now solemn, are a fit habit for the lyrical and epic seasons, and its garments are transformed, not only by the robings and disrobings of Spring and Winter, but at a point's change in the wind, at a rise or fall of temperature. These delicacies, with the more patent magic of fore-glow and dawn, sunset and after-glow, crepuscule and gloaming, are revealed under the most perfect imaginable conditions; for, by many chances and happy hazards, earth here responds to air in all its heights and depths so completely that each phenomenon finds all needful for fullest achievement. One might study the vision a thousand times, yet find no picture resemble another, even in detail of large forms; for the actual modelling changes, since light and atmosphere deal with forest, rock and ridge as though they were plastic—suppressing here, uplifting there, obliterating great passages at one moment and erecting into sudden prominence things concealed at another. The hill sinks at the pressure of a purple shadow; the unseen river suddenly sparkles its presence at a sunbeam.

In this hour, after noon on a day of mid September, the light was changing, not gradually at the sun's proper declension, but under the forces of a south-west wind bringing up vapour at twenty miles an hour from the distant sea.

From the rounded and weathered masses of the Beacon, the hill sloped abruptly and a receding foreground of dying fern and grey, granite boulders broke on a gap of such extent that earth, reappearing far below, was already washed by the milky azure of the air, through which it glimmered and receded and presently again rose to lofty lands beyond. The ground plan was a mighty cup, over which the valley undulated, rising here to knap and knoll, falling there into coombs and plains, sinking to its lowest depths immediately beneath the view point, where Dart wound about lesser hills, not small in themselves, yet dwarfed by the greatness of the expanse and the loftiness of the horizon's brim. Upon that distant and irregular line, now melting into the thick air, border heights and saliencies sank and rose, repeating on a vaster scale the anatomy of the river basin. They lifted through the hazes until they faded upon the sight into the gathering clouds, that loomed still full of light, above their grey confines. The sea was long since hidden.

A chief quality of this spectacle appeared in the three dissimilar and different coverings that draped it. The body of the earth lay wrapped in a triple robe, and each garment was slashed and broken, so that its texture flowed into and revealed the others. Every furlong of these rolling leagues, save only where the river looped and twined through the middle distance, was clad with forest, with field, or with wilderness of heath and stone; and all, preserving their special qualities, added character of contrast to their neighbours. There was not a monotonous passage from east to west in this huge spectacle. Tilth and meadow oozed out through coppice and hanger; the forests ascended the steep places and fledged the hills, only drooping their dark wings where furze and stone climbed higher still, until they heaved upon the sky. The immemorial heights changed not, save to the painting of the seasons; the woods, that seemed as ancient as they, were largely the work of man, even as the tesselated patterns of the fields that spread, shorn of their corn, or still green with their roots, among them. The verdant patchwork of mangel and swede, the grey of arrish, and the gloom of freshly broken earth bosomed out in gentle arcs among the forests, breaking their ragged edges with long, smooth billows of colour. They shone against the summer sobriety of the trees, for the solid masses of the foliage were as yet scarcely stained with the approaching breath of the fall. But woodlands welcomed the light also, and the sunshine, though already softened by a gathering haze that advanced before the actual clouds, still beat into the copse and spinney, to fringe with a nimbus of pale gold the boss of each great tree and outline it from the rest. Light rained and ran through the multitude of the trees, drowning their green and raying all their faces with a dim and delicate fire.

In a gap southward, shrunk to velvet tapestry among clumps and sheaves of pine and oak, spread the lawns of Holne Chase—great park lands, reduced by distance to a garden. There the last sun gleam wakened a transient emerald; then it was gone, as a jewel revealed for a moment and hidden in its casket again.

The woods of Buckland bear noble timber and each tree in many a glen is a giant, thrusting upward from vast bole to mossy branch, until its high top ascends among its neighbours to sunlight and storm. They are worthy of the hills that harbour them, and in their combined myriads affect the operations of the air, draw the rain clouds for their own sustenance and help to create the humidity that keeps Dart Vale so dewy and so green. Down and down they roll endlessly, sinking away into the likeness of a clinging moss; for seen afar, they look no more upon this great pattern of rising and falling earth, than a close integument. Their size is lost against the greater size of the undulations they clothe; they shrink to a close pelt for the land— no heavier than the leagues of the eagle fern, or the autumnal cloth of purple and gold flung upon the hills above them.

To-day the highest lights were in the depths, where Dart flashed at a fall, or shone along some placid reach. She was but a streak of polished silver seen from aloft, and her manifold beauties hidden; while other remote spots and sparks of light that held the eye conveyed no detail either. They meant a mansion, or the white or rosy wash on cottage faces. A grey smudge, sunk in the green to westward, was a village; a white lozenge in the woods beneath, the roof of a moorland church. Here and there blue feathers of wood smoke melted upward into the oncoming clouds; and thinly, through vapours beyond, like a tangle of thread, there twined high roads, ascending from invisible bridges and hamlets to the hills.

And then, little by little, detail faded and the shadows of the clouds grew denser, the body of the clouds extended. Still they were edged with light, but the light died as they thickened and lumbered forward, spreading their pinions over the Vale. The air gradually grew opaque, and ridge after ridge, height after height, disappeared in it. They were not blotted out, but washed away, until the fingers of the rain felt dumbly along the bosom of Buckland Beacon, dimmed the heath and furze to greyness, curled over the uplifted boulder, found and slaked the least thirsty wafer of gold or ebony lichen that clung thereto.

A young man, who had been standing motionless upon the Beacon, felt the cool brush of the rain upon his face and woke from his reverie. He was of a recipient, intelligent aspect, and appeared to admire the great spectacle spread before him; but whether, behind the thing seen, any deeper emotion existed for him; whether to the outward and visible sign there responded any inward and spiritual grace, was a question not to be answered immediately. He prepared to descend, where a building stood upon the hill below him half a mile distant. There he was expected, but as yet knew it not.

CHAPTER II
FALCON FARM

Beneath the Beacon, across the great slope that fell from its summit to the river valley, a road ran into the woods that hid Buckland village, and upon the right hand of this highway, perched among open fields, that quilted the southern slope of the heights, there stood a stone house. Here was Falcon Farm, and over it the hawks that had given it name would often poise and soar and utter their complaining cries. The cluster of buildings perched on the hillside consisted of a slate-roofed dwelling house, with cartsheds, a cowhouse, and stable and a fine barn assembled round the farm yard. About them stretched square fields, off some of which a harvest of oats had just been shorn; while others were grass green with the sprawling foliage of turnip. Beneath, between the farmhouse and the wooded road, extended meadows into which fern and heath were intruding ominously. A little wedge of kitchen garden was scooped out of the hill beside the yard and a dry-built wall fell from the shoulder of the Beacon above, broke at Falcon Farm, and with diverging arms separated its field and fallow from the surrounding wild.

The door of the dwelling faced west, and here stood a man talking to a woman.

He was of sturdy build with a clean shaved, fresh-coloured face and head growing bald. But he had plenty of grey hair still and his countenance was plump and little wrinkled. His eyes were grey and, having long learned the value of direct vision in affairs, he fixed them upon people when he talked. Mr. Joseph Stockman declared himself to be in sight of seventy; but he did not appear so much and his neighbours believed this assertion of age no more than an excuse for his manner of life.

Indeed, at this moment, his companion was uttering a pleasantry at the farmer's expense. She had come on an errand from Buckland village, a mile away, and loitered because she esteemed the humorous qualities of Mr. Stockman and herself found laughter a source to existence. She needed this addition. Her lot had not been one of great emotions, or pleasures, for Melinda Honeysett was a widow after three uneven years of marriage. They passed before she was five and twenty, when a drunken husband, riding a horse that would not "carry beer," was pitched off in the night on Dunstone Down and broke his neck. She had no children and now lived with a bedridden father and ministered to him in the village. This had been her life for nearly twenty years. She was a connection of Joseph Stockman through her marriage, for the Bamseys and the Stockmans and the Honeysetts were related, though neither family exactly knew how.

"A day of great events," said the farmer. "My two new hands both coming and, as my manner is, I hope the best, but fear the worst."

"A horseman and a cowman, so Susan said."

"Yes. But that means more than the words on a little place like this, as I made clear. In fact, they've got to do pretty much everything—with such help as I can give and Neddy Tutt."

"Hope they'll be all right. But they mustn't count on a poor, weak, old man like you, of course."

Mr. Stockman looked into Melinda's face. She was a chubby, red-haired woman built on massive lines with a bosom that threatened to burst its lavender print, and a broad, beamy body beneath. She had a pair of pale blue eyes and a finely modelled mouth, not devoid of character. Her teeth were neglected. She wore a white sunbonnet, which threw a cool shadow over her face, and carried a basket, now full of small carrots and large lettuces.

"You poke your fun at me, forgetting I've done ten men's work in my time and must slack off," he said. "Because, thanks to plain living and moderation in all things, and the widowed state with all its restfulness, I don't look my age, that's not to say I don't feel it, I can assure you. There's certain rights I owe to myself—the only person as ever I did owe anything to in my life—and even if I was fool enough to want to make a martyr of myself, which I'm not—even so Soosie-Toosie would never let me."

"I'm sure she wouldn't."

"My daughter knows where the shoe pinches; and that's in my breathing parts. Often I'll stand to work like a young man, knowing all the time I shall have to pay for it with a long rest after."

"Poor chap!"

He shook his head.

"You be among the unbelievers I see—that's your father's bad work. But since he don't believe in nothing, I can't hope he'll ever believe in me."

"But the new men. Tell me about them. What are they like?"

"Ah, you females! It's always the outside of a man as interests you. For my part it was what their papers and characters were like that I had to think about; and even so I've took one largely on trust."

"You're such a trustful creature, Joe."

"I like to trust. I like to do unto others as they should do unto me. But it's a disappointing rule of life. To be above the staple of your fellow creatures is to get a lot of shocks, Melinda; but you can only set a good example; you can't make people follow it. One man I have seen, t'other I have not. Thomas Palk, the horseman—so to call him—is in sight of middle-age and a towser for work. He's leaving Haccombe, down Newton Abbot way, because his master's son is taking up his job. A very good man by all accounts, and he understands the position and knows what lies before him. A faithful-looking man and I hope he'll prove so. Plain as a bit of moor-stone—in fact a mighty ugly man; but an honest face if I know anything."

"Sounds all right."

"T'other I haven't seen. He comes from up country and answered my advertisement. Can't give no character direct, because his master's died sudden. But he's been along with him for nearly five years, and it was a bigger place than this, and he writes a very good letter. In fact an educated man seemingly, and nobody's the worse for that if it don't come between them and work. Though I grant it be doing so."

"So father says."

"Lawrence Maynard he's called. I've engaged him and hope for the best. Both free men—no encumbrances. I hope, with my gift of making the darkness light where farming is concerned, they'll soon be pulling their weight and getting things all ship-shape."

"Father says nobody knows better than you what work means; but somebody else has always got to do it."

"A wonderful man your father; yet I'm very much afraid he'll go to hell when the end comes, Melinda."

"He's not."

A ginger-coloured lurcher appeared. It was a gaunt and hideous dog with a white muzzle. Behind it came a black spaniel and a white, wire-haired fox-terrier.

"Us must get to work," said Mr. Stockman. "Soosie-Toosie wants a brace of rabbits for supper to-night and I'd best to fight for 'em afore the rain comes. It have been offering since morning and will be on us afore nightfall."

The dogs, apparently understanding, sat round with their eye on Joseph.

"If your godless parent was to see these poor creatures to work, I can tell you what he'd say, Melinda. He'd say thicky spaniel was like me—knows her job very well indeed and prefers to see the younger dogs doing it. And why not?"

"No use growing old if you don't grow artful," admitted Melinda.

"Of course it ban't—here's the girl. What's the matter now, Soosie? The rabbits? I be just going after 'em."

But Miss Stockman, Joseph's only child, had not come about the rabbits. She was a woman resembling her father in no respect. Her hair was black, lustreless and rough, her brown face disfigured by a "port wine" stain that descended from her forehead to her cheek. Her expression was anxious and careworn, and though large-boned and powerfully made, she was thin. She had brown, dog-like eyes, a mouth with sad lips and a pleading voice, which seemed to have the same querulous note as the hawks that so often hung in air above her home.

"Mr. Maynard's box have come, father," she said. "Be he to live in the house, or to go in the tallet over the stables? Both rooms are sweet and ready for 'em."

"Trust you for that, Soosie," declared Melinda.

"The horseman goes over the stables, as being the right and proper place for him," said Mr. Stockman. "And if there was a dwelling room over the cows, the cowman would go there. But there is not, so he'll come in the house."

"Right then," answered his daughter. "Mr. Maynard comes in the house; Mr. Palk goes over the hosses."

Susan disappeared and Mrs. Honeysett prepared to depart.

"And you tell your father that so soon as the woodcock be back—not long now—he'll have the first. I don't bear no malice."

"We all know that. And when you shoot it, you come in and have a tell with father. You do him good."

"And you too I hope?"

"Of course you do—such a long-sighted man as you."

She descended down the farm road to the highway beneath, and Joseph, getting his gun, went upwards with his rejoicing dogs into the fern brakes on the side of the Beacon.

Here, in the pursuit of the only exercise he really loved, Joe Stockman forgot his alleged years. He was a wonderfully steady shot, though it suited him to pretend that failing sight interfered very seriously with his sport; but he excelled still in the difficult business of snapping rabbits in fern. Thus engaged, with his dogs to help him, he became oblivious of weather and it was not until the sight of an approaching stranger arrested him that he grew conscious of the rain. Then he turned up his collar over his blue woollen shirt and swore.

The man who had recently surveyed Dart Vale from the summit of the rocks above, was now descending, and seeing the farmer, turned his steps towards him. He was a slight-built but well-knit youth of seven or eight and twenty. He stood an inch under six feet and was somewhat refined in appearance. His face was resolute and cleanly turned, his skin clear and of a natural olive, that his open-air life had tanned. He wore a small, black moustache over a stern mouth, and his eyes were very dark brown and of a restless and inquiring expression. He wore rough, old tweeds, a little darned at the seat, and on his left arm over the elbow was a mourning band. His legs were cased in tawny gaiters; he had a grey cap on his black hair and in his hands he carried an ash sapling with which, unconsciously from habit, he smote his leg as he walked.

"Sorry to spoil sport," he said, in a quick, clear voice somewhat low pitched, "but I'm a stranger in these parts and want Falcon Farm. Be I right for it?"

"Very right indeed," answered Mr. Stockman. "In fact, so right that it's under your nose. There's Falcon Farm, and I'm the farmer, and I guess you're Lawrence Maynard, due to-day."

The other smiled and his habitual solemnity lifted off his face.

"That's right. I walked from Bovey, because I wanted to have a look at the country."

"And what d'you think of it?"

"Fine. After flat Somerset it makes your legs wake up."

"I dare say it would. There's nothing like a hilly country for tightening the muscles. The Shire hosses find that out when they come here. Yes, that's Falcon Farm. And there's the cows—all red Devons."

The newcomer looked down upon a little cluster of kine grazing in a meadow.

"A beautiful spot sure enough. And snug by the look of it."

"Nothing to grumble at for high land. But it calls for work. I've been here five and twenty year and made it what it is; but I'm old for my age, along of hard labour in all weathers, and can't do all I would no more. However, we'll tell about it later when my other new man, Thomas Palk, arrives. Horseman, he is; but, as I explained, you and him are going to be my right and left hand now, and I can see you're the quick sort that will justify yourself from the first."

"I hope so."

"Heave up them rabbits then, and we'll go down along. I can stop a bird or beast still, though getting cruel dim in the eye."

Maynard picked up three heavy rabbits and they went down the hill together.

"We're a small party," explained Joe, "but very friendly, easy people—too busy to waste time on differences. And you and Palk will find yourselves very comfortable I hope. There's only me and my daughter, Miss Stockman, who rules us men, and a young boy, Neddy Tutt, whose making up into a useful hand. At hay harvest and corn harvest I hire. We've just got home our oats. For the roots, we can pull them ourselves. Of the men who have left me, one went for faults, and we can let the past bury the past; t'other found the winter a thought too hard up here and have gone down to the in-country. He's wrong, but that's his business."

The newcomer felt favourably impressed, for Mr. Stockman had great art to win strangers. He promised to be a kindly and easy man, as he declared himself to be.

Lawrence patted the dogs, who sniffed round him with offers of friendship, and presently all returned together.

CHAPTER III
SUPPER

"I must go and change my coat," said the farmer as they entered the house place. "There was a time when I laughed at a wet jacket, same, no doubt, as you do; but that time's past. Here's my daughter. She'll show you your room."

Susan shook hands and her hurried, fitful smile hovered upon the new arrival.

"Your box be come and I'll give you a hand up," she said. "Your room's in the house at the end of the passage-way facing east. A very comfortable room I hope you'll find."

"Thank you, miss. But I'll fetch up the box if you'll show the way."

He shouldered it and followed her.

"Us'll be having dinner in a minute," she said. "Faither likes it at half after one. Mr. Palk ban't arriving till the afternoon."

During the afternoon Mr. Palk did arrive. He drove up from Ashburton in a trap hired at an inn and brought his luggage with him. He proved a broad and powerful man of fifty, iron grey, close bearded and close cropped. His head was set on a massive neck that lifted above heavy shoulders. His features were huddled together. His nose turned up and revealed deep nostrils; his mouth was large and shapeless; his eyes were steadfast. He proved a man with great powers of concentration. Thus his modest intelligence took him farther than many quicker wits lacking that gift. He did not see much beyond his immediate vision, but could be clear-sighted enough at close range. He had no humour and received impressions slowly, as a child; but grasped them as a child. A light touch was thrown away on Mr. Palk, as his new master soon found. Nod or wink were alike futile as means of suggestion: it was necessary to speak plainly that he might grasp a point. But, once grasped, the matter might safely be left. He never forgot.

At tea that night Joe Stockman expatiated on the situation and his new men listened, while the lad, Neddy Tutt, a big, fair youth, intently regarded them and endeavoured to judge their probable attitude to himself. He was inclined to like both, but doubted not they were on their best behaviour at present and might develop character averse from his interests.

"There's no manner of doubt that we're a little behind," confessed the master. "There are things you'll be itching to put right this autumn, I expect; and I doubt if men like you will rest till we're up to the mark again. When I was young, I had a hawk's eye for danger, and if I saw the thistles gaining on the meadow-land, or the fern and heath getting in while our backs was turned, I'd fight 'em tooth and nail and scarcely rest in my bed till they was down and out. On Dartmoor the battle's to the strong, for we're up against unsleeping forces of Nature as would rather hinder than help. In a word the work's hard, but I lead the way, so far as my weight of years allow it; and, what's more to the point, as you'll find, is my ideas on the subject of food and money. The money you know about; the food you don't. I attach a very great deal of importance to food, Mr. Palk."

Thomas Palk nodded.

"Them as work did ought to eat," he said.

"They did; and I'm often shocked in my observing way to see farmers that don't appear to think so. We keep a generous table here and a good cook likewise, for what my daughter don't know about a man's likes and dislikes in the matter of food ain't worth knowing. As to hours, what I say is that in private service, for that is how you must look at yourselves with me, hours are beside the question. Here's the work and the work must be done; and some days it's done inside seven hours I shouldn't wonder, and some days it's not done inside eight. But only the small mind snaps and snarls for a regulation hour, and it is one of the most mean things to a man like me, who never thought of hours but only the work, that poor spirits here and there be jealous of the clock and down tools just because of the time of day. For look at it. We ain't all built on the same pattern, and one man can do his sort of work an hour a day quicker than another, whether it is ploughing, or harvesting or what not; and the other man can do something else an hour a day quicker than he can. So I'm for no silly rules, but just give and take to get the work done."

"A very self-respecting sort of way, and much what I'm used to," said Maynard.

"Same with liquor," continued Joe. "On the subject of liquor, I take a man as I find him. I drink my beer and take my nightcap also, and there's beer and cider going; and if in drouthy weather a man says, 'I want another half pint,' the barrel's there. I'm like that. I like to feel the respect for my people that they always get to feel for me. But spirits, no. I might, or I might not of an evening say to you, 'Have a spot from my bottle, Palk'; but there wouldn't be no rule."

"I'm teetotal myself," said Maynard, "but very fond of cold tea in working hours."

"Good. You'll never have less cold tea than you want, be sure."

"I be a thirsty man," confessed the elder. "Beer's my standby and I'm glad you grant it; but I only drink when I'm thirsty, though that's often, owing to a great freedom of perspiration. But no man ever saw me bosky-eyed, and none ever will."

"All to the good, Palk. So there it stands. And one more thing: till you know the ropes and my manners and customs, always come to me when in doubt. Your way may be a good way, but where there's two ways, I like mine, unless you can prove yours better. That's reasonable—eh?"

"Very reasonable," admitted Maynard.

"The horses are a middling lot and can be trusted to do their work. I'm buying another at the Ashburton Fair presently. My sheep—Devon long wools crossed with Scotch—are on the Moor, and we'll ride out Sunday and have a look at 'em. I'm buying pigs next week at a sale over to Holne. The cows are a very fine lot indeed. We sell our milk to Ashburton and Totnes."

He proceeded amiably until the cows were lowing at the farmyard gate. Then Maynard departed with Neddy Tutt to the milking, and Palk, who would begin to plough the stubble on the following day, started alone to walk round the yard and inspect the horses and machinery.

"A quiet couple of men," said Joe to his daughter, when they had gone; "but I like the quiet ones. They save their wind for their work, which is where it ought to be."

"Mr. Maynard don't look particular strong," she said.

"Don't he? To my eye he's the wiry sort, that wear as well and better than the mighty men. Don't you go axing him after his health whatever you do. It often puts wrong ideas in their heads. We take health for granted. I'm the only person in this house where health comes in I should hope."

"You'd best turn 'em on to the fern so soon as you can," answered Susan. "Landlord was round again, when you were up over, seeing hounds meet at eight o'clock last week."

"What an early man he is!"

"Yes, and he said he'd hoped to see the work begun, because it frets him a lot that any land of his should go to rack. And he said that he'd have thought one like you, with a name for high farming, would have hated it as much as him."

"That's his cunning. The Honourable Childe's a very clever man, and I respect him for it. He knows me and I know him. The field will be as clean as a new pin before Christmas, I shouldn't wonder."

"You won't get your regular box of cigars from the man if it ain't, I expect."

"Oh yes, I shall. He's large-minded. He knows his luck. I like him very well, for he sees the amusing side of things."

"He weren't much amused last week."

Her father showed a trace of annoyance.

"What a damper you are, Soosie-Toosie! Was ever the like? You always take the dark view and be grim as a ghost under the ups and downs of life. If you'd only copy me there. But 'tis your poor mother in you. A luckier woman never walked you might say; yet she was never hopeful—always on the look out for the rainy day that never came."

"I'm hopeful enough to-day anyhow. I think the new men be the sort to suit you."

"Nobody's easier to suit than me," he answered. "Let a labourer but do his duty, or even get in sight of his duty, and I'm his friend."

Susan reminded her father that a kinsman was coming in the evening.

"You know Johnny promised to look in on his way home from Ashburton and take supper along with us."

"So he did. The man's affairs hang fire by the look of it. When's he going to be married I wonder?"

"Might ask him," answered Susan. "Not that he knows I reckon. It's up to her."

When night came John Bamsey duly arrived and shared the last meal of the day.

His father and Mr. Stockman were cousins, or declared themselves to be so, and John always called Joseph "Cousin Joe."

He was one of the water-bailiffs on the river—a position he had held for six months. But he had already given a good account of himself, and his peculiarities of character were such that they made him a promising keeper. He was keen and resolute, with the merciless qualities of youth that knows itself in the right. He was also swift of foot and strong. A poacher, once seen, never escaped him. John entertained a cheerful conceit of himself, and his career was unsullied. He echoed his mother's temperament and was religious-minded, but he had a light heart. He had fallen in love with a girl two years older than himself, and she had accepted him. And now, at twenty-two, John's only trouble was that Dinah Waycott would not name the day.

He was a fair, tall man, with a solid, broad face, small grey eyes and an expression that did not change. He wore an old-fashioned pair of small whiskers and a tawny moustache in which he took some pride.

He greeted the newcomers in friendship and talked about his work on the river. He was frank and hearty, a great chatterbox without much self-consciousness.

"And when's the wedding going to be?" asked Mr. Stockman. "Don't know; but it's about time I did; and I mean to know inside this month. Dinah must make up her mind, Cousin Joe. Wouldn't you say that was fair?"

"Certainly she should. Orphan Dinah took you very near a year ago, and the marriage ought to be next spring in my opinion."

"No doubt it will be," answered John; "but I will have something definite. Love-making is all right, but I want to be married and take the lodge at Holne Chase."

"The lodge Neddy Tutt's parents keep?" said Susan.

"Yes; and by the same token, Neddy, your mother expects you Sunday."

"I be coming," said Neddy Tutt, and John continued. "I'm lodging with 'em, but they're very wishful to be off, and they will be so soon as ever I'm spliced. The Honourable Childe wants me at the lodge and I want to be there."

Susan, who had a mind so sensitive that she often suspected uneasiness in other minds where none existed, was reflecting now, dimly, that the newcomers would not find this subject very interesting. They sat stolidly and quietly listening and eating their supper. Occasionally Maynard spoke to Susan; Palk had not made a remark since he came to the meal.

Now, however, Joe relieved his daughter's care. He enjoyed exposition and, for the benefit of his new men, he explained a relationship somewhat complicated.

"We be talking in the air no doubt for your ears," he said "But I hope you'll feel yourselves interested in my family before long, just as I shall be in your families, if you've got relations that you like to talk about. Me and this young man's father are cousins in a general way of speaking, and his father, by name Benjamin Bamsey, was married twice. First time he married the widow of Patrick Waycott, who was a footman at the Honourable Childe's, lord of Holne Manor, and she come to my cousin Benjamin with one baby daughter, Dinah by name. So the girl, now up home twenty-three, is just 'Orphan Dinah,' because her mother died of consumption a year after she married Mr. Bamsey. Then Benjamin wedded again—a maiden by the name of Faith West; and she's the present Mrs. Ben Bamsey, and this chap is her son, and Jane Bamsey is her daughter. And now Johnny here be tokened to his foster sister, 'Orphan Dinah,' who, of course, ain't no relation of his. I hope I make myself clear."

"Nothing could be clearer," said Lawrence Maynard.

"What did the footman die of?" asked Palk slowly.

"Consumption, same as his wife. In fact the seeds was in the poor girl when Ben took her. But she done very well with him as long as she lived, and he's terrible fond of Dinah."

Palk abstracted himself. One could almost appreciate outward signs of the mental retreat into his shell. He became oblivious with a frowning forehead, committing this family situation to a memory, where it would remain graven for ever.

John took up the talk.

"Father's too fond of Dinah for my peace in a way. You know father— how he dashes at a thing. The moment he heard from mother, who'd found out, that I was gone on Dinah, he swore as nothing would please him better. And he was on my side from the first. In fact if Dinah hadn't wanted me for myself, I believe father would have driven her to take me, for she'd do anything for him. She couldn't love a real father better. She doats upon him."

"He can't spoil her, however. Nothing would spoil Dinah," said Susan.

"And now," continued John, "now that the time's in sight and changes have got to come, father begins to sing small at the thought of losing her. He seemed to have a sort of notion I'd live on at home for ever, and Dinah too. He's like that. He dashes at a thing and forgets how it will touch him when it happens. He don't look all round a subject."

Maynard spoke.

"I hope the young woman is strong," he said. "'Tis rather serious for both parents to have died so young."

"A very natural and thoughtful thing to say," declared Joe. "It shows you've got intellects, Maynard. But, thank God, the girl is sound every way;

in fact, out of the common hearty and nice-looking too—at least Johnny reckons she is."

"A very bowerly maid," said Susan.

"That's right, Soosie-Toosie," chuckled John.

"If she's got a fault, she's too plain-spoken," said Mr. Stockman. "I'm all for direct speech myself and there's nothing like making your meaning clear. It saves time better than any invention. But Dinah—how can you put it? She's got such a naked way of talking. I don't say that the gift of language was given us to conceal our thoughts, because that's a very hard saying, though I know what it means; but I do say it was given us so as we should present our thoughts to our fellow creatures in a decent shape. She's a bit startling at times, Dinah is."

"That's because plain speech be so rare it's always startling," answered John. "We're so used to her, we never think of it at home."

"It ain't she says anything to shock you, when you come to think over it," argued Susan. "It's just plain thinking and going to the root of the matter, which ain't common with most people."

Maynard ventured a sentiment.

"If the young woman says just what she means, it's a very rare thing," he said.

"So it is then," admitted Mr. Stockman. "Few do so—either because they don't want to, or else because they haven't got the words to fit their feelings. There's lots feel more than they're educated to put into speech. But though Dinah haven't got any more words than any other young, ignorant creature, yet she's so inclined by nature to say what she means, that she generally manages to do it."

"Can make herself bitter clear sometimes,'" Johnny assured them. He spoke apparently from experience and memory, and his cheerful face clouded a little.

"No lovers' quarrels I hope," murmured Susan.

"Of course there are," chaffed Joe. "You that have missed the state, Soosie-Toosie, and don't know no more about love than a caterpillar, no doubt think that a lovers' quarrel be a very parlous thing. But it's no more parlous than the east wind in March—is it, Johnny? A frosty breeze may be very healthy and kill a lot of grubs and destroyers, if the ground be properly worked over and the frost can get into it. And so with lovers' quarrels, they do good, if both sides take 'em in a proper spirit."

Maynard laughed.

"I reckon that's true, Mr. Stockman," he said.

"What might you think, Mr. Palk?" asked Susan. She felt the heavy silence of Thomas and knew not, as yet, that he often clothed himself in silence for his own comfort. But he had listened with attention and she thought he must probably have experience.

He declared the reverse, however.

"Couldn't offer an opinion, miss," he replied. "I be of the bachelor persuasion and never felt no feeling to be otherwise. What you might call complete in myself, so far as a man can be."

"You're a loser and a gainer, Thomas," said his new master genially. "You may lose the blessing of a good son, or daughter, and a valuable wife; and you gain also, because you might not have had those fine things, but found yourself in a very different position. You might have had what's better than freedom; but on the other hand you might have had what's a long sight worse."

"And freedom's a very fine thing," added Maynard.

Mr. Stockman loved these questions. He proceeded to examine marriage in all its aspects and left a general impression on the mind of the attentive Mr. Palk that the ideal of achievement was to have loved and lost, and be left with a faithful, home-staying daughter: in fact, Mr. Stockman's own situation. He appeared to hold a brief for the widowed state as both dignified and convenient.

"All the same, father reckons you're the sort will marry again, Cousin Joe," Johnny told him. "He says that such a good-looking man as you, and so popular with the ladies, will surely take another some day, when you'm tired of sporting."

Mr. Stockman shook his head.

"That's like Benjamin—to judge by the outside and never sound the depths. He thinks that his own pattern of mind be the pattern of all. And not a word against him, for a finer pattern of mind and one fuller of the milk of human kindness don't live; but let nobody hope, or fear, any such adventure for me. Me and Soosie-Toosie will go our way, all in all to each other; and the less we have to trouble about ourselves, the more time and thought we can give to our neighbours."

Susan displayed her wan smile at these sentiments. She was in stark fact her father's slave and John well knew it; but he made no comment. Mr.

Stockman seldom said a word that was open to comment on any subject. He gave his views and opinions for what they were worth, but quarrelled with none who might differ from him. Indeed, he never quarrelled with anybody. It was his genius invariably to give the soft answer; and this he did from no particular moral conviction, but as a matter of policy. Life had taught him that friction was seldom worth the trouble; and he had an art to get his way rather by geniality of manner than force of character. He achieved his purpose, and that frequently a hard and selfish purpose, as often as a more strenuous man; but, such was his hearty humanity of approach, that people for the most part found themselves conceding his wishes. He did not, however, hoodwink everybody. A bad bargain is a bad bargain, no matter how charming may be the man with whom it is made; and there were neighbours who did not hesitate to say that Joe was a humbug always playing for his own hand, and better able so to do than many far less gracious and genial.

John Bamsey departed presently, and after he had gone the master of Falcon Farm praised him generously.

"A four-square, fine chap that," he said. "An example to the young fellows. A proper glutton for work. He'll be down on the river for hours to-night, to keep off they baggering salmon poachers. And he goes to church Sundays with his parents and always keeps his temper well in hand. For that matter a water-watcher ought to have a temper, so as the doubtful characters shall know he's not to be trifled with. A forceful chap—a little narrow in his opinions I dare say; but that don't matter when his opinions are sound and on the side of morals and good order. He gets 'em from both parents. And the larger charity will come in time. That's a question of mellowing and years. I can see you men are charitable minded, for I'm a student of character and read people pretty clever, owing to my large experience. Have a spot out of my bottle to-night for luck. Then, I dare say, you won't be sorry to turn in. We're early birds by night and early birds in the morning. I always say the hours before breakfast lay the foundation of the day and break the back of it."

Maynard took no liquor, but drank a cup of tea with Susan, whose solitary dissipation was much tea taken at all possible times. Thomas Palk accepted a glass of whisky and water.

Soon after ten all went to bed.

"Soosie-Toosie will call you at half after five," said Joseph, "and I like, in a general way, to hear Ned start with the milk cart to Ashburton before seven for the milk train. It's always a pain to me not to stir myself till breakfast. I lie awake and hunger for the hour; but lifelong rules have often got to be broke for failing health's sake in sight of seventy, as you'll find in your turn no doubt. Life, as I always say, be all cakes and cream to youth; but it's little more than physic when you be nearing the allotted span. Well, I wish you good night, and if there's anything you lack, tell my daughter to-morrow. I hope we shall be good friends and a lot more than master and man pretty soon."

He shook hands with them both, and while Palk contented himself by saying, "Good night, master," Maynard, who was clearly moved by such comfortable words, echoed them and thanked Mr. Stockman for the manner of his reception.

CHAPTER IV
AT BUCKLAND-IN-THE-MOOR

Like beehives cluster the thatched roofs of Buckland, for the cottages are dwarfed by the lofty trees which soar above them. Oak and ash, pine and beech heave up hugely to their canopies upon the hill slope, and the grey roofs and whitewashed walls of the hamlet seem little more than a lodge of pygmies sequestered in the forest. The very undergrowth of laurel has assumed giant proportions and flings many a ponderous bough across the highway, where winds a road with mossy walls through the forest and the village. Here and there green meadows break the woods and lay broad, bright tracts between the masses of the trees; then glimpses of the Vale beneath are visible through woodland rifts.

The cottage coverings were old and sombre of tone; but on this September day, before the great fall of the leaf, destined presently to sweep like a storm from tree top to earth, sunshine soaked through the interlacing boughs and brought light to the low-browed windows, to the fuchsias and purple daisies in the gardens. It flashed a ruby on the rays of Virginian creepers that sometimes clothed a wall and brightened the white faces of the little dwellings to pale gold. All was very silent about the hour of noon. For a few moments no human form appeared; only a brook poured down from the hills, foamed through its dark, hidden ways, rested at a granite drinking trough beside the road, then trickled on again. A robin sang, and far distant throbbed the note of a woodman's axe.

Midway between the squat-towered church, that stood at the limits of the village to the north-west, and the congeries of cots within the border of the woods, a second rivulet leapt in a waterfall from the hedge at the root of a mighty ash that shook out its serrated foliage a hundred feet above and made the lane a place of shade. The road bent here and the dingle was broken with great stones heavily clad in moss. Above stretched the woods, legion upon legion, their receding intricacies of branch and bough broken by many thousand trunks. Beneath, again the woods receded over steep acclivities to the river valley.

Though the houses were few and small, great distinction marked them. They held themselves as though conscious of their setting, and worthy of it. They fitted into the large and elaborate moulding of the hillside and by their human significance completed a vision that had been less without them. There was a quality of massive permanence in the scene, imparted by the gigantic slope of the hill whereon it was set. It fell with no addition of abrupt edge or precipice, but evenly, serenely from its crown on the naked Beacon above, by passages of heath and fern, by the great forests and sweeps of farmland and water meadows that broke them, down and down past the habitations, assembled like an ants' nest on its side to the uttermost depths of the river valley and the cincture of silver Dart winding through the midst of it.

At a point where the road fell and climbed again through the scattered dwellings there stood two cottages under the trees together. They adjoined, and one was fair to see—well-kept and prosperous, with a tidy scrap of garden before it and a little cabbage patch behind. The straw of the roof was trimly cut and looped heavily over the dormer windows, while above, on a brick stack, four slates were set instead of a chimney pot. But the neighbour cottage presented a forlorn appearance. It was empty; its thatch was scabbed and crusted with weeds and blobs of moss; at one place it had fallen in and the wooden ribs of the roof protruded. A mat of neglected ivy covered the face of the cot and thrust through broken windows into the little chambers. Damp and decay marked all, and its evil fame seemed reflected in its gloomy exterior. For the house was haunted, and since Mrs. Benjamin Bamsey had seen a "wishtness" peering through the parlour window on two successive evenings after the death of the last tenant, none could be found to occupy this house, though dwellings in Buckland-in-the-Moor were far to seek.

Now a man appeared in the road from the direction of the church. He was of an aspect somewhat remarkable and he came from Lower Town, a hamlet sunk in the Vale to the west. Arthur Chaffe combined many trades, as a carpenter in a small village is apt to do. He attended to the needs of a scattered community and worked in wood, as the smith, in iron. He boasted that what could be made in wood, from a coffin to a cider cask, lay in his power. And beyond the varied and ceaseless needs of his occupation, he found time for thought, and indeed claimed to be a man above the average of intelligence. His philosophy was based on religious principle and practice; but he was not ungenial for an old bachelor. He smiled upon innocent pleasure, though the lines that he drew round human conduct were hard and fast.

He was eight and fifty, and so spare that the bones of his face gave it expression. Upon them a dull, yellowish skin was tightly drawn. He was growing bald and shaved his upper lip and cheeks, but wore a thin, grey beard. His teeth were few and his mouth had fallen in. His cheeks puffed out when he ate and spoke, but sank to nothing under the cheek bones when he sucked his pipe. He had a flat nose, and his long legs suggested an aquatic bird, while his countenance resembled a goat and his large and pale brown eyes added to the likeness. His expression was both amiable and animated, and he could laugh heartily. Mr. Chaffe's activities were centripetal and his orbit limited. It embraced Lower Town and Buckland, and occasionally curved to Holne and outlying farms; but he was a primitive, and had seldom stirred out of a ten-mile radius in his life. Had he gone much beyond Ashburton, he had found himself in a strange land. He employed three men, and himself worked from morning to night. His highest flights embraced elementary cabinet-making, and when he did make a piece of furniture on rare occasions, none denied that it was an enduring masterpiece.

He left the high road now, approached the pair of cottages and knocked at the door of the respectable dwelling.

Melinda Honeysett it was who appeared and expressed pleasure.

"So you've come then, Mr. Chaffe. What a man of your word you are!"

"I hope so, Mrs. Honeysett. And very pleased to do anything for you and your father."

"Come in and sit down for five minutes. 'Tis a climb from Lower Town. But people say you can fly so easy as you can walk, and a hill's nought to you."

"We thin blades have the pull of the beefy ones in this country. I sometimes think I'll start a pony; but I like to use my legs and ban't often too tired."

"Will you have a drink and a piece of my seedy cake?"

"I will then and gladly. Milk for choice. How's the Governor?"

"Pretty middling for him. You must see him afore you go. You're one of his pets."

"I'm none so sure of that. But 'tis a longful time since we met. I've been busier than ever this summer. I surprise myself sometimes what I get into twenty-four hours."

"I dare say you do."

Melinda brought the wayfarer refreshment. They sat in a pleasant kitchen, whose walls were washed a pale ochre, making harmony with various brass and copper articles upon the mantel shelf and dresser. The floor was of stone, and in the alcove of the window some scarlet geraniums throve. They spoke of neighbours, and Mr. Chaffe asked a question.

"I hear from Ben Bamsey that his cousin have got two new men at Falcon Farm, and foreigners both."

"So they are. One's youngish, t'other's middle-aged; and Joe says they promise to be treasures. He's much pleased about them."

"Then they're gluttons for work without a doubt."

"So they are seemingly."

"How soft that chap do always fall," mused the carpenter.

"Because he's got the wit to choose where he will fall," answered Mrs. Honeysett. "Joe Stockman has gifts. He's a master of the soft answer."

"Because he knows it pays."

"Well, a very good reason."

"His cleverness and charity come out of his head, not his heart, Mrs. Honeysett. He's the sort may cast his crumbs on the waters, but never unless he sees the promise of a loaf returning."

"You don't like him."

"I wouldn't say I didn't like him. As a man of intellects myself I value brains. He's a clever man."

"He's spoilt a bit. He gets round one you know. There's a great power in him to say the word to a woman he always knows will please her. I properly like him some days; then other days he drives me frantic."

The gruff voice of Mrs. Honeysett's father intruded upon them. It came from a little chamber which opened out of the kitchen and had been converted into his bedroom. His lower limbs were paralysed, but he had a vehicle which he moved by handles, and could thus steer himself about the ground floor of his home.

"I hear Arthur Chaffe," rumbled the voice. "I'll see you, Arthur, afore you go, and larn if you've got more sense than when you was here last."

A gurgle of laughter followed this remark and the visitor echoed it.

"Ah! You bad old blid! No more of your sense, I promise you. We know where your sense comes from!"

"Don't you charge too much for my new gate then—sense, or no sense."

"Whoever heard tell of me charging too much for anything, Enoch?"

"Widow Snow did, when you buried her husband."

Again the slow, heavy laughter followed; but Mr. Chaffe did not laugh. He shook his head.

"Past praying for," he said.

Then he rose and suggested inspecting the old gate and making measurements for the new one.

That matter settled and the price determined, Arthur Chaffe returned to the cottage and found that Mr. Withycombe had travelled in upon his little trolley and lifted himself into a large, dog-eared chair beside the hearth.

He was a heavy man with a big, fresh face that had been exceedingly handsome in his prime, but was now a little bloated and discoloured, since fate had ended for the old sportsman his hard and active existence. He had hunted the Dart Vale Foxhounds for thirty years; then, maimed in the back by a fall, for five years he had occupied the position of indoor servant to a master who was deeply attached to him. Finally had come a stroke, as the result of the old injury, and Enoch was forced to retire. He had now reached the age of sixty-six and was a widower with two sons and one daughter. One boy was in the Royal Navy, the other lived at home and worked in the woods.

Mr. Withycombe had grey eyes, a Roman nose and cheeks of a ruddy complexion. He wore whiskers, but shaved his mouth and chin. He was a laughing philosopher, admired for his patience and unfailing good temper, but distrusted, because he permitted himself opinions that did not conform to the community in which he dwelt. These were suspected to be the result of his physical misfortunes; in reality they were but the effect of his environment. An admiration amounting to passion existed in the large heart of Mr. Withycombe for his former master, and during those years when he worked under his roof, the old fox-hunter had learned educated views on various subjects and modified his own to match them. The Honourable Ernest Childe, of Holne Chase, a lord of three manors, could neither do nor think wrong in Enoch's opinion. He was the paragon, and the more nearly did his fellow creatures take their colour from such a man and such a mind, the better it must be for all—so Mr. Withycombe declared. Others, however, did not agree with him. They followed parson rather than squire, and while admitting that the latter's sterling practice left little to be desired, yet suspected his principles and regretted that his pew in church was invariably empty. They puzzled at the discrepancy and regretted it, because it appeared a danger to the rising generation.

Mr. Chaffe shook the heavy and soft hand that Enoch extended to him.

"And how's yourself?" he asked.

"Half dead, half alive, Arthur. But, thanks be, the half that matters most is alive."

"And it be wise enough to feel patience for the weaker members."

"Now it do," admitted Enoch. "But I won't pretend. When this blow first fell upon me and I knew that my legs would be less use in the world than rotten wood, which at least be good for burning, then I cursed God to hell. However, that's past. I've got my wits and now, along of these spectacles, I can read comfortable again."

He pointed to a little shelf within reach of his hand where stood various works.

"I could wish you'd read some books of mine, Enoch," said Arthur Chaffe.

"So I will then—didn't know you'd got any books."

"Oh yes I have—Sunday reading."

"You chaps that limit yourselves to 'Sunday reading' get narrow-minded," declared Withycombe. "For why? You only see one side of life. I don't blame you, because you've got to do your work on weekdays; but you'd find there's a lot of very fine books just so good on Sunday as Monday. 'The Rights of Man,' for example. There's a proper book, and it don't interfere with the rights of God for a moment."

"Mr. Chaffe be going to ax seventeen and six for the gate and five shillings for the hinges and lachet," said Melinda.

"A very fair price and I shan't quarrel with it."

He handed his tobacco pouch to the visitor. It was covered with otter skin now grown shabby.

Arthur filled his pipe.

"We stand for different things, you and me," he said, "yet, thank God, agree in the virtues. Duty's duty, and a man that's honest with himself can't miss it."

"Oh yes he can, Arthur. There's plenty that be honest enough and don't want to shirk, yet miss the road."

"Because they won't read the sign-posts."

"Now stop!" commanded Melinda. "Talk about something interesting. How's 'Orphan Dinah'? Haven't seen her for a month."

"She's very well. Passed the time of day yesterday. Been helping in the harvest. Ben Bamsey have had the best wheat he remembers. 'Tis harvest thanksgiving with us Sunday week. And something out of the common to thank for this year."

"When's the wedding? You'll know if anybody does—Ben's right hand as you be."

"No, no; his wife's his right hand. But we'm like brothers I grant. In fact, few brothers neighbour so close I dare say. No news of the wedding; and that don't worry Ben. You know what Dinah is to him."

"Nearer than his own I reckon."

"Mustn't say that; but—well, now that the date is only waiting for Dinah, Ben begins to feel what her going will be. No doubt we shall hear soon. Faith Bamsey's at Dinah about it. She reckons it's not fair to Johnny to keep him on the hooks longer."

"More it is."

"Well, I dare say you're right, Mrs. Honeysett. Dinah's the sort that loves liberty; but the maids have got to come to it, and she's a good girl and will go into matrimony fearless."

"Fearless enough," said Enoch. "If she'd been born in a different station of life, how that creature would have rode to hounds!"

"She's more interesting than most young things in my opinion, because there's rather more to her," explained Mr. Chaffe. "With most of them, from the point of our experience, they are pretty easy to be read, and they do what you expect from their characters oftener than not. But she'll surprise you more than many grown-ups for that matter."

"It's something that a man who knows human nature so well as you should be surprised, Arthur," said the old hunter.

The other laughed at a recollection.

"You're pulling my leg I reckon—same as that sly publican, Andrew Gaunter, at the Seven Stars. 'Ah!' he said to me, 'you're a marvel, Chaffe; you get every man and woman's measure to an inch!' I told him I wasn't so clever as all that, because none but God knows all there is to know; but he swore he was right—and proved it by reminding me I'm an undertaker!"

Enoch laughed.

"One for him sure enough. Funny word, 'undertaker.' A good chap is Andrew Gaunter. Many a flip of sloe-gin I've had at his door when hounds met that way. He'd bring it out himself, just for the pleasure of 'good morning.'"

"You often hear the horn from here?"

"I heard it yesterday, and I finger my own now and again."

He looked up to where his hunting horn hung from a nail above the mantel shelf.

"There's no music like it as I always say, though not a sportsman."

"Is it true old Sparrow be gone to the workhouse?" asked Melinda, who loved facts concerning fellow creatures and reduced conversation to personalities when she could.

"It is true," answered Chaffe.

"A sparrow as fell to the ground uncounted then," said Enoch, but the carpenter denied it.

"You mustn't think that. What be the workhouse but a sign of the everlasting mercy put in our minds by a higher power?"

"A bleak fashion of mercy, Mr. Chaffe," answered Melinda.

"Many never know happiness till they get there. Human life have always been a hand to mouth business for most of us. It's meant to be, and I don't believe myself that Providence likes us to look much farther than the points of our noses."

"The great man is him that can, however," argued Mr. Withycombe. "Him as looks a few yards deeper into the mirk of the future than we can soon rises to be famous. He knows there can be no security against nature; but, outside that, he sees there did ought to be security between man and man, since we are reasoning creatures. And he thinks reasoning creatures did ought to be reasonable and he tries to help 'em to be—man and man and nation and nation."

"Good, Enoch. If everybody would fight to be friends as hard as they fight for other things, peace would set in, no doubt."

"To do it, you must come with clean hands, Arthur; but all the nations' hands are dirty. They look back into each other's histories and can't trust. Man's a brigand by nature. It's the sporting instinct as much as anything, and the best sporting nations are the best fighting nations. That's why we're up top."

"Are we?"

"The Honourable Childe always says so. He has chapter and verse for all his opinions."

"He'll drop in on the way home and tell you about a run now and again, same as he did last year, I shouldn't wonder."

"No doubt he will, Melinda."

"A puzzling gentleman," declared Chaffe. "Righteousness and goodwill made alive you may say; and yet don't go to church."

His daughter headed off her father's reply.

"What's this a little bird has whispered to me about Jane Bamsey?" she asked.

"Can't say till I know the particulars."

"That my brother, Jerry, be after her."

"Haven't heard nothing. But you ought to know."

"I've guessed it. Jerry's moonstruck and always looking that way."

"I hope it ain't true," said Enoch. "I don't much care for that maiden. She's spoiled, and she's shifty. She came to see us with her mother. Hard hearted."

"She's no more than a kitten yet, father."

"Yes; but the sort of kitten that grows into a cat devilish quick. I wouldn't wish it for Jerry's sake. He's a man likely to be under the thumb of his wife, so I'd hope a different sort for him."

"Jane's too young for Jerry," declared Melinda. "He's over thirty and she's but eighteen or so. Besides, when Dinah marries John and goes, then Jane will have to turn to and be more to her mother. She's terrible lazy."

Mr. Chaffe shook his head.

"They don't know what it will mean to that house when Dinah leaves it."

"Her step-father does," answered Enoch's daughter. "Dinah's the apple of his eye. But Mrs. Bamsey's looking forward to it on the quiet."

"It's natural in a way. She's always been a thought jealous of her husband's great love for Orphan Dinah. And so has Jane. She'll be glad enough when Dinah's away. And it's up to her, as you say, to fill the gap."

"Which she's not built to do," prophesied Mr. Withycombe.

"We must hope. With responsibility often comes the grace to undertake it."

They chatted a little longer and then, promising the new gate in a fortnight, Arthur Chaffe went on his way.

CHAPTER V
THE ACCIDENT

Though Lawrence Maynard was a man of intelligence far deeper than Thomas Palk, yet the latter began to arrive at a juster conclusion concerning his new life and his new master than did his fellow worker.

Nor was it experience of life that led the horseman to his judgment. Experience of life has little to do with duration of life; and as a gutter-snipe of eight will often know more about it and be quicker to read character than a rural boy of fifteen, so, with men, it is the native power to grind what life brings to the mill that makes the student. Maynard had both seen and felt far more than Palk, yet in the matter of their present environment, Thomas it was who divined the situation correctly. And this he did inspired by that most acute of prompters: self-interest; while precisely in this particular Lawrence Maynard was indifferent. His interests, for one with the greater part of his life still to live, were unusually limited. His own life, by the accident of circumstances, concerned him but little. Chance had altered the original plan and scope so largely that he was now become impassive and so emptied of his old former apprehension and appetite for living, that he did not at present trouble himself to use the good brains in his head. The very work he had chosen to do was not such work as he might have done. It was less than the work he once did; but it contented him now. Yet his activities of mind, while largely sharing an apathy from which it seemed unlikely the future would ever awaken him, were not wholly sunk to the level of his occupation. Sometimes he occupied himself with abstract speculations involving fate and conduct, but not implicating humanity and character.

So he took people at their own valuation, from indifference rather than goodwill, and in the case of his new master, found this attitude create a measure of satisfaction. He liked Mr. Stockman, appreciated his benevolence and took him as he found him, without any attempt to examine beneath the smiling and genial surface that Joe invariably presented. He had proved exceedingly kind and even considerate. He had, in fact, though he knew it not, wakened certain sentiments in the younger man's heart and, as a result of this, while their acquaintance was still of the shortest, moved by a very rare emotion, Maynard challenged his master's friendship by the channel of confidence. Nor did it appear that he had erred. The farmer proved exceedingly understanding. Indeed, he exhibited larger sympathies than he was in reality capable of feeling, for Mr. Stockman, among his other accomplishments, had a royal genius for suggesting that the individual who at any time approached him could count upon his entire and single-hearted attention—nay, his devotion. He appeared to concentrate on his neighbour's welfare as though that were the vital interest of his own life; and it was only the harder-headed and long-memoried men and women who were not deluded, but had presence of mind to wait for results and compare Joe's accomplishment with his assurance.

Thus, after a month at Falcon Farm, Lawrence Maynard honestly felt something like enthusiasm for the master, while Thomas Palk failed of such high emotion. Not that Thomas had anything to quarrel about actively; but weighing Joe's words against his deeds, he had slowly, almost solemnly, come to the conclusion that there was a disparity. He voiced his opinion on a day when he and Lawrence were working together on the great fern slopes under the Beacon. There, some weeks before, the bracken had been mown down with scythes, and now the harvest was dry and ready to be stacked for winter litter. They made bales of the fern and loaded up a haycart.

"The man tighteneth," said Palk. "I don't say it in no unkind spirit and I've nought to grumble at; but it ain't working out exactly same as he said it was going to. I wouldn't say he was trying to come it over me, or anything like that; but he's a masterpiece for getting every ounce out of you. If he worked a bit himself, he wouldn't have so much time to see what we was doing."

"Can't say he asks anything out of reason."

"No, no—more I do; but I warn you. He edges in the work that crafty—here a job and there a job—and such a scorn of regular hours. 'Tis all very well to say when our work's done we can stop, no matter what the hour is; but when is our work done? Never, till 'tis too dark to see it any longer."

Maynard laughed.

"We must suit ourselves. It's a free country. I find him a very understanding man, and friendly."

"So do I, so do I; but I mark the plan he goes on. 'Tis the same with the hosses. I won't say it's not a very good plan for a farmer. Feeds well and pays well and treats well; but, behind all that, will have a little more than his money's worth out of man and beast."

"Can't say I've found him grasping."

"Then I hope to God I'm wrong and 'tis my fancy. Time will show. I'm satisfied if you are; and if his daughter don't feel no call to be uneasy, why for should us?"

"For my part I like work," declared Lawrence. "I may not have been so keen once; but there's very little to my life but work. I've got used to looking at work as about the only thing in the world."

"The first thing, not the only thing," answered Thomas. "There's religion and, in the case of many people, there's their families and the rising generation. We'm bachelors and ban't troubled in that way; but I believe in regular hours myself, so far as you can have 'em in farming. I like to get away from work and just do nothing—with mind and body—for a good hour sometimes. 'Tis a restful state."

Palk started with a full cart presently, while Maynard began to collect fresh masses of the dry fern and bind it. He found himself well content at Falcon Farm. He was settling down and liked the place and the people. He did not observe, or attempt to observe, anything beneath the surface of his new neighbours; but they proved agreeable, easy, friendly; they satisfied him well. He liked John Bamsey; he liked Melinda Honeysett, and had visited her father and found a spirit who promised to throw light on some of his own problems.

Now he was to meet yet another from his new circle. He worked two hundred yards above the road that ran slantwise across the hillside to Buckland; and from below him now, whence the sound of a trotting horse's footfall ascended, he heard a sudden, harsh noise which spoke of an accident. Silence followed. The horse had ceased to trot and had evidently come down. Maynard dropped his hay fork, tightened his leather belt and descended swiftly to the hedge. Looking over into the deep lane below he saw a pony on the ground, the shaft of a light market-cart broken, and a girl with her hat crushed, her hair fallen and a bloody face, loosening the harness.

She was a brown, young woman with a pair of dark grey eyes and a countenance that preserved a cheerful expression despite her troubles. She wore a tweed skirt and a white flannel bodice upon which the blood from her face had already dropped. She was kneeling and in some danger of the struggling pony's hoofs.

"Stand clear!" shouted Lawrence. Then he jumped the sheer eight feet of the wall, falling for his own comfort on the mass of beech leaves that filled the water-table below. The girl rose. She was filled with concern for the pony.

"Poor chap; he's been down before. How's his knees? All my fault. I got thinking and forgot the road was slippery."

"You're badly cut I'm thinking."

"It's nothing much. I fell on top of him when he came down. 'Twas a buckle done it I expect."

The man freed the pony and pulled back the trap. The animal had not hurt itself, but was frightened and in a mood to run away. The cart had a shaft broken short off, but was not otherwise injured.

Its driver directed Lawrence.

"Thank you I'm sure. That comes of wool-gathering when you ought to be minding your business. Serve me right. I'll take the pony—he knows me. D'you think you could pull the trap so far as Buckland, or shall I send for it? I can put it up there in a shed and send to Lower Town for a new shaft."

"I'll fetch it along. Is your face done bleeding?"

"Very near. You'll be Mr. Lawrence Maynard I suppose?"

"So I am then. How d'you know it?"

"Guessed it. I'm Dinah Waycott. I expect my young man has told you about me. 'Orphan Dinah' they call me. I'm tokened to John Bamsey, the water-keeper, my foster-father's son."

He nodded.

"I've heard tell about you. John Bamsey often drops in at Falcon Farm."

He pulled the trap along and she walked beside him leading the pony. She spoke kind words to the creature, apologised to it and told it to cheer up.

Maynard had leisure to observe her and quickly perceived the nature of her mind and that outspeaking quality that had occasioned argument. Ac their present meeting it took the form of a sort of familiarity that impressed Lawrence as strange from a woman to a man she had never met before.

"I was wishful to see you, because Johnny likes you. But he's not much of a hand at sizing up people. Perhaps if he was, he wouldn't be so silly fond of me."

This was no challenge, but merely the utterance of her honest opinion. Nothing of the coquette appeared in Dinah. She had received his succour with gratitude, but expressed no dismay at the poor figure she cut on their meeting.

"He's a good chap," he said, "and terrible fond of you, miss."

Thus unconsciously he fell into her own direct way of speech. He did not feel that he was talking to a stranger; and that not because he had already heard so much about her, but because Dinah created an atmosphere of directness between herself and all men and women. She recognised no barriers until the other side raised them. There was a frank goodwill about her that never hid itself. She was like a wild thing that has not yet fallen in with man, or learned to distrust him.

"Are you a chap with a pretty good judgment of your fellow creatures?" she asked. "You've got a thoughtful sort of face as if you might be."

He smiled and looked at her.

"Your fellow creatures make you thoughtful," he answered.

"Don't they? Never you said a truer word! Your life all depends upon the people in it seemingly."

"They make or mar it most times."

"Yes, they're the only difficult thing about it."

"If we could live it all to ourselves, it might be easy enough."

"So I think when I look at a squirrel. But I dare say, if he could talk, he'd tell us the other squirrels was a nuisance, and cadged his food and worried him."

"I dare say he would."

"I'm one of the lucky ones," she said.

"Ah!"

"Yes. If I could put my finger on a trouble, which I can't, I should find it was of my own making."

"Like to-day?"

"This don't amount to a trouble—just an accident with nobody the worse. Only a cranky mind would call this a trouble."

"You might have broke your neck, however."

"But I didn't, nor yet the pony's knees—my luck."

"You may have marked your cheek for life."

"And what does that matter? Suppose I'd knocked half my teeth down my throat: that would have been something to worrit about."

"You're the hopeful sort. Perhaps that's your best luck—that you're built to take a bright view, miss."

"Perhaps it is. Aren't you?"

"We may be built to one pattern and then life come along and unbuild us."

"I wouldn't let life unbuild me."

He did not answer, and presently she asked him a question.

"What d'you think of Johnny Bamsey, Mr. Maynard?"

"Hardly know him well enough to say."

"You know him as well as he knows you—better, because Johnny will be talking more than thinking, same as me. But you're not like that seemingly. In fact, though he's took to you and sees you've got a brain, he says you're rather glum for a young man."

"I expect I am to the eyes of my own generation."

"Why? People ain't glum for nought."

"Oh yes, they are—often for less than nought. It ain't life, it's nature makes many downcast. You see chaps, chin-deep in trouble, always ready to forget it and laugh with the loudest."

"So you do then."

"And others—prosperous men, with nothing to grizzle about—always care-foundered and fretty."

"You'd say you was glum by nature then?"

"I wouldn't say I was glum—you've only got John Bamsey's word for it. Miss Stockman wouldn't tell you I was glum."

"She likes you very much. She told me so when she was over to my home last week. Soosie-Toosie's a woman quick to welcome a bit of luck, because she don't get much, and she likes you, and Mr. Palk also."

"I'm glad she does."

"And what d'you think of Johnny?"

"A very good chap I'm sure. Rather excitable, perhaps."

"He is, you might say a thought unreasonable sometimes."

"Never where you are concerned I'm sure."

"He's got the loveliest hair ever I saw on a man."

"Fine curly hair, sure enough."

"I believe temper always goes with that fashioned hair. I've noticed it."

"I'm sure his temper is good most times."

"He's sulky if he's crossed."

"He's young. Perhaps he hasn't been crossed often."

"Never—never once in his life—until now. But he's a thought vexed because I won't name the day."

"Who shall blame him?"

"Nobody. I'm sure I don't."

"I expect you will name it pretty soon, miss?"

"I expect so. How d'you like Cousin Joe?"

"Mr. Stockman? Very much indeed. I feel a lot obliged to him—a kindly, understanding man. He looks at life in a very wise way, and he's got a thought to spare for other people."

"I'm glad you like him. He's cruel lazy; but what does that matter? It takes all sorts to make a world."

"Everybody tells me he's lazy. I shouldn't call him particular lazy for his time of life. He's done a deal of work in the past."

"Glad you're so well suited. Where d'you come from, if I may ask?"

"Somerset."

They had reached Buckland, and Dinah hitched her pony to the hedge, opened a gate and directed Lawrence to wheel the trap into a byre close at hand.

"I'll tell Mr. Budge what's happened and he'll let father's cart bide there for the minute. Then I'll take the pony and my parcels home."

"You're all right?"

"Never righter. And thank you, I'm sure—a proper good Samaritan. I won't forget it; and if ever I can do you a good turn, I will."

"I'm sure you will. Very pleased to meet you, miss. And you see doctor for that cut. 'Tis a pretty deep gash and did ought to be tended."

"Foster-father'll put me right. And if you're in a mind to come over one day to Sunday dinner, I hope you will. He'll be wishful to thank you."

"No need at all. But I'll come some time, since you're so kind as to offer."

"Mind you do then. I want for you to."

They parted and Lawrence returned to his work in the fern. He came back as swiftly as he might, but the better part of an hour was past, during which he had been absent. He found Thomas Palk and his master. Joe had taken his coat off and placed it on a stone. He was handling Lawrence's fork and assisting Thomas to fill the haycart. As Maynard entered a gate beneath and ascended to the fern patch, Mr. Stockman laboriously lifted a mass of litter up to Thomas on the cart. Then he heaved a heavy sigh, dropped the fork and rubbed his side.

He spoke to Lawrence as he arrived.

"Here's the man! Well, Lawrence, you've been taking the air I see; but I can't help feeling, somehow, that it's a thought ill-convenient in the midst of a busy working morning, with the dry litter crying to be stored, that you should make holiday. I've filled the breach, of course, as my custom is. I've been doing your work as well as I was able—an old man, gone in the loins through over-work; but what d'you think? What d'you think about it, my son?"

"There was a good reason, master."

"Thank God! I'm glad of that. I told Palk I hoped there was; for, if I'd thought just for a thirst, or some wilful fancy to see a maid, or suchlike nonsense, you'd forgot your duty, I should have felt a lot cast down in my mind and wondered how I'd come to misread you. And what was the reason? Work while you tell me."

The young man explained, and Stockman was instantly mollified.

"Enough said as to you. You could do no less. A female in trouble is a very good excuse for leaving your duty. In fact you may say a female in trouble is everybody's duty."

The silent man in the cart made a note of this admirable sentiment, while Joe continued.

"To think that Orphan Dinah should let the pony down—such a very wide-awake young thing as her! Dreaming about Johnny no doubt. And hurt you say?"

"Miss had got a bad cut across her face; but she made nothing of it, for joy the pony wasn't scratched."

"A nice maid. Too large-minded for safety some might think; but she ain't. Hope she's not marked. Not that her face is her fortune by any means; her fortune's in her heart, for by the grace of God her heart is gold. But she's got a nice sort of face all the same. I like a bit hidden in a woman myself—for the pleasure of bringing it to light. But she's so frank as a young boy, and I dare say, to some minds, that would be more agreeable than tackling the secret sort."

"She says what she means, master."

"She does, and what's a lot rarer even than that, she knows what she means—so far as a human can. Many never do. Many in my experience find the mere fact of being alive such a puzzle to them that they ain't clear about anything—can't see clear and can't speak clear. They go through their days like a man who've had just one drop too much."

"Life be a drop too much for some people," said Lawrence.

"It is. Keep working, keep working. An hour lost is an hour lost, even though you'd knocked off to help the Queen of England. Oh, my poor side! There's a muscle carried away I'm fearing. Shouldn't wonder if I was in bed to-morrow. What a far-reaching thing a catastrophe may be! Orphan Dinah gets mooning and lets down her pony. Then you, as needs you must, go to the rescue, and drop your work and make a gap in the orderly scheme of things in general. Then I come along, to see how we'm prospering, and forgetting my age and infirmity, rush in to fill the gap. Then once more my rash spirit gets a reminder from the failing flesh, and I'm called to suffer in body as well as pocket. That's the way how things be always happening. Nobody to blame, you understand, but somebody to pay. Somebody's got to pay for every damn thing. Nature's worse than they blasted moneylenders."

"I'll put my part right."

"Yes, exactly so, Lawrence; and somebody always do offer to put their part right. Good men are always offering. But 'tis in the cranky nature of things that oftener than not the wronger ban't the righter. You can't call home sixty minutes of time, any more than you can order the sun to stay in his tracks. And you can't right my twisted thigh. So the harm's done for all eternity."

"The fern will be in to-night before milking."

"That's a brave speech, such as I should have spoken at your age," said Joe. "Now I must limp back afore I'm stiff, and see what my daughter can do for me. I dare say a valiant bout of elbow grease on her part may stave off the worst. If you use 'Nicholson's embrocation'—-the strength they make it for hosses—it will often save the situation. Many a day when I've been bone-tired after working from dawn till moon-up, I've refreshed the joints with 'Nicholson's'—hoss strength."

He left them, going slowly and relying much upon his stick. Then, when he was out of ear-shot, Thomas spoke.

"What d'you think of that?" he asked.

"Did he do much work?"

"Pitched three forks of fern, or it might be four—not a darned one more."

"He's a clever old man, however."

"I never said he weren't," answered Palk. "He's the cleverest old man ever I saw. I'm only telling you us may find out he's too clever."

"We'll get the fern in anyway."

Mr. Stockman had sat down two hundred yards from them by the grassy track to the farm.

"He's waiting for me to give him a lift home," said Thomas.

CHAPTER VI
ON HAZEL TOR

John Bamsey was a youth who had not yet felt the edge of life. His own good parts were in a measure responsible for this fortune, and the circumstances destined to make trial of his foundations and test what fortitude his character might command, were yet to come. He was quick minded and intelligent, and his success had made him vain. His temper was short, and in his business of water-keeper, he held it a virtue to preserve a very obstinate and implacable front, not only to declared evil-doers, but also against those who lay under his suspicion.

He was superior in his attitude to his own generation and therefore unpopular with it; but he set down a lack of friendship to natural envy at his good fortune and cheerful prospects. He liked his work and did it well. The fish were under his protection and no ruth obscured his fidelity to them. Into his life had come love, and since the course thereof ran smoothly, this experience had chimed with the rest and combined, by its easy issue, to retard any impact of reality and still leave John in a state of ignorance concerning those factors of opposition and tribulation which are a part of the most prosperous existence.

Dinah accepted him, after a lengthy period of consideration, and she was affectionate if not loverly. He never stayed to examine the foundation of her compact, nor could he be blamed, for he had no reason to suppose that she had said "yes" from mixed motives. A girl so direct, definite and clear-sighted as Dinah, seemed unlikely to be in two minds about anything, and John, knowing his own hearty passion and ardent emotions, doubted not that, modified only as became a maiden's heart, she echoed them. Yet there went more to the match than that, and others perceived it, though he did not. Dinah's position was peculiar, and in truth love for another than John had gone largely—more largely than she guessed herself—to decide her. There was little sex impulse in her—otherwise her congenital frankness with man and woman alike had been modified by it. But she could love, for a rare sense of gratitude belonged to her, and the height and depth of her vital affections belonged to her foster-father, Benjamin Bamsey. Him she did love, as dearly as child ever loved a parent, and it was the knowledge that such a match would much delight him, that had decided Dinah and put a term to her doubts. But she had become betrothed on grounds inadequate, and now was beginning, as yet but dimly, to perceive it. Her disquiets did not take any shape that John could quarrel with, for she had not revealed them. She was honestly fond of him, and if she did not respond to his ardour with such outward signs of affection as he might have desired, his own inexperience in that matter prevented any uneasy suspicion on his part. He judged that such reserve in love was becoming and natural to a maiden of Dinah's distinction, and knew not the truth of the matter, nor missed the outward signs that he might have reasonably expected.

The beginning of difficulty very gradually rose between them, and since they had never quarrelled in their lives, for all John's temper and Dinah's frankness, the difference now bred in a late autumn day gave both material for grave thought.

They met by appointment, strolled in the woods, then climbed through plantations of sweet-smelling spruce, till they reached great rocks piled on a little spur of the hillside under Buckland Beacon. Here the granite heaved in immense boulders that broke the sweep of the hill and formed a resting-place for the eye between the summit of the Beacon and the surface of the river winding in the lap of the Vale beneath.

Hazel Tor, as these masses of porphyry were called, now rose like a ridge of little mountainous islets from a sea of dead heath and fern. The glories of the fall were at an end, and on an afternoon when the wind was still and the sky grey and near, pressing down on the naked tree-tops, Dinah, sitting here with her sweetheart, chatted amiably enough. The cicatrix on her cheek was still red, but the wound had cleanly healed and promised to leave no scar.

Johnny, however, was doubtful.

"I won't say you won't be marked now."

"If kissing could make me safe, I should be."

"I wish you'd give me something to kiss you for; and that's the name of the day next Spring we're to wed."

"Isn't it enough if we say next Spring?"

"Quite enough, if you mean next Spring. But I don't know whether you do; and more do you know. And for that matter you never have said next Spring. If you say the word, then you'll keep your word; but you haven't, and patient though I am, I can't help wondering sometimes why you don't."

"You're not the only one that wonders for that matter."

"Of course I'm not. Cousin Joe wonders every time I see him, and father wonders, and mother does more than wonder. In fact it's getting to be a bit awkward and unreasonable."

"I know it is, Johnny. I never thought it would be so difficult when the time came."

"So you grant that the time has come—that's something."

"I do grant it. I dare say a man doesn't quite realise what a tremendous thing it is for a girl to lose her liberty like this."

He was irritable.

"Do chuck that! I'm fed up with it. If you think what you call liberty at the farm is better than living with me in your own house, you must be a fool, Dinah."

"No," she said. "I'm right. Marriage cuts into a woman's liberty a lot. It's bound to, and, of course, home along with foster-father must be a much freer sort of life than home along with you."

"You are a cold-blooded little devil sometimes," he said. "What's freedom, or slavery, or any other mortal thing got to do with a man and woman if they love one another? You don't hear me saying I shall lose my bachelor liberty."

"No, because you won't," answered Dinah. "I know you love me very dear, and I love you very dear; but marrying a woman don't turn a man's life upside down if he's a strong man and got his aims and objects and business. He goes on with his life, and the woman comes into it as an addition, and takes her place, and if all goes well, so much the better, and if all don't, then so much the worse for the woman—if the man's strong. A man's not going to let a woman bitch up his ways if he's strong. And you are strong, and no woman would spoil your show, because you wouldn't let her. But a woman's different. Marriage for her be the beginning of a new life. She can't take anything of the old life into it except her character and her religion. Marriage is being born again for a woman. I've thought of these things, Johnny."

"Well, what about it? If you know so much, you ought to know more. Granted it don't always pan out well, and granted I'm a sort of man that wouldn't be turned to the right or left, are you a sort of woman that would be like to try and turn me? Are you masterful, or cranky, or jealous of your fancied rights? If you'd been such a she as that, should I have fallen in love with you, or would you have fallen in love with me? People fall in love with character quite as much as looks. And as we've grown up side by side, our characters were laid bare to each other from the time we could notice such things."

She took him up eagerly.

"Now that's the very matter in my mind. I've been getting to wonder. There's a lot in it, John. Do we know one another so well as we think we do? And isn't the very fact that we're grown up under the same roof a reason why we don't know each other so well as we might?"

"You're always for turning a thing inside out, my words included. I say we must know each other as well as a man can know a girl, or a girl a man. We was little children together, when nothing was hidden between us, and grew up in perfect understanding which ripened at the appointed time into love—all natural and right and proper. Of course we know each other to the bottom of our natures; and so our marriage can't fail to be a good one. Any jolter-head would see that a man and a woman seldom come together on such a bed-rock of common sense and reason as us. And knowing all that, 'tis pure cussedness in you to argue different."

"You can be too near a thing to see it," she said. "I don't say we don't understand each other beautiful, John; but look at it without feeling—just as an interesting question, same as I do. Just ask yourself if we're all you say, how it comes about that, despite such a lot of reasons, I hang back from naming the date. You say you want to know why. Well, so do I. What makes me refuse to name it—an easy-going creature like me, always ready and willing to pleasure anybody if I can? It's interesting, and it's no good merely being cross about it. I don't want to fix the date. I don't feel no call to do it."

"Then you ought."

"That's what I'm saying."

"And since you're well used to doing what you ought, it's about time you let your duty master you."

"Granted. I allow all that. What I want to know is why I'm not so keen to name the day and get to the day as you are?"

"Along of this silly fooling about losing your liberty I suppose. As if a married woman wasn't a lot freer than a single one."

"Oh no, she isn't. The single ones was never so free as now. They can do scores of things no married woman would be suffered to do for a moment. That's because mothers and fathers care a lot less about what happens to their daughters than husbands care what happens to their wives. A daughter's good name be outside a parent's; but a wife's good name is her husband's. So the unmarried ones are a lot freer. There's few real parents nowadays be what your father is to me."

"If you think such a lot of him and feel you owe him such a lot, why don't you do what he wants you to do and fix the day?"

She did not answer, knowing well that old Mr. Bamsey, at the bottom of his heart, little liked to dwell on her departure. Indeed, she realised with growing intensity the reasons that had made her agree to marry John; and she knew more: she was aware that John's father himself had become a little doubtful. But the deed was done and Dinah appreciated the justice of her sweetheart's demands.

They talked and he pressed and she parried. Then he grew angry.

"Blessed if you know what love is despite all your fine talk. A little more of it, and I shall begin to think you're off the bargain and haven't the pluck to say so."

For answer she put her arms round his neck and kissed him.

"It's all very well; but you leave me guessing too often: and I'm not the sort that care to be left guessing. From a man I always get a plain answer, and I never leave him till I have. I hang on like a dog, and turn or twist as they may, they know they've got to come to it. But you—it's rather late in the day to begin all over again and ask you if you really love me, or not. It's putting a pretty big slight upon me; and perhaps, if I wasn't a fool, I should see the answer in that, without asking for it. For you wouldn't slight me— not if you cared for me one quarter what I care for you."

He showed temper, and the girl made no very genuine attempt to turn away wrath. She was in a wilful and wayward mood—a thing uncommon with her; yet such a mood was capable of being provoked by Johnny oftener than most people.

"I love your hair," she said, stroking it.

He shook his head and put on his cap.

"You're not playing the game and, what's a lot more, you know you're not. It's outside your character to do this—weak—feeble—mischievous. You know I smart a bit under it, because—fault or not—I'm a proud man. How d'you think that's likely to pan out in my feelings to you? Does it occur to you that with my very keen sense of justice, Dinah, I might begin to ask myself questions about it?"

She changed her manner and, from being idle and playful, gave him her undivided attention. He had said something that rather pleased her when he hinted that his own feelings might grow modified; but she knew well enough that such a remark ought not to have pleased her and was certainly not uttered to do so.

"There's a screw loose somewhere, Johnny," she said.

"Where then? And whose fault—yours, or mine? God's my judge I didn't know there was a screw loose, and it's pretty ugly news, I can tell you. Perhaps you'll let in a little more light, while you're about it, and tell me what the screw is and why i'ts loose?"

"I wish I could. Oh Johnny, don't you feel it?"

"No, I do not. And if I don't, then it's up to you to explain, not me."

"I don't know enough yet," she answered. "I'm not going to flounder into it and make trouble that can never be unmade again. I'll wait till I see a bit clearer, John. It's no use talking till we've thought a thing out and got words for it. A row will often happen just for lack of words to say what anybody really means. There is something—something growing; but since you've not felt it, then it can only be on my side. You shall know if it's anything, or nothing, pretty soon. Feelings never stand still. They fade out, or else get bigger. I love you very dearly, and, so far as we stand at present, it's understood we are to be married in the Spring."

"Then why hang it up any longer? You love me and you'm tokened and there's no reason why we shouldn't be wed and a great many reasons why we should. But now a screw's loose, or so you say. But you won't give it a name. Don't you see that instead of being yourself, Dinah—famed for thinking straight and seeing clear and saying what you mean—you're behaving like any stupid giglet wench, with no wits and not worth her keep to anybody?"

"Yes; and that's why a screw's loose. If I can feel like I do, and act away from my general plan, and dally with a thing—don't you see there's something wrong with me?"

"Well, if you know it, get it right."

"I must do that for all our sakes. I must and will, John."

"You certainly must. And the sooner you put a name to it and let me know what that name is, the better pleased I'll be. If I was the fast and loose sort, or if I'd ever done anything since we hitched up to give you a shadow of distrust, or make you look back in doubt, then it would be different; but this I will swear, that no man ever loved a woman better than I love you, or have been a better or truer lover. I must say that for myself, Dinah, since you've given up saying it."

"I did say it and I do say it. You're all right, and you've every reason to be pleased with yourself, Johnny. You're a wonder. But it's me. I'll work at myself. I can't promise more. I'll thresh it out and try to find where I'm wrong; and if you can help me, I'll tell you. It's not a happy thing; but at the same time it's not an unhappy thing—not yet. I owe you a very great deal—only less than your father. I'd sooner make anybody on earth unhappy before you; but it's no good pretending, and I couldn't hide worry from you even if I wanted to."

"Leave it then," he said, "and get it off your mind so quick as you can."

They talked about other things, and for the most part chimed harmoniously enough; but they did not always agree in their estimate of other people, or in their views of action and conduct. Dinah never conceded anything, nor pretended to see with his eyes if she did not, yet sometimes she praised him if he put a point and changed her own view by enlarging her vision of the subject.

John was in a better temper when presently the dusk fell and the lovers, leaving Hazel Rocks, passed through a clearing, reached the road to Buckland and presently climbed again to Falcon Farm, where they were to drink tea with Susan and her father.

Soosie-Toosie had a heavy cold in her head and appeared more unsightly than usual. Her large frame shook with her sneezes, and Joe, while humorously concerned for her and anxious that she should take steps to get well, soon dropped the humour for a little genuine trouble on his own account.

"There's some people I catch cold from, and there's some I don't catch cold from," he said, "just like some fires you catch heat from and some you never can. But Soosie-Toosie's colds be of the catching order. 'Tis the violence of her sneezes no doubt—like a fowling-piece going off. And though a cold be nought to her and here to-day and gone to-morrow, if I get 'em they run down the tubes and give me brownkitis and lay me by for weeks."

"Never seen you look better, Cousin Joe," declared John. "You be always at your fighting best when the woodcock comes back, so father says."

"He will have his bit of fun. There's only one thing wrong about your dear, good father, Johnny; and that is he ain't a sportsman. For a man to live in the Vale and not be a sportsman is like for a man to live by the sea and not care to go fishing. With a place in his heart for a bit of sport, I do believe Ben Bamsey would have been a perfect human. But as that's contrary to nature, no doubt the sport had to be left out."

"He is perfect," said Dinah, "and I've often told him so."

"He'd never believe it if you did," said Susan; "he's much too good a man to think he's good."

"As to that, my dear," answered Joe, "it's only false modesty and silliness to pretend you'm not good, when you know perfectly well you are. If I said I wasn't a good man, for example, it would be merely fishing for compliments; and if Soosie-Toosie said she weren't as good as gold, who'd believe her?"

"'Tis easy to be good if you're so busy as Soosie-Toosie and Johnny and a few more," answered Dinah; "but how you can be so amazing good with nothing on your hands, Cousin Joe? I'm sure that's wonderful."

"Nothing on my hands? you bad girl! Little you know. And me the mainspring. You ax Susan if I've got nothing on my hands, or Thomas here."

Lawrence Maynard was absent, but Mr. Palk took tea with the rest. He had not so far spoken.

"You'm the head of the house," he said.

"And if my hand have lost its cunning, my head have not—eh, Thomas?"

"It have not," admitted Thomas.

"Father makes his head help his heels, don't you, father?" asked Soosie-Toosie, following her question with an explosion.

"I should hope so; and do, for God's love, go out in the scullery when you feel a sneeze coming, there's a dear! You be scattering the evil germs around us so thick as starlings."

"I'm just going," she said, "they'll be done their tea in a minute; then I'll gather the things and get away for the wash-up."

Dinah soon departed to help the sufferer; then Joe smoked and bade the others do the like.

"'Twill lay Soosie's germs," he said.

They discussed Maynard, who had gone to see some cows for a neighbour.

"What he don't know about 'em ain't worth knowing," said Mr. Stockman. "A tower of strength the man is going to be."

"Is he growing a bit more cheerful?"

"If he's not cheerful, there's a reason for it. But he's very sensible, with a head rather old for his shoulders—eh, Thomas?"

"Made of sense, I reckon."

"And what is his opinion of me, Thomas, if I may ask?"

Mr. Palk was always rendered cautious at the hint of personalities. He did not reply immediately, though there was no need to hesitate. But he never replied immediately to any question.

"He thinks a great lot of you, master. He holds you to be a very good man indeed."

"Then I shall think higher of his opinion than ever," replied Joe; "and you may drop in his ear that I rate him high too, Thomas. All well within reason, of course—he ain't indispensable—nobody is, great or small. Still, I'm suited and I'm glad he is."

Thomas made no reply, but rose and went out. Then Joe addressed his kinsman.

"Have you got the date out of her?"

Johnny shook his head.

"She allows it must be in the Spring, but holds off naming the time any nearer."

"Not like her. We must all have a go at her. But if your father can't do it, who can?"

"If I can't, who can? That's the question, I should think."

They argued Dinah's delay and presently she returned.

"Susan did ought to go to bed," she said. "See me down the hill, Johnny; I must be off, else they'll wonder what's become of me."

CHAPTER VII
AT GREEN HAYES

To Dinah Waycott there came an experience familiar enough, yet fraught with shock and grief to any man and woman of good will who is forced to suffer it. By gradual stages the truth had overtaken her, and now she knew that what in all honesty she believed was love—the emotion that had made her accept John Bamsey and promise to marry him—was nothing more than such affection and regard as a sister might feel for a favourite brother. Their relations had in fact been upon that basis all their lives. She remembered Johnny as long as she remembered anything, for she had been but two years old when he was born, and they had grown up together. And now, being possessed of a mind that faced life pretty fearlessly, and blessed with clear reasoning powers, Orphan Dinah knew the truth.

First she considered how such an unhappy thing could have happened. She was young and without experience. She had never heard of a similar case. And what most puzzled her was why the light had been thrown at all, and what had happened to convince her that she had erred. When she accepted her lover, most fully and firmly she believed that her heart prompted. It did not beat quicker at his proposition, and for a time she could not feel sure; but before she accepted him she did feel sure and emphatically believed it was love that inspired her promise. But now she knew that it was not love; and yet she could not tell why she knew it.

For the usual experience in such cases had not proved the touchstone. There was none else who had come into her life, awakened passion and thus revealed the nature of her error with respect to John. No blinding light of this sort had shone upon the situation. But gradually, remorselessly, the truth crept into Dinah's brain, and she saw now that what she had taken for love was really an emotion inspired by various circumstances. Her step-father had desired the match and expressed his delight at the thought; and since he was by far the most real and precious thing in the girl's life, his opinion unconsciously influenced her. Then, for private reasons, she desired to be away from Benjamin Bamsey's home—that also for love of him. The situation was complicated for Dinah by the fact that Jane Bamsey, John's sister, did not like her and suffered jealousy under her father's affection for his foster-daughter. Dinah was some years older than Jane and far more attractive to Mr. Bamsey, by virtue of her spirit and disposition, than Jane could ever be. Ben himself hardly knew this, but his wife very clearly perceived it. She was a fair woman and never agitated on the subject, though often tempted to do so. But she was human, and that her husband should set so much greater store upon Dinah than Jane caused her to feel resentment, though little surprise. Astonishment she could not feel, for, though the mother of Jane, she admitted that the elder girl displayed higher qualities, a mind more loyal, a heart more generous. But Jane was beautiful, and she could be very attractive when life ran to her own pattern. Jane was not a bad daughter. She loved her mother and worshipped her brother. She might have tolerated Dinah too, but for the ever present fact that her father put Dinah first. This had been a baneful circumstance for the younger's character; and it had served to lessen her affection for her father. The fact he recognised, without perceiving the reason. On the contrary, he held Dinah a very precious influence for Jane, and wished his own child more like the other. Friction from this situation was inevitable; and now Dinah, considering the various causes that had landed her in her present plight, perceived that not the least had been a subconscious impulse that urged her, for everybody's sake, to leave Lower Town and the home of her childhood. Thus she had deluded herself as well as others, and declared herself in love with a man, while yet her heart was innocent of love. For a long time she had been conscious of something wrong. She had surprised herself painfully three months after her engagement by discovering that her forthright mind was seeing things in Johnny that she wished were different. This startled her, and instinct told her that she ought not to be so aware of these defects. Before they were engaged such things never clouded her affection; but in the light of altered relations they did. She grew to hate the lover's kiss, while the brother's kiss of old had been agreeable to her. Her kiss had not changed; but his had. She detected all manner of trifles, vanities, complacencies, tendencies to judge neighbours too hardly. These things did not make Dinah miserable, because her nature was proof against misery, and the emotion excited in her by ill fortune could never be so described. Indeed, under no circumstances did she display the phenomena of misery. But she was deeply perturbed and she knew, far better than Johnny could tell her, that serious reasons existed for her present evasion and procrastination. She also knew, as he did, that she was taking a line foreign to her character; but he did not guess the tremendous discovery that, for the moment, caused his sweetheart to falter and delay action.

He was in love, heart and soul, and Dinah understood that well enough. No hope of any revelation existed for him. He poured all his energy and quality into his plans for her future happiness. If he could be unselfish, it was with her; if he could be modest, it was with her. She awoke the best of him and influenced him as no other power on earth was able to do. He saw her pleasant face beautiful; he heard her pleasant voice as music; he held her laugh sweeter than a blackbird's song. She knew his adoration and it increased the threatening difficulties. But he was changing now, and the recent evidence of his irritation on Hazel Tor, Dinah recognised as perfectly natural and reasonable.

Still she hesitated before the melancholy conviction that she could not marry John, and the vision of the family when they heard it. She was waiting now in rare indecision; but she knew that such inaction could only be a matter of a very short time. The problem touched many, and she was aware that her change of mind would bring hard words to her ears from various quarters. She began to be sorry, but not for herself. She was concerned, first for John, and then for her foster-father. She was also in a lesser degree regretful for Mrs. Bamsey, and even for Jane; but she judged that their tribulation would be allayed by two things: first, in the conviction that John was well out of it; secondly, at the knowledge that Dinah herself would leave Green Hayes, Ben Bamsey's farm. She could not stop after the events now foreshadowed, and she felt tolerably certain that none would desire her to do so. Thus she hung on the verge, but had not taken the inevitable step upon a Sunday when Lawrence Maynard visited Lower Town according to his promise and came to tea.

Green Hayes was "a welcoming sort of place," as the owner always declared, though at first glance it did not seem so. The farmhouse was built of granite and faced with slate, which caused it to look sulky, but made it snug. A wide farmyard extended before the face of the dwelling, and pigeons and poultry lent liveliness and movement to it. A great barn, with a weathered roof of slate, extended on one side of the yard, and orchards and large kitchen gardens arose behind it; for fruit and vegetables were a feature of Mr. Bamsey's production. He better loved planting trees than rearing stock. Indeed, his neighbours denied him title to be farmer at all. But he did great things with pigs and poultry, and he grew plenty of corn in Dart Vale a mile below his home.

Maynard was welcomed and found that Dinah had made more of his past succour than seemed necessary. He discovered also whence the young woman had derived her directness of speech and clear vision, for Mr. Bamsey displayed these qualities, though in a measure tempered by age and experience. On the subject of himself he could be specially clear. He did not mind who knew his failings.

He was a man of moderate height, grey bearded and grey headed. His nose had been flattened by an accident in youth, but his face was genial and his eyes, behind spectacles, of a pleasant expression. He enjoyed humour, and a joke against himself always won his heartiest laugh. His wife was larger than himself—a ponderous woman, credited with the gift of second sight. She had been beautiful and was still handsome, with regular features, a clear skin, and large, cow-like eyes. Jane Bamsey, her daughter, a girl of eighteen, rejoiced in more than the beauty of youth. She was lovely, but she had a disposition that already made her beautiful mouth pout oftener than it laughed. She was jealous of Dinah, though the elder girl entertained no unfriendly emotion towards Jane. She admired her exceedingly and loved to look at her for the satisfaction of her fine curves, round, black eyebrows, lustrous, misty blue eyes and delicate, dainty nose. It was not her fault that she pleased Benjamin Bamsey better than his own child. Jane was spiteful, and Dinah's direct methods, which often defeated the younger in argument, never convinced her, but increased a general, vague feeling of resentment, the more painful to Jane, because she was no fool, and knew, at the bottom of her heart, that honest grounds of complaint against Dinah did not exist. The real grievance lay in the fact of her father's preference; but when, in a moment of passion, she had flung this truth at Dinah, the elder disarmed her by admitting it and also explaining it.

"If you thought for foster-father like I do, and loved him half as well as what I do, you'd have nothing to grumble about, and he'd love you so well as he loves me," said Dinah; "but you don't."

"I'd do all you do for him, and more, if you wasn't here," declared Jane, and met an uncompromising answer.

"No, you wouldn't, or anything like what I do; and well you know it, you pretty dear."

Mr. Bamsey thanked Lawrence heartily for his good offices in the past on Dinah's behalf, and Faith Bamsey, his wife, echoed him.

"The blessing is she ain't marked," said Ben. "I much feared she would be, for 'twas an evil cut, but such is the health of her blood that she healed instanter, and now, you see nought but a red mark that grows fainter every day."

The visitor regarded Dinah's face and admitted it was so.

"Wonderful," he said. "I never should have thought that ugly gash would have cleared up so well."

"Nature's on the side of the young," replied Benjamin. "She spoils 'em you may say. Not that anything could spoil Dinah."

"You can, and you do," she said.

"Oh, no. 'Tis the other way round. You'd keep me in cotton wool if you could. I'm feared of my life for Johnny that you'll make him soft."

"And tell him he's not to go out and fight the poachers by night, and silly things like that," added Jane.

"More likely offer to go out and help him fight 'em," said Maynard, and Ben applauded.

"That's right! You know her better than Jane do seemingly. Dinah won't stand between John and his duty—that's certain sure."

"No woman will ever come between my son and his duty," said Faith. "There's some young men be born with a sense of duty, and some gets it by their training and some, of course, never do. But John was doing his duty when he was five year old—came natural to him."

"And what's the duty of a five year old, ma'am?" asked Lawrence. He found himself easy and comfortable with the Bamseys.

"To obey his parents and trust in 'em first and last and always," answered Faith. "He was blessed with a very fine nature from his birth, and nothing ever happened to make him depart from it."

"One of the lucky ones, that finds it easier to be good than anything else."

"No, Mr. Maynard; you mustn't say that," answered Johnny's father. "You may be as good as gold, but you can't escape the old Adam. God Almighty don't make us angels, though he gives us the chance to imitate them."

"In fact, nobody can get high virtues by nature," summed up Mrs. Bamsey. "They've got to be worked for. And another thing—you can't win to goodness and then sit down and say, 'I've got the Lord, so now I'm out of the wood and safe for ever more.' That's not life. Nobody's ever out of the wood, and them that think they stand be often most like to fall. Things be sent to try our faith in God, and He sends 'em Himself."

Dinah, with proleptic instinct, looked ahead at her own affairs and wondered. Mrs. Bamsey, from whom moral principles flowed easily at a touch, proceeded awhile and Maynard's spirits began to fall. He was not religious and his own standards of conduct, upon which his past had been directed, had resulted from innate qualities of mind, rather than along the directions of dogma and creed. He perceived that Mrs. Bamsey's ideas ran in fixed channels and felt glad when Benjamin, upon some opinion of his wife, took up the conversation. She had been saying, with regard to her son, that while he owed certain qualities to herself, his father was also apparent in him. Dinah supported her, but Benjamin was not so sure.

"No," he said. "I can't flatter myself that John has to thank me for much. His mother stares out of him you may say, and all the best is hers. But there's a very wicked side of me that John haven't got, I'm glad to say. Leastways if he have, he's never let on about it."

Dinah laughed.

"Now I know what's coming," she said.

"And what might your wicked side be, Mr. Bamsey, if it ain't a secret?" inquired Lawrence.

"No secret at all. I've got no secrets. Hate 'em. It's just a queer bit of human nature."

"He's invented it," said Dinah. "It ain't true. He dreams it."

"It's very true indeed, and shows a weak spot where one didn't ought to be," confessed Ben. "If you'll believe it, Maynard, I often wake up of a night, somewhere about two o'clock, a changed man! Yes, I do; and then the whole face of nature looks different, and I find myself in a proper awful frame of mind against my fellow creatures. I mistrust 'em, and take dark views against 'em, setting out their wrongs and wickedness. At such times I'll even plan to sack a harmless chap, and lash myself up into a proper fury, and think the fearfullest things against man, woman and child. I'll go so far as to cuss the cat, because she haven't caught a mouse for a week! If the folk were to see me at such a moment, I dare say they wouldn't know me."

"What d'you say, ma'am?" asked Maynard.

"I say nothing, because I'm always asleep," answered Mrs. Bamsey.

"Do it pass off pretty quick, master?"

"It do. I slumber again after a bit, and come daylight, you may say butter wouldn't melt in my mouth. I don't write none of they rude letters I've invented, and I don't sack nobody—not even the cat. I wake up calm and patient with the neighbours and quite ready to forgive 'em, as I hope to be forgiven. After such a night I'm mild as old cider and only a bit tired."

"'Tis a sort of safety-valve I expect," suggested Lawrence.

"That's just what it is; and sometimes I've seen the like happen in daylight with other people. If you can send your neighbours to hell without them knowing it, it don't hurt them and comforts your nerves wonderful sometimes."

"A very shameful thought, Ben," declared his wife, "and you oughtn't to say such things."

"I know it's shameful. But I only tell the man these facts to open his eyes and show him how much better Johnny be than his father."

"May he never have nothing to cuss about," hoped Lawrence.

"I don't see how he ever can, when he's got Dinah."

"Yes—when," said Jane Bamsey. "He's got to wait Dinah's pleasure till the stroke of Doom seemingly."

Maynard had been admiring the younger girl. But he noticed that her beauty was clouded by discontent. There chimed also a note in her voice that carried with it slight, indefinite protest. His own voice embraced the identical note; but he was not aware of that.

"No politics, Jane," said Mrs. Bamsey. "You never did ought to strike into family affairs before a stranger."

"Mr. Maynard's not a stranger," argued Jane. "We're heard tell lots about him from Johnny, and Dinah too."

"That's right," said Lawrence.

Benjamin Bamsey nursed an old Skye terrier and scratched its back with a bunch of keys—a process the animal loved. He talked of dogs and cattle awhile; then they all went to tea. Faith Bamsey asked after Susan.

"She's quite recovered, ma'am. She was in a mind to come over herself to-day, being wishful to see you; but her father wanted her help. He's very busy with his figures this afternoon."

Faith shook her head.

"Just like him—to put off his duty all the week, then do it on the Lord's Day, when he didn't ought."

"He went to worship in the morning, however, as he generally does."

"That's to the good then."

"Soosie-Toosie's one of the best women on this earth," said Dinah, "only she's too much of a doormat. So cruel busy that she's never got time to think what she owes herself."

This struck the visitor as very true, but he had never been greatly interested in Susan. She was very unobtrusive and unchallenging in every way.

"She likes it," said Jane. "She likes being driven about and never getting even with her work."

"If work is prayer, her life is a prayer," said Mr. Bamsey.

"It's a prayer that never gets answered, then," replied Jane. "A dog's life really, only Susan don't see it, more than any other dog would, I suppose."

"Don't talk so free, Jane," urged her mother.

"She'll work herself to the bone and die afore her time I expect," continued Mrs. Bamsey's daughter. "Then very like you'll see her ghost, mother."

This gave Lawrence an opportunity to inquire concerning Faith Bamsey's famous gift.

"Is it true, as they tell, that you be a ghost-seer, ma'am?" he asked.

"I am," she replied placidly. "It runs in my family and I take no credit for it."

"Never afeared?"

"Never. They come and they go. 'Tis just something in my nature that lets my eyes see more than other people. There's animals have the gift also, so it's naught to brag about. I'll see the spectrums any time—just the ghostes of dead folk, that flicker about where they used to live sometimes; and if I be that way by chance when they be there, then I see 'em."

"And do they see you, ma'am?"

"I can't say as to that. I've never had no speech with them and they don't take no notice of me. Sometimes I recognise the creatures as people that lived in my time and memory; sometimes I do not. Only last week I see old Noah Parsons hanging over New Bridge, just as he did in life times without count, looking down over to see if there was any fish moving. An old poacher he was—till he got too feeble to do anything but right."

"And mother seed Lazarus Coomstock in Holne Wood not a month after he was teeled*—didn't you, mother?" asked Jane.

> * *Teeled*—buried.

"I did," answered Mrs. Bamsey. "I saw him outside his own house on the day of the sale, with live neighbours at his elbows—for all the world as though he'd come with the rest to bid for the things."

"A terrible queer gift," said Maynard. "Have you handed it on to Miss Jane here, I wonder?"

"No," declared Jane. "I've never seen a ghost ana never want to."

"You be young yet. Perhaps when you get up to years of discretion you'll see 'em."

"When Jane gets up to years of discretion, I'll give a party," laughed Ben; but Jane did not laugh.

"You always think I'm a fool, father; and you'll always be wrong," she snapped. Then she got up and left the room.

"You didn't ought to poke fun at her," said Faith. "You know she don't like being thought a child—least of all by you."

"If you make jokes, you must take 'em," said Ben. "Jane's got a very sharp tongue for her age and nobody doubts her wits; but if a father can't make a laugh at the expense of his child—no, no—we mustn't truckle under to Jane. Mayhap a good ghostey will teach her sense some day."

"She's that wishful to please you always," murmured Jane's mother.

"Well, well, she can do most things she sets her mind to. I ban't a man very difficult to please."

Lawrence struck in again. He had ignored these passages, and was still considering Mrs. Bamsey's alleged second sight.

"Would you say that John has got your gift, ma'am?" he asked

"Time will show," replied Faith. "He's a godly, plain-dealer is John, but I've never heard him say he's seen one."

"I hope he won't," said Dinah. "Because, in his business as water-keeper, and looking out against trespassers and such-like, it might confuse him and waste his time a lot, if he was to see shadow people about by the river and think them poaching."

Her foster-father exploded at the absurdity of the idea; but neither Lawrence nor Faith Bamsey saw anything amusing in it. Then Ben grew serious and set down his old dog, which had returned to his lap after tea was ended.

"There's church bell," he said, "and us be going. Have you worshipped at our church yet, Maynard?"

The thin tinkle of bell music fell from the wooded height above Green Hayes.

"No," said Lawrence. "I have not. I don't go to church."

Ben shrank, and his wife started and tightened her lips.

"Ban't you a Christian then?"

"Couldn't say as to that, ma'am; but I don't find church-going help me, so I don't go."

"Dear, dear—that's bad," said Mr. Bamsey, while his wife put further searching questions.

"Do you say your prayers, or do you not, if I may ask?"

"I say my prayers—yes."

She looked at him very suspiciously.

"We're bid to go," she said; "and you didn't ought to feel any doubt as to whether you're a Christian or not, did he, Ben?"

"Certainly he did not," answered her husband. Then he brightened and made a suggestion.

"You come along of us to-night. Won't hurt you, and you'll very like catch a grain that'll sprout. That's the beauty of church-going: 'tis like rough shooting—you never know what you're going to flush. And our parson's a man that abounds in plain truths. So like as not he'll get one home on you."

"Come, Mr. Maynard," said Dinah.

"Certainly I will if I may," he replied. "I've no feeling for, or against."

"If us can throw a light for your soul, you won't have come to tea in vain," suggested Mrs. Bamsey.

"And have got supper by it in the bargain," added Ben, "for you'll have to bide after."

"No, no—no occasion at all."

"Yes, you must," said Dinah. "They'll have finished at Falcon Farm long afore you can get back."

Therefore Lawrence Maynard joined the party at evensong and sat between Jane and Dinah. Jane was indifferent, but Dinah shared her hymn-book with him. He did not sing, however, though it gave him pleasure to hear her do so. She was devout and attentive; Jane was not. He praised the sermon afterwards and told Mr. Bamsey that it was full of sense. When supper had ended, he thanked them very earnestly for their great kindness to a lonely man, and Benjamin trusted that he would come again. Dinah also pressed him, and Jane, who was now in a very fascinating and gracious mood, ordered him to do so.

"If you don't, we shall think you don't like us," she said.

He was grateful, and left them in an amiable spirit.

They discussed him after he had gone, and Dinah praised him, but Mrs. Bamsey felt dubious.

"He's rather a secret sort of man in my opinion," she said.

"He is," admitted Ben; "but he's secret by accident, not nature, I believe. I took note of him. He's got a grievance against life I reckon; but what it may be, of course, we don't know."

"I'll get it out of him," said Jane.

"No you won't, my dear," answered her father. "Dinah's more like to than you."

"I don't want his secrets," declared Dinah.

"We'm often burdened with secrets we don't want," replied Ben. "It's part of duty sometimes to listen to 'em; though I grant the folk most ready to tell their secrets are often the hardest to help. Silliness is a misfortune that little can be done for."

"He won't be in no hurry to tell his secrets, if he's got any," prophesied Mrs. Bamsey. "He's not that sort."

CHAPTER VIII
THE OLD FOX-HUNTER

Joe Stockman had tried a new haricot bean for his own table and was now engaged in the easy task of shelling the brown husks and extracting the pearly white seeds. It amused him and put no strain upon his faculties. But he tired of it after ten minutes. He sat in an out-house with a mass of the dried pods beside him, and as the boy, Neddy Tutt, passed by, Joe's eye twinkled and he called.

"Look here, Ned—a-proper wonder—I'll show 'e something as no human eye have ever seen since the beginning of the world!" he cried out, and Neddy, agape, approached.

"Don't you be frightened," said Joe. "Won't hurt 'e."

Then under the lad's round eyes, he opened a bean pod and roared with laughter. Neddy also grinned.

"Now you go about your business, my son," said his master, and then, wearying of the beans, he stretched himself and looked out of doors. The day was mild and still. Mr. Stockman went into his kitchen and called Susan.

"Get on with they beans, there's a dear; I've been at 'em till my fingers ache; and we'll have a dish to-night for supper if you please. Such things be never so nice as when fresh and soft—far better than boughten beans. And I'll poke round and see if I can pick up a wood-pigeon to go with 'em. 'Tis soft by the feel of it this morning and a little exercise won't do me no harm."

She nodded, and getting a gun, Joe disappeared with his dogs. He skirted an outlying field, where Maynard and Palk were pulling mangel-wurzel. Bending low they plodded along, with the rhythmic swing and harmonious action proper to their work. Simultaneously with each hand they pulled up two roots from the earth, then jerked their wrists, so that the great turnips fell shorn of their foliage. The roots dropped on one side, the leaves were thrown down on the other, and behind each labourer extended long, regular lines—one of mangel awaiting the cart, one of heavy leaves. Mr. Stockman praised the roots, put a task or two upon Lawrence and Thomas for later in the day, and proceeded into the woods. It was Saturday, and when first they came, there had been a general understanding that on the afternoon of that day leisure might be enjoyed at Falcon Farm as far as possible; but slowly— so slowly that Lawrence had hardly remarked it—the farmer appeared to forget this vague arrangement; indeed, he exhibited a marked ingenuity in finding minor tasks for the later hours of that day. Thomas Palk, who had less to occupy his mind than his fellow labourer, was conscious of this fact, and when Joe had proceeded after the wood-pigeons he pointed it out.

"His hand tightens," he said. "You may have marked it, or you may not, and it don't matter to you seemingly, because you've got nothing to do of a Saturday afternoon; but I have."

Lawrence conceded the fact.

"He likes his pound of flesh. But you haven't got anything to quarrel with, Tom."

"I don't say I have."

"Best way is to tell him clear at the beginning of a week that you want next Saturday afternoon off—then he knows and it goes through all right."

"You might think it was the best way," answered Palk; "but it ain't, because I've tried it. If you do that, he'll run you off your legs all the week, and hit upon a thousand jobs, and always remind you about Saturday, and say he knows as you'll be wanting to put in a bit extra, owing to the holiday coming. Then he'll offer to do your work o' Saturday afternoon, though of course there ain't none, and make a great upstore about putting off a bit of pleasuring he'd planned for himself."

Maynard laughed and stood up for a moment to rest the muscles of his back.

"It'll take cleverer chaps than us to be even with him."

"A cruel, vexatious man, and knows how to balance the good against the bad so clever that nobody in his senses would leave him," grumbled the elder.

They continued to pull the great golden roots from the earth, and for a long time neither spoke. Then Palk, whose mind still ran on his Saturday afternoon, explained that he had intended to meet a man at Ashburton and would now be unable to do so.

"If that's it, don't bother. I'm free and I can do all he wanted," said Lawrence.

"If you can, then I'm obliged," answered the horseman. "It's somebody I'm very wishful to see, because he married my sister. She's dead, but she had a son, and I like to know, for his mother's sake, how he's going on."

Maynard was not interested and they spoke no more. At the side of the field they were building up the roots into a "cave" — packing them together and then heaping earth upon them. The hour was early noon, and at the end of the row they desisted, emptied the full cart at the hedge-side and presently went in to dinner.

"I'm going to see that old hunter, Enoch Withycombe, again tomorrow," declared the younger. "He's a queer man to meet. Wonderful the learning he's gotten, along of being crippled and nought much to do but read and think."

"Miss Susan says he's not a very good companion for you young men, however."

"Why, Tom?"

"Along of his opinions."

"He's taught me a lot."

"That you may have to unlearn. They clever men are dangerous. I don't like clever men. You never know where you are with 'em."

Mr. Stockman did not return for dinner and they ate it with Susan. She was perturbed at the necessity of going to Ashburton for her father.

"He wants half a dozen things, and I'm so properly busy here this week-end that I don't know how I'll do it," she declared, unaware that Thomas was going down.

Slowly it dawned over his mind that he might serve her. He hesitated, for he dreaded making any original proposition. He felt ready and even desirous to offer his services, but spoke not from native caution. Maynard, however, helped him.

"Tom's going in," he said. "Can't he do it?"

"I've no right to trouble him," answered Soosie-Toosie.

"Why not, then? I'm sure he'll do anything he can."

"He might be busy on his own account?"

"He'll make time if he can save you trouble."

They debated the question as though Mr. Palk were not present. He listened quite silently; but finally, when it became impossible not to state his opinion on the point, he spoke.

"I will certainly do so," he said. "If you'll write them down, I will carry out the items, miss."

"It's asking too much," hesitated Susan.

"It may be, or it may not," he answered. "But I'll do it—for you."

She thanked him very heartily. She was honestly most grateful.

"It's proper kind and will take a great weight off my mind, Mr. Palk."

"Set 'em down; and if there's anything to be carried, I'll carry it."

Susan evinced her gratitude, but repeated her fears that she was asking too much. She was almost excited and forgot her dinner.

"There's the patterns from the tailor first. Father wants a new, warm suit, and be hopeful Mr. West have got the same stuff as before; but tailor will give you a little book of patterns, as will go in your pocket I should think. And there's they cough drops made with black currants for father, and his boots, that went to be mended, and his new leggings."

"Nought for yourself?" asked Thomas.

"That'll be enough. What I want can wait."

"No," he said slowly. "If there's any chores for you, set 'em down. In for a penny, in for a pound."

"A reel of thread at Miss Bassett's shop and a pound of loaf sugar—but there, you've got enough without them."

"Put 'em down."

"And if tailor's shut, will you knock at the side door? 'Tis understood I be coming."

"I'll knock at the side door if tailor's shut," promised Thomas. He was really gratified at receiving this commission, but his vague, subconscious emotion on the subject, even if he had desired to declare it, was of a nature far too nebulous for any words.

He went and duly returned with the patterns for Joe's new suit, his cough lozenges and the rest. Both Susan and Mr. Stockman expressed the deepest thanks.

"Nevertheless, Thomas, another time it may be better, in my humble judgment, if each of us does his appointed task," said the master. "You see, if I may say so, it puts us out of our stride if you do my daughter's lawful work, and Maynard does yours. I'm a great believer in method, Thomas, as you are yourself, thank God; so I feel pretty sure you'll put duty afore pleasure another time. And now I hope you're going to take a spot out of my new bottle of whisky along with me."

Mr. Palk replied nothing, but accepted the drink and hid his thoughts.

Next day Lawrence kept his engagement to see the old huntsman, and their conversation advanced their friendship. Maynard was under a common experience and had found that one man might charm his confidence in one direction, while another could win him upon a different plane. One string in him had vibrated to the geniality, tolerance and worldly wisdom of his new master and he had responded thereto; while the bed-ridden man in the valley served to awaken a different interest and attract the young man on higher, impersonal grounds. Enoch Withycombe was friendly and fearless. He loved talking, for no other social activity remained to him, and he enjoyed to retail the experiences of his life and the results of his reading, both in season and out. He declared that there was no better way to remember the things that he best liked in his past, and in his books, than by restating them to any who would listen. Some indeed mourned Enoch's opinions; but others were impressed by his acquired learning, and humble men, though they failed to follow his arguments, felt flattered that he should be at the trouble to discourse with them on such large subjects.

Maynard had found a common bond, and with the enthusiasm of the young went farther in some directions than the veteran was prepared to follow. For Enoch had a great theory that nobody must move faster than his wits could carry him, or accept any truth beyond his intelligence to grasp and, if need be, explain again.

Thus it happened that while Joe Stockman knew most about Lawrence's actual history, Mr. Withycombe alone learnt the result of the young man's experience in terms of opinion and belief. The one had sympathy and understanding for the objective events in Maynard's life, the other listened to the subjective convictions arising from those events. To-day Enoch's visitor indicated the nature of his own ideas, in language that Mr. Withycombe felt was too definite.

Lawrence sat by the invalid's bed, for the day was cold and wet and Enoch had not risen. Melinda was out for the afternoon, and Maynard had undertaken to keep her father company and make the tea. Invited to give his views on the eternal question, the young man did so.

"You can only judge of things by your own experience," he said. "You must talk of life as you find it, I reckon, not as somebody else finds it. It's what God Almighty does to us must decide our honest view about Him — not what He does to our neighbours."

Enoch was alert at once.

"A doubtful view, but go on; I'll hear your argument first."

"My argument is that God Almighty have treated me like a cat treats a mouse—that's my argument. Let me go a little way in hope, then down comes His Hand again; let me think I'm clear and free of doubt and difficulty and begin to get my breath and look round, and He pounces again. Cruelty for certain, and makes you feel that what He taught the cat to do, He thinks is a very good plan and worth copying."

"That's too ownself a view—too narrow far. You're not everybody."

"No; but I'm somebody; and if God makes a mouse, He ought to respect it; and since He's made me, He ought to respect me, so long as I'm respectable. I've got my rights, same as everything that comes in the world. If you make a child, it's your duty to cherish it, and think for it, and be jealous for it."

"But God don't make us like we make our children," said Enoch. "We ain't His own flesh and blood, Maynard. With a child, the kinship's closer. Our blood be in them and our faults, belike, are handed on. In fact, 'tis a terrible serious thing, knowing yourself, to make a child in your own image; and that's why Nature tickles us to do it afore we've got the wits to think twice. But God—that's different."

"Why? Either He's our Eternal, loving Father, or He ain't? And we're told He is. Then why don't He go one better than our good, earthly fathers, Mr. Withycombe, and put a bit more of Himself into us to start us safer? Have God ever neighboured with me? Have He ever allowed for my weakness, or lent a hand to help me through the dark places, or shown a light when I needed it most? Never. I've had to go single-handed all my life. And, when I've done my best to be straight and honest, has He ever patted me on the back and rewarded me? Never. He's flung my pride and my blood in my face, and showed up the past, when I hoped and prayed it was buried, and landed me in new difficulties, when I thought by my own just acts I had the right to suffer no more. He won't come between a man and his past, or save your character from the tyrant things stuffed into it by your havage."*

* *Havage*—ancestry.

"The sins of the fathers are visited on the children, my lad, because the Lord's reasonable and can't strain His own laws for special cases."

"Then He's weaker than man, who can do so. A just judge will often strain a law in particular cases, when he knows that to enforce it would be unjust. No God of justice would visit the sins of the fathers on the children surely?"

"When you say 'justice,' you use a very big word. There's the justice of Nature, which often looks unjust to our eyes, the justice that makes the fittest to survive. Not the fittest in our point of view, very likely. We fight Nature there, because what we understand by 'fittest' be what makes for our own convenience and advancement. But she's not out for us more'n anything else, and if she was to set to work on our account, and banish our enemies, and serve our friends, that wouldn't be justice from her point of view. And the justice of God's the same as that, Maynard. You may be tolerable sure He ain't out for us first and last and always. God's got a darned sight more on His hands than Buckland-in-the-Moor, or the world for that matter; and if our intellects was big enough to fathom His job, or get an idea of the Universe and the meaning of the Creator of the Universe, then we should see that His justice must be something long ways different from ours. 'Tis a quality of sin that it plays back and forth, like an echo, and every human knows that the sins of the children be visited on the parents, quite as often as it goes t'other way. Law's law."

"You wouldn't whip your child for showing the sins you put into him yourself?"

"Yes, I would, if I could help whip 'em out of him by so doing. I know a man, who told me he never felt his own sins come back to roost so bitter cruel, as when he had to flog his son for committing the same. These things are dark mysteries, you must know, and we can only see 'em, not solve 'em. But you mustn't let your own faults and misfortunes make you a sour man. That won't help you."

"It comes down to this," said Maynard: "either you end in believing in God, or not. I can talk to you, because you're broadminded and a thinker."

"Yes, it comes down to God, or no God," admitted Enoch. "And if you do believe in Him, then it's no manner of use yelping at Him, or whining at the way He treats you. You've got to knuckle under and there's an end of it. And if you don't believe in Him, then it's equally silly to snivel; because, if there's no God, then you might as well be a hound and bay at the moon as talk hard words against Him. There's a lot I read in my books that shows me the free-thinkers ain't so much angry with God, as angry with their neighbours for believing in Him. And what's the sense of that?"

"Do you believe in Him, if I may ask?"

"Most certainly I do. But once I did not. For a time I did in my fox-hunting days. Then I was terrible frightened of Him and felt a lot of fear when I saw good men suffer bad things. Then, when I was smashed, I flung Him over, lock, stock and barrel, and didn't worry no more. But now I believe in Him again."

"I believe in Him too," said Lawrence.

"Then believe in Him, and don't waste your wind and fret your wits blaming Him, because He don't do to others as He teaches us to do to others. If you believe, you must hold that His ways ain't our ways and that He sees the end from the beginning and suchlike comforting opinions. To believe in Him and think that you could go one better than Him is silly."

"One thing's certain: you can't have it both ways."

"You never spoke a truer word," admitted Mr. Withycombe. "Foxhunting taught me that afore you were born; and life didn't ought to hurt a man that admits it. You've looked at life with seeing eyes no doubt, and you must have seen lots of men treated worse than you, as well as better. The machine treats the blades of grass much the same, whether they be tall or short, and to be under the harrow, or under the weather, is the common lot of us all. Only a man's self knows his luck—not them looking at him from outside. One primrose be set on the south side of the hedge, another on the north; but that never puzzles me, or troubles them."

Maynard was very silent before this philosophy. The ideas came as something new and the speaker's attitude of good-humoured, mental superiority did not tempt him to explain the reason for his own pessimistic attitude.

Presently Enoch challenged him.

"And what have you got to say against that?" he asked.

"Nothing at all. The point of view's everything, and if you, from your bed of sickness, can feel all's for the best, I suppose I ought."

"There's all sorts of beds of sickness," answered Mr. Withycombe, "and no doubt the highest wisdom would say that sickness of the body is a lesser evil than sickness of the mind. But it's a very natural thing that a young man like you should be more interested in your own case than any other, and think it harder than any other. You all do; I don't blame you for that. But, with your good wits and good health and the world before you, there's no reason why you should let the past make you too down-daunted, whatever it may have done to you. There's always the future for a young man."

"The past can bitch up the future past praying for, however," argued Maynard, and the hunter considered the statement.

"The future be at the mercy of the past in a manner of speaking I grant," he said; "but a lot depends on whether we hurt ourselves in the past, or was only hurt by other people. Of course bad blood in our veins and vices can maim our future past praying for, as you say; but, with an even-minded man like you, I should judge you'd always been master of your past, and so ought to face the future more hopeful than what you seem to."

Lawrence still felt no desire to go into details. He guessed that Mr. Withycombe must be a great talker and knew not as yet whether confidences would be sacred. Moreover, he was weary of the subject and thought that the other might be.

"I dare say you're right. It may be a fool's trick always to keep the past before your eyes and let it shadow the future. That is if you can help it. But—however, you'll be pretty tired of me and my affairs. The thing is to take big views."

"It is—and to take views that ain't got the figure of No. 1 stuck in front of 'em, Maynard. The first thing to do, if you be going to set up for a thinker, is to rule yourself out, and all you dread and fear, and all you wish and desire. You've got to clear yourself out of the way; and some can, and then, if they've got brains, they see things clearer; and some can't, and that sort will never add a mite to their own wisdom, or anybody's. Get me my tea now. Us'll drink some tea. It's good of you and other men to be here now and again, because it gives my daughter a chance to stretch her legs and get the news. Now I should call her a sensible pattern of woman."

"So she is then. And a very popular woman, Mr. Withycombe."

"She's one that haven't let ill fortune sour her. No childer, and a husband lost before his time. But there she is, fifty year old and facing life and its duties and the dull task of a bed-ridden father, all so quiet and seemly as need be. No grumbling—not a sigh. I'm devilish cranky when the pain's bad; and though we can all be very wise to our neighbours of a Sunday afternoon, like this, there's times when we ain't very wise to our relations on weekdays. The past—the past—small wonder we look back if it's been as good as mine."

Maynard got the tea from the kitchen and arranged a bed-table for the invalid.

"Fire's right for toasting," he said. "Shall I make some?"

"Do so. A good thought. You don't tell me the reasons for your dark view of things and I don't want 'em—don't think it. But I'll ax you something of a private nature, because you'll respect confidence. No need to answer, however, if you feel it's none of your business. And it certainly is not. But if you can reply in strict confidence, young man, you'll pleasure me. Does Joe Stockman ever tell about Melinda, or give his opinion upon her?"

"He does. He's got a mighty high opinion of her and says she's a burning light and a lesson to all the women. He don't hide his feelings. He was figuring up her age a bit backalong."

Enoch laughed.

"Ah! But you can't have it both ways, as we said just now. Master Joe's always crying out about being an old man, but he don't want to feel an old man, or look an old man where my Melinda's concerned. I read Joe like a book I may tell you. He often thinks what a fine thing it would be to wed Melinda; but he knows he couldn't make a servant of her, like he does of his daughter."

"He's always been uncommon friendly to me," said Lawrence.

"Long may he continue so. You're a good man at your job I doubt not, and he knows it. But—well, enough said."

Maynard sat another hour with the old man and the talk drifted to fox-hunting.

When Melinda returned, she found her father in the best of tempers and the tea things cleared away and washed up.

"My!" she exclaimed. "What a husband you'll make some of these days, Mr. Maynard!"

"And he's going to come again," said Enoch. "He's promised. We'll set the world right between us afore we've done—him and me. And next time you go up over to Falcon Farm, you've got to take the man a book. I can't put my hand on it for the minute; but he's got to read it."

"You let what my father says go in at one ear and out at the other," warned Melinda. "He's a dangerous old man and we all know it."

"You won't fright him," declared Enoch. "He's going to be a great thinker some day, same as me!"

Then Lawrence went his way.

CHAPTER IX
A HOLIDAY FOR SUSAN

The church of St. Peter's at Buckland-in-the-Moor has a fine waggon roof and a noble little oak screen. The windows are mostly of uncoloured glass and the light of day illuminates the building frankly. It stands, with its burying ground round about it, on a little plateau uplifted among sycamore and pine. A few old tombs lie in the yard with others of recent date; but for the most part, on this January day, the frosty grass glittered over the mounds of unrecorded dead. The battlemented tower, sturdy and four square, rose in the midst of meadows at a step in the great slope from the Beacon. Trees surrounded the gap, ascending above and falling below in their winter nakedness. It was a place of peace and great distinction, marked by the fine quality of the human care devoted to it.

The five bells rang through the frosty morning, and Melinda Honeysett, with her brother, Jerry Withycombe, stood by the parapet of the burying ground and looked across the valley, where Lower Town lay far beneath upon the other side. It glimmered pale grey amidst its dim orchards and ploughed lands, and beyond it Dartmoor flung out ragged ridges from south to north, clean and dark under the low sun. Beneath was a gorge where the land broke and fell steeply to the junction of the Webburn Rivers at Lizwell Meet; and so still was the day in the interval of the bell music, that Jerry and his sister could hear the sister waters mingling and sending a murmur upward.

The man's eyes sought the roof tree of Green Hayes, which made a respectable splash above the lesser habitations of Lower Town; and Melinda knew very well of whom he was thinking. Jerry resembled his father, the old fox-hunter. He was large and finely put together, but he lacked his father's intelligence and possessed no great individuality of character. At present he was in love, and the fact transformed him, lent its own temporary qualities and lifted him into a personality.

"If you'd only see it, Jerry, you'd understand she's too young and selfish to make any man happy yet awhile," said Melinda. "I don't say she won't be a good wife some day, when she's properly in love with a man, and cares for him well enough to put him first and his wishes and welfare above her own. That may come to her; but it haven't yet. She's young for her age and not wife-old up till now, however you look at her."

"She ain't young for her age."

"Yes she is—and a cat-handed, careless girl about the house. Never got her thought on her work, as her mother will find out when Dinah goes."

"Well, I shan't be no damn good in this world without her," answered Jerry frankly. "That's a cast iron certainty; and she haven't turned me down yet, whether or no."

"She don't take you serious, however."

"She don't take nothing serious. She's built that way. And I don't take nothing serious but her. We'd neighbour very well, and her father haven't got a word against me, knowing I'm Church of England and a good character."

"Nobody's got nothing against you," said Mrs. Honeysett. "I should think not—nor yet against anybody of the name. Lord knows I don't blame you for falling in love with the girl—or any man. She's a lovely creature, and where she came from exactly among they homely, nice people, who can say? A proper changeling; and if one believed the old stuff you might say she was a changeling. Only the fairy stories all made it clear they fairy-born girls weren't no good for humans."

"She ain't a fairy; but she's the only creature in the world that's any good to me."

"Well, you study her character when you're along with her, and don't let yourself be thrown all in a mizmaze by her looks. She ain't a very contented girl, remember."

"She would be if Dinah was away. 'Tis beastly hard on John, Dinah not saying the word. And I wouldn't suffer it if I was him."

"You wait. You don't know what you'd suffer, or what you wouldn't. The thing to find out for you is Jane's idea of your opinions and prospects. They like a man to know a bit and be wiser than them."

"She's as clever as they make 'em and sharp as a needle. 'Tis no good my pretending to be cleverer than her, because she knows I ain't."

"Don't you eat humble pie all the same. She's not the sort to take that in a very loving spirit. God help the man she masters."

They were still talking when a pair approached from Falcon Farm. Mr. Palk was a steadfast churchgoer and to-day he had brought Susan Stockman.

"Wonders never cease!" cried Melinda. "How did you get off to worship, Soosie?"

Susan was excited at her rare adventure.

"Father's away. He's gone down to a friend at Kingsbridge for a day or two's shooting. Decided yesterday and went off in the afternoon, and Mr. Palk and Mr. Maynard was quite content to let dinner look after itself and be a thought late."

"Why not? 'Tis less than human of Joe to keep you moiling Sunday morning. I've told him so for that matter."

"But he always comes himself," said Susan, "and he likes his dinner uncommon well Sunday."

Melinda shook her head.

"'Tis no good being religious if we won't let other people be," she answered. "Your soul did ought to be more to your father than a hot Sunday dinner."

The gaunt woman smiled.

"Well, here I be to-day anyway; and the walk, which Mr. Palk kindly allowed me to take along with him, have rested me wonderful."

"Very proud I'm sure," said Thomas.

They returned together after the service, and Mrs. Honeysett could not fail to notice that Susan's adventure had done her good. For a time her anxious eyes harboured a little rest. But her Sunday gown did not please Melinda.

"You ought to get yourself a new dress and a thicker jacket," she declared. "You could put your finger through that old thing and the moths be got in the neck of it."

"I hardly ever want go-to-meeting clothes," explained Susan, and the other woman grew mildly indignant.

"You be so meek as a worm, Soosie-Toosie. No doubt a very Christian virtue; but it do make me a thought wild off and on. Not a word against your father, of course, but a man's a man, and 'tis their nature to put on us; and 'tis our duty to see they don't. You've got to watch the best of 'em like a cat watches a mouse, else they'll come between you and your rights. The creatures can't help it. They be built so, like all the other male things. It's deep in 'em; and we've got to get it out. Why, I'll flare out against my own father, love him as I do, and a bed-lier though he is, if I find he's forgetting I'm flesh and blood and thinking I'm a machine. Once let 'em think we're machines and it's good-bye to our self-respect for evermore. We're no more machines than they be."

Mr. Palk nodded vigorously to himself at these sentiments, but he did not speak.

"I know my place," said Susan.

"That's just what you do not, and you'll make me cross in a minute and undo the good of church. You're a reasonable creature, ain't you?"

"I hope so, Melinda."

"You've got a soul, ain't you?"

"I believe so. It's a poor come-along-of-it if I haven't."

Susan looked almost frightened.

"Very well then, act according. You wouldn't cling after the next world so frantic if you was having a better time in this one. That's cause and effect, that is, as my father would tell you. It's your feeling for getting back a bit of your own after you be dead. If your Maker had meant you to be a donkey and a beast of burden, He'd have made you one."

"We're taught to bear other people's burdens, my dear."

"Yes, but we ain't taught to do other people's work—not if they can do it themselves."

"I only do my own work, Melinda."

"Not a chance! You do a cook's work and an all-work's work and you're a sewing machine thrown in, not to mention washing for three men and a boy, and all the thousand odd jobs from sun-up till you drop in your bed."

Mr. Palk could not contain himself.

"Gospel!" he said. "Gospel!"

"To do their work for 'em is to encourage our neighbours in selfishness and laziness; and Lord knows such vices don't want encouraging in the men," continued Melinda.

"What would you do if you was in power?" asked Susan. "What could you do for that matter?"

"I'd strike," replied the elder. "I'd strike for a maid-of-all-work first. I'd tell your father I was his daughter. He wants reminding."

"He's terrible fond of me, however. He looks to me if he scratches his finger."

"And right to do so, seeing he's got no wife. I'm not saying he's not a very fine man indeed, because we all know he is; but I'm saying you ought to help him to be finer still and open his eyes to a fault he could cure if he was minded to. What do you think, Mr. Palk?"

But, at a direct question, Thomas subsided. His caution thrust upon his private feelings and kept him quiet. He shook his head.

"Least said, soonest mended, ma'am. I wouldn't go for to offer an opinion—though I might have my views. A man's a right to his views, haven't he?"

Melinda snorted.

"See how they take sides against us!" she said.

But this Thomas would not allow.

"I won't take no sides, though you're made of sense and—and—well—there 'tis."

They parted presently and Susan proceeded homeward with the labourer. They spoke very little, but, apropos of some remark from Mr. Palk, Susan committed herself to the opinion that animals were very backward in their minds.

"They be," admitted Thomas. "Their ignorance is something awful. Take a cat, generally counted a clever creature. He's been catching mice since creation, no doubt, and yet don't know to this day what a mouse be called!"

With such reflections they beguiled their journey and each was cheered in a subconscious fashion by the companionship of the other.

Thomas framed a sentiment and nearly spoke it. He had it on his tongue to hope that Mr. Stockman might be inspired oftener to go away for a week's end; but he felt it unwise to commit himself to such a strong wish and therefore kept it hidden.

Soosie-Toosie, for her part, felt some increase of well-being from her religious exercises.

"You shan't suffer, you men," she said, as they entered the wicket gate. "Give me fifteen minutes and 'twill all be hotted up."

CHAPTER X
TALKING WITH DINAH

On a public holiday in early spring, Joe Stockman suddenly declared an urgent necessity to communicate with Arthur Chaffe at Lower Town on the subject of some hurdles.

"And if you saw your way to take the air in that direction, Maynard, I shall be more than a bit obliged," he said.

Susan mildly protested.

"'Tis a holiday, father, and Mr. Maynard's bound for pleasuring, be sure," she said.

"I know, and I hope he is," answered her father, "but I thought perhaps he might be taking a bit of a walk and would so soon go that way as another. 'Tis no odds, of course, if not convenient. I must meet a few men in Ashburton myself—more business than pleasure, however—else I'd ride down."

"I'll go then," suggested Susan. "I'm wishful to see Faith Bamsey."

Lawrence, however, declared himself very willing to go.

"I'm not for the fair," he said, "and would just so soon walk down to the carpenter as anywhere else. I've got no use for revels."

"I'm much to blame, mind you," confessed Joe. "I heap blame on myself, because I did ought to have written to Chaffe on the subject a month ago; but it slipped my memory along of my rheumatism, and being so busy helping you chaps afterwards to spread muck on the land. Then I was with the shepherd a lot too, and so on. But Chaffe's always got a little stock of seasoned hurdles in his big store, and he can send me just so many as ever he likes up to fifty yards of 'em; and if he can cart them up to-morrow, the better pleased I'll be. And if he can't, I must get 'em elsewhere, bitter sorry as I shall feel to do so. Make that clear, Lawrence. And say I'm blaming myself a good bit about it. I ought to have given Arthur time, I allow— wonder though he is."

Accordingly the cowman set out for Lower Town and took his holiday on foot. The day was fine, and he told Soosie-Toosie that he should not be back before milking. She was taking no pleasure herself, but glad to devote the day to some spring cleaning. Palk and the boy, Neddy Tutt, had started at daybreak for the old home of Thomas near Newton Abbot. Maynard had spent a second Sunday afternoon with the Bamseys, and now he called there on his way to Mr. Chaffe with Susan's message for Faith. But Mrs. Bamsey was from home with Benjamin. They and Jane had driven early to Ashburton and were taking holiday. Dinah had not gone, and she answered the door when Lawrence knocked. She was surprised to see him.

"I never!" she said. "Why ain't you gone to the fair?"

"No use for fairs. Why ain't you for that matter, miss?"

"No use for them either. I'm under the weather a bit. Come in and have a tell. There's nobody home but me."

Their acquaintance had ripened a little, for Dinah came to Falcon Farm sometimes with messages. Lawrence admired Dinah's straightforward mind, but was puzzled at some things about her; while she, inspired by her step-father's opinion, that the man had some hidden grievance against life, found him interesting. She did not think he had a grievance, for he was not particularly gloomy with her or anybody else; but she had found him reticent concerning himself and he never spoke about his own experiences, or earlier existence, though she had invited him to do so.

"Where's Johnny?" asked the visitor.

"Fairing—or so he said; but if truth's known I expect he's to work. He often gives out he's away when he isn't. He's catched a chap once or twice like that."

"Ah! He knows his business. I expect he's down on the water somewhere. I should have guessed, now, you would have been up to his plans and going to take him his dinner by the river presently."

Dinah was rather aghast at this pleasantry. It argued an intimate knowledge of lovers' ways on the part of the other.

"You might think so," she said. "And often I have for that matter. But we're out—my fault, too."

"Never!"

"Yes—and that's why I say I'm under the weather."

"Well, Miss Susan wants Mrs. Bamsey to lend her the cheese press. We're going to have a try at cheese-making. Mr. Stockman's got an idea the thing be well worth trying; and Miss Susan wants to come over and have a tell about it and learn Mrs. Bamsey's wisdom. And the clutch of chickens be ready for you."

"Didn't you hear me say I was under the weather?"

"Twice. Yes. Sorry. It'll come right. Lovers' quarrels be naught."

"What have you heard Cousin Joe say about me and Johnny?"

"D'you want to know?"

"I do then."

"He says you're not treating John fair, and that it's a very black mark against you not fixing up the wedding."

"So it is, and nobody knows it better than me."

"You've got your reasons, no doubt."

"God knows if I have."

He said nothing, and she asked a curious question.

"Be you faithful, Mr. Maynard?"

"I hope so."

"I can talk to you. Funnily enough I've wanted to talk to you for a month, but held off. And now's the chance. I can trust you?"

He was a little uneasy.

"Don't you tell me anything you'll be sorry for."

"I'll tell you this. Johnny's sworn he won't see me no more till I name the day. And his people are on his side—very properly. And why don't I name the day? Can you answer that?"

"No, I can't—nor anybody else but your own self I should think."

"What's love like?"

"You did ought to know."

"So I did; and that's the trouble. I did ought to know; but I don't. Only I know this bitter clear: I'm not in love with Johnny. And it's hurting me and it's wrong."

He was sorry for her, but not astonished to learn the truth. Indeed he had already guessed it. Others also suspected it. Susan had spoken plainly on the subject one night to her father.

"'Tis whispered you took him for Mr. Bamsey's sake."

"No, I can't be let off like that. I wouldn't have done that, though it helped me to decide, of course. But I took him, because I thought I did love him, and now, after keeping company just on a year, I know I do not. Now you're a man that understands things."

"Don't you fancy that. None on God's earth is more puzzled about things than me. I've had a puzzling life I may tell you."

"I haven't. Till now my life's been as clear as sunshine. But now—now I'm up against a pretty awful thing, and it's cruel hard to make up my mind. Was you ever really in love?"

"Never mind me."

"Was you ever in doubt, I mean?"

"Never."

"I don't ask for rudeness, but reason. There's nobody you can ask in my life, because they be all biased. I'm not thinking of myself—God judge me if I am. I'm just wondering this: Can I be the right down proper good wife Johnny deserves to have if I don't love him? And the question that's so hard is, ought I to marry him not loving him? Not because of my feelings, but because of his future. Think if you was him, and loved a woman as truly as he loves me, and you had to say whether you'd marry her and chance the fact she didn't love you, or, knowing she didn't, would give her up."

"That's not how it is, though. Johnny don't know you don't love him. He don't know what you're feeling. I judge that by what he says, because he often drops in and talks openly, finding all on his side."

"What would you do?"

"If I wanted to marry a woman and she'd said 'yes,' but afterwards found herself mistook, I shouldn't love her no more."

"Then you don't know much about love."

"Very likely I don't."

"It's a selfish thing. If I was in love, I'd be like Johnny—and worse. A proper tigress I expect."

"Are you in love?"

"No, I swear I'm not. Not with anybody. I've growed up, you see, since I said 'yes' to John. I was a child, for all my years, when I said it. Growing up ain't a matter of time; it's a matter of chance. Some people never do grow up. But I have, and though I don't know what it would be like to fall in love, I know parlous well I'm not, and never was. And it comes back just to what I said. Would it be better for Johnny to marry him not loving him, because

I've promised to do so, or would it be better for him if I told him I wasn't going to? That's the question I've got to decide."

"You'll decide right," he said. "And you don't want other people's views. You know."

"I know what I'd like to do; but just because my own feeling is strong for telling him I won't marry him, I dread it. Of course he'll say I'm only thinking of myself."

"You can't be sure what he'll say."

"Yes, I can: I know him."

"If he knew you didn't love him — —"

"He'd only say he'd larn me how to later. But he wouldn't believe it."

"If you was to hold off much longer, he'd chuck you perhaps."

"Never. I'm his life. He says it and he means it."

"But to marry him would be your death?"

She nodded.

"Yes, I think."

"Perhaps you're wrong, however."

"Very likely. My first thought was to tell him how it was with me and leave it to him. But I know what he'd do. He'd only laugh at me and not take it serious, or let me off."

"You are thinking for yourself then?"

"I suppose I am."

"It's natural. You've got your life to live."

"Be sporting," she said. "Don't think of me and don't think of him. Put us out of your mind and just say what you'd do if you was me."

He felt a little moved for her. It is pathetic to see a resolute creature reduced to irresolution. The manhood in him inclined Lawrence to take her part against the man. It seemed an awful thing that her life should be ruined, as it must be if she married one she did not love. He liked Dinah better than Johnny, for the latter's arrogance and rather smug and superior attitude to life at large did not attract Maynard.

"It's never right under any circumstances for a woman to marry a man she does not love," he said.

"You think so?"

"I do—I'm positive."

"Even if she's promised?"

"Your eyes are opened. You promised because you thought you loved him. Now you know right well you don't. A proper man ought to bend to that, however much it hurts. And if you still think it's your duty to marry him, I say duty's not enough to marry on."

"It's hurting me fearfully, and there's something awful wrong about it. They want me away from here—Mrs. Bamsey and Jane—that's natural too. Though why I'm confiding in you I don't know. Something have drove me to do it. But I know you'll be faithful."

"I wish I could help you, miss. I can only say what I think."

"You have helped me I reckon. You've helped me a lot. I was half in a mind to go and see Enoch Withycombe; but he's old, and the young turn to the young, don't they?"

"I suppose they do; though I dare say the old know best, along of experience."

"The old forget a lot. They always begin by telling you they remember what it was to be young themselves; but they don't. They can't. Their blood runs slower; they're colder. They've changed through and through since they were young. They can't remember some things."

"I dare say they can't."

"Will you come for a walk with me one day and show me that stone you was telling about—the face?"

"You remember that?"

"Yes; you was going to say more about it the last Sunday you was here; then you shut up rather sudden."

The idea of a walk with Dinah had certainly never entered Maynard's head. He remained silent.

"D'you think it would be wrong, or d'you only think it would be a nuisance?" she asked.

"It's a new notion to me. I'd like to pleasure you and it wouldn't be a nuisance—far from it I'm sure; but as to whether it would be wrong—it would and it wouldn't I fancy. It couldn't be wrong in itself; but seeing you're tokened to another man, you're not free to take walks with Dick, Tom, or Harry. No doubt you see that."

"John wouldn't like it?"

"Certainly he wouldn't. You know that."

"Would you mind my walking with another man if you was engaged to me?"

"Yes, I should, very much indeed; especially if I was in the same fix that John Bamsey is."

"Poor John. There's such a thing as liking a man too well to love him, Mr. Maynard."

"Is there?"

"I'm beginning to feel—there—I've wasted enough of your time. You won't go for a walk with me?"

"I'd like to go for a walk with you."

"I'll ask you again," she said. "Then, whether I marry John, or don't marry John, there'll be no reason against."

"I quite understand."

"To see that face on the stone. You'll find Mr. Chaffe in his workshop. Holidays are naught to him. Good-bye. Truth oughtn't to hurt honest people, ought it?"

"Nothing hurts like truth can, whether you're honest, or whether you're not."

He went forward turning over with mild interest the matter of the conversation. He was little moved that she should have asked him to go for a walk. From any other young woman such a suggestion had been impressive; but not from her. He had noticed that she was never illusive and quite unpractised in the art of lure, or wile. The stone he had mentioned was a natural face carved by centuries of time, on the granite rocks of Hey Tor, some miles away. He had mentioned it in answer to a remark from Benjamin Bamsey, and then, for private but sufficient reasons he had dropped the subject. His connection with the stone belonged to a time far past, concerning which he was not disposed to be communicative. That she should have remembered it surprised him. But perhaps the only thing that had really interested her was the fact he dropped the subject so suddenly.

He fell to thinking on his own past for a time, then returned to Dinah. That she could confide in him inclined him to friendship. He admired her character and was sorry for the plight in which she found herself. He hoped that she might drop Bamsey and find a man she could love. He was aware that her position in her step-father's house held difficulties, for the situation had often been discussed at Falcon Farm. Whether she decided for John, or against him, it was probably certain she would leave Green Hayes; and that would mean distress for Benjamin Bamsey. He was sorry for all concerned, but not inclined to dwell over-much on the subject. His own thoughts were always enough for him, and his experience had tended somewhat to freeze the sources of charity and human enthusiasm at the fount. He was not soured, but he was introspective to the extent that the affairs of his fellow creatures did not particularly challenge him. Thus it was left for Thomas Palk to see the truth of the situation at Falcon Farm; Lawrence had never troubled to realise it for himself. It seemed improbable that he would be woven into the texture of other lives again. Indeed, he had long since determined with himself that he would never be.

Arthur Chaffe was making a coffin.

"The dead can wait for no man," he said. "A poor old widow; but I'm under her command for the moment; and she shall have good work."

Lawrence told the matter of the hurdles and Mr. Chaffe promised to do what he could.

"Joe treats time with contempt," he declared. "He did ought to have told me long ago; but I always reckon with the likes of him. I think for a lot of people and save them from their own slow wits. Not that Stockman's got slow wits. His wits serve him very well indeed, as no doubt you've found."

"He's a good farmer and a kind-hearted sort of man."

"So he is, so he is. You'll not hear me say a word against him."

"Yet a few do."

"They do. But mind you, when he says he worked as a young man, it's true. He did work and took a long view, so now you find him as he is. But he never loved work for itself, same as I do. Work never was meat and drink to him; and when it had got him what he wanted, he was very well content to play and let others work for him. And knowing well what work means, nobody he employs will ever deceive him on the subject."

"He sees that we earn our money. But he's fair."

"Ah! To be fair with your neighbour is a great gift. Few are, and who shall wonder? Now Joe's a man who takes a generous view of himself. But 'tis better to be hard on yourself and easy with other people—don't you think?"

"A fine thing, to be hard on yourself, no doubt," admitted Lawrence.

"Yes, and them who are hardest on themselves will often be easiest with their neighbours. But that's a high position to reach, and few can."

"It's very easy in my opinion not to judge other people. But when life demands you to judge, then the trouble begins."

"When our own interest comes in, we often make a mess of it and judge wrong," admitted Mr. Chaffe. "And what I always say to anybody in a fix is this: to get outside the question and think how it would be if it was all happening to somebody else. If you've got the sense to do that, you'll often be surprised to find the light will shine. And you'll often be surprised, also, to find how much smaller the thing bulks, if you can wriggle out of it yourself and take a bird's-eye view."

"I expect that's true."

"Oh yes, it's true. I've proved it. A thing happens and you're chin deep in it. Then you say to yourself, 'Suppose I was dead and looking down on this job from my heavenly mansion, how would it seem then?' And if you've got the intellects to do it, then you often get a gleam of sense that you never will while you're up against the facts and part of 'em. It's like the judge trying a case, without having any interest in it beyond the will that right shall be done."

"Men haven't the gift for that."

"They have not; yet even to try to do it stills passion and breeds patience and helps religion."

"Very good advice, no doubt."

"This coffin will go along early to-morrow morning, and I'll bring half the hurdles this week in two or three loads; and tell Joe the price be up a thought since last year. He knows that as well as I do."

Maynard noted the instructions in a little pocket-book and presently departed. He took a meal of bread and cheese and cider at the inn hard by, then set out on an extended round, walked to Widecombe, tramped the Moors, watched the swaleing fires, that now daily burned upon them, and did not return home until the hour of milking.

CHAPTER XI
NEW BRIDGE

On New Bridge, over Dart, stood Dinah with the sun warm upon her face, while a first butterfly hovered on the golden broom at water's edge. She had sent a message to Johnny by his sister that she would meet him here, and now, while she waited, she speculated on the difference between the beauty of the May day and the ugliness of what she was about to do. But she had decided at last, and having done so, she could only wonder why it had taken her so many weeks to reach a decision. To her direct instincts delay had been a suffering and produced a condition of mental bad health; but it was not for her own sake that she had delayed, and she knew now that her hesitation had been no kindness to Johnny, though endured largely out of affection for him. She was convinced, beyond possibility of doubt, that her regard could not be called love and she had determined with herself, as she was bound to do, that to marry under such circumstances would be no marriage in any seemly interpretation of the contract. She had the imagination to know, however, that what was beaten ground to her—a way exploited a thousand times by day and sleepless night—was no such thing for him. He had said that he would have nothing more to do with her until she named the day, and he was coming now under expectation of hearing her do so. Instead he must learn that the day could never be named.

She was full of sorrow, but no fear. Dinah had long discounted the effect of the thing she was called to do. She did not expect anybody to be patient, or even reasonable, save her step-father.

Johnny appeared punctually, with his gun on his shoulder. They had not met for more than a month, but he ignored the past and greeted her with a kiss. She suffered it and reflected that this was the last time he would ever kiss her.

"At last," he said. "I've hated this job, Dinah; and you'll never know how much I hated it; but what could I do?"

"I don't know, Johnny. You could have wondered a bit more why I held off perhaps."

"And didn't I wonder? Didn't I puzzle myself daft about it? I don't know now—such a downright piece as you—I don't know now why you hung back. It wasn't natural."

"Yes it was—everything's natural that happens. It couldn't happen if it wasn't natural—old Arthur Chaffe said that once and I remembered it."

"If it was natural, then there was a reason," he answered, "and I'd like to hear it, Dinah—for curiosity."

"The reason is everything, John. I didn't know the reason myself for a good bit—the reason why I held away from you; and when I did, I was so put about that it seemed to alter my whole nature and make me shamed of being alive."

"That's pretty strong. Better we don't go back then. I'll ask no questions and forget. We'll begin again by getting married."

"No; the reason you've got to hear, worse luck. The reason why I behaved so strange was this, John: I'd made a terrible mistake—terrible for both of us. I thought the love that I had for you, and still have for you, and always shall, was the love of a woman for the man she's going to wed. Then, like a cloud, it came over me, denser and denser, that it was not. Listen— you must listen. I examined into it—give me that credit—I examined into it with all my senses tingling night and day. I never worked so hard about anything after I'd got over my first fright. And then I saw I'd slipped into this, being young and very ignorant about love—much more so than many girls younger than me; because I never was interested in men in the way they are. I found that out by talking to girls, and by the things they said when they knew I was tokened to you. They looked at marriage quite different from me, and they showed me that love is another thing altogether seen that way than as I'd seen it. They made me terrible uncomfortable, because I found they'd got a deep understanding that I had not got about it; and they laughed at me, when I talked, and said I didn't know what love meant. And—and—I didn't, Johnny. That's the naked truth."

He was looking at her with a flushed face.

"Get on—get on to the end of it," he said.

"Be patient. I'm bitter sorry. We was boy and girl for so many years, and I loved you well enough and always shall; but I don't know nothing about the sort of love you've got for me. The first I heard about it was from Jane. She knows. She understands far deeper about what love is than I do. I only know I haven't got it, and what I thought was it didn't belong to that sort of love at all. Haven't you seen? Haven't you fretted sometimes—many times—because I couldn't catch fire same as you, when you touched me and put your arms round me? Didn't it tell you nothing?"

"How the devil should it? Women are different from men."

"Not they—not if they love proper. But how could you know that—you, who was never in love before? I don't blame you there; but if you'd only compare notes with other men."

"Men don't compare notes as you call it about sacred things like love."

"Don't they? Then they're finer than us. Women do. Anyway I found out, to my cruel cost, I was only half-fledged so far as you were concerned."

"I see. But you needn't lie about it—not to me. You loved me well enough, and the right way too. You can't shuffle out of it by pretending any trash about being different from other girls. You loved me well enough, and if you'd been on-coming like some creatures, I'd have hated you for it. That was all right, and you knew what you were doing very well indeed. And you're lying, I say, because it wasn't women have brought you to this. It was men. A man rather. Be plain, please, for I won't have no humbug about this. You've found some blasted man you hanker after and think you like better than me. And it's not the good part in you that have sunk to any such base beastliness; it's the bad, wicked part in you—the part I never would have believed was in you. And I've a right to know who it is. And I will know."

"Hear me then, Johnny. May God strike me dead on this bridge, this instant moment, if there's any man in the world I love—or even care for. I tell you that I've never known love and most likely never shall. 'Tis long odds it be left out of me altogether. And I can't marry you for that good reason. I didn't come to it in a hurry. For one of my nature I waited and waited an amazing time, and for your sake I hoped and hoped I'd see different, and I tried hard to see different. I thought only for you, and I'm thinking only for you now. It would have been far easier for me to go on with it than break. Can't you see that? But afterwards—you're a quick man and you're a man that gives all, but wants all back again in exchange for all; and rightly so. But what when you'd found, as find you must, that I'd not loved you as you thought? Hell—hell—that's what it would have been for you."

"You can spin words to hide your thoughts. I can't. You're a godless, lying traitor—and—no—no—I call that back. You don't know what you're saying. Have some mercy on a man. You're my all, Dinah. There's nothing else to life but you! Don't turn me down now—it's too late. You must see it's gone too far. You can't do it; you can't do it. I'm content to let it be as it is. If you don't love me now, I'll make you love me. I'll—all—I'll give all and want nothing again! It's cruel—it's awful—no such thing could happen. I believe you when you say there's not another man. I believe you with all my heart. And then—then why not me? Why not keep your solemn oath and promise? If anything be left out of you, let me put it in. But there's nothing left out—nothing. You're perfect, and the wenches that made you think you wasn't ban't worthy to black your boots. For Christ's sake don't go back on me—you can't—it wouldn't be you if you did."

"Don't make it worse than it is, dear John. I'm proud you could care for me so well; but don't you see, oh, don't you see that I can't act a lie? I can't do it. Everything tells me not to do it. I'm in a maze, but I know that much. I must be fair; I must be straight. I don't love you like that. I thought I did, because I was a fool and didn't know better. It can't be. I'm fixed about it."

For a moment he was quiet. Then he picked up his gun, which he had rested against the parapet of the bridge. His face was twisted with passion. Then she heard him cock the gun. For a moment she believed that he meant to shoot her. She felt absolutely indifferent and was conscious of her own indifference, for life seemed a poor possession at that moment.

"You can kill me if you like," she said. "I don't want to go on living—not now."

He cursed her.

"Lying bitch! Death's a damned sight too good for you. May your life be hell let loose, and may you come to feel what you've made me feel to-day. And you will, if there's any right and justice in life. And get out of Lower Town—d'you hear me? Get out of it and go to the devil, and don't let me see your face, or hear your voice in my parents' home no more."

A market cart came down the hill and trundled towards them, thus breaking into the scene at its climax. John Bamsey turned his back and strode down the river bank; Dinah hid her face from the man and woman in the cart and looked at the river.

But the old couple, jogging to Poundsgate, had not missed the man's gestures.

The driver winked at his wife.

"Lovers quarrelling!" he said; "and such a fine marnin' too. The twoads never know their luck."

With heavy heart sat Johnny by the river under great pines and heard the rosy ring-doves over his head fluttering busily at their nest; while Dinah leant upon the parapet of the bridge and dropped big tears into the crystal of Dart beneath her.

CHAPTER XII
AFTERWARDS

The shock of Orphan Dinah's sudden action fell with severe impact in some directions, but was discounted among those of wider discernment. The mother of John had seen it coming; his father had not. In a dozen homes the incident was debated to Dinah's disadvantage; a few stood up for her—those who knew her best. In secret certain of John's acquaintance smiled, and while expressing a sympathy with him, yet felt none, but rather satisfaction that a man so completely armed at all points, so successful and superior, should receive his first dose of reality in so potent a shape.

The matter ran up and down on the tongues of those interested. His mother and sister supported Johnny in this great tribulation, the first with dignity, the second with virulence, hardly abated when she found herself more furious than John himself.

For after the first rages and intemperate paroxysms in which Jane eagerly shared, she fancied Johnny was cooling in his rage; and, such are the resources of human comedy, that anon her brother actually reproved Jane for some particularly poignant sentiments on the subject of Dinah. He had set her a very clear-cut example in the agonised days of his grief; but presently, to the bewilderment of Jane, who was young and without experience of disappointment, John began to calm down. He roughly shut up the girl after some poisonous criticism of Dinah, and a sort of alliance into which brother and sister had slipped, and into which Jane entered with full force of love for John and hate for Dinah, threatened to terminate.

Jane lessened nothing of her fervid affection for John, however, and it remained for another man to explain what seemed to her a mystery. He was not a very far-seeing, or competent person, but he had reached to the right understanding of Johnny's present emotion.

With Jerry Withycombe Jane fell in beside a track through the forest, where he was erecting a woodstack, and since their relations were of the friendliest and Jane, indeed, began to incline to Jerry, she had no secrets from him and spoke of her affairs.

"What's come to them I don't know," she said. "Father's plucking up again, and I can see, though Dinah's trying to get a place and clear out, that he'll come between and prevent it very likely. Mother's at him behind the scenes, but God knows what they say to each other when they go to bed. You'd think Dinah wouldn't have had the face to bide in the house a day after that wickedness; but there she is—the devil. And John ordered her to go, too, for he told me he had."

"It's your father," answered Jerry. "My sister was telling about it. Melindy says that Mr. Bamsey's troubled a lot, and though he knows Dinah has got to go, he's taking it upon himself to decide about where she shall go and won't be drove."

"I see through that; mother don't," said Jane. "Father only cares for Dinah really, and he thinks, in his craft, that very like, given time, things may calm down and her be forgiven. That's his cowardly view, so as he shall keep her. But nobody shan't calm down if I can help it. I won't live with the wretch, and so I tell John. Men ban't like us: they don't feel so deep. They're poor things in their tempers beside us. A woman can hate a lot better than a man. Why, even Johnny—you'd never believe it; but you'd almost think he's cooling a bit if it was possible."

"He is," answered Jerry. "And why not? What the hell's the good of keeping at boiling point over what can't be helped? Especially if, on second thoughts, you begin to reckon it can be helped."

"What d'you mean by that?" asked Jane.

"Why, you see John's a very determined sort of customer. He's never took 'no' for an answer from anybody, and he's got an idea, right or wrong, that a man's will is stronger than a woman's. I thought so, too, till I got to know what a rare will you've got. But there it is in a word; not two days agone I met Johnny, and he said where there was life there was hope."

Jane gasped.

"That's what be in his head then! That's what made him stop me pretty sharp when I was telling the truth about her?"

Jerry nodded.

"Very likely it might have been. In fact, he ain't down and out yet—in his own view, anyway. You see, as John said to Lawrence Maynard, and Maynard told me, 'If Dinah ain't got no other man in sight, she's what you may call a free woman still.' And I believe that John be coming round to the opinion that Dinah may yet live to see she was wrong about him."

Jane stared and her thoughts reeled.

"D'you mean to tell me that a man like my brother could sink to think again of a girl that had jilted him?" she flamed.

"Don't you turn on me," protested Jerry. "It ain't my fault men are like that. You know John better than I do. But it wouldn't be contrary to nature if he did want her still. A man in love will stand untold horrors from a woman; and though it may make you, looking on, very shamed for him — still, life's life. And I believe, if John thinks he can get Dinah back, he'll come down off his perch yet and eat as much dirt as she likes to make him."

"It's a beastly thought — a beastly thought!" cried Jane. "But he shan't — he never shall have her now if I can prevent it. I'd be a miserable woman if I had to suffer her for a sister-in-law now."

Jerry saw danger in this attitude.

"I always feel just like you feel," he said, "but for God's love, Jenny, don't you go poking into it. It's a terrible good example of a job where everybody had best to mind their own business. You let John do what he's minded to do. Men in love be parlous items, and if he's still that way, though wounded, then 'tis like a wild tiger a man have fired at and only hurt. He's awful dangerous now, I shouldn't wonder; and if he wants her still and counts to get her, God help anybody who came between. He'd break your neck if you tried to: that I will swear."

But Jerry was more perturbed at the vision he had conjured than Jane. For his information she was able to give facts concerning the other side.

"If that's what John's after, he's only asking for more misery then," she said. "I hope you're wrong, Jerry, for I should never feel the same to John if I thought he could sink to it; but anyway he needn't fox himself that she'll ever go back on it again. That much I'm positive certain. Cunning as she is, I can be more cunning than her, and I know all her sorrow about it and pretended straightness and honesty was put on. She weren't sorry, and she never was straight, and I've sworn before to you and will again, that she's got somebody else up her sleeve."

"Who then?" asked Jerry Withycombe.

"I can't tell you. Lord knows I've tried hard enough to find out; but I haven't — not yet. Only time will show. It's a man not worthy to breathe the same air with John you may be sure. She was too common and low ever to understand John, and his high way of thinking; and she'd be frightened to marry such a man, because she knows she'd always have to sing small and take a second place. She's a mass of vanity under her pretences."

"We all know you don't like her; and more don't I, because you don't," answered Jerry. "But if you are positive sure she'll never come round to Johnny again, it might be truest kindness to tell him so. Only for the Lord's sake do it clever. You may be wrong, and if there's a chance of that, you'd do far better to leave it alone."

"I'm not wrong; but all the same I shall leave it alone," said Jane. "What mother and me want is for her to get out of the house, so as we can breathe again. It's up to father, and father's going to have a bad time if he stands against mother."

"Dinah won't stop, whether your father wants for her to or not," prophesied Jerry.

But a few evenings after this meeting, the situation was defined for the benefit of Jane and her mother and, with Dinah out of the way at Ponsworthy, her foster-father endeavoured to ameliorate the existing strain. He had confided his difficulties to Arthur Chaffe and been counselled to speak plainly. Indeed, at his wish, the carpenter joined his circle and supported him.

Mr. Bamsey tried to conceal the fact that Arthur had come to help him, for his friend not seldom dropped in to supper; but on this occasion Faith felt aware of an approaching challenge and was not surprised when, after the evening meal, her husband led the conversation to Dinah Waycott.

"Arthur's my second self," he said, "and I know he'll lift no objection to listening, even if he don't see with our eyes."

"You needn't say 'our eyes,' father," replied Jane, quick to respond. "Me and mother——"

But her mother stopped her. Mrs. Bamsey was all for law and order.

"Listen, and don't talk till you're axed to," she said.

"Give heed to me," began Ben. "There's been growing up a lot of fog here, and Arthur, the friend that he be, was the first to mark it. He pointed it out to me, all well inside Christian charity, and what I want to do is to clear it off this instant moment, now while Orphan Dinah's out of the way. We stand like this. When she threw over Johnny, because her eyes were opened and she found she couldn't love him in a way to wed him, John ordered her out of Lower Town. Well, who shall blame him? 'Tweren't vitty they should clash, or he should find her here in his parents' home. She was instant for going, and though you think I withheld her from doing so, that ain't fair to me."

"You do withhold her, father," said Faith Bamsey quietly.

"No, I do not. I come to the subject of Dinah from a point you can't grasp. For why? She was left to me by my dead first as a sacred and solemn trust. Mind, I'm not letting my affection for Dinah darken my reason. I grant I'm very fond of her, and I grant what she's done haven't shook my feelings, because, unlike you, mother, I believe she's done right. My heart's bled for my own—for your great trouble and for John's. Nothing sadder could have come to shake John's faith, and for a time I was fearful for John. The devil always knows the appointed hour when a soul's weakest, and, coward that he is, 'tis in our worst moments, when life goes wrong and hope's slipping away, that he times his attacks. We all know that; and you remember it, Jane. For he forgets neither the young nor the old. But John has justified his up-bringing; and the mother in him is bringing him back to his true self."

"You may think so; but——" began Jane.

She was, however, silenced.

"Hear me, and if you can throw light after, Jane, we'll hear you," continued Mr. Bamsey. "I say what I think and believe. My trouble be still alive for John; but my fear be dead. So that leaves Dinah. Her wish and will is to be gone. She's seeking a proper and fitting place—neither too low nor too high. She'd go into service to-morrow—anywhere; but I won't have that."

"And why for not, father?" asked Mrs. Bamsey; "your first was in service once."

"That's different," he answered. "You must see it, mother. The situation is very tender, and you must remember my duty to the dead. Would Jane go into service?"

"No, I would not," answered Jane; "not for anybody. I'd go on the street first."

Mr. Chaffe was shocked.

"Do I hear you, Jane?" he asked.

"God forgive you, Jane," said her father; then he proceeded.

"My foster-daughter is a much more delicate and nice question than my own daughter; and mother, with her sharp understanding, knows it. From no love for Dinah I say so. She's a sacred trust, and if she was a bad girl, instead of a good one, still she'd be a sacred trust. I'm not standing here for my own sake, or for any selfishness. I've long been schooled to know she was going, as we all hoped, to Johnny. And go she must—for her own sake—and her own self-respect. And if anybody's fretting about her biding here, it's Dinah's self. But the work she must go to is the difficulty, and that work has not yet been found in my opinion. Her future hangs upon it and I must be head and obeyed in that matter."

"She's turned down such a lot of things," said Jane.

"She has not," replied Mr. Bamsey. "She'd do anything and take anything to-morrow. She was at me to let her go for barmaid to the Blue Lion at Totnes. And I said, 'No, Dinah; you shan't go nowhere as barmaid while I live.' And I say it again, meaning no disrespect to the Blue Lion, which is a very good licensed house."

"She's of age, and if she was in earnest, she could have gone, whether you liked it or not," said Jane.

Mr. Bamsey grew a little flushed and regarded his daughter without affection.

"You would—not Dinah," he answered. "Dinah looks to me as her father, and she won't do nothing I don't hold with, or take any step contrary to my view. That's because she's got a righter idea of what a girl owes her father than you have, Jane."

"And what is your view, father?" asked Mrs. Bamsey.

"You know, mother. I want for Dinah to go into a nice family, where the people will receive her as one of themselves, and where she'll take her place and do her proper work and go on with her life in a Christian manner, and not feel she's sunk in the world, or an outcast, but just doing her right share of work, and being treated as the child of a man in my position have a right to expect to be treated."

"You won't find no such place, father," said Jane.

"I hope we shall. She's out to Ponsworthy with Mrs. Bassett to-day; and the Bassetts are God-fearing people in our own station of life."

"If she was to go there, she'd only be nursemaid to four young children," declared Faith.

"Then, if that's all there is to it, she won't go there," answered Ben.

"And what if nothing to suit your opinions can be found, father?" asked his wife.

"Then—then she'll be forced to stop here, I'm afraid, my dear."

"And what if I said I wouldn't if she did?" flashed out Jane.

"There's some questions beneath answering, Jane, and that's one of them," replied Mr. Bamsey.

In the pause that followed, Mr. Chaffe, who had been smoking in the chimney corner of the house-place where they sat, addressed the family.

Jane, however, did not stop to listen. She began to remove the supper things and came and went.

"Ben's so right as he can be in my opinion, and if you think, you'll see he's right, Faith," said Arthur. "He founds what he says upon the fact that Dinah has done the proper thing to give John up; and if you could only see that, instead of blaming her and thinking hardly of her for so doing, you'd admit she was not to be punished for what she done. We all make mistakes, and though I don't know nothing about love from personal experience, I've seen it working in the world, for good or ill, these fifty years very near. And a tricky thing it is, and Dinah ain't the first that thought she was in love when she wasn't, and won't be the last. There's some would have gone on with it and married Johnny just the same, for one reason and another; but in my humble judgment a girl who can marry a man she doesn't love, for any reason, be little better than a scarlet woman. And when Dinah found there weren't love on both sides, very properly she owned up and said so."

Faith Bamsey listened quietly.

"I've pretty well come to that myself, Arthur," she said. "I may say I go that far now. It was a burning shame, of course, as Dinah couldn't make up her mind months and months ago; but when I tell her that, she says she didn't know her mind. And so not a word against her. She's a saint and worthy of all praise, and I dare say we ought to kiss her feet and bless her. But what next? That's all I humbly want to know? Ben, you see, is very jealous indeed for Dinah; but, on the other side, I like John to be free to come and go from his mother's home; and you won't say that's unnatural. But while she's here, angel though she may be, come John can't; and that's not unnatural either."

She smouldered bitterly under her level speech and self-control.

"All good—all good," declared Mr. Chaffe. "And if I may speak for Ben, I should say he grasps the point as firm as you do, Faith. Dinah's wishful to go; she'd go to-morrow if it was only to be a goose-girl; but that wouldn't be seemly, and you can leave Ben to do his duty in that matter and not let any personal feelings interfere. In fact the more he cared for Dinah, the more he would see she must go out into the world now, for the sake of all parties. The rightful place will be found for her, and I always say that when people do their part up to the point where they may fairly look to Providence to go on with it, then Providence be very quick to take up the running. And if Providence don't, it's because our part have not been done right."

"This very night," said Ben, "Dinah may come back in sight of work at Ponsworthy."

"There remains John," continued Mr. Chaffe, "and John's gone through the fire very brave indeed by all accounts, without a crack, thank God. You've every right to be proud of him; and his turn will come. The Lord tempers the wind to the shorn lamb, and no doubt his future mate will be along in due course for his comfort and uplifting."

Dinah returned a few minutes later and she expressed a desire to go to Ponsworthy; but Mrs. Bamsey's prediction was correct: her work with the Bassetts must be that of a nurse and no more.

"Providence haven't spoke yet then," said Mr. Bamsey; "but as Arthur very truly says, we've reached a point when we may fairly count to hear a seasonable word afore long; and doubtless we shall do."

Mr. Chaffe presently went home. But for all his smooth speeches, none knew better than he where the fret and difficulty began; and he was aware that it would never end while Dinah remained at Green Hayes.

"If nought's done, in less than no time, she'll make a bolt," he reflected. "She's that sort of woman; and for all us can say, it may be the will of Providence to cut the knot in that manner. I hope not, however, for 'twould be a bitter blow to Ben and fill his old age with sorrow."

He was so impressed with this dark possibility that he decided to see Dinah at the first opportunity and warn her against it.

"A very curious, puzzling thing," thought Mr. Chaffe, "that the price for well-doing be often stiffer than the price for bad. But the good man should keep in mind that the credit side be growing for all he suffers. If we can't trust the recording angel's book-keeping, who should we trust? The wicked may flourish like the green bay; but the end of the green bay be fire, come soon, or come late."

He passed a neighbour in the darkness going home and published his reflection.

"Be that you, Nicholas Gaunter? So it is then. And here, on my way, I was filled with a great thought, Nicholas."

Mr. Gaunter—a hedge tacker of low repute—had drunk too much beer; but not too much not to know it. He concealed his error and Arthur failed to observe the truth.

"A oner for thoughts you be, Mr. Chaffe," he said.

"Yes—they come; and it just flashed over my mind, Nicholas, that goodness breeds life and a good deed can't perish out of the land; but the payment of evil is death—sure and certain."

"Only if you done a murder," said Mr. Gaunter.

"Pass on, Nicholas, pass on. The thought be too deep for your order of mind I'm afraid," replied the older man.

CHAPTER XIII
JOE ON ECONOMICS

On a June evening Lawrence Maynard fell in with Dinah at Buckland, near the cottage of the old huntsman. Accident was responsible for their meeting, and they had not seen each other since the girl's engagement was at an end. Now the cowman was on his way to spend an evening with Enoch Withycombe, while Dinah intended to visit Falcon Farm and beg Susan and Mr. Stockman to interest themselves on her account and find her work.

"I can't get anything to do that will pleasure foster-father," she said. "He's so hard to please where I'm concerned, and he don't quite see so plain as I do that it's bad for me and everybody else my biding there."

"I dare say it is."

"Where's your black armlet what you wore for your dead master in Somerset?" she asked.

"I've left it off now with these new clothes."

She nodded.

"I'm going to see Cousin Joe and Susan. She's always been terrible kind to me. So has he for that matter. How have they took this? If they're very much against me, perhaps I'd best not go."

"It's interested 'em a lot. They've heard John's side mostly, because he comes up over now and again. But they keep fairly open minds about it."

"They don't know why I done it?"

"Yes. I ventured to say a word or two. No business of mine; but I just went so far as to explain that I'd seen you last bank holiday, and you told me what you thought to do, and why."

"Thank you I'm sure."

"No call for that. Common fairness. Mr. Stockman's very good to me and lets me talk if I've a mind to. He's a far-sighted, fair man, or so I find him."

"They won't jump down my throat, then?"

"Not likely. I'm going in to have a tell with Mr. Withycombe now. He's poorly, and a neighbour cheers him up and makes him forget his pains."

"What did he think about it, Mr. Maynard?"

"He thought you was right, I believe."

"I'm very glad of that. And what did you think?"

"You know what I thought, miss. I thought you was dead right."

She kept silent for a moment. Then she spoke.

"I wish to God Johnny would see it."

"He will—some day. He don't yet. He——"

Maynard stopped. She put her hand on his arm eagerly.

"Is there anything I could do or say to help him, should you think? If there was, I'd do it if it killed me."

"Nothing much to help him I should reckon."

"What was you going to say when you stopped?"

"Nothing worth saying—at least, something better not spoken for the minute."

She considered this.

"Please tell me if it can help him," she begged.

Now it was his turn to weigh his thoughts and the thing he had on his lips. He decided that he ought to tell her.

"It's this, then. They think at Falcon Farm that, if Johnny is patient, things may yet come right."

Dinah was cast down.

"Oh, I'm sorry they talk like that. Why do they?"

"Because they've seen him and not you, perhaps."

"I don't reckon I'll go now," said Dinah, but continued, before he could advise: "Yes, I will. I must. If there's any feeling like that about, it's only right they should know. I'm not the sort to play with a chap, and it's cruel to let Johnny think I am. But does he?"

"I dare say not."

They talked for another ten minutes. Then she prepared to go up the hill.

"You've done me good," she said, "and I'm very glad I met you. And I'd like to meet you again, please. D'you mind that walk I wanted to go? Will you take it now?"

He hesitated.

"Not if you don't want."

"It's like this, Miss Waycott. If there's a ghost of a chance that you go back to Johnny Bamsey, then I'd rather not, because it wouldn't be vitty and might add to trouble. So if you're in doubt—even a hair's breadth—we'd better wait."

"I'm not in doubt. I wouldn't have given myself all the hateful grief of doing it, nor yet him, if I hadn't made up my mind. I kept my mouth shut so long as there was a shadow of doubt—and long after there was no doubt for that matter. And you can tell 'em so at Falcon Farm, or anywhere."

"Then I'll be very pleased to take a walk any Sunday if you've a mind to."

"Sunday week then, if I don't find work before. I'll meet you—where?"

He considered.

"If 'tis fair and offering a fine afternoon, I'll be—but that's too far. If we're going to Hey Tor Rock, it's a long way for you anyhow."

"How if I was to come to dinner at Falcon Farm first?" she asked, and he approved the suggestion.

"A very good thought, then we can start from there."

"Sure you don't mind?"

"Proud."

They parted then and Dinah, cheered by the incident of this meeting, went on her way.

She liked Maynard, not for himself, but his attitude to life. Yet, had he been other than himself, she had probably not found him interesting. He was always the same—polite and delicate minded. Such qualities in an elderly man had left her indifferent; but, as she once said to him, the young turn to the young. Maynard was still young enough to understand youth, and it seemed to Dinah that he had understood her very well. She was grateful to him for promising to take the walk. He would be sure to say sensible things and help her. And she wanted to tell him more about her own feelings. Life had unsettled her, and she was learning painful rather than pleasant facts about it. She began dimly to fear there must be more painful than pleasant facts to learn. Several desires struggled with her—the first to see Johnny again and be forgiven and resume a friendly relation, if that were possible. His sustained anger she could not comprehend; and if, as she began to hear, her old lover still hoped to make it up, the puzzle became still greater.

She reached Falcon Farm with two determinations: to talk to Johnny and declare that she could never change again; and to ask herself to dinner, for the sake of the walk with Lawrence Maynard. To make any mystery of the walk had not occurred to her, or him. She did not even think that anybody might put any particular interpretation upon it.

When she reached the farm on the hill, Joe Stockman and Thomas Palk had been for an hour in conversation. It was an evening when in good heart and more than usually amiable, Joe had offered his horseman a "spot of whisky" from his own bottle, and Thomas, accepting it, had cautiously entered upon a little matter for some time in his mind.

Susan sat at the table mending her father's socks, while the men were by the hearth, for the kitchen fire never went out at Falcon Farm and Joe always found it agreeable after sun-down, even in high summer.

Mr. Palk crept to his theme with great strategy. He spoke of the price of commodities in general and the difficulties that confronted even a bachelor with a good home and satisfactory work.

"The thought of a new black coat do make you tremble nowadays," he said.

"Then put the thought away from you, Thomas," advised Mr. Stockman. "I'm often wishful for little comforts myself, as is natural at my time of life; but I say to myself, 'The times are hard and these ban't days to set an example of selfishness.' The times are lean, Thomas, and we've got to practise the vartue of going without—high and low alike."

"Everybody knows one thing: that everybody else did ought to be working harder," said Susan. "You hear it all round. Where I go, up or down, I always seem to find men loafing about saying the people did ought to be working harder."

"True for you, Soosie-Toosie. I've marked the like. 'Tis all very well for Thomas here to say the prices be cruel; but the question is, 'Why are they?' And I'll tell you for why. Labour says Capital ought to give more; and Capital says Labour ought to work harder; and so they both stand chattering at each other like magpies and saying the country's going to the devil. Whereas, if they'd take a lesson from us of the land and put their backs into it with good will, the sun would soon come from behind the cloud. If each man would mind his own business and not waste his time judging his neighbour and envying him, we'd get a move on. You don't find the professional people grizzling and whining for more money—doctors and lawyers and such like. Nor farmers neither."

"No," said Thomas, "because their job pays and they fetch in the cash and have enough to put by. I'd be so cheerful as them if I could make so much. I'd work like hell pulling mangel if I could get half as much by it as a dentist do pulling teeth. And the great puzzle to me is why for should pulling teeth be worth a fortune and pulling mangel deny me a new Sunday coat?"

"Never heard you to say such a foolish thing afore, Thomas," answered Joe. "My dear man, you voice the whole silly staple of Labour when you say that. And I always thought you was above the masses in your ideas, as we all are to Buckland—or most of us. A thing is only worth what it will fetch, Thomas, and the root of our trouble at this minute is because Labour is forcing Capital to pay it more than it did ought to fetch."

"Labour's worth what it can get," ventured Susan, and her father rebuked her.

"A very wicked thought and I'm sorry you can sink to it," he said. "It's that opinion and a weak Government that's ruining the kingdom. Look at it, Thomas. Here's a man has three pounds a week for doing what an everyday boy of fifteen could do as well. That's false economy to begin with, because that man can't honestly earn three golden pounds in a week. He haven't got the parts to do it. And if millions of men are getting more than they can earn, what's happening?"

"They must have the money to live," said Thomas.

"For the moment they must," admitted his master, "and they're getting it, but where half their time be wasted is in wrangling over keeping it. The fools won't work, because they're afraid of their lives if they do, their wages will come down; and they don't see, so kitten-blind they are, that the very best thing that could happen to them would be that their wages should come down. For what would that mean? It would mean things was returning to their true values, and that a pound was in sight of being worth twenty bob again."

"That's it," answered Thomas. "If three pound be worth only thirty shilling, they must have three pound."

"Listen to me, my son. Would you rather have three pound, worth thirty shilling, or two pound, worth forty? You'd rather have two worth forty; and when Labour sees that two worth forty be better than three worth thirty, then, very like, Labour will set to work to make two worth forty again. That's what their leading men know so well as me; but they're a damned sight too wicked to rub it into the rank and file, because 'twould ease Capital so well as Labour and they've no wish to do a stroke for Capital or the nation at large. They be out for themselves first and last and always. And while the people be so busy fighting for money that they ain't got time to earn it, so long the English sovereign and the world at large will have to wait to come into its own."

"And meantime three pound be worth less than thirty bob; and that's what interests me most for the minute," said Mr. Palk.

"Don't look at it in a small way, Thomas. Don't darken counsel by thinking of number one," urged Joe. "That's what everybody's doing, God forgive 'em. You preach work, in season and out, for at this gait the younger generation will never know what work means. They be hungering to eat without working, and that means starvation for all. Paper's only paper, Thomas, and gold's always gold, till man ceases to think in the pound sterling. So what we want is to get back on to the sure ground of solid gold and establish ourselves again as the nation with the biggest balance at the bank. But us must take these high questions in a high spirit, and not let little things, like a new black coat, blind the sight."

"You speak for Capital, however," murmured Mr. Palk. "I can't withstand 'e, of course, because I haven't been aggicated; but——"

"I speak for Labour quite so much as for Capital," declared Mr. Stockman. "I began life as a labouring boy and I'm a labouring man still, as you can vouch for. I'm only telling Labour, what it don't know and won't learn, that if it worked harder and jawed less, it would be putting money in its pocket. As things are it's a child yowling for the moon."

"Then I suppose I be," said Thomas, "for I was going to put it to you, man to man, that it would be a Godsend to me if you could lift me five bob, or even three."

Soosie-Toosie cast a frightened glance at Mr. Palk and another at her father; but Joe was smiling.

"More money—eh? Now that's a great thought, Thomas—a very great thought. Fancy! And why for, Thomas, if I may ask without making a hole in my manners?"

"For my dead sister's boy," said Mr. Palk. "There's no money, because his father's out of work and I'm very wishful to lend a hand on his account."

"And very creditable to you, Thomas; and how comes it his lawful father's out of work?"

It was at this moment, to the joy of Susan, that Dinah knocked at the door. She leapt up and thankfully brought the visitor back with her.

Mr. Stockman, too, was pleased.

"Company, Thomas," he said. "We'll take this subject up at another time. Don't think I'll forget it. I never forget anything, for though the body's weak, worse luck, the mind is clear. Dinah, I see—and why not? You'll always find friends here, Orphan Dinah."

Thomas emptied his glass and disappeared, while Dinah plunged into the first object of her visit.

"I'm glad you haven't throwed me over for what I've done," she said.

"Far from it," replied Mr. Stockman. "Is Soosie-Toosie the sort that judges, or be I?"

"We're only terrible sorry for all parties, Dinah," said Susan; "and we hope it will come smooth again."

"So do I," answered the younger; "but not the way you mean, Soosie. For it to come smooth is for John to understand I didn't do a wicked thing, only a mistaken thing. And I had to put the mistaken thing right."

She went over old ground and made it clear that none must expect her to go back.

"I hope I'll live to see John happily wedded," she said. "And I never shan't be happy, I reckon, till he is."

"And what about you?" asked Joe. "What's the truth, Dinah?"

She explained that she was not constituted to love.

"I'm like Soosie," she said. "Us be the sort that's happier single." But Miss Stockman laughed.

"You're a good few years too young to tell like that, Dinah. You wait till all this here storm be blowed over and 'tis calm weather in your mind again. You'm born to be married to the right one. If he don't come along, then, with your experience of making a mistake, you never will be married I dare say; but 'tis any odds he will come along I expect."

Dinah, however, shook her head.

"A mistake like what I've made be a very shattering thing," she said. "I wouldn't have the nerve to go into it no more. There's a lot of unmarried women wanted to carry on the work of the world nowadays."

"And always was," declared Joe. "There's plenty of the sensible sort about, like Soosie-Toosie, who know where they stand and be helping on the world very nice indeed. And though some, here and there, may cast a side glance at marriage, it's often because they don't know when they be well off. However, education's opening their eyes a good deal. The deepest minded sort, such as Susan, don't marry; and even them that do wed put it off a good bit because they see in their wisdom it's better to have a certainty to go to than a hope; and better to be the mother of two than ten. I understand these things, I may tell you, and the moment the world gets wise and puts war away for ever, then us won't hear no more from the parsons about breeding, and the populations will go down and prosperity will go up. A time is coming when a man with ten children will be a disgrace and a quiverful a proper laughing-sport."

"I dare say it will," agreed Dinah.

"Yes—the women will see to that. There was a time when a labouring man bred like a rabbit, in hopes that his dutiful childer would keep him out of the workhouse at the end; but that time's past. The poor women begin to see, like the better-most females, that child-bearing ain't the only use for 'em and not the best fun in the world anyhow."

They promised her to remember her need for work, and Joe undertook to see a friend or two at Ashburton who might be able to find it. Then, thanking them very heartily, she asked a question.

"May I come to dinner Sunday week?"

They approved, and Joe hoped by that time he might be able to report progress.

"I've got another reason," she explained. "Mr. Maynard is a very understanding man and he's promised to go for a walk and show me a stone on the moor I'm wishful to see."

Susan was interested.

"Lor, Dinah!" she said.

Mr. Stockman appeared to be buried in thought for a moment.

"Did he ask you, or did you ask him to go for a walk, Orphan Dinah?" he inquired.

"I asked him. I asked him a long time back and he wouldn't go, because he reckoned Johnny wouldn't like it. But I wanted to see the stone, and I wanted to hear Mr. Maynard talk, because he's a very sensible chap and has said several things that did me good. And so I asked him again, and he's got no objection—not now."

"He's a very sensible man as you say," declared Joe, "a more sensible man for his years I haven't met. In fact he's old for his years—for various reasons."

"Would you have any objection, Cousin Joe?" asked Dinah.

He considered.

"No," he decided. "I wish John could have been of the party, I'm sure; but since that's off for all time, then there's nothing wrong in your taking a walk with Maynard. Nor would there be any harm in any case. I know all about Maynard. He's all right; and, of course, if you asked him to go for a walk, Dinah, he couldn't very well refuse to do so."

"He's a very seeing man," said Dinah, "and he thinks a lot of you, Cousin Joe."

"And why not?"

"He might marry himself," said Susan.

"He's not the sort to hurry it," answered the girl. "He don't care for women overmuch seemingly."

Dinah drank a cup of milk and presently set out to walk home. Susan admired her courage.

"Nothing daunts you," she said. "I wouldn't go down through the woods in the night by myself for the world."

"Night's got no more to it than day," declared the other. "I like it—specially when you have such a lot of trouble on your mind."

She met Maynard returning home, but did not stop more than a moment.

"I'm coming Sunday week," she said, "and Cousin Joe's got no objection to us going out walking."

"Good night, miss. I hope we'll have a fine day for it. Can't go else," he answered.

"How's Mr. Withycombe?"

"Suffering a good bit I'm sorry to say."

"I'm sorry, too."

Lawrence had forgotten the question of the walk while with the old huntsman. Now he considered it and was glad that Dinah had spoken about it in her open fashion. He apprehended pleasure from it, yet doubted a little. There hung a shadow over his reflections—something to which he could not have set a word. In so much that the shade should hover over his own thoughts it amused him, and assured that it could not cloud Dinah's, he dismissed the futility from his mind.

CHAPTER XIV
THE FACE ON THE ROCK

The day came for Dinah's walk with Lawrence Maynard, and though the sky lowered at dawn, before noon the wind had travelled north of west and there was no longer any fear of rain.

They set out, climbed the Beacon and advanced by those rolling stretches of heath and stone that extend to the north of it.

John Bamsey had been to see the Stockmans, and it seemed that his mother, or sister, had now made it plain to him that Dinah would never change her mind.

"He's taking it ill," said Lawrence. "He's not standing up against what he's got to suffer in a very good spirit."

"Us must pray that the right one will come along," answered Dinah.

They talked but little on their way, reached the White Gate, held to the winding road awhile, then returned to the moors and presently stood looking down into the deserted quarries of Hey Tor.

"I'll show you the face on the rock when we turn," he said. "I wanted for you to see this first. A very interesting place and known to me since I was a boy."

Thus he opened a measure of the confidence he designed for her. All the truth about himself he did not propose to tell; but there were things that he could trust to her; and he meant to do so. His purpose was vague and sprang from no deep emotion. He thought only to distract her mind, perhaps amuse her, and for a time arrest the melancholy flow of her thinking. For she was not cheerful and as yet no outlet for her life and energies had been discovered. Benjamin Bamsey proved obdurate in the matter of her future, and there was come a new and painful element into the life at Green Hayes.

They sat and looked into the quarry. The weathered place was hung with ferns and heath. Deep, green pools lay in the bottom of it and a ring-ousel sat and sang his elfin song, perched on a rusty fragment of iron, driven into the granite by men long since in their graves.

"This was my playground and a place of magic to me when I was a child," said Lawrence, to the surprise of the listener.

"I thought you was a foreigner," she said.

"No. But let everybody else go on thinking so, please. I want it a secret, though it's of little consequence really. I was born a mile from here. The cottage where I lived with my family is a ruin now—I'll show it to you—and me and a little sister used to play on the heath and make our games. They're all gone except that sister. She married and went to Australia. The rest are dead."

"You'm a lonely man then?"

"Used to it. It's only my childhood that the face on the rock comes into, and this deserted quarry. I met a gentleman here once, who told me all about the place. He knew its history and cared for such things. And his talk put great thoughts in my head, for I was thirteen by then and full of ideas already. I got 'em from my mother. She was better bred and born than father and wishful to see me higher than a labourer some day."

Dinah threw herself into his narrative.

"To think of that," she said. "How terrible interesting everybody is, the moment you begin to know the least bit about 'em!"

"I suppose they are. Not that there's anything interesting in me. Only I often catch myself turning back to when I was a boy. The gentleman told me that a lot of the stone cut out from this place is in London now. London Bridge be made of it, and part of the British Museum too. And I never forgot that. I envied those stones, because it seemed to me it would be better to be a bit of London Bridge than what I was."

"What a queer thought," murmured Dinah.

"'Tis a queer thought, but true, that there's plenty of dead stones doing better work in the world than plenty of live men. I used to dream like that when I was a nipper, but I soon had to earn my living, and then there was an end of dreams. Poor folk haven't got no time to dream."

"And not much to dream about most times."

"Plenty to dream about," he assured her, "but we pay our leaders to do the dreaming for us; then, when they've fixed up the dream, they come to us to turn the dreams into reality."

"You'd like to be doing something better than milking cows perhaps?"

"No, I shouldn't—not now. I had ideas, but life knocked 'em out of me."

"Not at your age, I'm sure. You talk as if you was old."

"The heart knows its own bitterness, and a head like mine knows its own weakness," said Lawrence. "If things had gone as I expected, I should never have thought of large questions, and been quite content with the business of running my own life. But things happened to change my outlook and make me think. Then I found I'd got a poor set of brains. I'd just got brains enough to know I was a long way nearer a fool than lots of other men; and I'd just got eyes to see the gulf between. And yet to wish you'd got more brains is only a fool's wish, come to think of it, for the pattern of a man's brain ain't of his own choosing. I suppose nobody's satisfied with what he's got."

"You must be a pretty clever sort of chap to think such things at all," answered Dinah. "And you're a good man, and most times the good ones ain't the right down clever ones. You can't help seeing that."

"For a long time, owing to one thing and another, I was a chap overcome by life," confessed Maynard. "Things fell out that properly dazed me; and it was not till then I began to see the real meaning of life at all. It's much the same with John Bamsey at this minute. While all went smooth, he never saw much beyond the point of his own nose, and never wanted to; then came trouble, and we'll hope it will make his mind bigger when the smart dies. For trouble's no use if it don't do that. Anyway life made me take larger views for a bit. A storm clears the air. Then with time, I settled down again, same as I am now."

"Contented?"

"As near content as I'm ever likely to get. I've simplified my life to the limits. I said to myself, 'Since you can't have what you wanted, have nothing.' And I have nothing."

"That cuts both ways, I reckon," declared Dinah; "you escape a lot of bother, but you lose a good few things that make life better, don't you?"

"To cut a loss is a very wise deed," he answered. "So it seemed to me anyway. That may be wrong, too, in some cases; but if you've got no choice, then you must. Now let me show you where I was born, if you're not tired."

Presently, in the valley far beneath these downs, where the hillside fell to the north and a stream ran in the bottom of a woody coomb, Maynard pointed to a little building. It stood where the land began to ascend again and climb to those rugged piles of granite known as Hound Tor Rocks.

"D'you see that ruin alongside the green croft beside the edge of the woods? That was a fair-sized cottage twenty years ago. My father worked at Hedge Barton, near by, and we lived there till he died. Then we scattered."

Dinah regarded the spot with interest.

"To think of that," she said.

"My playmate was my sister Milly," continued Lawrence. "We were the eldest, and after us came two girls, who both died. Then my mother was with child again, and that brings me to the face on the rock, what you want to hear about."

Dinah, as her custom was, had flung herself entirely into these interests of another being. She had an instinct to do this: it was no art, but a natural impulse in her. At this moment nothing on earth seemed more important and desirable to know than these passages from the boyhood of Lawrence Maynard.

"Such things bring you home to my mind," she said. "Now I'll have a better idea about you; and then you'll be more interesting."

He laughed at that.

"Not very interesting, even to myself, so it's sure I can't be to anybody else," he answered. "Now we'll take Hey Tor Rock on our way back. It'll throw a bit of light on one or two things you've asked me."

They approached the granite bosses of the tor and stood presently beside it, where high on the cliff above them a face bulked enormous and stared into the eye of the westering sun.

The chisels of Nature carve slowly on granite, but once a masterpiece has been wrought, it will outlast many generations of mankind. Such things chance out of slow mouldings, or by sudden strokes. They may be the work of centuries, or the inspiration of a moment—plastic, moulded by patient Time, as the artist models his clay, or glyphic—struck with a blow of lightning, or earthquake, from the stone.

The great rock idols come and go, and haunt lonely cliffs, crown lonely heights, gaze out upon the surges of lonely seas. To Nature these whimsical figures, near enough to man to challenge him, are but faces in the fire, peeping to-day from the flux, and cinders again to-morrow; but, to the short-lived thing they imitate, they endure, while his own generations lapse.

This giant's head was smaller than the Sphinx and of an antiquity more profound. The countenance lacked majesty and was indeed malignant—not with the demoniac intelligence of man-cut fiends, such as "Le Stryge" on Notre Dame, but rather with the brutish, semi-human doubt and uncertainty of a higher ape. So the Minotaur might have scowled to seaward. The expression of the monster trembled on the verge of consciousness; it suggested one of those vanished beings created near the end of our hundred thousand years' journey, after man's ancestors descending from the trees set forth on the mighty march to conscious intelligence.

The face belonged to the forefathers of the neolithic people: it burlesqued hugely those beetle-browed, prognathous paleoliths of old time, and for them, perchance, possessed an awe and sublimity we cannot grant it to-day.

But it had challenged a boy and girl, who were still many thousands of years nearer to prehistoric ancestors than their parents. For children still move through the morning of days, and through minds ten and eleven years old the skin-clad dreamers and stone men were again reflected and survived.

Now Dinah heard with what force the discovery of the stone Titan had struck upon the boy and girl.

"A new baby was coming," said Lawrence, "and sister and me were each given a bit of food and told to run out on the moor and play till nightfall. That pleased us very well and we made our games and wandered and picked hurts.* And then I suddenly found yonder face and shouted to Milly and made her see it too. It excited me a lot, and Milly always got excited when I did. She said 'twas like father, but I said, 'No, 'tis a lot grander and finer than father.' Then she was frighted and wanted to run away; but I wouldn't have that. 'He'd blow out of his mouth and scat us to shivers if we ran,' I told her. I took pleasure in giving great powers to the monster, and wondered if he was good, or wicked. And little sister thought he must be wicked, but I didn't see why he should be. 'Perhaps he's a good 'un,' I said; and then I decided that he might be good. Milly was for sloking off again, but my child's wits worked, and I very soon lifted up the stone into a great, powerful creature. 'Us'll say our prayers to him,' I told Milly, but she feared that also. 'I never heard of nobody saying no prayers except to Gentle Jesus,' answered Milly to me. 'The Bible's full of 'em,' I told her. 'How would it be if we offered to be his friends?'"

* *Hurts*—whortleberries.

"Tempted your little sister to turn heathen!" exclaimed Dinah.

"Yes, and she soon fell. I minded her how we had once prayed with all our might to Gentle Jesus to kill father, because he wouldn't take us to a circus as had come to Bovey. 'Gentle Jesus have got His Hands full without us,' I said to Milly. 'He haven't got no time to think about two little squirts like us. But this here great creature might be a good friend to us; and nobody the wiser!'"

"You was a crafty little boy."

"No craft, only a queer twist of the brain. I smile sometimes, looking back, to see what thoughts I'd gotten. But child's thoughts die like flowers. We can never think 'em again when we grow up. Milly held out a bit, yet she never withstood me very long. She was only afraid that Gentle Jesus would hear tell about it and punish us; but I said, 'Not Him. If harm comes, I'll take the blame. And we won't put anything very hard upon this monstrous old rock till we know how strong he be.' We thought then what we should pray for, and Milly had a bright idea. 'Ax him to make the new baby a boy,' she advised, and I agreed, for we was very wishful to have a boy home, and so was our mother. Then Milly had another thought. 'What be us to call him?' she asked me. 'Something terrible fearful,' I said—'the fearfullest thing we can think upon.' We strove after the most dreadful words we knew, and they were our father's swear-words. 'Let's call him "Bloody,"' I said; and Milly thought we ought to say 'Mr. Bloody.' But I told her 'Mister' was a name for a gentleman, with nothing fierce or grand to it. 'We'll call him "Bloody" and chance it,' I said; and so we did. I prayed to the stone then. I said, 'Dear Bloody, please let mother's new babby be a boy. Amen'; and Milly done the same; and when we got home in the dimpsy light, all was over and father eating for the first time that day. There had come a little boy and mother was happy. Milly whispered to me, 'That's one for him!'"

Dinah laughed with delight. Her own troubles were for the time forgotten.

"I'll mind that story so long as I live," she said, gazing up at the iron-black, impassive features above her.

"That's not all, though. We got terrible friendly with our great idol, and then, a week later, the baby fell ill and seemed like to die. For the nurse that waited on mother had come from whooping-cough and the poor child catched it afore it was five days old. We were in a terrible upstore about that, and I minded this rock; and when a day came and the little one was at his last gasp, me and Milly went up and stood here, where we sit now. I said we must bring offerings, but us hadn't nothing but my knife and Milly's pet bunny rabbit. But such was the fearful need, we determined to sacrifice both of 'em; and we did. Lord knows how we could, but I killed her little rabbit for 'Bloody,' and I dropped it and my knife in that cleft below the rocks at his feet. We used to call 'em his paws. The rabbit and my knife went down there, and we asked for our new-born brother, and prayed the creature to save him alive. And we wept a good bit, and I remember Milly felt glad to see me cry as well as her. We went home a lot comforted—to find the baby was dead."

He broke off and the listener expressed sorrow.

"You poor little things—to think of you trotting back together—to that! I could cry for 'e now."

"We cried for ourselves I warrant you. We was terrible upset about it, and I properly gnashed my teeth I remember. Savage I was, and loved to hear father damn to hell the nurse that had done the mischief. 'Douglas Champernowne' the poor child was called. My mother doted on high-sounding names. And the day he was buried, my sister and me roamed on the moor again in our black after the funeral, bewailing our loss; and it was Milly that called my mind to our stone god, for I'd forgot all about him just then. 'There he is—aglaring and agrinning!' she said, and I looked up and saw we'd come to him without thinking. It had been raining all day, and his face was wet and agleam in evening sunlight. We liked him that way, but now I turned my hate on him and cursed him for a hard-hearted, cruel devil. 'Beast—hookem-snivey beast!' I yelled up at the tor; 'and I wish to God I was strong enough to pull you down and smash your face in!' Milly trembled with fear and put her arms around me, to save me, or die with me if need be. But I told her the idol couldn't hurt us. 'He can only kill babbies,' I yelled at him. Then I worked myself up into a proper passion and flung stones and mud at the rock, and Milly, finding our god helpless, egged me on. We made faces and spat on the earth and did everything our wits could hit on to insult him. Then, tired out, we turned our backs on him, and the last he heard was my little sister giving him the nastiest cut of all. 'We be going back to Gentle Jesus now,' screamed Milly."

Maynard ceased and lighted his pipe.

"It's a sad, lovely story. I don't wonder you come and have a look at the face sometimes. So shall I now. May I tell it again?" asked Dinah.

"No, miss, don't do that—I'd rather none heard it for the present. I've my reasons for not wishing to be linked up with these parts."

"Call me 'Dinah,' and let me call you 'Lawrence,'" she said. From her this was not a startling suggestion. Indeed she had already called him "Lawrence" sometimes.

"If you like," he answered. "It's easier. We see a good many things the same."

"I suppose we do. And did you and Milly go back to 'Gentle Jesus'?"

"Certainly we did; and I'll make bold to say she never left Him no more."

"But you—you ain't exactly a Christian man, are you? When did you change?"

He looked into the past and did not answer for a moment.

"I don't know," he said at last. "It's hard to tell sometimes when we change. Them that come to the penitent bench, or what not, know to an hour when they was 'saved,' as they call it; but them that have gone the other way, and heaved up anchor, and let their reason steer the ship and their faith go astern—such men can't always answer exactly when the change came. Sometimes it's just the mind getting bigger and the inner instinct dropping the earlier teaching; and sometimes things happen to shake a man for ever out of his hope and trust."

"A very sad thought," she said.

"It's always sad to see a thing fall down—whether it's a god or a tree. The sound of the woodman's axe be sad to some minds."

"It is to me," said Dinah.

He looked up at the features above them, carved on the mass of the tor. Beyond swung out Rippon's granite crown against the sky, and nearer stretched miles of wild and ragged heath. Then, in long, stone-broken curves the moor rose and fell across the western light to Honeybag and Chinkwell and huge Hameldown bathed in faint gold. The sun kneaded earth with its waning lustres until matter seemed imponderable and the wild land rolled in planes of immaterial radiance folding upon each other. The great passages of the hills and dales melted together under this ambient illumination and the stony foreground shone clear, where, through the hazes, a pool glinted among the lengthening shadows and reflected the sky. Quartz crystals glittered where the falling rays touched the rocks, and as the sun descended, great tracts of misty purple spread in the hollows and flung smooth carpets for the feet of night.

For a moment "Bloody" seemed to relax his brutal features in the glow. Sunset lit a smile upon the crag, and nature's monstrous sculpture appeared to close its eyes and bask in the fading warmth.

"It would be a pity if ever Hey Tor were thrown down, as I wanted to throw it, when I was that little angry boy," said Lawrence.

She put out her hand to him.

"Don't you fling over God," she said very earnestly.

"I hope never," he answered.

After they had talked awhile longer he looked at his watch.

"Half after seven," he exclaimed.

They set off for home and she asked for another tale.

"Tell me what happened to you when you went out into the world," she begged; but this he would not do. He made no mystery, but definitely declined.

"You've heard enough about me, I reckon. Speak of yourself a bit."

She obeyed and described her life in childhood, while he listened to the simple story, interested enough.

He reminded her of his desire as their walk ended and they reached the door of Falcon Farm.

"Don't say nothing of my past in this, or tell the tale of the rock again, Dinah. I'm not wishful for the people to know anything about me."

She promised.

"I can keep secrets," she assured him.

CHAPTER XV
BEN BAMSEY'S DOUBTS

As the summer advanced, Jane Bamsey let it be known that she proposed to wed Enoch Withycombe's son, Jerry. For some time her parents refused to believe it, but as Jane persisted and brought Jerry to see them, they began to accept the fact. Benjamin felt hopeful of the match, while Jane's mother did not. In the first place she was disappointed, for while a fine and amiable man, of good repute, not lacking in respect, Jerry could not be considered a very promising husband. He was too old; he was only a woodman and would always remain a woodman. Mrs. Bamsey held that a daughter of hers should have looked higher.

Jane, however, now declared her undying love, and, for the moment, it was undoubtedly true that she did love and desire the son of the huntsman better than anything in the world. She did not share her parents' estimate of him but perceived possibilities and believed that, with her help and supported by the dowry she expected to bring him on their marriage, Jerry would prove—not her head, but her right hand. For Jane had her own private ambitions, and though they staggered Jerry when he heard them, such was his devotion that he agreed to propositions for the future inevitably destined to upset his own life and plunge it into a wrong environment. Their absurdity and futility were not as yet apparent to him, though Jane's ideas from anybody else had been greeted with contempt. They embraced a radical change in his own existence that had been unbearable to contemplate save in one light. But that light his sweetheart created; and when she described her ambitions to leave Dart Vale and set up a little shop in town, Jerry, after some wondering protests, found that the choice might actually lay between this enterprise and Jane herself. Therefore, he did not hesitate. He stated his case, however, when she agreed to marriage on her own conditions.

"Away from trees, I'm much afraid I should be but a lost man," declared Jerry.

"And in the country, I'm but a lost woman," replied Jane. "I'm sick of trees, and fields too."

She had never hinted at the possibility of accepting him at all before the occasion of these speeches; and it was natural that no stipulation could long daunt Jerry in the glorious hour of success. Jane was actually prepared to accept him at last, and since life with Jane in a dungeon had been better than life without her under any conditions whatsoever, Jerry, after a display of argument that lasted not five minutes, agreed to her terms, and found his sweetheart on his knees, his arms round her, the astounding softness of her cheek against the roughness of his own.

How far Jane might be looking ahead, neither her future husband, nor anybody else knew; but one guessed; and since it was Enoch Withycombe who received this spark of divination, he kept it to himself for the present. Now the invalid spoke to Jane's father, who came to see him upon the subject; but both old men considered the situation without knowledge of the facts, because Jane, with greater insight than Jerry and shrewd convictions that her terms would meet with very hearty protests from her lover's family, if not her own, had counselled Jerry, indeed commanded him, to say nothing of their future intentions until the marriage day was fixed.

"And how's yourself, Enoch?" asked Benjamin, as he smiled and took Mr. Withycombe's hand.

"Middling, but slipping down, Ben. The end's getting nearer and the bad days getting thicker sprinkled in the pudding. I shan't be sorry to go."

"Well, well, if you ban't, there's a cruel lot will be when you do," said Mr. Bamsey. "And often and often I catch myself asking if the deaders do really go at all. Married to Faith, as I am, I can't help but feel we've got a cloud of witnesses round about. How it may be in other places, of course, I can't say, but there's no doubt that the people who drop around here, hang about after; and if you've got Faith's amazing gift, they ban't hidden. She see widow Nosworthy last week, down by the stile in 'five acre,' where there's a right of way. She was standing there, just like she used to stand time without count waiting for her drunken son of a night, to steer him past the pond to his home. I say naught, however, whatever I may think."

Mr. Withycombe showed a little impatience.

"'Tis no good prattling about ghosts to a man who'll damn soon be one himself," he said. "As you very well know I don't believe in 'em, Ben; and if us understood better, we'd be able to prove, no doubt, that your wife don't see nothing at all, and that the ghosts be in her own mind's eye and nowhere else. Not a word against her, of course. I respect her very much. But' second sight,' so to call it, be just a thing like gout, or bad teeth—handed down, and well inside nature, like everything else. I don't believe in no future life myself, but I don't quarrel with them that do. I'm like my old master—large-minded, I hope. And if another life there is, then this I will swear, that the people as be called home have got their senses, and the next world have its duties and its upper ghosts set over the unknown country to rule and direct it. You can't suppose that everybody's on his own there, to moon about and poke about, like a lot of birds, with no law and order. When the men and women go out of this world, they've done with this world, and I never will believe they be allowed back, to waste our time and fright the silly ones and talk twaddle to people in dark rooms and play senseless tricks we'd whip a child for."

"Leave it," said Ben. "I go largely along with you, and for that matter my wife herself thinks no more of it than her power to make butter."

"How's Johnny?"

"Got a lot more silenter than he was. Comes and goes; and he's civil to Dinah now, but don't see her alone. Us be a bit hopefuller about him, but not her. In fact Dinah's one of the things I be come to tell about. I'm a bit afeared in that quarter. I might see a ray of light where she's concerned; but John, being what he is, the light, even if there is any, looks doubtful."

"Leave him then. You want to talk of this here match between my Jerry and your Jane."

"I do. I'm very wishful to hear you speak out on the subject, Enoch. For myself, being a great believer that marriages are made in heaven and 'tis only our human weakness mars 'em on earth, I'm always willing to hope the best and trust true love. And true love they've gotten for each other I'm very sure indeed, though I wish they was nearer of an age."

"What does Faith Bamsey say?"

"It don't so much matter as to her. She's a right to her opinions, and seldom we differ, but in this affair, to be honest, we don't see eye to eye. In marriage, the woman be more practical than the man."

"I'll tell you what she says, Ben. She don't like it. All her reasons I cannot tell: one I'm dead sure about. It's a come-down for her Jane to marry Jerry. I grant that. I've told Jerry so too."

"Perfect love casteth out any such thought," said Mr. Bamsey.

"It may cast it out, but it will come back. In some girls it wouldn't. In Jane it will. Jane's on powerful good terms with herself, as you'll grant. The toad knows she's a beauty, and she knows a lot else—a lot more than Jerry knows for that matter."

"You don't like her," said Mr. Bamsey.

"I do not; and she don't like me."

Ben was silent.

"She came up to tea Sunday, and I seed 'em side by side. She's sly and she's making Jerry sly. How the devil she's larned such an open sort of creature as Jerry to keep secrets I don't know. But secrets they've got. I dare say they'll be married. But I agree with Faith Bamsey that it won't come to overmuch good. I don't think Jane is a very likely pattern of wife."

"She's young and there's bright points to her. She wasn't saucy nor anything like that I hope?"

"Oh no—butter wouldn't melt in her mouth."

"What does Melinda think about her?"

"Melinda thinks better of her than what I do. She didn't before the match, but now, womanlike, she's all for it."

"That's to the good then. They talk of late autumn."

"Have you asked your girl where she thinks to live?"

"We haven't raised that yet."

"I did, and she put me off. There's things hidden. What are you going to give her?"

"Five hundred pound, Enoch."

"Don't, Ben. Keep it against their future. That's a hugeous lot of money and Lord knows what she'd do with it. I hope you haven't told her no such thing."

"My only daughter must have a good start. It's none too much; she knows about it."

Mr. Withycombe considered.

"Then I'll tell you what she's doing, Ben. She's marrying for money! Yes, she is. Not Jerry's, because he won't have a penny till I die, and then he can only have one-third of the lot, which ain't much. But Jane's marrying for your money, and I'll lay my life that she's going to spend it, thinking that there'll be plenty more where that comes from."

"You mustn't say such things. She knows the value of money better than most."

"Then have it out and learn what's in their minds. They've no right to secrets if you're going to pay the piper and start 'em in that generous way. Keep her money and let her have the interest on it and no more, till you see how they get on."

"Secrets there didn't ought to be I grant," said Benjamin. "But, mind you, I'm not allowing there are any. You may be mistook."

"Then find out where they be going to live and how Jane thinks to handle that dollop of cash," warned Mr. Withycombe. "You've a right to know: it's your duty to know, and your wife will tell you the same. And don't let Jane throw dust in your eyes. She's a tricky piece, like most of them beauties. I wish she'd took after the pattern of Orphan Dinah."

"So do I," admitted the other. "And now, to leave this, I'd like to speak a word about Dinah, because there's some things you may know bearing upon her that I do not. I'm struck with doubt, and I've been keeping her on along with me for two reasons. Firstly, because the right sort of place in my opinion don't offer."

"It never will," said Enoch. "Truth's truth, and the truth is you can't part from her."

"No, you mustn't say that. She's a very great deal to me, but I ban't selfish about her. I'm thinking of her future, and I don't want her placed where her future will be made dark and difficult. There's a lot to consider. And while I've been considering and withstanding Faith, here and there, and Dinah also for that matter, there's drifted into my mind the second point about Dinah. And that's in my mind still. But I begin to feel doubtful, Enoch, whether it's very much use for us old people to worry our heads as we do about the young ones. This generation will go its own way."

"Pretty much as ours did before them no doubt," answered the sick man. "We ancient folk love to bide in the middle of the picture so long as we can, and when I was a lot younger than now, yet not too young to mark it, I often thought it was rather a sad sight to see the old hanging on, and giving their opinions, and thinking anybody still cared a damn for what they said, or thought."

"Yes, only the little children really believe in us," confessed Mr. Bamsey; "and that's why I say we squander a good bit of wisdom upon the rising race, for they'll go on rising, for good or evil, without much troubling their heads as to whether we approve, or don't. They put education before experience, so, of course, what we've got to offer don't appeal to 'em. But Dinah—she does heed me, and now there's come a shadow of a suspicion in my mind about another man for her. That's why I'm so content to mark time a little and get hard words for doing it. She don't know herself, I believe, and very like the man don't know yet. Or he may know, and be biding his time. But more than once or twice—more, in fact, than she guesses—Dinah, when she's been talking to me, have named a certain person. I very near warned her against it, for women's ears are quicker than ours, and if Jane and my wife had marked it, evil might have risen out of it at once. But Dinah says a lot more in my hearing than in theirs and they don't know so far. And, as I tell you, Dinah herself don't know. But the name echoes along. In a word, what do you think of Maynard at Falcon Farm? You know him better than I do, though the little I've seen of the man leads me to like him. He's a sensible soul and none too cheerful—rather a twilight sort of man you might say; but that's a way life have with some of the thinking sort. It turns 'em into their shells a bit."

"He's a kindly, well-meaning chap and old for his years," said Withycombe. "I should say he's not for a wife."

"How d'you know?"

"I don't know. We never talk about himself, nor yet myself. He gives me his company sometimes and we tell about pretty high matters, not people. He's got a mind, Ben."

Melinda Honeysett joined them at this moment and entered their conversation.

"He's got a mind, no doubt," said Mr. Bamsey. "But he's also got a body, and it would be unnatural in a young, hearty man of his years, prosperous too I suppose, because, with his sense, he's sure to have put by a bit—it would be unnatural, I say, if he'd never turned his thoughts to a home of his own."

Enoch spoke to his daughter.

"Here's Ben trying to hatch up a match for Dinah," he said.

"No, no—too wise, I'm sure," answered Melinda.

"Far too wise," declared the visitor. "But if such a thing was possible in fulness of time, it would cut a good many knots, Melindy."

"Dinah likes freedom now she's got it, I believe, and I wouldn't say she was too fond of children neither," answered Enoch's daughter.

"They never like children, till they meet the man they can see as father of their own children," answered Ben; "and if Dinah ever said she didn't want 'em, that's only another proof that she never loved poor John."

"The love of childer be knit up with other things no doubt," admitted Enoch.

"There's lots love childer as never had none, like myself," answered Melinda.

"True, my dear. There's lots love game as never shot it. But the snipe you brought down yourself be always the one that tastes best. A mother may love her own children, or she may not; but it depends often enough on the husband."

It was Mrs. Honeysett's father who spoke.

"There's some child-lovers who only wed because that's the way to get 'em," he continued. "Such women don't think no more of the husband than the doctor—I've known such. But perfect love of childer did ought to begin with the perfect love of the man that got 'em. Take me. I had but three, but they were the apple of my wife's eye, because they was mine as well as hers."

"My brother, Robert, be coming home presently," said Melinda. "My sailor brother, Mr. Bamsey. How would you like him for Dinah? I'm sure she'd make a proper wife for him. He's like Jerry, only quicker in the uptake. But not so clever as father."

"Wouldn't like Dinah to marry a sailor man," confessed Ben. "I know Robert is a fine chap; but they've got a wife in every port. A sailor sees a lot more than the wonders of the deep."

Mr. Withycombe laughed.

"He ain't that sort, I promise you," he said.

"The point is, in strictest confidence, Melindy," explained Ben, "that I believe, though she scarce knows it herself, Dinah's interested in the Falcon Farm cowman. She's seen him off and on and, in my ear alone, speaks of the man. And your father here has nought but good to say of him."

"He's not for a wife, so Joe tells me. He was naming him a bit agone," answered Melinda, "and he said that the most comforting thing about him, and Mr. Palk also, was that they were cut out for the bachelor state for evermore. Perhaps you'd best to name that to Dinah. Though, for my part, I should hope it would be years after her last adventure afore she ever dared to think upon a man again."

"So it would be—so it would be in the course of nature," granted Ben. "No doubt you're right; and yet—there it is. He seems to attract her—against her own reason I dare say."   •

"When that happens, it means love," declared Enoch.

Melinda spoke like a woman. She was fond of Dinah, but had been exceedingly sorry for Johnny.

"Queer—sure enough," she said. "If Dinah, now, was to feel drawn to a man as hadn't any use for her, it would be fair justice in a manner of speaking, wouldn't it, Mr. Bamsey?"

"In a manner of speaking I dare say it might, Melindy," he admitted. "But I'll not hear Dinah tongue-handled over that no more."

"I'll sound Lawrence on his next visit," promised Enoch. "But he's very shy where his own affairs are concerned."

"And another thing be certain," added Melinda, "Joe Stockman would be terrible put about if he thought any such doings as that was in the wind."

Then Mr. Bamsey went his way, as doubtful as when he came.

CHAPTER XVI
SUNDAY

Jerry and his sweetheart wandered together along the lane from Buckland on an afternoon when Jane had been visiting the Withycombes. The sun beat down through the trees and even in the shade it was too hot to tempt the lovers far.

"We'll climb up the Beacon a little ways and quott down in the fern," said Jerry, "and I'll smoke in your face and keep the flies off."

Jane, however, objected.

"I'm going to Hazel Tor I reckon, and then to Cousin Joe's for tea. We'll meet John at Hazel Tor. Shall we tell him our secret plans, Jerry?"

"I don't care who knows it. If you feel there's no more need to hide up what we've ordained to do, then tell everybody."

"There's every need to hide up for that matter. Only Johnny's different from others. Me and Johnny are pretty close pals and always were. He won't mind us having a shop in a town. I've often told him I was set on the thought of a shop."

"The doubt will lie with me," said Jerry. "I know very well my father and Melindy and everybody will say I ban't the sort of man to shine at a shop."

"There's shops and shops," answered Jane, "and it's a very difficult question indeed to decide what to sell. If we sold some things you'd be a lot more useful than if we sold others. But there's a lot of things I wouldn't care about selling."

They had already debated this matter many times, and never failed to find it attractive.

"There's certain goods ruled out, I know," he said. "You don't hold with butching, nor yet a fish shop."

"Nothing like that. I won't handle dead things," declared Jane. "It lies in my mind between three shops now. I've brought 'em down to three. There's a shop for children's toys, which I'd very much like, because new toys be clean and bright and interesting to me; but you wouldn't be much use in that."

"I should not," admitted Jerry.

"Then," continued Jane, "there's a green-grocer's; and there's a great deal to be said for that, because we should have father behind us in a manner of speaking, and he'd let us have tons of fruit and vegetables at a very small price, or no price at all I dare say."

"Only if he comes round, Jenny. You grant yourself he'll little like to hear you be going to spend your capital on a shop."

"He'll come round when he sees I'm in earnest. And it might help him to come round if we took a green-grocer's. But I'm not saying I'd specially like a green-grocer's myself, because I shouldn't. 'Tis always a smelly place, and I hate smells."

"All shops have their smells," answered Jerry. "Even a linen draper to my nose have a smell, though I couldn't describe it in words."

"They have," admitted she. "And the smell I'd like best to live in be tobacco. If I'd only got myself to think for, it would be a tobacco shop, because there you get all your stuff advanced on the cheap, I believe, and if you once have a good rally to the shop, they bring their friends. And it's quite as much a man's job as a woman's."

"My head spins when I think of it, however," confessed Jerry. "The only shop I see myself in is the green-grocer's, and only there for the cabbages and potatoes and such like. The higher goods, such as grapes and fine fruits, would be your care."

Jane shook her head.

"Half the battle is to feel a call to a thing," she said, "same as I felt a call to you. And as I'll be shopwoman most of the time, it's more important as I shall be suited than you."

"Certainly."

"There's more money moving among men than women: you must remember that too," continued Jane. "Men have bigger views and don't haggle over halfpennies like women. A green-grocer's be a terrible shop for haggling; but with tobacco and pipes and cigars, the price is marked once for all, and only men buy 'em, and the clever shop women often just turn the scales and sell the goods. I've watched these things when I've been in Ashburton along with father, or Johnny; and I've seen how a pleasant, nice-spoken woman behind the counter, especially if she's good-looking, have a great power. Then, again, the bettermost sort of men go into a tobacconist; but never into a green-grocer. Buying vegetables be woman's work."

"I can see you incline your heart to tobacco," said Jerry. "And so, no doubt, it will be tobacco; but I must work, and if there's no work for me in our shop, then I'll have to find it outside our shop. Lots of women keep a shop and their men do something else."

"Why not?"

"Us may say the lot's pretty well cast for tobacco then. Shall us tell Johnny to-day and get his opinion?"

"I'll see what sort of frame he's in," replied Jane. "He's been dark lately, because he's getting slowly and surely to know that Dinah Waycott ain't going back on her word. It makes me dance with rage sometimes to think that John can want her still, and would forgive the woman to-morrow if she offered to take up with him again."

"Love's like that, I dare say," guessed Jerry. "It'll sink to pretty well anything."

"Well, I hate to see it—a fine man like my brother. He comes and goes, and they've made it up and are going to be friends; at least, father thinks so—as if anything could ever make up a job like that. If I was a man, and a woman jilted me, I know when I'd make it up. I'd hate her to my dying day, and through eternity too."

"You oughtn't to say things like that, Jane."

"It ain't over yet," she continued. "I shouldn't wonder much if there was an upstore before long. Dinah can't keep secrets and she's shameless. There's another in her eye as I have told you—talk of the devil!"

They were abreast of Falcon Farm and a man descended from it by a path to the main road as Jane spoke. Maynard was on his way to Buckland. He met them and gave them "good day" pleasantly enough. Jerry responded and praised the weather, but his sweetheart did not speak.

"Your brother be coming up to tea at the farm," said Lawrence.

"I know that," was all Jane answered, and he went his way without more words.

"There!" she exclaimed, when he was out of earshot.

"Why did you say 'talk of the devil'?" asked Jerry. "Surely nobody have a quarrel with that chap? My father says he's a very proper sort and a lot cleverer than you might think."

"I dare say he is a lot cleverer than some people," answered Jane; "but he ain't a lot cleverer than me. He's a tricky beast, that's what he is, and us'll know it presently."

Jerry was much astonished.

"I never! You're the first person as I've heard tell against him. Joe Stockman thinks the world of him. What have he done to you? If you have got any fair thing against the man, I'll damn soon be upsides with him."

"I'll tell you this," she replied. "I believe Dinah's hanging on at home and letting father have his way, not because she cares two straws for father really. She's a heartless thing under all her pretence. But she's on that man's track, and she's too big a fool to hide it from me. And him that would look at her, after what she done to Johnny, must be a beast. And I hope you see that if you're not blind."

Jerry scratched his head and stared at her.

"I'm sure I trust you be wrong, Jenny. That would be a very ill-convenient thing to happen, because Farmer Stockman would be thrown very bad."

"What does he matter? Can't you see the insult to John? And can't you see that, if they be after each other on the quiet, it must have been Maynard that kindiddled Dinah away from John in the first place? What I believe is that he came between Dinah and John, and got round her, and made her give John up."

"For God's sake don't say such things," begged Jerry. "Don't you rush in like that, or you'll very likely wish you hadn't. 'Tis too fearful, and you can't tell what far-reaching trouble you might make if you was to tell John such a thing. Him being what he is, you might land him—Lord knows where!"

She considered this.

"You're right so far I suppose; all the same I've had it on the tip of my tongue to whisper this to John and bid him watch them."

"Don't then—for the Lord's love, don't," implored Withycombe. "It would be playing with fire. If she's given over John once for all, then let him think no more about the woman. 'Tis no good spying, nor nothing like that. It ain't your business; and for that matter, it might be the best thing to happen for somebody to get hold of Dinah, and marry her, and take her far ways off. John have got to come to it, and when he found she loved somebody else, surely that would show him 'twas wasting his time to grizzle any more about her."

"I'll thank you to look at it different, Jerry," said Jane sharply. "If I hate a man, for very good reasons, then you ought to do the same. I can see into things a lot deeper than what you can, as you've always granted, and I can see into Maynard. He's the silent, shifty sort, deep as a well—and I won't have you sticking up for him against me, so now then."

Jerry whistled.

"I've nothing for, or against him," he answered slowly. "I scarcely know the man, but there's my father and others speak well of him; and I'm always wishful to think well of everybody, unless there's a reason against."

"I'm the reason against then," she declared, "and you've got to put me and my opinions first, I should hope. I'm a kindly creature enough, God knows, and ban't quick to think evil."

"Certainly not," admitted Jerry.

"But I look to you to pay me the respect due," she continued, "and if I tell you a man's doubtful, then 'tis for you to believe me and act according."

"I will," he promised. "We'm all doubtful for that matter. Us will speak and think of the man as we find him. We needn't go out of the way to make trouble."

"I ban't one to make trouble," she retorted; "but, next to you, John's more to me than anybody, and I won't stand by and see him wronged by that hateful woman, nor yet by that man, if I can stop it."

Jerry felt this attitude unreasonable, but decided the subject had better be dropped.

"If wrong's done, I'll help to right it, that I'll swear," he promised.

"I'd right it myself," she said. "If I could prove the man had stole her from my brother, I'd lie behind a hedge for him!"

"Do shut up and stop telling such dreadful things," he answered roughly. "'Tis hateful to hear such words from your mouth—Sunday and all. I won't have it, Jane. What the hell's the matter with you?"

They were silent for a time; then having reached Hazel Tor, Jerry helped his sweetheart to climb the great rocks. Soon they were perched high on the granite, and Jane opened a white and blue parasol, while he stretched his vast limbs at her feet and smoked his pipe. His elephantine playfulness and ideas on the tobacco shop won Jane's smiles presently, and at heart Jerry regretted the moment when his future brother-in-law ascended through the pine-trees from the river and joined them.

The fret and sting of his hopeless quest had marked John Bamsey, and now he was come to the knowledge that no hope remained. His dream dissolved. Until now he had defied reason and lived on shadows spun of desire. He had sunk beneath his old pride and returned to Dinah's hand. He had not grovelled; but he assumed an attitude, after the passing of the first storm, that astonished his family. And Dinah it astonished also, filling her with fresh pain. He had hung on; he had asked her to forgive his words upon the bridge; he had returned into the atmosphere of her and gone and come from home as before. Dominated by his own passion, he had endured even the wonder in his mother's eyes, the doubt in Jane's. Dinah could not be explicit to him, since he had been careful not to give her any opportunity for the present. But, under his humility, he had bullied her. The very humility was a sort of bullying, and she felt first distracted and then indignant that he should persist. To him she could not speak, but to Faith Bamsey and Jane she could speak; and to the former she did.

Mrs. Bamsey therefore knew that Dinah was not going to marry John, and in her heart she was thankful for it; while none the less indignant that John's perfections should have failed of fruition for Dinah. She resented Dinah's blindness and obstinacy, and felt thankful, for John's sake, that the girl would never be his wife. As for Jane she had never shared her brother's whispered hope that Dinah would return to him. She hated Dinah, and while hot with sympathy for her brother, rejoiced that, sooner or later, her father's foster-daughter must disappear and never be linked to a Bamsey.

Johnny's present attitude, however, she did not know; and it was left for this hour amid the tree girt rocks of Hazel Tor to teach her. She longed to learn what he would say if any other man were hinted of in connection with Dinah. She much wanted Johnny to share her opinion of Dinah, and now, ripened for mischief by the recent sight of Maynard, she prepared to sound Johnny. Jerry suspected what was in her mind and hoped that she would change it. They spoke first of their own secret, and informed John, after exacting from him promises of silence.

He was moody and his expression had changed. Care had come into his face and its confidence had abated. He had always liked to talk, and possessed with his own wrongs, of late, began to weary other ears. To his few intimate friends he had already spoken unwisely and salved the wounds of pride by assuring them that the rupture was not permanent. He had even hinted that he was responsible for it—to give the woman he designed to wed a lesson. He had affected confidence in the future; and now this was not the least of his annoyances, that when the truth came in sight, certain people would laugh behind his back. Upon such a temper it was easy to see how any mention of another man in connection with Dinah must fall; and had Jane really known all that was tormenting her brother's mind, at the moment when it began to feel the truth, even she might have hesitated; but she did not.

John considered their dreams of a shop without much sympathy and doubted their wisdom.

"You're a woodman and only a woodman—bred to it," he declared. "What the mischief should you make messing about among shops and houses in a town? You know you'd hate it, just so much as I should myself, and you know well he would, if he don't, Jane."

"You forget his feeling for me, Johnny," explained his sister. "It wouldn't be natural to him I grant; but there's me; and what's my good be Jerry's good when we'm married."

"You ought to think of his good, too, however. I shouldn't hide this up. You'd do well to talk to mother before you do anything."

"You don't think father will change about the five hundred pound?" asked Jane. "'Twas fear of that kept us quiet."

"No; he won't change. I was to have had the same."

"And so you will have," she said. "'Tis only a question of time."

"You'll get one as feels for you, same as Jane feels for me, presently," ventured Jerry.

"And Dinah Waycott will get hell," added Jane; "and I dare say it may happen to her afore so mighty long, for that matter."

Jerry shrank, for Jane's brother fastened on this.

"What d'you mean?" he asked, and she was glad he did.

"Nothing, Johnny; only I've got eyes. I ban't one to think evil; but I can't help being pretty quick where you are concerned. You're next to Jerry, and I shan't be a happy woman till you're a happy man, and you know it."

"What then, Jane?"

"We met Lawrence Maynard walking down the road a bit ago."

"And if you did?"

She dared greatly.

"I suppose you haven't ever heard his name along with hers?"

"'Hers'? D'you mean Dinah's? No, by God—nor any other man's! If I did——Out with it. What are you saying, Jane?"

To hear him swear made Jerry wonder, for John had never sworn in the past. The woodman, regarding him very anxiously, now perceived how his face and the tone of his voice had altered. That such phenomena were visible to Jerry's intelligence argued their magnitude.

"She went for a long walk with him a few weeks back," said Jane. "She made no secret about it. He took her to see a stone out Hey Tor way."

"Did he? And why didn't you tell me?"

"I was going to; but I waited to see if there was more to tell. There is no more than that—not yet."

Johnny fell silent. His mind moved quickly. Love had already begun to suffer a change, half chemical, half psychological, that would presently poison it. Such passion as he had endured for Dinah would not fade and suffer extinction in Johnny's order of mind. He came to the ordeal untried and untested. He had till now been a thief of virtue, in the sense that he was good and orderly, peace-loving and obedient by native bent and instinct. He fitted into the order of things as they were and approved them. Nothing had ever happened to make him unrestful, to incite class prejudice, or to foment discontent with his station. He had looked without sympathy on the struggle for better industrial conditions; he had despised doubt in the matter of religion. He was born good: his mother had said the Old Adam must surely be left out of him. But now came the shock, and pride prevented John from admitting his failure to anybody else; pride, indeed, had assured him that such a man as he must have his own way in the end.

He debated the past, and his self-respect tottered before his thoughts, as a stout boulder shakes upon its foundations at the impact of a flood. He stared at Jane and Jerry unseeing, and they marked the blood leap up into his face and his eyes grow bright. This idea was new to him. What Jane said acted perilously, for it excused to himself his gathering temper under defeat and justified his wrath in his own sight.

"Be careful," he said. "D'you know all it means you'm saying, Jane?"

"For God's sake, unsay it, Jenny," urged her sweetheart. "You can't know—nobody can know."

"If any other man thinks he'll have that woman——"

John said no more; but his own thoughts surged up and seemed to be bursting his head. A mountain of wrongs was toppling down upon him. He forgot his companions; then became suddenly conscious of their eyes staring into his. He looked at them as though they had been strangers, started up, went down the rocks at a pace to threaten his neck and then was gone through the trees, plunging straight ahead like a frightened animal.

Jerry Withycombe declared great alarm; Jane only felt the deepest interest.

"Now you've done it," said the man.

"So much the better," she answered. "It was bound to come. I'm glad."

Meantime Maynard, musing on Jane Bamsey's curt attitude, had reached Buckland to spend an hour or two by invitation with Enoch Withycombe.

"Time drags for you sometimes I expect," said Lawrence.

"No, I wouldn't say time drags," declared the sick man. "Time don't run more than sixty minutes to the hour with me, though I can't say it runs less, like it does for the young and hale and hearty people. Give me a new book and life don't drag. And there's always memory. I've got a very good memory—better than many who come to see me I reckon. My mind keeps clear, and I still have the power to go over my great runs with hounds. And I don't mix 'em. I can keep 'em separate and all the little things that happened. You'd think they'd get muddled up; but they do not."

"That's wonderful," said Lawrence.

"Yes, I can shut my eyes and get in a comfortable position and bring it all afore me and feel my horse pulling and my feet in the stirrups. And once or twice of late I've dreamed dreams; and that's even better, because for the moment, you're in the saddle again—living—living! When I wake up from a dream like that, I make a point of thanking God for it, Maynard. I'd sooner have a dream like that than anything man can give me now."

"They're terrible queer things—dreams," declared the younger. "I've had a few of late. They take hold of you when your mind's more than common full, I reckon."

"Or your stomach—so doctor says. But that's not right. I've stuffed once or twice—greedy like—just for the hope that when I went to sleep I'd be hunting, but it never did anything but keep me awake. No, dreams hang on something we can't understand I reckon; and why the mind won't lie down and sleep with the body, sometimes, but must be off on its own, we can't tell. But there's things said about dreams that ban't true, Lawrence. I read somewhere that you never see the faces of the dead in dreams. That's false. You do see 'em. I saw my brother none so long ago—not as he was when he died, but as a little boy. And dreams be very reasonable in their unreason, you must know, for I was a little boy too. I saw his young face and flaxen hair, and heard him laugh, and we was busy as bees climbing up a fir-tree to a squirrel's dray in a wood. A thing, no doubt, we'd done in life together often enough, sixty years agone; and 'twas put into my dream, and I woke all the better for it."

"Don't you get no sad dreams?" asked Lawrence.

"They come too. They leave you a bit down-daunted, I grant. And some be lost, because you can't call 'em home when you wake up. You'll dream a proper masterpiece sometimes and wake full of it; and yet, for some mysterious working of the brain, 'tis gone, and you try to stretch after it, but never can catch it again. I woke in tears—fancy! Yes, in tears I woke once, long ago now; and for the life of me I didn't know what fetched 'em out of my eyes."

"Perhaps you'd had a cruel bout of pain while you was asleep?"

"No, no; pain don't get tear or groan out of me. I'll never know what it was."

He broke off suddenly, for a previous speech of his visitor gave him the opening he desired.

"You said just now you'd been dreaming, along of your mind, that was more than common full. Was it anything interesting in particular on your mind, or just life in general?"

"Just life as it comes along I reckon."

Enoch regarded him.

"You be looking ahead, as you've the right to do. You're a man a thought out of the common in your understanding. You don't want to work for another all your life, do you?"

"I never look much ahead. Sometimes the past blocks the future, and a man's often less ambitious at thirty than he was ten years before. I don't particular want a home of my own. A home means a lot of things I've got no use for."

"Pretty much what some of the maidens think," said Enoch with craft. "For them a home means a man; and for us it means a woman, of course, because we can't very well establish anything to be called home without one. Orphan Dinah wants badly to be off, so Ben Bamsey, her foster-father, tells me. And yet he's in a quandary; because he feels that if a happy home were in sight for her, he'd far sooner she waited for it, a year or more, than left him to go somewhere else."

"A very reasonable thought. But these things don't fall out as we want 'em to."

They fenced a little, but Lawrence was very guarded and committed himself to no opinion of Dinah until Enoch, failing in strategy, tried a direct question.

"What do you think of Orphan Dinah as a woman?" he asked.

"I like her," answered the other frankly. "Since you ask, there's no harm in saying I think she's a very fine character. She haven't shone much of late, because there was a lot of feeling about what she done; and it's been made the most of I can see by women, and some men. But she's made it clear to me and to you, I hope, that she did right. She's built on a pretty big pattern and she's had a lot to put up with, and she's been very patient about it."

"A bit out of the common you'd say?"

"I think she is."

"I may tell you, for your ear alone, Maynard, that she thinks very well of you."

Lawrence tightened his lips.

"No, no—don't you say that. She don't know me. I dare say, if she was to, she'd feel different."

"Dinah can't hide herself from her foster-father's eyes," explained Enoch. "She don't try to for that matter, and Ben sees that there's something about you that interests her; and you've told me there be something to her that interests you. And what follows? I'm only an old man speaking, and you mustn't take offence whether or no."

"There's no offence," answered Lawrence. "You'd not offend anybody. But I'd rather not have any speech about it, Mr. Withycombe."

Enoch had said all he desired to say and learned all he wanted to learn.

"And quite right and proper," he answered. "These things are very safe where they belong, and I wouldn't rush into a man's private affairs for money."

"You've been a very good friend to me and made my mind bigger," declared Lawrence. "A man that can preach patience from your bed of pain, like you do, did ought to be heard. It ain't easy I should reckon."

They talked of Enoch's books and his master, who had lately been to see him.

"There's one who fears not to look the truth in the face," said the huntsman. "He told me things that only I say to myself, because the rest are too tender to say them. Doctor looks them, but even he won't say them out. But master could tell me I'd soon be gone. He believes in the next world, and don't see no reason in the nature of things why there shouldn't be fox-hunting there."

Another visitor dropped in upon Mr. Withycombe. It was Arthur Chaffe in his Sunday black.

"If one's enough at a time, I'll be off," he said, "and fetch up again next Sunday."

But Enoch welcomed him.

"I'm in good fettle, Arthur, and be very willing to make hay while the sun shines."

Arthur, however, doubted.

"You'm looking so grim as a ghost, my old dear," he answered, "and so white as a dog's tooth."

Mr. Withycombe laughed.

"You be a cheerful one for a death-bed, sure enough," he answered.

"There's no death, Enoch, and you know it so well as what I do."

"And you an undertaker! Mind you deal fair and square with me, Chaffe; for death, or no death, 'tis as certain as life that I shall want some of your best seasoned elm afore very long."

But Mr. Chaffe steadied the conversation.

"You be quiet, Enoch," he said. "This is the Lord's Day and us didn't ought to be joking, like as if 'twas Monday."

The hunter took up the challenge and they went at it again, in the best of humour, till Melinda returned and gave the three men tea.

They spoke of Dinah and gave examples of her quality and difference from other young women. Mrs. Honeysett tended rather to disparage her of late, having been influenced thereto in certain quarters; but Arthur Chaffe supported Dinah, and Lawrence listened.

He presently, however, quoted.

"Long ago, before she had to break with poor Bamsey, I remember a word she said to me," he remarked. "It showed she knew a bit about human nature and was finding out that everybody couldn't be relied upon. She asked me if I was faithful. It seemed a curious question at the time."

"And you said you was, no doubt?" asked Melinda.

"We must all be faithful," declared Arthur Chaffe. "Where there's no faith, there's no progress, and the order of things would run down like a clock."

"The world goes round on trust," admitted Mr. Withycombe, "and the more man can trust man, the easier we advance and the quicker. 'Faithful' be the word used between us in business and it wasn't the one we fixed upon for nothing. 'Yours faithfully' we say."

"Yes, oftener than we mean it, God forgive us," sighed Mr. Chaffe. "'Tis often only a word and too few respect it. Us have all written so to people we hate, and would like to think was going to be found dead in their beds to-morrow. Such is the weakness of human nature."

"We must be civil even to enemies," said the sick man.

"I wonder," mused Melinda. "It's a bit mean to hide our feelings so much."

"Warner Chave was a fine example," answered Mr. Chaffe. "Foes he had a plenty, as such a straight and pushing chap must; but he never quarrelled with man or mouse. He never gave any living soul a straw to catch hold of. His simple rule was that it takes two to a quarrel, and he'd never be one; and he never was. Why! He got on with his relations even!"

"How?" asked Maynard.

"Never criticised 'em. Such was his amazing skill that he let them live their lives their own way, and treated 'em with just the same respect he showed to everybody else."

They enjoyed tea in a cheerful temper, and Arthur Chaffe had continually to remind them it was Sunday.

Then he prepared to depart and Maynard left with him. In the high road they, too, separated, for their ways were opposite.

"I laugh, but with sorrow in my heart," said Arthur, "for that dear man be going down the hill terrible fast to the experienced eye. We shall miss him—there's a lot of Christian charity to him, and I only wish to God he'd got the true Light. That's all he wants. The heart be there and the ideas; but his soul just misses the one thing needful."

"I hope not," said Maynard. "He's earned the best we can wish for."

"It may come yet," prophesied Arthur. "It may flash in upon him at the last. Where there's life, there's hope of salvation. Us must never forget that the prayers of a righteous man availeth much, Maynard."

"And the life of a righteous man availeth more, Mr. Chaffe," answered Lawrence.

"That we ain't told," replied the elder. "We can only leave the doubter to the mercy of his Maker; and there's many and many got to be left like that, for doubt's growing, worse luck. Us say 'sure and certain hope' over a lot of mortal dust, when too well our intellects tell us the hope ban't so certain nor yet sure as us would like to feel."

He perked away on his long, thin legs, like a friendly stork, and Maynard set his face upward for his home.

CHAPTER XVII
DINAH

Though circumstances had of late baffled Dinah Waycott and tended sometimes to beget a reserve and caution foreign to her; though she found herself hiding her thoughts in a manner very unfamiliar and keeping silent, where of old she would have spoken, or even allowing by default an opinion to pass unquestioned as hers which of old she would have contradicted; there was still no confusion in her mind when she communed with herself. Therefore, when she found that she stood face to face with a new thing, she pretended no doubt as to the name of it. Bewilderment, none the less, filled her mind, and elements of joy, that might be supposed proper to such an experience, could not at present live with the other more distracting sensations her discovery awakened. Something like dismay she did feel, that any such paramount event should have overtaken her at this stage in her life; for Dinah was not insensitive, though so plain-spoken, and now painfully she felt this was no time to have developed the burning preoccupation that already swept into nothingness every adventure and emotion of the past.

There had happened a precious wonder beyond all wonders, but Dinah felt angry with herself that, under present conditions of stress and anxiety, any loophole existed for such a selfish passion. It had come, however, and it could not stand still; and selfish she had to be, since the good and glory of the thing must be shared with none at present.

Silent, however, she could not be for long. There was one to whom she never feared to talk and from whom she had no secrets. To him, her foster-father, Dinah had taken every joy and sorrow, hope and fear since she could talk. Only once, and that in the matter of his own son, John, had she hidden her heart from Ben Bamsey, yet found it possible to show it to another.

She remembered that now; and it was that same 'other,' who, from the first, had possessed a nameless quality to challenge and arrest Dinah. Gradually he had occupied a larger and larger domain in her mind, until he overwhelmed it and her gradual revelation was complete. For gradual it had been. Together they walked once more at her wish, after their first long tramp, while, agreeably to the invitation of Mr. Bamsey, Lawrence Maynard again visited Green Hayes upon a Sunday afternoon. Then, indeed, under the eyes of Jane and her mother, Dinah had hidden her heart very effectually, and even made occasion to leave the house and go elsewhere before Maynard's visit was ended; but she knew by signs in her body and soul that she was in love. The amazing novelty of her thoughts, the transfiguration they created in her outlook upon all things, the new colours they imparted to any vision of the future, convinced her that there could be no doubt. Against this reality, the past looked unreal; before this immensity, the past appeared, dwarfed and futile. That cloudy thing, her whole previous existence, was now reduced to a mere huddled background—its only excuse the rainbow that had suddenly glowed out upon it.

She was honestly ashamed that love could have happened to her at this moment and thrust so abruptly in upon her sad experience with Johnny. It seemed, in some moods, callous and ungenerous to allow such wayward delights and dreams to enter her heart while well she knew that his was heavy. But, at other times, she would not blame herself, for her conscience was clear. Maynard had meant nothing to her when she gave up her first lover, and it was no thought of him, or any man, that had determined her to do so.

Her love at least was pure as love well could be, for she did not know that he returned it; sometimes, at first, she almost hoped he would not. But that was only in the dim and glimmering dawn of it. Love cannot feed on dreams alone. She put it from her at first, only to find it fly back. So she nursed it secretly and waited and wondered, and, meantime, strove to find a way to leave Green Hayes. But still Ben opposed her suggestions, and then there came a time when, from the first immature fancy that to love him secretly, herself unloved, would be enough, Dinah woke into a passionate desire that he should love her back again. Now she was mature, accomplished, awake and alert, lightning quick to read his mood, the inflexion of every word he uttered when he was beside her, the faintest brightening of his eyes, his dress, his walk, the inspiration of every moment.

She could not help it. Often she returned dull and daunted, not with him but herself; and as she began to know, from no sign of his but by her own quickened sex endowment that he cared for her, she grew faint and ashamed again. He had taught her a great deal. He seemed to be very wise and patient, but not particularly happy—rather unfinished even on some sides of his experience. There were a great many things he did not know, and he seemed not nearly as interested in life as she was, or as desirous to have it more abundantly. Johnny had evinced a much keener appetite for living and far greater future ambitions than Maynard. Lawrence was, in fact, as somebody had said, "a twilight sort of man." But it was a cool, clear, self-contained twilight that he moved in, and he appeared to see distinctly enough through it. Dinah thought it was twilight of morning rather than night. She imagined him presently emerging into a wonderful dawn, and dreamed of helping him to do so. She checked such fancies, yet they were natural to her direct temperament, and they recurred with increasing force. Her native freedom of mind broke down all barriers to private thinking, and sometimes she longed for him; then she chastened herself and planned a future without him and found it not worth remaining alive for. She began to sleep ill, but hid the signs. She plotted to see Maynard and was also skilful to conceal the fact that she did so. He always welcomed her, sometimes with a merry word, sometimes with a sad one. The milch cows grazed upon the moor now, and once or twice, sighting them a mile off upon her way home, Dinah would creep near and wait for Lawrence and the sheep dog to round them up and turn them to the valley for milking. She would hide in a thicket, or behind a boulder, and if he came would get a few precious words; but if Neddy Tutt appeared, as sometimes happened, then she would lie hid and go her way when he was gone.

She knew now that Maynard cared for her; but she discounted his every word and granted herself the very minimum. She was fearful of hoping too much, yet could not, for love's sake, hope too little. She longed to set her mind at rest upon the vital question; and at last did so. Making all allowance, and striving to chill and belittle his every word, she still could not longer doubt. He was often difficult to understand, yet some things she did now clearly comprehend. She had already seen a man in love, and though the love-making of Johnny differed very widely from that of Lawrence, though indeed Lawrence never had made a shadow of love to her, yet she knew at last, by mental and physical signs that curiously repeated Johnny's, he did love her.

She hugged this to her heart and felt that nothing else mattered, or would ever matter. For a time she even returned to her first dream and assured herself that love was enough. He might tell her some day; he might never tell her; but she knew it, and whether they came together, or lived their lives apart, the great fact would remain. Yet there was no food in any such conclusion, no life, no fertility, no peace.

She came to Ben Bamsey at this stage of her romance, for she hungered and thirsted to tell it; and to her it seemed that her foster-father ought to know. She came to him fresh from a meeting with Lawrence, for she had been, at Mr. Bamsey's wish, with a message to Falcon Farm, and she had met Maynard afterwards as she returned over the foothills of the Beacon.

The year was swinging round, and again the time had come for scything the fern, that it might ripen presently for the cattle byres.

He stopped a moment and shook hands with her.

"Just been up to see Soosie-Toosie," said Dinah. "Terrible sorry Mr. Palk's cut his hand so bad."

"Yes; it'll have to go in a sling for a bit. He thought it would mend and didn't take no great count of it, and now it's festered and will be a fortnight before it's all right."

"I wish I could help," she said. "If you was to do his work and Mr. Stockman would let me come and milk the cows for a week — —"

"No, no—no need for any help. Tom can do a lot. It's only his left hand and master's turning to. He says if he can't do the work of Tom's left hand, it's a shame to him."

"Did Mr. Palk get his rise he was after?"

"He did not, Dinah. But Mr. Stockman put it in a very nice way. He's going to raise us both next year. And you? Nothing turned up?"

She shook her head.

"A funny thing among 'em all they can't find just the right work. I wish you was away from Green Hayes."

She had told him all about her difficulties and he appreciated them. He thought a great deal about Dinah now, but still more about himself. He had been considering her when she appeared; and for the moment he did not want to see her. His mind ebbed and flowed, where Dinah was concerned, and he was stubborn with himself and would not admit anything. He persisted in this attitude, but now he began to perceive it was impossible much longer to do so. If Dinah had read him, he also had read her, for she was not difficult to read and lacked some of the ordinary armour of a woman in love with a man. He knew time could not stand still for either of them, yet strove to suspend it. Sometimes he was gentle and sometimes he was abrupt and ungenial when they met. To-day he dismissed her.

"Don't you bide here now," he said. "I'm busy, Dinah, and I've got a good bit on my mind too."

"I'm sorry then. You ask Soosie if I shall come and milk. That would give you more time. Good morning, Lawrence."

He had seen how her face fell.

"I wish I could think of a way out for you. Perhaps I shall. I do have it on my mind," he said. "But there's difficulties in a small place like this. Pity you ain't farther off, where you could breathe easier."

For some reason this remark cheered her. She left him without speaking again and considered his saying all the way home. The interpretation she put upon it was not wholly mistaken, yet it might have surprised the man, for we often utter a thought impelled thereto by subconscious motives we hardly feel ourselves. He did not for the moment associate himself, or his interests, with the desire that Dinah should go away, yet such a desire really existed in him, though, had he analysed it, he had been divided between two reasons for such a desire. He might have asked himself whether he wished her out of her present difficult environment in order that his own approach to her should become easier and freer of doubtful interpretation in the mouths of other people; or he might have considered whether, for his own peace, he honestly wished to see Dinah so far away that reasonable excuses should exist for dropping her acquaintance. Between these alternatives he could hardly have decided at present. He lagged behind her, for love seldom wakens simultaneously, or moves with equal pace on both sides. He might continue to lag and fall farther behind, or he might catch her and pass her. He was at a stage in their approach when he could still dispassionately consider all that increase of friendship must imply. He hardly knew where the friendship exactly stood at the moment. Actual irritation sometimes intervened. He suffered fits of impatience both with himself and her. Yet he knew, when cool again, that neither was to be blamed. If blame existed, it was not Dinah's.

She went home now, and after dinner on that day, found opportunity to speak with her foster-father. They were cutting oats and she descended to the valley field beside Ben and made a clean breast of her secrets, only to find they were not hidden from him. He treated her as one much younger than she really was, and seeing that she was indeed younger than her age in many particulars of mind, this process always satisfied Dinah and made her feel happier with Ben Bamsey than his family, who made no such concession, but, on the contrary, attributed qualities to Dinah she lacked.

"Foster-father," she said, "I'm wishful to have a tell and here's a good chance. I be getting in a proper mizmaze I do assure 'e."

"You must be patient, my little dear," he answered.

"I've been patient for six months, though it's more like six years since I changed about poor Johnny. And other people, so well as I, do feel I'd be better away."

"Have I ever said you wouldn't be better away, Dinah? I know only too well how it is. But a father can look deeper into life than his child. I'm wide awake—watching. I understand your troubles and try to lessen 'em where I can."

"If you wasn't here, I'd have runned away long ago. For a little bit, after that cruel come-along-of-it, I wouldn't have minded to die. Now that's passed; but you, who never did such a thing, can't tell what it is to know that you're fretting and galling two other women. And Mrs. Bamsey and Jane have a right to be fretted and galled by me. I can well understand, without their looks, how I must be to them; and 'tis a sharp thorn in your flesh to be hated, and it's making me miserable."

He had not guessed she much felt this side of the position.

"You'm growing up, I see, like everybody else," he said. "I forget that I can't have it both ways, and can't have you a loving, watchful daughter and a child too. And if you can think for me, as you do so wonderful, then you'm old enough to feel for yourself, of course. Still you'm so parlous young in some ways, that it ain't strange I still think of you a child in everyway. I suppose you must go and I mustn't find nothing against no more. And yet——"

He broke off, his mind upon Maynard.

While he was hesitating and wondering whether he should name the man, Dinah saved him the trouble.

"Only this morning coming home from Falcon Farm I met Lawrence—Lawrence Maynard and he—even he, an outsider so to say, said he thought I'd be better far ways off. And I well know it. I didn't ought to be breathing the same air as Johnny. It ain't fair to him, especially when you know he's not taking it just like I meant it. And I wouldn't say it's right, foster-father."

He, however, was more concerned for the moment with the other man than his own son.

"Johnny's beginning to understand. His good sense will come to help him," he answered; "but when you say 'Lawrence Maynard,' Dinah—what do you say? Why for has he troubled his head about your affairs?"

"You like him?" she answered.

"Granted. And so do you seemingly. And how much do you like him? Do you like him as much as I think you do, Dinah?"

She was astonished but pleased.

"I'm glad you ask me that; but I hope Mrs. Bamsey and Jane——?"

"So do I. No, they haven't marked nothing; or if they have, they've hid it from me very close. But Faith wouldn't hide nothing. Tell me."

She hesitated.

"What do you think?" she asked.

"I think you care about the man."

"I love him then."

"Ah!"

"It sounds a fearful thing spoke out naked. But truth's truth, and I'm very thankful to tell you. Don't you call it wicked nor nothing like that. It only happened a very little while—not till long, long after I dropped Johnny. But it has happened; and now I know I never loved dear Johnny a morsel."

He reflected.

"The man himself told you to go—Maynard, I mean? What was in his mind when he said that?"

"I've been wondering. It ought to have made me sad; but it hasn't. Ought it to have made me sad?"

"Has Lawrence Maynard——? What about his side?"

"I don't know—yet I do. There's some things you feel. I don't think I could have loved him if I hadn't known he loved me first. Could I?"

"He's never said it, however?"

"A man's eyes and ways say things."

"Don't you talk like this to anybody but me, Dinah," urged Mr. Bamsey.

"Not likely. Is it wrong?"

"I'm moving in the matter; I'm moving," he answered. "You can't hide much from me, and already I've had Maynard in my thoughts."

"You haven't?"

"Yes. I've seen a very good, common friend. And I'll tell you this. I sounded Mr. Withycombe—the bed-lier. The young man often goes of a Sunday to see him, and Enoch thinks well of him. But more than that. He's spoke cautious with Maynard, and Maynard likes you. He granted you was out of the common, in fact a remarkable pattern of woman."

She had his arm and her own tightened upon it.

"Foster-father!"

"So enough said. And now you'll understand why I'm marking time. The rest be in the hands of God. You keep out of his way for a bit—Maynard, I mean; and we'll watch how it goes."

"Nothing else matters now," she said.

"A lot matters now; but what matters be up to him."

"I didn't think it was possible to be so happy as I be this minute, foster-father."

"Put it out of your mind, however, so far as nature will let you. We be groping in the dark."

"No, no—it's all light—all light now."

"So far as he's concerned, we be in the dark," he repeated. "No doubt the time's near when he'll offer for you, Dinah. And then he's got to come to me. I remember the first evening he was to Green Hayes, and seemed a thought under the weather and a little doubtful about his Maker. I said he'd got a grievance against life, and I must hear all about that grievance, if such there is."

"You'll never hear anything but the truth from him. He wouldn't do anything that you wouldn't like. I'm feared of him in a way. He's very strict and very stern sometimes. He's not what you call easy on wrongful doing. He's better'n me."

"That no man ever was, or will be," said Ben. "I'm very glad you came to me with this; for if you'd hung off much longer, I'd have had to see the man. Now I shan't, and I'm not sorry. We know where we stand, because you'm so open-minded, thank God, along with me. But we don't know—at least we can't be sure we know—where he stands. It's up to Mr. Maynard to unfold his feelings. And for sure he very soon will."

"And why should you reckon he advised me to be off from here so soon as I could?" asked Dinah again. "Queerly enough I liked him for saying it, and yet—yet you might think there might be a frosty reason."

"There might be. Time will show. You can't be off till we've found the proper place for you to be off to. Now you run home about your chores. Mother wants you in the garden. There's the last lot of rasps to be picked. I didn't count on no more, but I was surprised to see enough to market yet."

She ran up the hill and he descended to a field of heavy oats. The weather after a spell of sunny days began to break up and Mr. Bamsey hoped to get his crop off the ground before it did so. But his mind was not on his oats. He believed that Dinah must indeed leave him now, and guessed that Maynard would think it wise to abandon his present work and take her far away. Mr. Bamsey knew what this must mean for him. He did not disguise from himself that he loved Dinah better than anything on earth, while blaming himself unfeignedly for doing so.

CHAPTER XVIII
MAYNARD

Mr. Stockman, having decided that sea air and a fortnight of rest were desirable to fortify him against another winter, had been absent from his home and was only recently returned. He had visited a friend, who farmed land in the neighbourhood of Berry Head, above Brixham, and he declared himself very much better for the change of scene and companionship. He related his adventures, told how he had trusted himself to the sea on more than one occasion in a Brixham trawler, and also expatiated in Soosie-Toosie's ear upon a woman whom he had met—the daughter of his friend.

"Mr. King has but one stay-at-home child, like me," he said, "and I could wish you were able to see the way Ann King runs her father's house. Not a breath against you, Susan—you know how I thank my God every night on my knees for such a daughter; but there's a far-sightedness and a sureness about Ann as I don't remember to have marked in any other female."

"How old might she be?" asked Susan.

"Older than you by ten years I dare say; but it's not so much that as her way of dealing with life and her sure head. The Elms Farm is bigger than ours and mostly corn. They grow amazing fine wheat, to the very edge of the cliffs; and Ann King reigns over the place and the people in such a way that all goes on oiled wheels. She's always ahead of time, that woman— bends time to her purpose and never is run about, or flustered. A great lesson to a simple man like me, who never seems to have enough time for his work."

Mr. Palk heard these things. There was growing between him and Joe a shadow of antagonism. So faintly did this contest of wills begin that neither appreciated it yet.

"And how many females do Miss King have at her word of command, master?" asked Thomas, his subconscious self up in arms as usual when Susan was even indirectly assailed.

Joe stared blandly at him.

"Hullo! I didn't know you was there, Thomas. I was talking to my daughter, Thomas, not you, if you'll excuse me; and if you've got nothing on your hands for the moment, perhaps you won't mind having a look over the harness and reporting to me to-morrow. I was put about when I came home to see a bit of rope where there did ought to be leather, Thomas. You know what I mean."

"I was going to name it," answered Mr. Palk.

"Good; I'm sure you was; we'll go over the lot at your convenience—to-morrow perhaps. I admire you a lot for making shift and saving my pocket. It shows a spirit that I value in a man; but we must keep our heads up, even under the present price of harness if we can; and when we've had a tell over it, I'll go down to saddler at Ashburton and put it to him as an old customer."

Joe returned from his holiday full of energy. He had to-day been at a sale of sheep at Hey Tor village and was tramping with Maynard by road behind fifty fine ewes from a famous breeder. He discoursed of sheep and his man listened without much concentration.

They trudged together behind the raddled flock with a sheep-dog attending them.

"The rare virtue of our Dartmoors is not enough known," declared Mr. Stockman. "In my opinion, both for flesh and coat, there's no long-wooled sheep in the world to beat 'em and few to equal 'em. Yet you'll find, even to this day, that our Devon long-wools be hardly known outside the South Hams and Cornwall. Mr. King had a friend from Derbyshire stopping at Brixham—a very clever man and wonderful learned in sheep; but he knew naught about our famous breed. They did ought to be shown at all the big shows all over England, and then, no doubt, they'd come into their own, and some of us who rears 'em would earn our just reward."

"That class ought to be included in all important shows certainly," admitted Lawrence. "At their best they can't be beat."

"And they ought to be shown in their wool," added Mr. Stockman. "The difficulties ought to be got over, and it should be done for the credit of the county, not to say Dartmoor."

They debated this question till the younger man wearied of it and was glad when a farmer on horseback overtook them. He had been a seller, and he approved of Joe's opinions, now repeated for his benefit. Maynard walked a little apart and found leisure to think his own thoughts. They revolved about one subject only, and reverted to it with painful persistence.

He was in love with Dinah Waycott and knew that she was in love with him. The something that was left out of her made this all the more clear, for she relied on no shield of conventions; she had a way to slip a subject of the clothes it generally wore, in shape of speech.

She had exerted no wiles, but she could not be illusive, and the obvious qualities of Dinah which had appealed to Johnny's first love had also, for different reasons, overwhelmed Maynard. Many men by these very qualities in her would have been repulsed. Experienced men might have missed those elements in Dinah that, for them, make a woman most provocative and desirable; but in the case of this man, his own experience of life and his personal adventure combined to intensify the charm that her peculiar nature possessed. He had known nothing like her; she contrasted at almost every possible point with what he had known; she shone for him as an exemplar of all that was most desirable in feminine character. He could not believe that there were many such women, and he doubted not that he would never see such another. He had tried to adopt a fatherly attitude to Dinah and, for a considerable time, succeeded. The view he took of her at their first acquaintance, when she was betrothed to John Bamsey, persisted after the breaking of the engagement; but the very breaking of the engagement enlarged this view, and the freedom, that could no longer be denied to her after that event, had improved their knowledge of each other until both learned the same fact. Then Maynard could play a fatherly friendship no more, nor could the figment of an elder brother serve. He loved her and she loved him. A thing he had never considered as possible now complicated a life that for seven years he had striven with all his might to simplify; and the new situation extended far beyond Dinah, for it was calculated to alter his own agreement and undertaking with himself. These covenants had been entered into with himself alone. Circumstances had long ago combined, at a certain period of his early, adult life, to change the entire texture of existence, deflect its proposed purpose and throw down the goal he set out to attain. And with the changes wrought in temporal ambitions had come others. Life thus dammed ceased to flow. His future collapsed and in its place appeared a new purpose, if negation could be called a purpose. That had sufficed, though at a cost of mental corrosion he did not guess; but now it seemed that a closed book was thrown open again and he stood once more facing outlets to life that even implied happiness. His existence for seven years, it appeared, had not been a progression, but a hiatus. Yet he knew, even while he told himself this, that it must be a delusion and a juggle with reality; since no man can for seven years stand still.

There was need for a jolt forward now, and the problem appeared simple enough as to the thing he must do, but shattering when he saw it done. He was deeply agitated, yet through the inexorable shot a thread of unexpected hope and beauty. To cut this thread, which had crept so magically into the grey fabric of existence and touched the days of his crepuscular life with the glimmering of an unguessed sunrise, promised to be a task so tremendous that it was not strange he hesitated. For did any vital necessity exist to cut it? He could not immediately convince himself, and every natural instinct and impulse combined to cry out against such a necessity.

He had reached an attitude of mind, and that long before he met Dinah Waycott, which now suffered no shock from the personal problem. He had dealt in generalities and pondered and meditated on human conduct in many aspects. The actual, present position, too, he had debated, and even asked himself how he might expect to act under certain circumstances. But the possibility of those circumstances ever arising had not occurred to him, and now that they had done so, he saw that his view and his judgment were only one side of the question in any case. The visionary figure of a woman had turned into a real one, and as such, her welfare and her future, not his own, instantly became the paramount thing. What he might have deemed as sudden salvation for himself, namely, a good and loving woman in his life, took another colour when the woman actually appeared. The temptation now lay in this. He knew Dinah so well, that he believed, from her standpoint, she might look at the supreme problem as he did; and for this very reason he delayed. Reason argued that, did Dinah see eye to eye with him, no farther difficulty could exist, while if she did not, there was an end of it; but some radical impulse of heredity, or that personal factor of character, which was the man himself, fought with reason at the very heart of his being and made the issue a far deeper matter for Maynard now.

The horseman left Mr. Stockman and galloped forward, while Joe regarded his retreating figure with mild amusement and turned to Lawrence.

"Did you hear that?" he asked, and the other replied that he had not.

"I've vexed him—just the last thing ever I meant, or intended. It's a funny world. If you mind your own business and stick to it, the people say you're a selfish, hard-hearted creature, with no proper feeling to humans at large. And if you seek to mind other people's business, and serve 'em, and help the folk along, and lend a hand where you may, then they lift their voices and call you a meddling Paul Pry and a busybody and so on. That man's just told me to look after my own affairs, because I went out of my way to give him a valuable tip about his!"

"More fool him," said Maynard. "The fools are the hardest to help."

"Nothing but the people themselves keep me from doing a great deal more good in the world than I might," declared Joe. "The will is there, and I think I may say the wit is there; but my fellow creatures choke me off."

"They're jealous of your sense I reckon."

"No doubt some be, Lawrence. But 'tis cutting off your nose to spite your face, when you quarrel with a man who might be useful, just because you hate to think he's got a better brain than you have."

"A very common thing."

"Not a mistake of the wise, however. For my part I've lived long enough to see that jealousy, look at it all round, is the feeblest and silliest vice we humans suffer from. There's nothing to it but wretchedness and wasted energy. Jealous I never could be of any living creature, I assure you."

But though Joe despised jealousy, such was his humour, that within an hour, for the sake of personal amusement he sought to awake the futile flame in another breast.

Melinda Honeysett was waiting at Falcon Farm when the men returned, but she had come to see Lawrence Maynard, not Mr. Stockman. He, however, entertained her while his man was looking after the sheep. Indeed, he insisted on Melinda joining him in a cup of tea. He had not seen her since his return from Brixham, and now the rogue in Joe twinkled to the top and he began to enumerate the rare qualities of Miss King. He knew that Melinda regarded herself as holding a sort of proprietary right over him, and he much enjoyed this shadowy bondage and often pretended to groan under it. But now he launched on the task of making Melinda jealous for his private entertainment. With Soosie-Toosie the enterprise had failed. She humbly accepted the accomplishments of Ann King and praised her genius so heartily that Joe soon dropped the subject; but for Melinda it came as a new idea, and this enthusiasm on Mr. Stockman's part for a paragon at once unknown and eligible, caused Mrs. Honeysett just that measure of exasperation her first male friend desired to awaken.

"My!" said Melinda, after listening to the glowing story of the farmer's daughter, her virtues, her resource, her financial ability and her practical knowledge of affairs; "I didn't know there were any angels to Brixham. Do she fly about, or only walk, like us common women?"

"No, she walks," said Joe, delighted at his instant success; "but even in walking she never wastes a footstep, like most of us. Never wastes anything, and yet not close. Just a grasp of all that matters and a large scorn for all that don't. And as to being an angel, Melinda, you may say she is that—just in the same sense that you and Soosie-Toosie and all nice women are angels. Only that. She's a thorough human woman and, simply judged as a woman, a very fine piece indeed."

Mrs. Honeysett laughed somewhat harshly.

"Don't you drag me and Susan in. I'm sure he needn't do that, need he, Soosie? Such poor creatures as us—not worthy to hold a candle to this here Jane King."

"Ann King," corrected Joe.

"You and me will go and take lessons, and ax her to teach us how to look after our poor fathers," said Melinda to Miss Stockman. "We're such a pair of feckless, know-naught fools that it's time we set about larning how a parent did ought to be treated. And, by the same token, I must get back to mine. He's bad and getting worse. I only came to see Maynard, because father wants to have a tell with him—to-night if possible. Poor father's going down hill fast now—all, no doubt, because I've not understood how to nurse him and tend him and live my life for him alone. If he'd only had Ann King to look after him, I dare say he'd be well again by now."

Joe, greatly daring, pushed the joke a little deeper.

"You mustn't say that. There's nobody like you to look after a sick man, Melinda, and I'm sure Miss King couldn't have done it very much better and steadier than you have. But perhaps it might be a clever thought to invite her up along. I dare say she'd make time to pay us a visit, if I told her as you and Soosie-Toosie were very wishful to make her acquaintance and gather in a bit of her far-reaching sense. She's always as willing as I am myself to throw a bit of light."

"Ax her to come then," said Mrs. Honeysett. "'Twill be a great blessing for me and Susan to go to school to her. And something to see a really wise creature in Buckland, because we'm such a lot of God-forsaken zanies here—men and women alike."

She rose breathing rather deeply.

"No tea, thank you," she said. "I've changed my mind. I'll go home and pray for the light of Ann King to fall on my dark road. And when she comes along, you ask her if she'll give a poor, weak-minded widow a little of her sense. Tell her I'm one of they women that thinks the moon be made of green cheese, will 'e? And say I believe in pixies, and charms for warts, and black witches and white witches and all that. And you can add that I was one of them idiots that always gave men credit for nice feeling and good sense and liked to believe the best about some men and stuck up for 'em, even when I heard 'em run down and laughed at. Tell her all that; and say as I'm going to give certain parties a rest in future, because, though a poor worm and not worthy to be seen alongside her, yet I've got my pride, like the cleverest of us. And give Lawrence Maynard father's message, Soosie, if you please."

"Come back, you silly gosling!" shouted Joe; but Melinda did not come back. He laughed very heartily, yet not loud enough for the departing woman to hear him.

"Lord! To think now!" he said. "I've took a proper rise out of her, eh?"

"You have," admitted Susan ruthfully. "And if you done it on purpose, it weren't a very clever thing to do. Melinda's fiery, but a good friend and a great admirer of yours, father. Now you've vexed her cruel."

"You never larn all there is to know about a female," he said. "I meant to get her wool off—just for a bit of honest fun; but I can't say as I ever understood she felt so deep how clever she was. She's a vain, dear creature."

"It weren't that," explained Susan. "She ain't vain, though she knows her worth, and so do everybody else know it; but what she is proud of, naturally, be your great fondness for her. She knows you put her first, and she knows you're a clever man and wouldn't put her first if there wasn't a reason. And her father be going to die presently and—and God knows what's in her thoughts, of course. And then to hear that Miss King be worth all the women you've ever seen in your life put together, and be the top flower of the bunch, and such a wonder as was never seen by mortal man— why, of course, Melinda took it to heart a bit. Who wouldn't?"

"You didn't," said Joe.

"No, I didn't, because I know my place, father. I'm not so clever as Melinda. I'm a poor thing, though well intending. But Melinda's a fine thing and you know in your heart that a virgin woman, like Miss King, however clever she be, couldn't teach Melinda nothing about how to look after a man."

"Fun be thrown away on you creatures," said Joe. "You're terrible thick-headed where a joke's the matter, Soosie; but I did think as Melinda was brighter."

He turned to Palk, who had just entered for his tea. Thomas had heard the word thick-headed applied to Susan.

"Did you ever know a woman as could see a clever bit of fun, Tom?"

The horseman reflected.

"Women's fun ban't the same as ours," he answered. "No doubt they've got their own pattern of fun. But there ain't much time for Miss Stockman to practise laughing in this house."

"Ah! You can be so comical as any of us when you'm in a mind for it, Thomas," said his master.

CHAPTER XIX
LIGHT OF AUTUMN

Sent to find granite and bidden to choose a boulder that would split out, so that needful stone posts might be fashioned from it, Lawrence Maynard climbed the Beacon and loitered here and there, examining the great stones that heaved their backs or sides from the earth. For the master of Falcon Farm was a Venville man and claimed moor rights extending over stone and turbary.

Lawrence marked certain masses and thrust in sticks beside them, that presently Joe Stockman might himself ascend and determine, from his better knowledge, which blocks would yield the needful pillars. For the farmer was skilled in granite and declared it to be a good-natured stone in understanding hands.

Lawrence was mastered by his own thoughts presently, and with the pageant of late autumn flung under his eyes, he sat down where a boulder protected him from the fierce wind and brooded. From time to time the vision of things seen broke in.

Upon this canvas, so hugely spread, Nature painted her pictures in punctual procession, and in some measure Maynard valued them. Indeed, under the present stress and storm that unsettled the weather of his mind, he found himself more pervious than of old to the natural impressions of the Vale.

To-day a north wind shouted overhead, drove the scattered clouds before it and hummed in organ notes upon the great mass of granite that capped the Beacon. Then copper red ribbons of beech fell broadly into the depths below—and, against their fire, the plantations of the pine wove darker patterns, where they descended in a gradual arc over the shoulders of the hills, until the air and space wrought magic upon their distances and swept them together in one glowing integument for the low lands. There it was as though a mighty tiger skin had been flung down upon the undulating earth, so rich in orange-tawny and russet were the forest reaches, so black the slant shadows thrown by the low sun at spinney edge, along the boundary of hanging woods, or where open fields broke horizontally into the kingdom of the trees. There shone green meadows against the flame of the fall around them; and the ploughed fallows heightened colour by their contrast. They intruded their tessellate designs, wrought out in a network of squares and triangles and rhomboidal forms; they climbed the hills, penetrated the valley depths and ceased only where the upland ramparts barred their progress with heath and stone. Shadows flew to dim the splendour and then again reveal it; nor was the clarity of the air purchased without cost, for unseen moisture drenched it and sometimes took shape of separate storms, sweeping in a low, grey huddle over the earth they hid, yet divided by great sunny spaces. They drew their veils over half a league of the land at a time, then dislimned and vanished again. And far away, beyond the last peaks and saliencies southward, stretched a horizon of dazzling and colourless light, where sea girdled earth and Devon rolled dark against the liquid brilliance of the Channel lifted beyond it.

The Vale, with its river winding through the midst, was a frame for these far-away passages of light and darkness—a setting and boundary, rich but restrained; for under the sleight of distance, the glories of the colour, each touch a tiny leaf of gold or crimson, were cooled and kneaded with shadow and tempered by the blue November air.

To appreciate the detail of the spectacle, the throb and palpitation of so much fire, it had been necessary to descend among the forest glades, where were revealed the actual pigments of all this splendour and the manner of Nature's painting, touch by touch. Thence the scene, whose harmonies rang so subdued from the height of the Beacon above, resolved itself into a riot of colour. Larch and ash were already grey, and the lemon of the birch, the gold of the elm flashed out against the heavier bronzes and coppers of oak and beech. The wood smoke that rose so thinly seen from aloft, here ascended from a fire in a column of gentian blue under the sunshine, purple against shadow. Carpets of colour extended where the trees broke—textures of scarlet whortle and crimson blackberry, bright ivy, jewels of moss and glittering dead grass. The spindle flashed its fruits, and aglets and haws sparkled beneath it on briar and bough. There, too, the sheltered fern had not been beaten flat as on the open heaths above. It rose shoulder high, delicate in dead but unbroken filigrees, with many a spider's gossamer and iridescent web twinkling rainbows upon its amber frondage. The dusky regiments of the conifers intensified the blaze. Green, or glaucous green, or of a solid darkness, they massed, and, against them, stems of maiden birches leapt upward to the last of their foliage, like woodland candlesticks of silver supporting altar-flame within these far-flung sanctuaries.

Intermittently Maynard allowed his thoughts to dwell upon these things spread under his eyes; and he even dipped sometimes into the communion of the trees and pictured all that lay beneath him; he could spare a moment to reflect upon the ceaseless battle under the splendour, and how every tree of these countless thousands had fought through half a century for its place in the sun. But for the most part his reflections turned upon himself, though unconsciously the outward pageant became enwoven with the inward gloom, as long afterwards he discovered.

He had taken life in an uncompromising spirit of old; he had displayed a strength of purpose and a grip of his own values in some measure remarkable for a man, at that time barely beyond his majority. And now, into a life that he had deemed cut away once and for all from all further human complexities, was come this unexpected and supreme problem. Yet such rifts and gleams as had of late been thrust through his grey existence must now be shut out. For a time he considered with himself whether this should be so; but he weighed Dinah's fate more tenderly in the balance than his own. For him, indeed, the facts did not preclude possibility of actual temptation; but he had yet to learn how they would affect her. Had he cared to take consolation there, he might have done so; but what had encouraged hope in another man, discouraged him. His temptations were not proof against his principles, and he foresaw that more than a narration of facts might be necessary when the day came for bare speech with Dinah. The necessity for any return to the past had never been anticipated by Maynard; but he had long seen now that one certainly involved the other. The need for confession troubled him little; the time of trial must come with Dinah's reception of his confession. He hoped that she might take such an instant decision that deeper distresses would be avoided; and yet the very hope seemed cowardly to him; and sometimes he felt a desire above or below his own view of rectitude. What promised distress in one mood opened the gates to a new and a blessed life in another.

He was come, however, to the inevitable place of open dealing: he must tell her all that still remained hidden from her. With a sense of relief he felt that more could not be done until that position had been reached; and for the present he put away from himself any thought of what would follow his revelation in her mind, or the great final decision that must be called for from his own.

Then he dropped his affairs for a little while and let the sense of the immense and outspread earth drift into his thoughts. It heartened him and inspired him to a dim resolution that a man might glean something from the purposes of a world so large and splendid, so that he, too, should rise worthy of his place in it, and largely and splendidly order his own part amid the great scheme of things. But he guessed all the time that such poetry only played over the surface of forthcoming events. It had less power of reality, than the bubbles on a wave to influence its way. The final pattern of things lay deep within himself. No man or woman could ever alter the terms of his own destiny, or change the principles under which he willed to live. So he imagined.

CHAPTER XX
THE HUNTER'S MOON

The thought of their next meeting was in the minds of both Dinah and Lawrence, and the girl also guessed that they had reached a position only to end in one way. Even so, her own unconscious desires were running before the facts. It is certain that she had gone a little farther along the road of love than he had; but only because upon her path there were no obstacles and she could not guess, or imagine, the hindrances lying upon his. She knew that he loved her and conceived of no reason why he should not tell her so. She had, of course, come to lift him into the supreme reality of her existence.

She waited for him and began to wonder at the delay. Sometimes, indeed, as time passed and for two weeks they had not met, a shadow fell upon her; but it was fleeting. She could not long doubt of him even in the small hours, when life was at its lowest.

The days began to close in and winter was at the door again before he spoke. Then only chance precipitated the event, when, to the unhidden joy of both, they met in the street at Ashburton, on a Saturday afternoon of late November.

Any passing fear that Dinah might have felt vanished before his look as he shook her hand, and he was inspired to action by the pure happiness that lighted her face and shone without restraint upon it.

"I was going to write to you to-morrow if you'll believe me," he said. "But this is better. Are you free?"

"Yes. I've come in to do some chores for Mrs. Bamsey."

"And I'm running errands for Falcon Farm. Neddy Tutt's milking this evening. How would it be if we were to have a cup of tea together?"

"I'd love it. Lord! I am thankful to see you, Lawrence! Sometimes I began to think I never was going to no more."

"You had to see me once more, anyway. Where shall we go out of the way, so as I can talk?"

"Anywhere you please."

He considered.

"There's a little teashop in Church Street with a back parlour. I've been there once or twice, but they don't know nothing about me. We'd have the room to ourselves I reckon. I must go to gunsmith for the governor and get a hundred cartridges. Then I'm free."

"I never thought I was in for such a treat when I woke up this morning," said Dinah.

"No treat, my dinky maid. I wish to God it was a treat. I've got a lot on my mind when I look at you."

"A shared trouble soon grows light," she said; yet his heavy voice chilled her. They walked side by side, and to walk by him cheered Dinah again. The cartridges awaited Lawrence and in twenty minutes they were at the little eating-shop in Church Street. It was a languishing establishment, out of the beaten track. A woman behind the counter smiled at Maynard and recognised him.

"A pot of tea and some bread and butter and cake, missis," he said; then he entered a small parlour behind the shop. The woman lighted a gas jet over their heads, in the corner that Lawrence chose farthest from the door. Presently she brought a tray with their tea upon it, and then she left them. The time was past four.

"Will you pour the tea, Dinah?"

"Yes, I will then," she said. "Be you happy to see me, Lawrence?"

"You know it. I'd sooner see you than anything in the world. Shall I tell her to light a blink of fire? She would. 'Tis a thought cold in here."

"No, no; I'm not cold. Talk—talk to me. Let me hear you talk."

He leant across and took her hand.

"Let me hold it a minute. I like to feel it. You know a bit of what I'm going to tell you; but only a terrible little bit. I wish there was no more than that to tell."

She held his hand tightly.

"I love you. I've known it a long time, Dinah. That's the little bit I think you know. If that was all——"

"It is all—all on earth that matters to me," she said quietly. "And I did know. I wouldn't believe myself for a long time; but it was vain fighting against it. If it happens to you, you must know. I wouldn't have doubted, perhaps, if I hadn't loved you back so fierce. That made me doubt, because it seemed too good to be true and a long way past my deserving. Now the rest don't signify. Nothing's so big as knowing you love me, Lawrence."

"The bigger thing is that it can't be."

She shrank and he felt her hand grow limp. He took his from it and considered how to begin speaking. Meantime she spoke.

"That's a hard thing—not a bigger thing," she said quietly; "it can't alter what is."

"You must hear from the beginning. If I'd ever thought this would happen, I'd have gone long ago. But it came like a thief, Dinah."

"Same with me. Go on—tell why not—quick."

"I'm married," he said.

She bent her head and leant back and shut her eyes.

"That's the only thing that could come between you and me. I'm married. It's a mad tale, and I was the madman, so most people said. Maybe you will, too; maybe you won't. I shall know in a minute. Yet, if I thought what I was going to say would make you hate me, I wouldn't say it. But it won't do that."

She was looking at him with wet eyes.

"How could I hate you? Love's love. I'd see a way to love you through it if you killed her."

"When I went into the world after father died, I was took by a relation of my mother's at Barnstaple, you must know; and there was that in me that made for getting on. I done very well, and when my mother's sister, who had a little dairy, found the sort I was, she reckoned to do me a good turn and suit herself also. By twenty years old I knew the business inside out and all that goes to it; and when I was twenty-one, my aunt, who was a widow, bargained with me to let her go out and drop the shop and be paid a regular income for her lifetime. When she died I was to have all. It worked very well for a year and a half, and I found I'd got a turn for the business, and opened out a bit, and bought a few cows for myself and even had thoughts of going higher up into the middle of the town and starting a bigger place and having a department for teas and refreshments and so on.

"But that wanted a woman, and then, just at the right moment as it seemed, a woman came along—the very woman on all the earth for the business. It looked as if Providence was out on my side and nothing could go wrong."

"You loved her?"

"I did. Yes, I loved her, Dinah. I wouldn't have thought twice about marrying any woman I didn't love."

"I suppose you wouldn't."

"No more than you could. She was called Minnie Reed, and she came to live not far ways off from where my aunt lived. She was twenty and had a widowed mother along with her, and they didn't lack for means. My old lady took to Mrs. Reed and didn't think it amiss when, presently, I began to make chances for seeing Minnie. In a way it was her great cleverness, more than herself, that took me first. I was all for cleverness at that time, Dinah— all for knowledge and learning; and I found, a good bit to my surprise, that Minnie Reed had got a lot more book learning than any young creature I'd ever come across before. Her mother explained she'd been educated above her station and so on; and she certainly had. Her very speech was nice—far ways above what you'd expect. And from admiring her cleverness, I got to admire her. She had a bit of money too—a thousand pounds put away in a very fine investment. Her mother told my aunt that; and she took good care to tell me; because my old lady was as thick as thieves with Mrs. Reed by now, and they both wanted to see Minnie married to me.

"Looking back I can't say much about what I felt. I only knew I was very wishful to win her if possible, and I soon found she was quite agreeable. Always pleasant, cool, collected she was. She liked me and had an easy, friendly manner; yet I'll swear she always held herself a cut above me. She never said so, perhaps she didn't even think so, but unconsciously she let me feel, somehow, that was in her mind. Not that I cared. I was in a stage to her then that I thought so too. My havage was of no account, and I felt she was superior, along of education and natural quick wits. An old head on young shoulders she had. I do believe most honest that she cared for me, and felt happy to think she was going to share my life and push on my business. But from the day we got tokened she didn't turn half so much to love-making as work. And I wasn't the soft, cuddling sort neither; and if anything could have drawed me to her more than I was drawed, it would have been the fashion she set to mastering my business and all its details. She took it up with all her wits, and soon showed that she was a masterpiece at it. She liked business and she had a head for saving. She understood more about money than I did, though I thought myself pretty clever at it. But I felt a gawk beside her, and she soon showed me how to make more. In fact, her thoughts soared higher than mine from the start, and I knew I'd have such a right hand in that matter as few men in my position could ever have expected.

"I think I knew my luck, and it suited me very well, as I say, that she didn't want a lot of love-making, for I was busy as a bee and not given to that sort of thing. And she was on the cold side too—so I reckoned. In fact she made it clear in words. For she'd thought about that, like most subjects. She held the business of love-making and babies and so on was only a small part of life, and that men thought a lot too much about that side of marriage and took women too seriously. She said certain things with an object, and gave me an opening to ax a few questions; but I was too green to take up the hint, and she said afterwards that she thought I agreed with her.

"We were married and started in the train for our honeymoon. We was going to Exeter for a week and then coming home again, for neither of us had much use for honeymooning, but felt full of business.

"We had a carriage to ourselves by the kindness of the guard—a Barnstaple man. And we talked. And when I got out of the train at Exeter, I left her; and I've never seen her again and never shall. She was a stranger woman to me for evermore."

He was silent for a time, but Dinah said nothing.

"It was her work, not mine. She'd got a dim sense of what she owed me, I suppose, or else a fear of something. Yet, looking back, I often wondered she troubled to tell me the truth, for she knew well enough I was much too inexperienced and ignorant to have found it out. She might have lied. Perhaps it was a case where a lie would have been best—if a lie's ever best. Anyway it's to her credit, I suppose, that she told me. Not that she would have done so if she'd known how I should take it. She reminded me of her nest-egg and how I'd asked her how she came by it, and how she'd said an uncle left it to her under his will. 'That's not true,' she said to me. 'And I don't want to begin our married life with a secret between us, specially as it happens to be such a trifle. I dare say some fools would pull a long face,' she said, 'but you ain't that sort, else you'd never have fallen in love with me.' Then she told me that for two years she'd been the mistress of a gentleman at Bristol—a rich, educated man in business there. He'd kept her till he was going to be married, and they parted very good friends and he gave her a thousand pounds. He'd used her very well indeed and never talked any nonsense about marrying her, or anything like that. It was just a bargain, and he had what he wanted and so had she. Then she bent across the carriage and put her arms round my neck and kissed me. But she kissed a stone. I kept my head. I didn't go mad. I didn't curse or let on.

"I put her arms off me and bade her sit down and let me think; and all the passion I felt against her kept inside me. I was man enough for that. She looked a pretty thing that day. In pink she was, and if ever a man could swear he looked at a virgin, he might have sworn it afore her grey eyes.

"I told her it was all up; and she kept her nerve too. A funny sort of scene for any onlooker, to watch a newly-married man and woman starting on their honeymoon and lost to all but a future bargain. Guard looked in and had a laugh sometimes when the train stopped, and we ruled our faces and grinned back at him.

"She began by trying hard to change me. She poured out a flood of reasons; she used her quick brains as she'd never used them afore. But she kept as keen and cool as a dealer to market, and when she found I wasn't going on with it, she bided still a bit and then asked me what I was going to do.

"That I couldn't tell her for the minute. 'Us'll begin at the beginning,' I said, 'and have every step clear. You've got my name now, and you're my wife in the law, and you've got your rights. And I shan't come between you and them. But my love for you is dead. I don't hate you, because, I suppose, women are mostly built like you and I won't waste my strength hating you. You've gone. You're less to me now than the trees passing the window. You'll live your life and I'll live mine,' I said to her; 'but you're outside mine in future and I'm outside yours.'

"'That can't be,' she said. 'I've got a claim, and if you turn me down, though I pray to God you won't—but if you do, you've got to think of my future as well as your own.' I granted that and promised her she need not trouble for herself. Being what I am, for good or evil, I saw very quick this blow would fall on me, not her. She wouldn't miss me so long as everything else was all right, and my feelings were such that I wasn't particular mindful of myself, or my ruined hopes at that minute. I got a sudden, fierce longing to cut a loss and be out of it. And that first driving impulse in me—to get away from her and breathe clean air—stuck to me after twenty-four hours had passed. Once knowing what she'd been, my love for her went out like a candle. That may be curious, but so it was. I didn't fight myself over it, or weaken, or hunger for her back. Never once did I. She was gone and couldn't have been more gone if she'd dropped dead at my feet. All my passion was a passion to get out of her sight.

"She tried with every bit of her cleverness to change me. Yes, she tried hard, and I saw the wonder of her brains as I'd never even yet seen them. She made a lot clear. She scorned the thing we call sin. She said to give a man what she'd given was no more than to give another woman's baby a drink from her breast if it was thirsty. She talked like that. She said she never loved the man as she loved me, and she prayed very earnest indeed for me to take a higher line and not be paltry. But it was all wind in the trees for me and didn't shake me by a hair."

He stopped for a moment and Dinah asked him a question. She had followed him word by word, her mouth open, her eyes fixed upon his face.

"If she'd told you before instead of after, would it have made a difference?"

"Yes, it would," he said. "God's my judge, it would have made all the difference between wanting her and loathing her. I'm the sort of man that could no more have brooked it than I'd willingly touch a foul thing. That may be silliness and a narrow understanding of life. Where women are concerned, I may have wanted better bread than is made of wheat—I don't know and I don't care; but that's me. And nothing could change me. She tried hard enough—part for my own sake, I do believe, and part for hers. She was wonderful and I'll grant it. She knew me well enough to waste not a minute of her time in coaxing, or tears, or any foolery. She just kept to the argument as close and keen as a man, and if she was feeling as much as me, which ain't likely, she certainly didn't show it.

"She said a strange thing—bare-faced it seemed to me then, but I dare say in strict fairness to her, I might have been shook by it. She reminded me that it was what that blasted, rich man had taught her had made her what she was. She said he'd lifted her above her class and woke up her brains and educated her with books and lessons; and that what had drawn me was just what she had to thank him for. She said, 'You'd never have looked at me twice for myself. A pretty face means nothing to you. It was my sharpened sense took you; and now you turn round and fling me off for just what made you marry me.' Cunning as a snake she was—the wisdom and the poison both. Or so it seemed to me. But what she said didn't alter the facts. Nothing could alter them, and I wasn't built to take any man's leavings.

"She worked at me till we were very nearly to Exeter. Then she stopped and said it was up to me to say what I intended. And I told her as to that she needn't fear, because I'd do all that was right, and more. Her talk, you see, had done this much. It made me understand that from her point of view—hateful though it was—she had her rights. And so I bade her take her luggage to one inn and I'd go to another; and next day I wrote to her that she'd get a letter from me when I'd looked all round and decided what was proper to do. She left me still hoping; I could see that. But she didn't hope no more when she got my letter."

"You never went back on it?"

"Only once, for five minutes, that first night in bed, turning over my future life and hers. For five minutes a thought did creep in my mind, and for five minutes it stuck. It was such a thought as might have been expected I dare say—a sort of thought any man might think; but it stank in five minutes, and I shook it out. And the thought was how would it be if I said to her she must give up her nest-egg and get rid of it for evermore, and then I—— But what real difference did that make? None."

"Perhaps she wouldn't have let it go," said Dinah.

He nodded. It was another woman's view.

"Perhaps she wouldn't. She earned it—eh? Anyway the idea was too dirty for me. Next morning I wrote and said what I was going to do. It was pretty definite and that was where people said I was mad; but, looking back, I can swear I'd do pretty much the same again. The thought was to be quick—quick and away and out of it. Everything I'd done up to then tumbled down that day. It was all gone together—not only her, but everything. I dare say that was curious, but that's how I felt. I only asked for the clothes on my back, and to get away in 'em and never see a bit of the past no more and begin again."

"You'd feel like that."

"I did. I took a line she couldn't quarrel with. She made a fight; but business was her god, and though I was a fool in her eyes, that didn't make her inclined to play the fool. She hadn't to drive a bargain, or any such thing. I cut the ground from under her feet, threw up the lot, handed her over the business, lock, stock and barrel, and was gone, like a dead man out of mind, so soon as I'd signed the proper papers."

"She let you?"

"She couldn't do no otherwise, and as what I planned was well within her sense of what was right and proper, she made no question. She pointed out that she'd lost a good bit in any case with a mystery like this hanging over her; and she also wrote, when all was fixed up, that she hoped I'd live to change my mind and come back to her and very thankful she would be if I was to. I dare say she truly thought I would.

"We were in Exeter for a week and came and went from a lawyer's—but never there together. I ordained to give her what I'd got and leave her to do as she pleased. She was sorry I saw it like that; but the sense of the woman never allowed nothing to come between her and reason. The lawyer tried to change me too. He was a very kindly man. But it went through. She took over the dairy and carried on my engagements to my aunt, and no doubt developed the shop same as I meant to. She gave out I'd gone away for a bit and might be back in a month. I don't suppose anybody ever heard more, and when I didn't come back, she had a search made for me all very right and regular; but I'd gone beyond finding, and she carried on; and no doubt the nine days' wonder died in course of time. Only my aunt knew I'd gone of my own accord; but why I'd gone, only one creature beside my wife ever knew; and that was her mother; and I doubt not she sided with her daughter. I dare say there's a lot more the other side could tell; but I made a clean cut. I dropped every creature and began again out of their reach. That's the story of me, Dinah. I've most forgotten many of the details myself now. It's seven and a half years agone. I saw in a North Devon paper my old aunt was dead, and so Minnie's free of them payments and standing alone. Half my savings she had also."

There was silence between them for more than a minute. Then Dinah spoke, went back to his first word and asked a question.

"D'you call that being married?"

"Yes—that's my marriage. There ain't much more to tell. I was for going to Canada, and started unknown with fifty pounds of money, which was all I kept. I was going to get a state-aided passage from London and begin again out there. It sounds a big thing to fling over the whole of your life, like as if you was taking off a suit of old clothes; but it didn't seem big to me then— only natural and proper. I comed even to like it. But chance willed different, and the accident of meeting a stranger in the train kept me in England after all. Chance done me a very good turn then. A farmer got in the train at Taunton and between Taunton and Bath, fate, or what you like to call it, willed I went to that man. We got talking, and I told him I was going abroad, being skilful at cows and the butter and milk business. He got interested at that and reckoned I might be such a man as he needed; but I said plainly that I was cutting losses, and my past must bide out of sight, and I'd best to go foreign in my opinion. By that time, however, he'd got a fancy he'd trust me. He was a very good man and a judge of character, which most good men are not in my experience. I found after that he was a rare sort of chap—the best and truest friend to me—such a man as inclined me slowly to think the better of the world again. He only asked me one question and that was if, on my honour, I could tell him I'd done no dishonest or wicked thing from which I was trying to escape. And I swore by God I had not. He believed me, and when, a day or two later, I told him the whole story, he didn't say whether in his judgment I'd done right or wrong, but he granted that I'd done right from my point of view and thought no worse of me for it. I hesitated a bit at his offer; but I liked him, somehow, from the first, and I was cruel tired, and the thought of getting to work right away was good to me. Because I knew by then that there was nothing like working your fingers to the bone to dull pain of mind and make you sleep.

"My life with him is another tale. I look back upon it with nothing but content. I did well by him, and he was as good as a father to me. It's near eighteen months ago he died, and his two sons carried on. Very nice men, and they wanted me to stop; but I couldn't bide when the old chap dropped out. He left me two hundred pounds under his will, Dinah; and his sons didn't object that I should take it, for they were well-to-do and liked me. Then I saw Joe's advertisement in the paper and had a fancy to come back alongside where I was born."

"And Mrs. Maynard never found you?"

"No; but she isn't Mrs. Maynard. Maynard's not my name and Lawrence ain't my name."

She sighed.

"Man!" she said, "you be sinking and sinking—oh, my God, you be sinking out of my sight! I thought you was one creature, and now you be turning into a far-away thing under my eyes."

"I don't feel like that. I'm Lawrence Maynard to myself, Dinah. T'other be dead and in his grave. My name was Courtier. There's some of the family about on Dartmoor yet. My great-grandfather was a Frenchman—a soldier took in the wars more than a hundred year ago. And the moor folk traded at the war prisons to Princetown, so he got to know a good few at prison market. Then he was tokened to a farmer's daughter, and after the peace he married her and stopped in England and started a family."

"What's your other real name then?"

"Gilbert, same as my father."

"Us must be going," she said.

"Shall I tell her to hot some more tea for you?"

"No—I don't want no tea."

He drank his cold cup at a draught and pressed her to eat a little; but she shook her head.

"I'll see you home by New Bridge and then get up back through the woods, Dinah."

"I can travel alone."

"No, you mustn't do that."

She said very little during the long tramp through a night-hidden land. The darkness, the loneliness, the rustle of the last dead leaves and the murmur of the wind chimed with her thoughts. She seemed hardly conscious of the man at her side. He strove once or twice to talk, but found it vain and soon fell into silence. At New Bridge Dinah spoke.

"You'll always be 'Lawrence' to me," she said. "Tell me this. When are you going to see me again, after I've thought a bit?"

"Like you to want to. We can meet somewhere."

"You love me?"

"Yes; as I never thought I could love anything. But how should you love me any more?"

She did not answer immediately. For some distance they walked by the river. Then they reached a fork of the road where their paths divided; for here Dinah climbed to the left by a steep lane that would bring her to Lower Town and home, while Maynard must ascend into the woods.

They stopped.

"Will you do this?" she said. "Will you put the story of your life before Enoch Withycombe?"

"Why, Dinah?"

"To get his opinion on it—all—every bit."

"Yes, if you like."

"I do like. I'm very wishful to know what a man such as him would say."

"If he's well enough, I'll see him to-morrow. It's been in my mind to tell him about myself before to-day."

"I wish you had."

"He shall hear it. I set great store by his sense. He might— — Can you get home from here? I'll come with you if you like."

"No."

"You've forgiven me?"

"I'll think and think. Be there anything to forgive?"

"I don't know. And yet I do. Yes—you think—then you'll find you've got to forgive me for ever loving you, Dinah."

"You're life—you're life to me," she said. "Don't say small things like that. I'm only being sorry for all you've had to suffer all these years and years. I'll go on being sorry for you a long time yet. Then I'll see if I'm angry with you after. I can only think of one thing at a time."

She tramped up the hill and he stood, until her footfall had ceased. Then he went his own way and had climbed to within half a mile of Buckland, when a strange thing happened. He heard the winding of a hunter's horn. Through the darkness, for all listening ears at Holne or Leusden, Buckland or the neighbour farms and hillsides to hear, came the melodious note. It rang out twice, clear and full; and kennelled hounds a mile distant caught it and bayed across the night—a farewell, good to the heart of Enoch Withycombe if he had heard them.

CHAPTER XXI
FUNERAL

Enoch Withycombe had always promised to sound his horn again in sight of his end, and three days after he woke the echoes of the Vale he died. On the night that his music vibrated over hill and valley for the last time, Melinda had pushed his chair to the cottage door. When Lawrence called on the following Sunday afternoon, though he sat for a while beside his bed, the old hunter had already drifted into a comatose state, and the story Maynard had hoped to tell was never heard by him.

A bitter grey day dawned for a funeral attended by unusual mourners. The dead sportsman's master had made a promise and he kept it. Hounds did not meet that day; but the master, the huntsman and the whipper-in both clad in pink, and two brace of hounds were at the grave side—a bright flash of colour in the sombre little crowd that assembled.

Melinda Honeysett and her brother, Jerry, were chief mourners, while behind them came the fox-hunters; and of those who followed, some took it amiss to see such an addition to a funeral; while others held it most seemly and fitting.

Indeed for many days afterwards the question was heavily debated, and Arthur Chaffe and Ben Bamsey, who were both at the grave side, considered squire and parson alike to blame for an impropriety; while Joe Stockman, who came with Susan, Maynard and Thomas Palk, highly approved of the innovation. John Bamsey and Lawrence were among the bearers. They had also helped to carry the dead man from his home to the grave, for it was a walking funeral. Half a dozen private carriages followed it, and Melinda was bewildered to arrange the many gifts of flowers that came to her from her father's old friends of the countryside.

"Fox-hunters have long memories seemingly," said Jerry to his sister, as they read the cards attached to wreath and cross.

After the funeral was ended and when Enoch lay beside his wife, on the north of the church tower beneath a naked sycamore, it happened that Maynard found Dinah Waycott beside him in the press of the people. She had come with the Bamseys and, knowing that he would be there, now reached his side, bade him "good day," and unseen put a letter into his hand.

For a moment he picked up the thread of their conversation, where they had left it on the night by Dart River a week before.

"I couldn't tell him—he was too far gone next day," he said quietly, taking her letter.

"No matter," she answered, and then moved away.

The crowd drifted down the lanes and up the lanes. The men in pink mounted their horses and rode away with the hounds. Enoch's old master also departed on horseback, as did a dozen other men and several women. Soon only Melinda and Jerry were left to see the grave filled in and dispose the wreaths upon it. Mr. Chaffe kept them company. He cheered them by saying that never in his long experience, save once, had he known any man of the people enjoy such splendid and distinguished obsequies.

"A magnificent funeral despite the hounds," he said, "and Buckland did ought to be proud of it. There was a journalist from a Plymouth newspaper there, Jerry, so you'll be able to keep a printed history, with all the names, for future generations of your family to read aloud."

But Jerry was weeping and paid no heed; while his sister also, now that the strain had passed and the anticlimax come, hid not her tears.

Soosie-Toosie, her father and the two labouring men walked home together and Joe uttered a vain lament.

"A thousand pities the man's sailor son, Robert, couldn't be there," he said. "It would have been a fine thing for him to see what his father was thought of. And he'd have supported Melinda. She stood up very well and firm; but I know she'll miss him a terrible lot—her occupation gone you may say; for there's nobody leaves such a gap as an invalid that's called for your nursing for years. When the place is suddenly emptied of such a one, you feel as if the bottom was knocked out of your life, same as I did when my wife went."

Joe was in a mood unusually pensive and his daughter felt anxious. She tried to rally him, but failed.

"I'm looking forward," he said. "In that great rally of neighbours there was a lot of old blids from round about—a good few up home eighty years old I shouldn't wonder; and such was the bitter cold in the churchyard that you may be certain death was busy sowing his seeds. I hope to God I be all right, and I thank you for making me put on my heavy clothes, Soosie."

Palk walked behind them and talked fitfully to Maynard.

"'Twill ruin Christmas," said Thomas. "He was a famous man and there'll be a gloom fall over the place now he's dropped out."

"It won't make any difference," answered the younger.

"It may make a valiant lot of difference, and that nearer home than you think for," answered Palk.

But Maynard shook his head.

"There's nothing in it. Joe won't offer for her—Mrs. Honeysett—if that's what you're thinking; and if he did, 'tis doubtful if she'd take him. I've heard her tell about him to her father."

"And what did she tell?"

"Nothing but good. She knows his worth and all that. But Enoch didn't set very high store on master. I wondered why sometimes."

"Did you? I lay he knew him better than what you do. And he knew this—that a man who worked his only child like Stockman works his would make his wife a proper beast of burden."

"Everybody's selfish. I dare say when the news of the rise reaches us presently, you'll think better of him."

Then Stockman called Lawrence and Susan fell back to the horseman.

"He wants to tell Maynard about some ideas he's got, and it will distract his mind to do so," she explained.

"Be master under the weather about Mr. Withycombe, or is he only pretending?" asked Thomas bluntly.

"He's a very feeling creature is father," answered the woman. "He didn't care much for poor Mr. Withycombe, and Mr. Withycombe never quite saw father's good points, like most of the people do; but father's down-daunted to-day. 'Tis a landmark gone; and death's death; and he's fearful that another old person here and there may be took presently, along of the cruel cold in the churchyard."

"The wind curdled down off the Beacon like knives," admitted Palk. "Mrs. Honeysett kept her face very steady."

"She did. But she's a brave creature."

"She've got the cottage for her life, however."

"Yes. Squire's left it to her for naught, so long as she likes to bide there."

"A deep thought—how long she will bide there."

"Yes, it is. Jerry will be gone, come presently; but she'll have a neighbour. There's a widow man and his daughter took the cottage—the haunted house that joins hers. He's a new gardener to Buckland Court and don't fear ghosts."

"So I heard tell."

They were silent and then Thomas, now on very friendly terms with Susan, asked a question.

"Will it make a difference to Mr. Stockman, Mrs. Honeysett being set free of her father, miss?"

"I couldn't tell you, Tom. I've axed myself that question. But I'm not in father's thoughts."

His caution made him hesitate to speak again, but he knew that another question would go no farther than his listener.

"And if I may venture to put it, would you like to see him wed, miss?"

Susan slowed her steps that no sound of their voices might reach Joe. Her eyes were on his back as she answered.

"Yes, I think I would. A wife would add to his peace and comfort."

"She might add to yours."

"She might; but I'm not troubling as to that. Still, if she was a nice woman, I dare say she would."

"A wife—nice or otherwise—would open your father's eyes," declared Thomas. "In all respect I say it; but where you be concerned, he's got to make such a habit of you, and got to take you so terrible much like he takes his breakfast, or his boots, or any other item of his life, that it would be a very good thing for his character if he found out what you was."

"He don't undervalue me I hope," answered Susan. "Because a man don't say much, it don't follow he don't feel much, Thomas."

"But he do undervalue you cruel, and for that reason I'd be very pleased indeed if he was to get a woman for himself. Because no female he'm likely to find will show your Christian power of taking everything lying down. In fact no woman as ever I heard tell about can rise to such heights in that partickler as you; and your father have got so used to you, like a good pixy about the place, ready and willing to work night and day; and if he was up against another woman, he'd very soon have the surprise of his life."

"If a wife was so fond of him as what I am, she'd treat him so faithful as what I do," argued Soosie-Toosie; but Thomas assured her that she was mistaken.

"Don't think it," he said. "No wife ever I heard tell about would drudge for nought same as you. However, I be going beyond my business, and no doubt you'll tell me so. But 'tis only on your account, I assure you."

"I know it, Tom, and I thank you for your good opinion. But father's built in a higher mould than you and me. He's born to command, and I'm born to obey. Us generally do what's easiest, to save trouble; and if he was to marry again, he'd still be born to command, and any woman, knowing him well enough to take him, would understand that."

"They might, or they might not," argued Mr. Palk. "When a man goes courting, he hides a lot in that matter and, strong though the governor may be, there's women very well able to hold their own against any man born; and Melindy Honeysett is one. But it may happen. The mills of God may be grinding for it; and then master would look at you, and the scales would fall from his eyes I expect."

As soon as he was alone, Lawrence Maynard read the letter from Dinah. It was the first time he had ever seen her writing, and he found it a large, free hand with a hopeful slope upwards at the end of each line.

But the note was very brief. She committed herself to no opinions and only begged Lawrence to come to her in Lizwell Woods, a mile or two from her home, on the following Sunday afternoon.

"I'll be where the Webburn rivers run together, so soon after three o'clock as I may," she said.

CHAPTER XXII
AT WATERSMEET

Dinah was first at the tryst and doubted not that Maynard would come. The lonely, naked woods swept round her and she sat on a fallen trunk not far from where the Webburn sisters shot the grey forest with light and foamed together beneath the feet of trees. The day was dull and windy with rain promised from the south. Withered beech leaves whirled about Dinah's feet in little eddies, then rushed and huddled away together in hurtling companies—with a sound like a kettle boiling over, thought Dinah. Her mind was not wholly upon Maynard, for Joe Stockman's gloomy prophecy had come true in one case and Mr. Bamsey was indisposed from a chill caught at the funeral. As yet they were not concerned for him; but he had grown somewhat worse since the preceding day and Faith had sent Jane to fetch the doctor. Jane never declined a commission that would take her into Ashburton.

A smudge of black appeared in the woods and Maynard stood on the east bank of the river. Dinah rose and waved to him; then he ascended the stream until a place for crossing appeared. Here he leapt from stone to stone and was soon beside her. They wandered away and he found a spot presently, where the ground was dry with fallen needles from a pine above it.

"Sit here," he said, "a little while."

She had not spoken till now, save to tell him her foster-father was ill. But when they sat side by side, with the bole of the great pine behind them and its lower boughs sweeping about them to the ground, she answered all the questions he wanted to put in one swift action. For a moment she looked at him and her face glowed; and then she put her arms round his neck and kissed him.

"Dinah—d'you mean it?" he said. "Oh, d'you mean all that?"

"I want you; I can't live my life without you, Lawrence."

"After what I've told you?"

His arms were round her now and he had paid her fiercely for her kiss.

"What is marriage? I've been puzzling about it. I've been puzzling about it for years, for it seems years since you told me you was married. And if you knew what I'd been feeling, or how I fought not to kiss you at the funeral, you'd be sorry for me. But you've only been sorry for yourself I expect, you selfish man."

He did not answer. He had released her, but was still holding one of her hands.

"I'd make you a good wife, Lawrence," she said.

"By God you would!"

"And what is marriage then? Why d'you tell me you're married to her—any more than I'm married to John Bamsey—or anybody?"

"Marriage is a matter of law, and a man can only marry one wife."

"And what's a wife then?"

"The woman you are married to—she that's got your name."

"Would you say your wife was married?"

"Certainly she is."

"A widow then?"

"Not a widow if her husband is alive."

"Then why d'you say that Gilbert Courtier died when Lawrence Maynard came to life? If Gilbert Courtier's dead, then his wife is a widow."

Her literal interpretation was not a jest. He perceived that Dinah presented no playful mood. She was arguing as though concerned with facts, and not recognising any figurative significance in what he had told her about himself. For a moment, however, he could hardly believe she was in earnest.

"If it was as easy as that," he said.

"How d'you feel to it then?"

"I feel to it as you do, with all my heart. God knows what I want—one thing afore all things and above all things: and that's to have you for my own—my own. And whether I can, or can't, my own you will be from this hour, since you want to be my own, Dinah."

"And I will have it so. You're my life now—everything."

"But you can't make me less than I am. It's no good saying that Gilbert Courtier's dead; and though I change my name for my own comfort, that's not to change it against the facts."

"D'you want to go back to it then?"

"Not I. I'll never go back, and 'tis no odds to me what I'm called; but a wife's a wife, and my wife must stand safe within the law—for her own safety—and her husband's honour."

She stared at this.

"D'you feel that?"

"I do, Dinah."

"That things like safety, or the law, matter?"

"To you—not to me."

"What do I know about the law—or care? D'you think I'm a coward? You've only got one name for me, and ban't the name I love best in the world good enough? Who else matters to you, if you're Lawrence Maynard to me? And what else matters to you if I love you? Words! What are words alongside the things they stand for? I want you, same as you want me. And whose honour's hurt?"

"You feel all that?"

"Not if you don't. But you do."

His own standards failed for the time and he said somewhat more than he meant. Such love as Dinah's, such certainty as Dinah's, made doubt, built on old inherited instincts, look almost contemptible. Trouble of old had shaken these deep foundations; now happiness and pride at his splendid achievement similarly shook them.

"Yes I do," he said. "There's naught else on God's earth; I'd let all go down the wind afore I'd lose what I've won. I can keep off words as easy as you; and the word that would come between me and such love as I've got for you was never spoke and never will be. Words are dust and can go to the dust. But——"

He had recollected a fact beyond any power of words to annul.

"There's a hard and fast reality, Dinah, and we've got to take it into account, for it can't be argued down, or thought away."

"Then let it go—same as everything else have got to go. There's only one thing matters, I tell you, and we feel the same about it. Love's far too strong for all other realities, Lawrence. There's only one reality: that you and me are going to live together all our lives. What fact can stand against that? If facts were as big as the Beacon, they're naught against that fact. You be my own and I'm your own, and what else signifies?"

"You make me feel small," he said, "and love so big as that would make any man feel small, I reckon. And for the minute I'll put away the ways and means and machinery, that always have to be set running when a man wants to wed a woman."

"What's machinery to us? We didn't love each other by machinery and us shan't wed by machinery."

"Us can't wed without machinery."

"You say that! Ban't us wed a'ready? Be the rest of it half so fine as what brought us together, and made us know that our lives couldn't be lived apart? Ban't you wed to me, Lawrence?"

"I am," he said, "and only death will end it. But there's more than that for you; and so there's got to be more for me. And if I'm going to be small now and talk small, it's for you I do, not for myself. You're a sacred thing to me and holy evermore mind."

"And you be sacred to me," she said. "You've made all men sacred and holy to me; and you've made me feel different to the least of 'em, because they be built on the same pattern as you. I swear I feel kinder and better to everybody on earth since I know you loved me so true."

"It's this, then—a bit of the past. When I first came here I felt, somehow, that in Stockman I'd had the good luck to hit on just such another as my old master up country. He seemed to share the same large outlook and understanding, and I found him a man so friendly and charitable with his neighbours that I told him about myself, just like I told the other; and he was just the same about it—generous and understanding. In fact, he went further than my old master, and agreed with me right through, and said it was a very manly thing to have done, and that if more people had the pluck to cut a loss, the world would go smoother. He praised me for what I'd done, and I remember what he said. He said, 'To let sleeping dogs lie be a very wise rule; and to let sleeping bitches lie be still wiser.' But I know a lot more about Joe Stockman now than I did then; and though I've got no quarrel with him, yet, if the time was to come again, I wouldn't tell him. He'd never tell again, or anything like that; but he knows it, and if I was to say to him that I held I wasn't married and wanted another, he'd laugh at me."

Dinah admitted that Mr. Stockman was a serious difficulty.

"What would trouble him wouldn't be that; but the thought of losing you," she said. "That would make him nasty, no doubt, and quick to take a line against you."

"Joe knows about Barnstaple. He said to me once, 'Good men come from Barnstaple; my father did.' He has relatives up that way. But I only told him I knew the place; I never said I'd come from there."

She was silent for a moment staring straight before her with her elbows on her knees, her chin on her hands.

"All this means," he continued, "that we can't do anything small, or cast dust in people's eyes about it, even if we were tempted to, which we're not. For the minute we must mark time. Then we'll see as to the law of the subject and a good few things. All that matters to me is that you can love me so well as ever, knowing where I stand, and don't feel no grudge against me."

But she was not sentimental and his general ideas did not interest her. She had gone far beyond generalities. Her only thought was their future and how best and quickest it might be developed and shared.

"As to doing anything small, nothing's small if the result of it is big," she said. "There's no straight wedding for us here anyway, since Cousin Joe knows, but Buckland ain't the world, and what we've got to satisfy be ourselves, not other people. I hate to hear you say we'll see about the law. People like us did ought to be our own law."

"We've got enough to go on with, and we've got ourselves to go on with—everything else is naught when I look at you."

"If you feel that, I'm not afeared," she said. "That means firm ground for me, and all the things that balked and fretted me be gone now."

They talked love and explored each other's hearts, very willing to drop reality for dreams. They were a man and woman deeply, potently in love, and both now made believe, to the extent of ignoring the situation in which they really stood. Time fled for them and the early dusk came down, so that darkness crept upon them from every side simultaneously. Rain fell, but they did not perceive it under the sheltering pine. They set off anon and went down the river bank.

"Now we must go back into the world for a bit," said Dinah, "and we'll think and see what our thoughts may look like to each other in a week. Then we'll meet here once more, unbeknown'st. For I reckon we'd better not moon about together in the sight of people overmuch now. If Joe knows about you—and yet perhaps that's to the good in a way, because he knows you be straight and honest, so he'd feel I was safe enough, and only laugh at the people if they told him you and me were friends beyond reason."

Maynard wondered to see how quickly Dinah's mind moved, and how she could see into and through a problem as it arose. But he approved her opinion, that they had better not be seen too often together.

Yet they did not separate before they ran into one who knew them both. Thomas Palk met them on a woodland road below Watersmeet.

He stood at the edge of an ascent to Buckland.

"Hullo, Tom! What's brought you out this wet evening?" asked Maynard, and the elder explained that he had been to Green Hayes for news of Mr. Bamsey.

"Master was wishful to hear tidings," he said. "And I had naught on hand and did his pleasure. The doctor was along with Benjamin Bamsey when I got there; so I be taking home the latest."

"And what is it, Mr. Palk?" asked Dinah.

"Bad," he answered. "He's got a lung in a fever and did ought to have seen doctor sooner."

"Good night, then. I must be gone," she said, and without more words left the men and started running.

Palk turned to Lawrence.

"I shouldn't wonder if Bamsey was a goner," he prophesied. "If the breathing parts be smote, then the heart often goes down into a man's belly, so I believe, and can't come up again. And that's death."

The other was silent. For a moment it flitted through his mind that, if such a thing happened, it might go far to simplify Dinah's hold upon the world and make the future easier for them both; but he forgot this aspect in sympathy for Dinah herself. He knew that danger to her foster-father must mean a very terrible grief for her.

"He's a hard, tough old chap. He'll come through with such care as he'll get. But Stockman said as that biting day might breed trouble among the grey heads. He was right."

He talked with a purpose to divert Tom's mind from the fact that he had met him walking alone with Dinah; but he need not have felt apprehension: Mr. Palk was immersed in his own thoughts, and no outside incident ever influenced his brain when it happened to be engaged with personal reflections.

"Stockman always looks ahead—granted," he answered as they climbed the hill together, "and for large views and putting two and two together, there's not his equal. But self-interest is his god, though he foxes everybody it ain't. For all his fine sayings, there is only one number in his mind and that's number One. He hides it from most, but he don't hide it from me, because the minute you've got the key to his lock, you see how every word and thought and deed be bent in one direction. And under his large talk of the greatest good to the most, there's always 'self' working unseen."

"You ain't far out, yet in honesty there's not much for you and me to quarrel with," said Maynard.

"When you say that, you'm as ownself as him. And if you and me was everybody, I wouldn't feel what I do. He don't quarrel with us, though he often says a thing so pleasant and easy that you don't know you're cut, till you find the blood running. But we ain't everybody. He may see far, but he don't see near. He's fairly civil to us, because he don't mean to lose us if he can help it; but what about her as can't escape? How does he treat his own flesh and blood?"

Maynard was astonished. He had not given Thomas credit for much wit or power of observation. Nor had he ever concerned himself with the inner life of the farm as it affected Susan.

"Would you say Miss was put upon?" he asked.

"God's light!" swore Mr. Palk. "And be you a thinking man and can ask that? Have you got eyes? If Orphan Dinah had to work like her, would you ax me if she was put upon?"

The challenge disturbed Lawrence, for it seemed that Thomas had observation that extended into the lives of his neighbours—a gift the younger man had not guessed.

"What's Miss Waycott to do with it?" he asked.

"Naught. Nobody's got nothing to do with it but master. And he's got everything to do with it; and he's a tyrant and a damned slave-driver, and treats her no better than a plough, or a turnip cutter."

They were silent and Thomas asked a question.

"Have you ever heard tell they port-wine marks be handed down from generation to generation, worse and worse?"

"No, I never did."

"I heard Stockman tell Melindy Bamsey they was."

"I dare say it might be so."

"And yet again, when the subject come up at Ashburton, a publican there said that if a man or woman suffered from such a thing they was doomed never to have no children at all. He said he'd known a good few cases."

"A woman might," answered Lawrence, "because, if they're afflicted that way, they'd be pretty sure to bide single. But it would be a nice question if a marked man couldn't get childer. I wouldn't believe anybody but a doctor on that subject."

Thomas turned this over for ten minutes without answering. Then the subject faded from his mind and he flushed another.

"What about our rise?" he said.

"We'll hear after Easter."

They discussed the probable figure. Maynard seemed not deeply interested; but Palk declared that his own future movements largely depended upon Mr. Stockman's decision.

CHAPTER XXIII
IN A SICK-ROOM

Dinah could not think of her foster-father all the way home. Though deeply concerned, her thoughts left him fitfully to concentrate on Lawrence Maynard. She felt a little puzzled at a streak of mental helplessness that seemed to have appeared in him. Just where it appeared most vital that he should know his own mind, she could not help feeling he did not. He groped, instead of seeing the way as clearly as she did. For him, what he had to tell her seemed serious; for her, as she now considered it, the fact that Mr. Stockman knew Maynard was married sank in significance. She found that it was only because Lawrence regarded it as grave, that she had done so. That it made a simple situation more complex she granted; but it did not alter the situation; and if it was impossible to be married at Buckland, there would be no difficulty, so far as she could see, in being married elsewhere.

She had examined the situation more deeply, however, before she reached home and perceived that Lawrence, after all, was not groping, but rather standing still before a very definite obstacle. They could not be married at Buckland; but could they be married anywhere else without first vanishing far beyond reach and hearing of Buckland? For him that was easy; for her impossible, unless she deliberately cut herself off from her foster-father and, not only that, but prevented him from knowing where she might be. For it was idle to tell him, or anybody, that she had married Maynard, while Mr. Stockman could report from Maynard's own lips that he was already married.

Now indeed Dinah's soul fainted for a few moments. She hated things hid; she loved events to be direct and open; but already some need for hiding her thought, if not her actions, had become imperative and now she saw a complication arising that she had never taken into account: the collision between Lawrence and Ben Bamsey. What might be right and honest enough to her and her lover—what was already clean and clear in her mind, and would, she did not doubt, be presently equally clean and clear to Lawrence—must emphatically be neither righteous nor thinkable to the generation of Mr. Bamsey. None else indeed mattered; but he did. Great vistas of time began to stretch between her and her lover. He retreated; but the gathering difficulties did not daunt her since the end was assured.

For a season life was now suspended at the bedside of an old man, and Dinah returned home to plunge at once into the battle for her foster-father's existence. It was a battle fought unfairly for her, and not until the end of it did Dinah discover the tremendous effect of her exertions on her own vitality; for she was in a position false and painful from the first, being called at the will of one very sick to minister to him before his own, and to suffer from the effects of his unconscious selfishness, under the jealousy of the other women who were nearer to him.

Ben rapidly became very ill indeed, with congestion of the lungs, and for a time, while in the extremity of suffering, his usual patient understanding deserted him and facts he strove to keep concealed in health under conditions of disease appeared. They were no secret to Faith Bamsey and she was schooled to suffer them, being able the easier so to do, because she was just and knew the situation was not Dinah's fault. Indeed they created suffering for the girl also. But to Jane, her father's now unconcealed preference for Dinah, his impatience when she was absent and his reiterated desire to have her beside him, inflamed open wounds and made her harsh. Her mother argued with her half-heartedly, but did not blame her any more than she blamed Dinah. She knew her husband's armour was off, and that he could not help extending a revelation of the truth beyond her heart, where she had hoped it was hidden; but she was human and the fact that everybody, thanks to Jane, now knew that she and her own child were less to Benjamin than his foster-daughter, distressed her and sometimes clouded her temper.

One only stood for Dinah and strove to better the pain of her position. Tossed backward and forward still, now, when at last he was minded to accept the situation and admit to his own mind the certainty he could never win her, a ray of hope flushed wanly out of the present trouble; a straw offered for him to clutch at. John Bamsey came to Green Hayes daily, to learn how his father did, and he heard from Jane how Dinah was preferred before his mother or herself. Then inspired by some sanguine shadow, he took Dinah's part, strove to lessen the complication for her and let her know that he understood her difficulties and was opposing his sister on her account.

He quarrelled with Jane for Dinah's sake and told Dinah so; and she perceived, to her misery, how he was striving yet again to win her back at any cost. Thus another burden was put upon her and she found that only in the sick-room was any peace.

Mr. Bamsey much desired to live, and proved a good patient from the doctor's point of view. A professional nurse, however, he would not have and, indeed, there was no need. All that could be done was done, and it seemed that the crisis was delayed by the sleepless care of those who tended him. He was not unreasonable and sometimes solicitous both for his wife and Dinah. He desired that they should take their rest and often demanded Jane's attention, for the sake of the others; but, as he reached the critical hours of his disease, his only cry was for Dinah and his only wish appeared to be that he should hold her hand. Thus sometimes she had to sit beside him while his wife did nurse's work. The torture was sustained; and then came a morning when, still clear in his mind, Mr. Bamsey felt that he might not much longer remain so. He then expressed a wish for his family to come round him, while he detailed his purposes and intentions.

John was also present at this meeting, and when Dinah desired to leave them together, he and not his father bade her stop.

"You're one of us," he said. "Sit where you are and don't leave go his hand, else he'll be upset."

The sufferer had little to say.

"'Tis all in my will," he told them. "But I'm wishful to speak while I can; and if mother has got anything against, there's time to put it right. All mine is hers for her life—all. But I'll ax her, when each of you three come to be married, to hand each five hundred pounds. That won't hurt her. She'll bide here, I hope; and presently, when Jane weds, it would be very convenient if Jerry was to come here and go on with the farm. But if mother wants to leave here, then she can sublet. And when mother's called, the money's to be divided in three equal portions for Dinah and John and Jane."

He stopped, panting.

"Heave me up a bit, Dinah," he said.

Nobody spoke and he looked into their faces.

"Well?" he asked impatiently.

"That will do very right and proper, my dear," answered Faith. "Don't you think no more about it. A just and righteous will I'm sure."

But Jane had left the room and her father observed it.

"Have that woman anything against?" he asked.

"No, no—a very just and righteous will," repeated his wife soothingly. "I could wish you'd trusted me with the capital, father; but there—I'm content."

"I put you first, Faith."

"I've put you first for five and twenty years."

"You ban't content?"

"Well content. Rest now. Us'll go and leave you with Dinah Waycott."

She tried to resist using Dinah's surname, but could not. Then she left the room.

"I've done what I thought was my duty, John," said Mr. Bamsey.

"You've never done less. I'm very willing that Dinah should share. So's mother I'm sure."

"Try and get a bit of sleep now, my old dear," said Dinah. "And thank you dearly—dearly for thinking on me; but—no matter, you get off if you can. Will you drink?"

He nodded and she gave him some warm milk.

"I'll drop the blind," she said and did so.

In her thoughts was already the determination to forego any legacy under any circumstances. She longed to tell Jane that she meant to do so.

Mr. Bamsey shut his eyes and presently dozed. The steam kettle made a little chattering in the silence, but the sick man's breathing was the loudest sound in the room.

He slept, though Dinah knew that he would not sleep long. To her concern John began talking of what had passed.

He proceeded in undertones.

"Don't think I don't approve what father's done. I do; and I wish to God you'd take two-thirds—mine as well as your own—in fulness of time. Which you would do, Dinah, if you came to me. Why can't you see it?"

"Why can't you, John?"

"What is there for me to see? Nothing, but that you don't know your own mind. Haven't I been patient enough, waiting for you to make it up? What's the good of going on saying you don't love me, when you know I've got love enough for me and you both? Can't you trust me? Can't you judge the size of what I feel for you, by the line I've took for very near a year? You loved me well enough back-along, and what did I ever do to choke you off? You can't tell me, because you don't know. Nobody knows. You bide here, and you understand I'm not changed and won't be blown away by all the rumours and lies on people's tongues; and you can let me live on in hell—

for what? You don't know If you had a reason, you'd be just enough to grant I ought to hear it."

"Don't say that, Johnny. You never asked me for a reason more than I gave you from the first. I told you on New Bridge that I was bitter sorry, but I found my feeling for you was not the sort of love that can make a woman marry a man. And that was the sole reason then. And that reason is as good now as ever it was."

"It's no reason to anybody who knows you like what I do. Haven't you got any pity, or mercy in you, Dinah? Can you go on in cold blood ruining my life same as you are doing—for nothing at all? What does a woman want more than the faithful love and worship of a clean, honest man? Why did you stop loving me?"

"I never began, John; and if you say that reason's not enough, then—then I'll give you another reason. For anything's better than going on like this. To ask me for pity and mercy! Can't you see what you're doing—you, who was so proud? D'you want a woman to give herself up to you for pity and mercy? Be you sunk to that?"

"I'm sunk where it pleased you to sink me," he said; "and if you knew what love was, pity and mercy would rise to your heart to see anybody sinking that you could save."

"I do know what love is," she answered. "Yes, I know it now, though I never did till now. When I begged you to let me go, I didn't know anything except what I felt for you wasn't what it ought to be; but, since then, things are different; and I do well know what love is."

"That's something. If you've larned that, I'll hope yet you'll come to see what mine is."

"You can't love a man because he loves you, John. You may be just as like to love a man who hates you, or love where mortal power can't love back—as in your case. Where I've got now be this: I do love a man."

"You thought you loved me. Perhaps you're wrong again and was right before."

"I love a man, and he loves me; and nothing on God's earth will ever keep us apart unless it's death."

"So you think now. I've heard some talk about this and gave them that told it the lie. And I'm most in the mind to give you the lie. I can't forget all you've said to me. It's hard—it's horrible, to think you could ever speak such words to anybody else."

She smiled.

"I don't want to be cruel; I don't want to be horrible, John. But what I've ever said to you was naught—the twitter of a bird—the twaddle of a child. How could I talk love to you, not knowing love? You never heard love from me, because I didn't know the meaning of the word till long after us had parted for good and all. Find a woman that loves you—you soon might—then you'll hear yourself echoed. I never echoed you, and that you know very well, because I couldn't."

"Who is he?"

She expected this and was prepared. None must know that she loved Lawrence Maynard—least of all John Bamsey. He would be the first to take his news red hot to Falcon Farm and Joe Stockman. The necessity for silence was paramount; but she voiced her own desire when she answered.

"I wish to Heaven I could tell you, Johnny. Yes, I do. I'd like best of all to tell you, and I'll never be quite, quite happy, I reckon, until you've forgiven me for bringing sorrow and disappointment on you. 'Tis not the least of my hopes that all here will forgive me some day; for I couldn't help things falling out as they have, and I never wanted to be a curse in disguise to foster-father, or any of you, same as I seem to be. You can't tell—none of you—how terrible hard it is; and God's my judge, I've often wished this dear old man could have turned against me, and hated me, and let me go free. But he wouldn't send me out and I couldn't go so long as he bade me stop."

"You're wriggling away from it," he said. "Who's the man? If there's any on earth have the right to know that much, it's me."

"So you have—I grant it. And if it ever comes to be known, you'll be the first to hear, John. But it can't be known yet awhile, for very good reasons. My life's difficult and his life's difficult—so difficult that it may never happen at all. But I pray God it will; and it shall if I can make it happen. And more I can't tell you than that."

"You hide his name from me then?"

"What does his name matter? I've only told you so much for the pity you ask. I needn't have gone so far. But I can see what knowing this ought to do for you, John, and I hope it will. You understand now that I care for a man as well, heart and soul and body, as you care for me. And for Christ's sake let that finish it between us. I hate hiding things, and it's bitter to me to hide what I'm proud of—far prouder of than anything that's ever happened to me in all my born days. So leave it, and if there's to be pity and mercy between us—well, you're a man, and you can be pitiful and merciful now, knowing I'm in a fix, more or less, and don't see the way out at present. It's a man's part to be merciful, so be a man."

The turning point had come for him and he knew that his last hope was dead. This consciousness came not gradually, but in a gust of passion that banished the strongest of him and exalted the weakest. Hate would now be quickly bred from the corpse of his obstinate desires, and he knew and welcomed the thought.

"Yes," he said, "you'm right; it's for men to be merciful. No woman ever knew the meaning of the word. So I'll be a man all through—and there's more goes to a man than mercy for them that have wickedly wronged him."

He forgot where he stood and raised his voice.

"And I'll find him—maybe I know where to look. But I'll find him; and there won't be any mercy then, Dinah Waycott. 'Tis him that shall answer for this blackguard robbery. I can't have you; but, by God, I'll have the price of you!"

He woke his father, and Ben, choking, coughed and spat. Then he heaved himself on his arms and pressed his shoulders up to his ears to ease the suffocation within.

Dinah ministered to him and John went from the sick-room and from the house.

CHAPTER XXIV
"THE REST IS EASY"

Ben Bamsey survived his illness and had to thank a very pains-taking doctor and most devoted nurses for his life. He was unconscious for four and twenty hours, and during the fortnight that followed the crisis remained so weak, that it seemed he could never regain strength sufficient to move a hand. Then he began to recover. He prospered very slowly, but there were no relapses, and the definite disaster left by his illness remained unknown to the sufferer himself until the end of his days. Nor did other people perceive it until some months had elapsed. The physician was the first to do so, but he did not speak of it directly, rather leaving Ben's own circle to discover the change and its extent. The doctor had feared early; but it was not a fear he could impart.

Meantime it became known to those who had already bidden farewell to the master of Green Hayes that he would live; and not one of all those known to Mr. Bamsey but rejoiced to learn the good news.

On a day some time after Christmas, while yet the sick man's fate was undetermined and it could not be said that he was out of danger, Lawrence Maynard went down to Green Hayes, that he might learn the latest news. Life ran evenly at Falcon Farm and Mr. Stockman's first interest at present was his kinsman. Now Lawrence brought a partridge, with directions from Joe that it was to be made into broth for Mr. Bamsey.

He saw Ben's wife and heard the morning's news, that her husband was now safe and would recover.

Faith looked haggard and pale, and Maynard expressed a fear that the ordeal must have been very severe. She admitted it, but declared that such relief as all now felt would be a tonic and swiftly restore them.

"We're about beat," she said, in her usual placid fashion. "We've worked hard and, between us, we've saved my husband with the doctor's help. That man's a miracle. I've got a very great respect for him. You'd best to come in and rest yourself before you go back."

He entered, in secret hope of seeing Dinah, whom he had not met for several weeks. Once, however, she had written him a brief note to say that she was well.

Faith Bamsey spoke of Ben and praised his fortitude.

"If he'd wavered, or thrown up the sponge for an hour, he'd have died; but so long as he kept consciousness he determined to live, and even when he thought and felt positive he must go, he never gave up doing the right thing. He won't be the same man, however; we mustn't expect that. He'll be in his bed for a month yet and can't hope to go down house for six weeks. He mustn't think to go out of doors till spring and the warm weather; then it remains to be seen how much of his nature he gets back."

She entertained Maynard for half an hour, while he drank a cup of tea. She did not share Jane's suspicion and dislike of him and felt no objection to the idea of his wedding Dinah and removing her from Lower Town. She was almost minded in his quiet and inoffensive presence to raise the question, and went so far as to tell him Dinah had driven to Ashburton that afternoon. But he showed no apparent interest in the fact and Faith did not continue on the subject. She could be generous, however, in the blessed light of Ben's promised recovery, and she admitted that Dinah had been of infinite value in the sick-room. Indeed Mrs. Bamsey did not hide from herself that Dinah had doubtless made the difference between life and death for her husband; and since she desired above all things that Ben should live, some of her dislike was softened for the time. She wished her away very cordially, but knew the hour of Dinah's departure must now be protracted indefinitely, for no question could at present be put to her foster-father.

With her personal anxieties ended, Faith Bamsey found it possible to consider other people again.

"I've never had time to think of what Enoch Withycombe's death meant yet," she said, "because it brought such a terrible time to us. But now us can lift up our heads and look round at other folk again and inquire after the neighbours. Melinda was down axing after my husband a bit ago, but I didn't see her. Jerry comes and goes. I hope Melinda gets over it. To nurse a father all them years and then lose him, must have left her stranded in a manner of speaking."

"Mrs. Honeysett comes to see Miss Susan and farmer sometimes."

"I warrant. Would you say Cousin Joe be looking in that direction now she's free?"

Maynard shook his head.

"I wouldn't. I don't reckon Mr. Stockman will marry again. He's very comfortable."

"Yes—one of them whose comfort depends on the discomfort of somebody else, however."

"So people seem to think. It's a hard home for Miss Susan; but it's her life, and if she's not a cheerful sort of woman, you can't say she's much downcast."

"No—she dursn't be cast down. He wouldn't stand cast-down people round him. Mind to say I'm greatly obliged for the bird, and I hope Ben will eat a slice or two presently. I'll come up over and drink a dish of tea with them afore long. I'm properly withered for want of fresh air."

"I dare say you are, ma'am."

"I saw Enoch Withycombe last week," she said. "The old man was standing down in the Vale, not far from the kennels—just where you'd think he might be. And always seeing him lying down, as we did, it gave me quite a turn to mark how tall his ghost was."

To see a dead man had not astonished Faith; but the unremembered accident of his height had done so.

"How did he look, Mrs. Bamsey?" asked Maynard.

"I couldn't tell you. The faces that I see never show very clear. You'm conscious it is this man, or this woman. You know, somehow, 'tis them, but there's always a fog around them. They don't look the same as what living people look."

"The haunted house that adjoins Mrs. Honeysett's is taken at last," he said. "Mr. Chaffe has been up over a good bit putting it to rights, and they've stripped the ivy and are going to put on a new thatch. It's a very good house really, though in a terrible state, so Mr. Chaffe told master."

"I've heard all about it," she answered. "There's a new gardener come to Buckland Court—a widow man with a young daughter. And he don't care for ghosts—one of the modern sort, that believe naught they can't understand. And as they can't understand much, they don't believe much. So he's took it."

"Harry Ford, he's called," added Lawrence. "A man famous for flower-growing, I believe."

"I'm glad then. I hate for houses to stand empty."

He asked after Jerry.

"I met your young people back-along, and I'm afraid Miss Jane have put me in her black books—why for I don't know very well. I suppose they'll wed come presently?"

Again Mrs. Bamsey was tempted to speak, but felt it wiser not to do so. She ignored Maynard's first remark and replied to the second.

"Yes; they'll be for it now no doubt. After Easter perhaps; but not till my husband is strong enough to be at the church and give Jane away of course. Jerry's come into a bit of money since his father died. They must have their ideas, but they're close as thieves about the future. All I can hear is that they be wishful to go away from here come they're married."

"Folk like to make a change and start life fresh after that."

"I suppose they do."

He talked a little longer and it was impossible for Faith to feel dislike or anger. Had he come between her son and his betrothed—had he been responsible for the unhappy break, she would have felt differently; but she knew that he was not responsible and she perceived that if he indeed desired to marry Dinah, the circumstance would solve difficulties only ignored by common consent during her husband's illness. She had not heard what John said to Dinah in the sick-room and supposed that now her son must appreciate the situation, since he had quite ceased to speak of Dinah. His purpose, avowed in a passion, had not overmuch impressed Dinah herself, for it was outside reason and she doubted not that Johnny would be ashamed of such foolish threats in a cooler moment. But, none the less, she meant to warn Lawrence and now an opportunity occurred to do so.

For Maynard availed himself of Mrs. Bamsey's information, and hearing that Ben's foster-daughter was gone to Ashburton, knew the way by which she would return home and proceeded on that way. He had not seen her since the Sunday afternoon at Lizwell Meet; neither had he written to her, doubting whether it might be wise to do so and guessing that her whole life for the present was devoted to the sufferer.

He left Mrs. Bamsey now and presently passed the workshops of Arthur Chaffe at Lower Town, then sank into the valley. By the time he reached New Bridge, Dinah had also arrived there and he carried her parcels for half a mile and returned beside the river.

She was beyond measure rejoiced to see him and he found her worn and weary from the strain of the battle; but its victorious issue went far already to make her forget what was passed. She talked of Mr. Bamsey and gave Maynard details of the sick-room and the alternate phases of hope and despair that had accompanied the illness. To her these things bulked large and filled her thoughts; but he was well content, because Dinah adopted an implicit attitude to him that indicated beyond doubt her settled consciousness of their relation. She spoke as though they were lovers of established understanding. She seemed to take it for granted that only an uncertain measure of time separated them.

This much she implied from the moment of their meeting and presently, when they approached the parting place, she became personal.

"Don't think, for all I'm so full of dear foster-father, that you've been out of my thoughts, Lawrence," she said. "You was there all the time—the last thing in my mind when I went to get an hour or two of sleep, and the first thing when I woke. You ran through it all; and once or twice when he was rambling, he named your name and said you was a very good sort of man—civil and thoughtful and peace-loving. And I told him you were; and he hoped we'd come together, for he said he could trust me with you. He wasn't far from himself when he said it, but only I heard; and whether he ever named you in his fever dreams when I wasn't there—to Jane, or Mrs. Bamsey—I don't know. They never let on about it and so I hope he didn't."

"I've just seen his wife," he said. "She's long ways happier for this great recovery. She's sensible enough. She looked a few questions, but didn't ask them, and you're not bound to answer looks."

Then Dinah told him of John's threats and how he had again begged her to wed.

"I felt things was at a climax then; and I told him straight out that I knew what love was at last. I was gentle and kind to the poor chap; but he wasn't gentle and kind to me. He wanted to know the man, and that, of course, I couldn't tell him, though dearly I longed to. But things being as they are, I can't name you, Lawrence, though 'tis terrible hateful to me I can't. I said to Johnny 'twas no odds about the man for the present, and then he lost his temper and swore he'd find him out and do all manner of wicked deeds to him. Only his rage, of course, and nothing to trouble about, but so it is and I meant for you to know."

He considered and she spoke again.

"It makes me mad to think all we are to each other have got to be hid, as if we was ashamed of it instead of proud—proud. But Cousin Joe would abide by the letter against the spirit no doubt. He'd tell everybody you was married if we blazed out we were tokened; and now Mr. Withycombe's dead, there's not any in the Vale that would understand."

"Certainly there is not, Dinah—or beyond the Vale I reckon."

"All's one," she said. "In my eyes you're a free man, and just as right to find a mate as a bird in a tree. Yes, you are. I know what marriage means now, and I know what our marriage will mean. For that matter we are married in heart and soul."

"It's good to hear you say so," he answered. "My love's so true as yours, Dinah; but there's more mixed with it."

"Away with what be mixed with it! I won't have naught mixed with it, and no thought shall think any evil into it, Lawrence. You couldn't think evil for that matter; but men be apt, seemingly, to tangle up a straight thought by spinning other thoughts around it. And I won't have that. What be your thoughts that you say are mixed with the future? Can you name them? Can you think 'em out loud in words and look in my face while you do? I lay you can't! But, for that matter, I've been thinking too. And what I think mixes with what I feel, and makes all the better what I feel."

In her eagerness Dinah became rhetorical.

"I was turning over that widow at Barnstaple," she said—"the woman called Courtier, married to a dead man. And I was wondering why I thought twice of her even while I did so; for what be she to me? Not so much as the grass on the field-path I walk over. And what be she to you more than the dead? Be she real, Lawrence? Be she more real and alive to you than Gilbert Courtier, in his grave, beyond sight and sound of living men for evermore? Let the dead lie. You'm alive, anyway, and free in the Eye of God to marry me. And what matters except how soon, and when, and where?"

"You're a brave wonder," he said, "and the man you can love, who would miss you, must be a bigger fool than me. What's left be my work— and a glorious bit of work I reckon."

"Easy enough anyway."

"For the things to be done, easy enough I doubt not; for the things to be thought, none so easy. Them that sweep fearless to a job, like you, have got to be thought for. And love quickens a man and makes him higher and deeper and better—better, Dinah—than himself—if love's got any decent material to work upon and the man's any good. And pray God that will turn out to be so in my case. A bit ago, when first I came here, I'd have gone bare-headed into this—same as you want to. But I've larned a lot from a dead man since I came to Falcon Farm. Withycombe looked deeper into life than me, being taught by his master and his own troubles and also out of books so to do. He steadied me here and there, and maybe it was for this great business that the words were put in his mouth. And it's that that be mixed with what I feel for you. God knows it don't lessen the love; but it—how shall I say—it lifts it a bit—into sharper air than a man breathes easy. I ban't going to be selfish if I can help it. We're young and the world's before us. But afore we come together, I want you to be so strong and sure-footed that nothing shall ever shake you after, and naught that man can do or say — — "

"Oh, my dear heart!" she cried, "what do you think I'm made of?"

"I know—I know. It's what I be made of, Dinah darling. I've got to find that out."

"Let me show you then. You don't frighten me, Lawrence. I know what you're made of, and I know if I know naught else, you won't be a finished thing till you share what I'm made of. We be halves of one whole as sure as our Maker fashioned the parts; and that you know—you must know. And I tell you the rest is easy, and you know it's easy so well as me."

He said no more. In her present mood it must have only hurt to do so, and every human inclination, every reasonable argument, every plea of common sense and justice prompted him to acquiesce whole-heartedly. But something other than reason possessed his mind at that particular hour. For the moment he could not smother thoughts that were selfless and engaged with Dinah only.

After a silence he answered her last words.

"Yes, I know it," he said. "If the rest goes that way, then the rest is easy enough."

"What other way can it go, unless like our ways to-night—mine up one hill—alone—yours up another hill—alone?"

"Never, by God! I'm only a man."

"And my man! My man!"

They talked a little longer, then parted, where they had parted on a previous great occasion. But they did not part until Maynard had made her promise to meet him again and that quickly.

"You'll be a lot freer now," he said.

"I shall and I shan't too, because all the fighting for foster-father have made me closer than ever to him somehow. There's such a lot of different loves in the world seemingly. I love the dear old man with my whole heart— every bit of it. He can't do nor say nothing I don't love him for—he's an old saint. And I love you with my whole heart too, Lawrence. I properly drown in love when I think of you; and I can almost put my arms round you in my thoughts, and feel we ain't two people at all—only one."

They kissed and went their ways, and he considered all that she had said even to the last word. The thought of these things in themselves rejoiced him. To run away with Dinah and vanish from this environment would not be difficult. Indeed he had already traversed the ground and considered the details of their departure. He would give notice a month before they disappeared, and while his going might be orderly enough, Dinah's must be in the nature of a surprise. He considered whether they should leave in such a manner that their names would not be associated afterwards; but it seemed impossible to avoid that. It mattered little and not at all to her. In any case the details were simple enough; there was nothing whatever to prevent their departure when they chose to depart. To Canada, or Australia, they might go when they willed, and he had retraced the old ground and reconsidered the question of state-aided passages and his own resources, which were ample for the purpose.

But not with these things was Maynard's mind occupied when he left Dinah. He was not a man of very complex character, and the independence of thought that had marked the chief action of his life had never been seriously challenged until now. He had been guided by reason in most questions of conduct and never recognised anything above or outside reason in the action that led him to desert his wife on their wedding day; but that same quality it was that now complicated reason and made him doubt, not for his own sake or well being, not of the future opened for him by the immense new experience of loving Dinah, but by the consequences of such a future for Dinah herself. Here reason spoke with a plain voice. His wits told him that no rational human being could offer any sort of objection to their union; and the tribal superstitions that might intervene, based on the creed morals under which his nation pretended to exist, did not weigh with him. What did was the law of the land, not the religion of the land. Under the law he could not marry Dinah, and no child that might come into the world as a result of their union would be other than a bastard. That would not trouble her; and, indeed, need not trouble anybody, for since Gilbert Courtier, as Dinah had said, no longer existed for them, and was now beyond reach as completely as though indeed he lay in his grave, there could be none to rise and question a marriage entered into between him and Dinah—in Canada, or elsewhere. But there were still the realities and, beyond them, a certain constituent of his own character which now began to assert itself. There persisted in his soul a something not cowardly, but belonging to hereditary instincts of conscience, mother-taught, through centuries. It made Lawrence want to have all in order, conformable to the laws of the world and his own deeply rooted sense of propriety. He had no desire to run with the hare and hunt with the hounds: he knew that for nothing you can only get nothing, but he longed, before all else, that the inevitable might also be the reputable, and that no whisper in time to come should ever be raised against his future wife. The desire rose much above a will to mere safety. It was higher than that and, indeed, belonged to Maynard's ethical values and sense of all that was fitting and good of report among men and women. It echoed the same influence and radical conception of conduct that had made him leave his wife on his wedding day; and the fact that no such considerations controlled Dinah, the truth that she regarded the situation on a plane of more or less material reality and felt no sympathy with his shadowy difficulties, promised to increase them. He hardly saw this himself yet, but though he felt that she was right, yet doubted, in that secret and distinctive compartment of his inner self, whether she might be wrong. He was, for the moment, divided between agreeing with her utterly and feeling that he must allow no natural instinct and rational argument to let him take advantage of her. And when he looked closer into this, a new difficulty arose, for how could he ever make Dinah understand this emotion, or set clearly before her comprehension what he himself as yet so dimly comprehended?

Her grasp of the situation was clear and lucid. From the moment when she had said in the teashop, "D'you call that being married?" he guessed how she was going to feel, and how she would be prepared to act. Nor would the suggested confession to dead Enoch Withycombe have made any difference to Dinah, whatever view the old hunter might have held. Dinah's heart was single, and while now Maynard longed with a great longing to find his own heart seeing eye to eye with hers in every particular, he knew that it did not, and he could not be sure that it ever would. He regarded the situation as lying entirely between her and himself, and entertained no thought of any possibility that others might complicate it, either to retard, or determine the event. She had, indeed, told him of John Bamsey's threats, but to them he attached no importance. From within and not from without must the conclusion be reached.

CHAPTER XXV
JOHN AND JOE

John Bamsey now threatened to run his head into folly. He was an intelligent man; but out of the ferment that had so long obscured his vision and upset his judgment, there had been developed a new thing, and a part of him that chance might have permitted to remain for ever dormant, inert and harmless, was now thrust uppermost. He developed a certain ferocity and a sullen and obstinate passion bred from sense of wrong, not only towards Dinah, but the unknown, who had supplanted him with her. For that he had been supplanted, despite her assurance to the contrary, John swore to himself. Thus, indeed, only could Dinah's defection be explained; and only so could he justify his purpose and determination to treat this interloper evilly and rob him, at any cost, of his triumph. He built up justification for himself, therefore, and assured himself that he was right, as a man of character, in taking revenge upon his unknown enemy. He convinced himself easily enough and only hesitated farther because his rival continued to be a shadow, to whom his sister alone was prepared to put a name. She resolutely swore that Maynard was the man, and she declared that her father had mentioned him and Dinah together, more than once, when rambling in his fever dreams.

This brought John, from a general vague determination to stand between Dinah and any other man, to the necessity for definite deeds that should accomplish his purpose; and when he considered how to turn hate into action, he perceived the difficulty. But the folly and futility he declined to recognise, though his reason did not omit to force them upon him and declare that any violence would be vain.

There was still a measure of doubt whether Maynard might be the culprit, and while now practically convinced, John took occasion, when next at Falcon Farm, to satisfy himself and learn whether Susan, or her father, could add certainty to his suspicion. It seemed impossible that, if such an intrigue were progressing, Joe Stockman should have failed to observe it.

He inquired, therefore, and learned more than he expected to learn.

John ascended from his work at dusk of a March evening. The sky was clear and the wind, now sunk, had blown from the north all day. The weather had turned very cold again after a mild spell, and already, under the first stars, frost was thrusting its needles out upon the still woodland pools.

From Hazel Tor arrived young Bamsey, and though tea was done at Falcon Farm, Susan brewed another pot and Joe listened to Johnny and spoke very definitely upon the subject of his concern.

"You say there's a murmur come to your ear that Orphan Dinah be tokened in secret, John; and as for that I know naught. It's a free country and she's a right to be married if the thought pleasures her; but when you ax if my cowman be the other party to the contract, then you ax me what another busy-body here and there have already axed, and I can say to you what I've said to them. Melindy was also wondering, and more than her; but I'll tell you most certain sure. Lawrence Maynard is a very understanding chap and I admire his parts and consider him, between ourselves, as about the best I've ever had in my employment. He thinks a lot of me also, as I happen to know, and he don't keep no secrets from me. 'Tis his fancy, perhaps, that I've got my share of intellects and know enough to be useful to the rising generation; but so it is, and he've come to me many a time with such cares as the young have got to face, being gifted with the old-fashioned idea that the wisdom of the old may be worth the trouble of hearing. That's a tip for you, Johnny, I dare say. And I can tell you that Maynard, though a kindly and reasonable creature, as would do any man, woman, or child a good turn, have no thought whatever of marrying. He's not for marriage—that's a cast-iron certainty; and you might so soon think Thomas Palk would venture—or even sooner. Tom have a poor pattern of mind that inclines him to discontent. My reading of him is that he might take the plunge if he was to find a big enough fool to go in with him."

"I wouldn't say that," argued Susan. "Thomas ain't blind to women, father. I've heard him say things as showed he marked their ways."

"Mark their ways the male must," replied Joe. "Their ways be everywhere, and they are half of life, and we admire 'em, according as they do their appointed duty, or shiver at 'em, when they get off the rails and make hateful accidents for the men, as often happens. But that's neither here nor there, and, be it as it will, of one thing you can clear your mind, Johnny. If there's any man after Dinah, it ain't my cowman, no more than it's my horseman, or anybody else I know about."

"He may be throwing dust in your eyes, however," argued John Bamsey.

"My eyes be growing dim, worse luck, along of using 'em to work as I would year after year—just for love of work; but they ain't so dim that the rising generation can throw dust in 'em yet. And now, since you seem so busy about it, let me ax in my turn what it matters to you anyway? We've all granted you had very hard luck, because Dinah changed her mind; but she did, as women be built to do, so what's the matter with you, and why be you making this upstore about her and her plans?"

"Because no living man shall have her while I'm above ground," answered the younger. "She's ruined my life, for nothing but cold-blooded wickedness and without any decent reason. And there is a man, and I'll find him. And Jane says it's Maynard."

"Then Jane's a damned little fool," answered Joe; "and you're a damned big one, if you can talk like that."

"It's wicked, John," declared Soosie-Toosie. "You ought to let the dead past bury the dead, I'm sure. And Jane is wicked too, and didn't ought to want for other women to be miserable, now she's going to be happy herself."

"'Tis a bee in your bonnet, John; and you'd best to get it out afore it stings you into foolishness," advised Joe. "You're talking evil nonsense and very well you know it. You mustn't think to spoil a woman's hopes of a home because she ain't got no use for yours. Be there only one girl in the world? Don't you properly tumble over the wenches every time you go into Ashburton? If you want to be married, set about it, and whatever you do, mind your own business, and don't talk about marring the business of other people—else you'll end by getting locked up."

Soosie-Toosie also rated the sufferer.

"And you brought up as you was, John," she said. "And thought to be the cleverest young man out of Lower Town. There's no rhyme nor reason in any such bad thoughts; and even if it was Lawrence Maynard, what quarrel have you got with him? Dinah's free and all the world to choose from, and if she's found a man she likes better'n she liked you, 'tis very ill-convenient for you to thrust between 'em. And no man worth his salt would stand it."

"Don't you talk," he answered roughly. "You don't know nothing about what it is to love and then be robbed. Love, such as I had for Dinah, be a thing too big for you neuter women to understand, and it's no more sense than a bird twittering for you to say anything on the subject. Dinah was mine, and if she's gone back on that, she's the wicked one, not me; and I'll do what I will."

"Don't you call Soosie-Toosie names anyhow," warned Joe. "She tells you the truth, John, and you'm making a very silly show of yourself—so funny as clown in a circus, my dear. And most men would laugh at you. But me and Susan are much too kind-hearted to do that. And as to Soosie being a neuter creature, that's great impertinence in you and I won't have it. And thank God there are neuter creatures, to act as a bit of a buffer sometimes between the breeders and their rash and wilful deeds. A pity there ban't more of 'em, for they're a darned sight more dignified and self-respecting than most of the other sort, and they do more good in the world nine times out of ten. You pull yourself together, John, else no decent girl will have any use for you. They want balance and common sense in a man, and something they can look up to and trust. All of which you had; so you get back to your proper mind and mend your manners and your way of speech."

"What better than that Dinah should come by a husband and get out of Green Hayes?" asked Susan. "You know very well it would be a good thing for all parties, and, I dare say, you'd very soon feel better yourself if she was out of your sight for good and all. And if there's a man ready and willing, it would be a most outrageous deed for you, or anybody, to try and stop it."

"Never heard better sense," declared Joe. "That's turning the other cheek that is; and if you find a female that's half as fine a Christian as Soosie—neuter or no neuter—you'll get more luck than you deserve."

John, however, was not minded to yield. He talked nonsense for half an hour, explained that he had been wickedly wronged and marvelled that they were so frosty and narrow as not to see it. He opened a spectacle of mental weakness, and when he was gone, Joe took somewhat gloomy views of him.

"Us'll hope the poison will work out," said Susan. "But who could have thought it was there?"

"I look deeper," answered her father. "Yesternight I met Chaffe, and he whispered to me, under oaths of secrecy, which you'll do well to keep, Susan, that Ben Bamsey won't never be the same again. His body's building up, but Arthur, who's very understanding and quick, fears that Ben's brain have took a shock from this great illness and be weakened at the roots. It weren't, even in his palmy days, what you might call a first class brain. He was a sweet-tempered, gentle creature with no great strength of mind, but so kindly and generous, that none troubled whether he had big intellects or no. Sometimes he did rage up wildly against injustice and wrong; and perhaps, if we understood such things, we should find he hadn't handed down to John such good wits and clear sight as we thought he had. Johnny was always excitable and a terror to a poacher and doubtful blade. And now it looks as if he was going to be a terror to himself—if nobody else."

"He'm so unforgiving," said Susan. "If he goes on like this, folk will very soon think they see why Dinah threw him over. 'Tis so silly to be obstinate over such a job. Surely, when a female tells a man she haven't got no use for him, that did ought to be a plain hint of her feelings."

"There be them whose memories are merciless," said Mr. Stockman. "God pity that sort, for they need it. If your memory's so built that it can't pass by a slight, or wrong, or misfortune, you have a hell of a life and waste a lot of brain stuff and energy. They can't help it; they stand outside time and it don't act on 'em. There are such people; but they're as rare as madmen— in fact hate, or love, that won't die decent is a form of madness; and that's how it is with Johnny."

"He ought to pray about it, didn't he? A parlous, withering thing for the chap."

"So it is, and I wish he could get it drawed out, like we draw out a bad tooth. For such torments foul the mind, and naught does it quicker than love carried beyond reason. That's one thing you'll always have to be thankful for, Soosie—one among many, I hope—that you was never tangled up with a man. 'Neuter' the rude youth called you; but that ain't the word, and even if it was, there can't be no sting to it seeing the shining angels of God be all neuters and our everlasting Creator's a neuter Himself."

"'Tis quite enough to have a soul; and you can't be a neuter ezacally if you've got that," said Susan.

"More you can then. And every human woman should take her consolation out of the thought," declared Joe. "Even the caterpillars turn into winged creatures, and when a left female be disposed to envy the wives and mothers, let her remember she's as safe for her wings and crown as the best of 'em and safer than many; and more likely to be happy up over when her time comes; for the larger the family, the more chance for black sheep among 'em; and where's the woman in heaven will have such peace as you, if she's always fretting her immortal soul out over some lost boy or girl in t'other place?"

These consolations, however, awoke no answering enthusiasm in Soosie-Toosie.

"I've heard Melindy say she didn't miss a family; but nature's nature," she answered, "and 'tis a great event to have bred an immortal creature, whether or no."

"When you say 'Melindy,' you lead my thoughts into another direction," declared the farmer. "To be plain, she's in my mind. She'll be a terrible lonely one for the future—unless—— In fact I'm turning it over."

This matter interested Soosie-Toosie more than most, for her own views were clear. She would have welcomed Mrs. Honeysett at Falcon Farm and believed that, from her personal point of view, such an advent must be to the good; but she felt by no means so sure whether it would result in happiness for her father.

"I could, of course, have her for the asking, if that was all that stood to it," mused Joe. "She'd come, and there's another here and there who'd come. Then I say to myself, 'What about you?'"

"No, you needn't say that. Your good's mine and I'm very fond of Melindy. She'd suit me down to the ground, father. You need only think of yourself; and the question is whether the sudden strain of another wife would interfere with your liberty."

"I know. You may be sure I shall look all round it. I've been married; but marriage in youth is far ways different from wedding in sight of seventy. If I was a selfish sort of man, I might take the step—for my own convenience—like David, and a good few since him; but I put you first, Soosie, and I'm none too sure whether a character like Melinda might not cut the ground from under your feet."

"She wouldn't do that. I know my place. But, of course, it would be terrible sad to me if she was to cut the ground from under yours, father."

"She's wonderful," admitted Joe. "But, on the whole, she ain't wonderful enough to do that. My feet be a lot too sure planted for any woman to cut the ground from under 'em, Soosie. However, 'tis a bootless talk—feet or no feet. I'm only mentioning that she'd come if I whistled—just a pleasant subject to turn over, but no more."

He smiled at his own power and Susan admired him.

"She would come, not being a fool and knowing the man you are; and if you want her, you can put out your hand and take her; but there's a lot would go with Melinda besides herself, if you understand me."

"What?" asked Mr. Stockman.

"I don't mean her bit of money; I mean her strong character and far reaching ideas and steadfast opinions."

"And think you I don't know all that? But such a man as me might very well rub off the edges of a woman's mind where they was like to fret."

Thus Joe, albeit he had not the smallest present intention of offering marriage to Melinda, liked to ponder on the thought that this fine woman would take him. The idea tickled his fancy, and Susan knew it; but she had not the discernment to perceive that it was only an idea—a vision from which her father won greater entertainment than the reality could promise.

CHAPTER XXVI
MR. PALK SEEKS ADVICE

An observer of life has remarked that it is pleasanter to meet such men as owe us benefits, than those to whom we owe them. When, therefore, Thomas Palk appeared one Saturday afternoon in the workshop of Arthur Chaffe at Lower Town, the carpenter, guessing he came for gratitude, was pleased to see him. It was a half holiday, but Mr. Chaffe ignored such human weaknesses. He held that the increased demand for shorter working hours was among the most evil signs of the times, failing to appreciate the difference between working for yourself and other people in this regard.

Thomas plunged into an expression of gratitude immediately while the carpenter proceeded with his business.

"We've got our rise, master, and Mr. Stockman named your name and said we had to thank you for the size of the lift—me and Maynard, that is. And hearing that, I felt it was duty to do it."

"And thank you also, Thomas. Few remember such things. Joe's a wonderful man and, like yourself, ain't above giving credit to them who earn it."

"He wouldn't have gone so far single-handed."

"Don't say that. I only pushed him along the road he was taking. The employer be always reluctant to see things are worth what they'll fetch, except when he's selling his own stuff. But the Trades Unions be bent on showing them. A world of changes, as poor Enoch used to say. Not that he had much use for Trades Unions. He'd read about the Guilds of the old days and held they was powerfuller and better for some things. And they thought of the workmanship: Trades Unions only think of the worker. What I call workmanship, such as you see in this shop, I hope, be a thing of the past, save among old men like me. But the joy of making be gone."

"There's some things have got to be done right and not scamped, however."

"True; the work on the land must be done right, or the face of the earth will show it. There's only one right way to drive a furrow, or milk a cow. You can't scamp and 'ca'canny' when you'm milking a cow, Thomas. But the joy of the workmanship be gone out of work in the young men. Wages come between them and the work of their hands, and while the bricklayer jaws to the hodman, the bricks go in anyhow. Patience be the first thing. Human nature's human nature, and 'tis no use wanting better bread than's made of wheat."

"If everybody was patient," said Mr. Palk, "then the hosses, and even the donkeys, would come into their own no doubt. But patience be too often mistook for contentment; and when the masters think you'm content, they be only too pleased to leave it at that."

"Yet impatience is the first uprooter of happiness," argued Mr. Chaffe. "Take a little thing like habits. Only yesterday a particular nice, clean old woman was grumbling to me because her husband's simple custom was to spit in the fire when he was smoking; and sometimes he'd miss the fire. A nasty vexation for her no doubt; but not a thing as ought to cast a shadow over a home. Our habits are so much a part of ourselves, that it never strikes us we can worry our friends with 'em; but if you consider how the habits of even them you care about often fret you, then you'll see how often your little ways fret them."

"No doubt 'tis well to be patient with your neighbour's habits, so long as they'm honest," admitted Mr. Palk.

"Certainly; because if you don't, you'll set him thinking and find you'll get as good as you give. Patience all round be the watchword, Tom, and it would save a power of friction if it was practised. Nobody knows where his own skeleton pinches but himself, and to rate folk harshly may be doing a terrible cruel thing and touching a raw the sufferer can't help."

"Like Ben Bamsey," said the horseman. "'Tis whispered he've grown tootlish since his famous illness. That'll call for patience at Green Hayes."

"True love's always patient, my dear. Yes, the poor old man be sinking into the cloud, and the only bright thought is that he won't know it, or suffer himself. But them with brains will suffer to see him back in childhood. Yet he was always a childlike man and none the worse for it. The light's growing dim, and doctor says he'll fade gradual till he don't know one from another. And then, such is human nature, his family will change gradual too, and forget what he was, and come slow and sure to think of him as a thing like the kettle, or washing day—just a part of life and a duty and not much more."

"Better he'd died."

"You mustn't say that. He may very like have a stroke and go soon, doctor says; but he'll live so long as he's useful here to his Maker. He'll be a reminder and a lesson and a test of character. His wife will see he don't come to be just a shadow, like a picture on the wall—so will I, so far as I can. He's been a very great friend of mine and always will be, wits or no wits."

Mr. Palk, impressed with these opinions, was inspired to ask a question that had long troubled him. He had never made a very close confident of Maynard, feeling the man too young, and also doubting his ideas on various topics; but here was a Christian of general esteem and one older than himself. He debated the point while a silence fell, save for the noise of Arthur's plane.

"Tell me this," he said suddenly. "By and large would you reckon that if a man sees a wrong thing being done—or what seems a wrong thing in his eyes—did he ought to seek to right it? It ain't his business in a manner of speaking; and yet, again, wrong be everybody's business; and yet, again, others might say it weren't a wrong at all and the man's judgment in fault to say it was wrong."

Arthur cast down his plane and pondered this somewhat vague proposition. But his quick mind, even while considering the case, found a subconscious way of also speculating as to what lay behind it. He knew everybody's affairs and was familiar with a rumour that Maynard secretly paid court to Dinah Waycott. For some reason he suspected that this might be in the mind of Maynard's fellow-worker.

"You put the question very well, Tom, and yet make it a bit difficult to answer," he said. "For it ain't a straight question, but hemmed about with doubt. If you was to say you saw wrong being done and asked me if you ought to try and right it, than I should answer you that it was your bounden duty to try to right it and not let anything come between. But you ban't sure in your mind if it is wrong being done, so that's the point you've got to fasten on and clear up; and until I know more of the facts of the case, I couldn't say more than that you must be sure afore you set about it."

Thomas Palk considered this speech and did not immediately reply, while Arthur spoke again.

"Have you heard anybody else on the subject, or be it a thing only come to your own notice? Mind I don't want to know a word about it—only to help you, or, if it ain't you yourself, whoever it may be."

"It is me," answered the other. "And I see what I take to be a wrong thing going on. I don't feel no doubt myself; but I can't say as anybody else but me seems to see it. And if I was to up and say I thought so, which I ban't at all feared to do, I might open his eyes, or I might not."

"Would you be harming anybody if it was took in a wrong spirit?"

"It didn't ought to."

"There's no anger to it, nor nothing like that, Thomas?"

"Not a bit. I'm very friendly disposed to all concerned."

"Mind—don't you answer if you don't want; but is there a woman in it, Thomas?"

Mr. Palk considered.

"If there was?"

"Then be terrible careful."

"There is—and that's all I be going to tell you," answered Mr. Palk, growing a little uneasy.

The carpenter doubted not that here lay direct allusion to Dinah and Lawrence; but he had no motive, beyond inherent curiosity, for going farther into that matter then. Indeed, he saw the gathering concern of Mr. Palk and sought only to put him at his ease.

"You're not a boy," he said. "And you have got plenty of experience of human nature and a Christian outlook. I should fall back on my religion if I was you, Tom, for you can trust that to lead over the doubtfullest ground. You're not a joker-head, as would rush in and make trouble along of hasty opinions; and if you think what's doing be wrong, and if you think a word in season might do good and make the mistaken party hesitate afore he went on with it, then, in my judgment, you'd do well and wisely to speak. But keep the woman in your mind and do naught to hurt her."

Mr. Palk expired a deep breath of satisfaction at this counsel.

"So be it," he said. "I'll do it; and for the sake of a female it will be done."

"Then you won't have it on your conscience, whether or no, Thomas."

"'Tis my conscience be doing of it," said Mr. Palk; "it can't be nothing else."

Nevertheless he felt a measure of doubt on this point. His motives were beyond his own power of analysis.

"I might come and let you know the upshot one day," he said.

"You'll be welcome, and all the more so if I can do you a good turn," promised Mr. Chaffe; then Thomas went his way.

There now awaited him a very formidable deed; but he was determined not to shrink from it, while still quite unable to explain to himself the inspiration to anything so tremendous.

CHAPTER XXVII
DISCOVERY

Circumstances swept Thomas to action sooner than he had intended and, though slow of wits, he was quickened to grasp an opportunity and essay his difficult and dangerous adventure. He had convinced himself that conscience must be the mainspring of the enterprise and assured his mind that, with such a guide, he might feel in no doubt of the result. Even if he failed and received the reward that not seldom falls to well doing, he would be able to sustain it when he considered his motives.

There came an occasion on which Joe Stockman declared himself to be ill in the tubes; and as the fact interfered with certain of his own plans, it caused him much depression and irritation. Indeed he was greatly troubled at the passing weakness and took care that Falcon Farm should share his own inconvenience. He railed and was hard to please. He reminded Palk and Maynard of their rise and hoped they would not imitate the proletariat in general and ask for more and more, while doing less and less. He criticised and carped; and while the men suffered, his daughter endured even more than they. It was possible for Lawrence and Thomas to escape to their work, and since Joe held the open air must not for the present be faced, they were safe for most of their time; but Soosie-Toosie found herself not so happily situated and when, after dinner on a wet and stormy day in early May, her father decided that he must have a mustard and linseed poultice that night, a bottle of brown sherry and a certain lozenge efficacious for the bronchial tubes, despite the atrocious weather, she gladly consented to make the journey to Ashburton.

"'Tis too foul for you to go. Better let me," ventured Thomas, when the need arose; but Mr. Stockman negatived his proposal.

"The weather's mending as any fool can see," he said, "and if it comes on worse, you'd best to take a cab home, Susan. 'Twill be the doctor to-morrow if I ban't seen to; and Lord He knows how such as me can pay doctors, with wages up and prices down same as now."

"I'm wishful to go," answered his daughter. "You bide close by the fire and I'll be gone this instant moment. Washing up can bide till I come back."

"If the pony wasn't in sight of foaling, you could have took the cart," answered Joe; "but that's outside our powers to-day. And I wouldn't ax you if I didn't think a breath of air would do you good. I know what 'tis to pine for it."

"It will do me good," she answered, and soon was gone, through lanes where the mad, spring wind raved and flung the rain slantwise and scattered fields and roads with young foliage torn off the trees.

Thomas Palk saw her go and his heart grew hard. He proceeded with his work for an hour, then the ferment within him waxed to boiling point and he prepared to strike at last. He went indoors, changed his wet jacket and entered the kitchen, where Joe sat sighing and gurgling over the fire with a tumbler of hot whisky and water beside him.

"You!" he said. "God's light! Be you feared of the weather too?"

"You know if I'm feared of weather, master. But I be taking half an hour off. There's naught calling for me special and I'm going over some weak spots in the stable timber where we want fresh wood. The big plough hoss chews his crib and us must run a bit of sheet tin over it I reckon; and there's dry rot too. But I want a word, and I'll be very much obliged to you if you'll bear with me for a few minutes."

"I bear with life in general, including you, Thomas; so speak and welcome," answered Mr. Stockman, "though I hope it's nothing calling for any great feats of mind on my part. When I get a cold in the tubes, it withers my brain like a dry walnut for the time being."

Thomas felt rather glad to know this. It might mean that his master was less able to flash retort.

"No, no," he said. "I couldn't put no tax upon your brain—ain't got enough myself. 'Tis a small matter in one sense and yet in another a large matter. Lookers on see most of the game, as they say; and though I ban't no nosey-poker, and far too busy a man, I hope, to mind any business but my own, yet, there 'tis: I live here and I can't but see us did ought to have another female servant under this roof."

"And why for, Thomas, if you'll be so good as to explain?" asked Mr. Stockman.

"Now we be coming to it," answered the horseman. "And I beg you in Christian charity to take it as it is meant—respectful and as man to master. But there 'tis: the reason why for we want another woman here is that there be a lot too much for one woman to do. And that means, as I see it, that Miss Stockman's doing the work of two women. And such things be easily overlooked, especially in her case, because she's a towser for work and don't know herself that she's got far too much upon her. She's just slipped into it, and 'tis only by looking at the affair from outside you see it is so; and through nobody's fault in particular but just by chance; yet certainly she's doing more than a human creature ought; for her work's never ended. You say you done the work of ten in your palmy days, master, so perhaps it don't fret you to see her doing the work of two at least; but the female frame ban't built to do more than a fair day's work, and in my humble opinion, as a friend of the family and proud so to be, Miss Susan's toiling a lot harder than be safe for her health; and I feel cruel sure as some day the strain will tell and she'll go all to pieces, like a worn-out engine. Not that she'd ever grumble. This very day she'll be properly drowned out afore she comes home; and I dare say will be too busy working at you when she comes back to put off her wet clothes, or think of herself. But there it is; I do believe she moils and toils beyond the limit, and I point it out and hope you'll take it as 'tis meant, from a faithful servant of the family. And if it was the other way round and I had a girl I was making work too heavy—from no unkindness, but just because I'd got used to it—if it was like that and you called my attention to it, I'd be very thankful, master."

"Capital, Thomas," said Mr. Stockman. "Never heard your tongue flow so suent afore. You go on and say all you feel called to say, then I'll answer you, if you'll allow me."

"That's all," answered Palk. "And I hope all well inside civility and my place. And, as man to man, I do pray you won't be put about nor yet feel I've said a word beyond my duty."

Joe appeared quite unangered and indeed only mildly interested. He sipped at his glass; then lighted his pipe and drew at it for half a minute before he replied.

"Every man has a right to do and say what he feels to be his duty, Thomas. And women likewise. It's a free country in fact—or so we pretend—and I should be very sorry to think as you, or Maynard, or the boy even, was bound to endure my tyrant manners and customs a minute longer than your comfort could put up with 'em. But that cuts both ways, don't it? An all-seeing eye like yours will grant that?"

"I ain't got an all-seeing eye, master. 'Tis only the point of view. And of course we could go if we was wishful to go, which we are not I'm sure. But a man's daughter be different. She can't go very well, can she?"

"She cannot," admitted Mr. Stockman. "And I've yet to hear she's fretting to do so. This place is her home, and she's stood at her father's right hand ever since he was doomed to widowhood. And I may be wrong, of course, but I've always laboured under the opinion she loved her parent and was proud and pleased to be the crown of his grey hairs. She can't well desert me, as you say. But in your case, Thomas, the position is a bit otherwise. You can go when you please, or when I please. 'Tis well within your power to seek other work, where your kind heart won't be torn watching a daughter do her duty by a sick father; and 'tis well within my power to wish you to go. And I do wish it. I'm wishing it something tremendous this moment."

Mr. Stockman smiled genially and continued.

"In a word, fine chap that you are and a willing worker, with good methods and worthy of my praise—which you've had—I'm going to get along without you now, and so we'll part Monday month, if you please. And delighted I shall be to give you a right down good character for honesty and sound understanding—where the hosses are concerned."

Mr. Palk had not expected this. He was much bewildered.

"D'you mean it, master?" he asked, with eyes not devoid of alarm.

"I do, my dear. I never meant anything with a better appetite. A great loss, because with one like me—old and stricken before my time, along of working far too hard, which was a foolish fault in my generation—it was a comforting thing to feel I'd got a hossman in you worthy of the name. You be the pattern of a good, useful sort, that's dying out—worse luck. But when you said you wasn't a nosey-poker, Thomas, you said wrong, I'm afraid; and a meddlesome man, that has time to spare from the hosses for the women, and thrusts in between parent and child, be very much against the grain with me. And though, of course, you may be quite right, and know better how to treat and cherish a grown-up daughter than a stupid creature like me—and you a bachelor—yet even the worm will turn, Thomas. And, worm though I am, I be going to venture to turn. You're great on the point of view; and so will I be: and, from my point of view, I can see you haven't got enough work to do in this little place. You must go in the world and find a bigger and a harder job, that won't leave you time for other people's business, which at best be a kicklish task and avoided by men of much wits as a rule."

"I meant well, master."

"And don't you always mean well? Why, you're the most well-meaning man, after myself, I ever had the luck to meet, Thomas. But you've fixed a gulf to-day, and I feel terrible sure we shan't suit each other no more. So we'll part friends Monday month."

Joe spoke with far greater cordiality than when raising Mr. Palk's wages six weeks before. He beamed graciously on Thomas and lighted his pipe again.

"The talk be at an end now, because I mustn't strain my tubes," he said. "And I'll beg you not to return to the subject. Both me and my God are very well satisfied with the way I brought up Soosie-Toosie, and so's she; and if she feels there's anything on this earth I can do for her, to make her home a happier place, rest assured she'll ax me herself. She's my master-jewel and always will be, though she'll never know all I've done for her, because no child ever can know the heights and depths of a good father's love. 'A good father,' mark me, Thomas."

"Monday month then, master?"

"If quite convenient to yourself."

Then Palk went out into storm and gathering dusk. The woods of Buckland waved grey through the gloaming and rain swept them heavily. The wind shouted over the granite crown of the Beacon; sheep and cattle had crept down from the high land and stood in the shelter of walls and woods.

Thomas considered with himself. He was in a state as perturbed as it was possible for such a stolid spirit to be; but he remembered that the innocent cause of this revolution was now returning heavy laden up the long hill from the market town.

He decided that he would go and meet Susan. His upheaval took the form of increased solicitude for Miss Stockman.

"She shall hear the fatal news from me—not him," he reflected.

He set off and presently sighted the woman tramping up the hill in the rain. Under the wild weather and fading light, she looked like some large, bedraggled moth blown roughly about. Her basket was full and her left arm held a parcel in blue paper. It was the only spot of colour she offered. They met, greatly to her surprise.

"Good Lord!" she said. "Have father put more chores on you? Be you going to Ashburton?"

"I am not," he answered. "I came out with my big umbrella to meet you."

She was fluttered.

"How terrible kind! But 'tis no odds. I be bone-wet."

Nevertheless, Mr. Palk unfurled a large, faded, glass-green umbrella over her.

"Give me the basket," he said, "and I'll walk betwixt you and the weather. I come for more reasons than one, Susan. Something's happened while you were to town and I'd sooner you heard it from me than him."

"Nought gone wrong with father?"

"That's for others to say. But something have gone parlous wrong with me."

She started and hugged her blue paper parcel closer. It contained the bottle of brown sherry.

"I hope not, I'm sure."

"In a word, I'm sorry to say I leave Falcon Farm Monday month. It have fallen with a terrible rush upon me—and my own fault too. I can't tell you the reason, but so it is. The master's sacked me; and every right to do so, no doubt, in his own eyes."

Miss Stockman stood still and panted. Her face was wet with rain; her hair touzled; her hat dripping.

"Be you saying truth?" she asked, and fetched a handkerchief from her pocket and dried her face.

"Gospel. I done a thing as he took in a very unkind spirit I'm sorry to say."

The blue parcel trembled.

"Going—you? Never!"

"Monday month it have got to be."

"Why for? What have you gone and done? It must have been something properly fearful, for he thought the world of you, behind your back."

"To my face, however, he did not—not this evening. And as to what I done, I hope he won't feel called to name it in your ear. It was a very dangerous task, as I reckoned when I started on it; but I felt drove—Lord knows why! I meant well, but that don't amount to much when you fail. No doubt he'll get somebody he likes better; and he won't withhold a good character neither."

"This be a cruel come-along-of-it," she said blankly. "I couldn't have heard nothing to trouble me more, Thomas. You was the bestest we've ever had to Falcon Farm—and kindness alive."

"Thank you I'm sure. We've been very good friends. And why not?"

"I can't picture you gone. 'Twas a rit of temper. I'll speak to father."

"Don't you do that. There weren't no temper, nor yet language. He meant it and he's an unchanging man."

"Whatever did he say? What did you do? I will know! It shan't be hid. Perhaps 'tis only his tubes fretting him."

"No—nothing to do with his tubes. He was well within his rights. Not that I'll allow he was right, however."

"Why can't you tell me what it is then? If you want to stop—but perhaps you don't?"

He considered.

"I never thought to go, and I never wanted to go less than what I do at this minute, seeing you cast down. I be very much obliged to you in a manner of speaking for not wanting me to go."

She looked up drearily at him and sniffed.

"We never know our luck," she said. "Not you, but me."

To his intense amazement he perceived that Susan was shedding tears. She shook her head impatiently and it was not rain that fell from her face. If a small fire can kindle a great one, so surely may a drop of water swell into a river.

Light began to dawn in the mind of the man and it much astonished him by what it revealed there. He was, in fact, so astounded by the spectacle that he fell into silence and stared with mental eyes at the explanation of the mysteries that had long puzzled him. His next remark linked past with present.

"Be damned if I don't begin to know now why for I done this!" he said with a startled voice. "I've wondered for weeks and weeks what was driving me on, and I couldn't put no name to it, Susan; but 'tis coming out in me. Shut your mouth a minute and let me think."

She kept silence and they plodded on. At the top of the hill a gust caught the umbrella and it was in peril. Thomas turned it against the wind.

"Come under the lew side of the hedge," he said. "I thought 'twas conscience driving at me—but I begin to see it weren't. There's a wonder happening. Fetch in here under the trees a minute."

She followed him through a gap at the summit of the hill and they left the road for the partial shelter of spruce firs. They escaped the wind, but the rain beat from the branches upon Mr. Palk's umbrella.

"You're a woman of very high qualities and a good bit undervalued in your home—so it seems to me. You're the light of the house, but 'twas left for others to find that out seemingly—not your father. He's a man with a soft tongue, but a darned hard heart—to say it respectful."

"I'm naught and less than naught. But I was always pleased to pleasure you," she answered.

"The light of the house," he repeated. "And 'tis the light be far more to the purpose than the candlestick. I can speak to you straight, Susan, because I'm ugly as sin myself and not ashamed of it. I didn't have the choosing of my face, and my Maker didn't ax me what I'd like to look like come I grew up. And same with you. But you be a living lesson to us other plain people, and show us that the inside may be so fine no thinking man would waste a thought on the outside."

Susan was not concerned with his philosophy: she had fastened on a question of fact.

"You're not particular ugly, Thomas. I've seen scores plainer. You've got a very honest face and nice grey eyes if I may say so."

"Certainly you may say so, and I'm very well content as you've been to the trouble to mark the colour of my eyes. 'Tis a way women have. They always know the colour of their friends' eyes. And if my face be honest in your opinion, that's good news also. And as for your eyes, if they was in a prettier setting, they'd well become it."

Susan grew a dusky red, but kept to the point.

"If you can say such things as that, surely you can tell me why you're going?"

"I meddled—I—but leave the subject. 'Tis all dust and ashes afore what's stirring in my head now—now I know why I meddled. You'd like me to bide at Falcon Farm seemingly?"

"I should then. You've got nice ways, and—and you've always been amazing pitiful to me."

"Where would your father be if you left him?"

"I'll never leave him. He knows that."

"How old might you be?"

"Thirty-five—thirty-six come October."

"Some say port-wine marks are handed down, and again some say they are not. And if you was to hand it down, you'd hand down what's better too, I shouldn't wonder."

She did not answer, but gasped and stared in front of her.

"Look here," he said. "Now I see so plain why for I done this, why the mischief shouldn't you? 'Twas done because I've risen up into loving you, Susan! I want you—I want to marry you—I'll take my dying oath I do. It have just come over me like a flap of lightning. Oh, hell!"

The bottle of wine had trembled dangerously in Soosie-Toosie's arm before; now it dropped, broke on a stone, and spread its contents at their feet. The sweet air suddenly reeked of it. But Susan ignored the catastrophe.

"Me! Me! My God, you must be mad!"

"If so, then there's a lot to be said for being mad. But I ain't. I see the light. I've been after you a deuce of a time and never grasped hold of it. I didn't think to marry. In fact my mother was the only woman I ever cared a cuss about till I seed you. And no doubt, for your part you've long despaired of the males; but you'm a born wife, Susan; and you might find me a very useful pattern of husband. I love you something tremenjous, and I should be properly pleased if you could feel the same."

"'Tis beyond dreaming," she said regarding him with wild eyes. "'Tis beyond belief, Thomas."

"It may be," he admitted, "but not beyond truth. We can make it a cast-iron fact; and 'tis no odds who believes it, so long as it happens."

"You be above yourself for the minute. Your face is all alight. Best to think it over and go to church and let a Sunday pass. I can't believe you really and truly mean it."

"God's truth I do then."

"Father—did I ought to put love of you afore love of him, Thomas?"

"Certainly you did ought, and you've got the Bible behind you. If you love me, then you did ought to put me afore every damn thing, and cleave to me for ever after. Say you'll do it, like a dear woman. I want to hear you say it, Susan. 'Twill cheer me up a lot, because I've never had the sack afore in my life and don't like the taste of it. I be feeling low, and 'twill be a great thing to get back on farmer afore I go to bed to-night."

She was suspicious at once.

"You ban't doing this out of revenge, however?" she asked.

"For naught but love—that I'll swear."

"To be loved by a fine man—a go-by-the-ground creature like me!"

"And never no female better fit for it."

"I'll take you, Thomas; but if you change your mind after you've slept on it, I shan't think no worse of you. Only this I'll say, I do love you, and I have loved you a longful time, but paid no attention to it, not understanding."

"Then praise the Lord for all His blessings, I'm sure."

He held her close in his arms and they kissed each other. She clung to him fervently.

"Now, if you'll take the basket, I'll go back and buy another bottle of sherry wine," she said.

"Not at all. But we mustn't shatter the man at one blow. He'll want more than pretty drinking when he hears about this. I'll traapse down for another bottle, and you go home under my umbrella; and change every stitch on you, and drink something hot, else you might fall ill."

"Ah! That's love! That's love!" she said, looking up at him wet-eyed.

"No—only sense. I'll show 'e what love be so soon as I know myself. You get home, and say as you dropped your bottle and was just going back for another when I met you, on my way to Ashburton, and offered to get it. And on the whole us'll keep the fearful news for a few days till he's well again. 'Twill be more merciful."

"You'm made of wisdom, Tom. 'Tis a great relief to keep it from father a bit till I've got used to the thought."

"Kiss me again then," he answered, and put his arms round her once more.

"There's a brave lot of 'e to cuddle whether or no."

"'Tis all yours I'm sure, if you really want it, dear Thomas."

"I be coming to want it so fast as I can, woman!"

CHAPTER XXVIII
THE LAW

For Dinah Waycott the sole difficulty of her position began to clear itself; and since she was now convinced that she and Lawrence saw the future with the same vision, she felt that future approach quickly. It seemed, however, that for her, pure joy could only be reached through sorrow, and on an occasion of meeting Maynard upon the moor, she said so.

"Nothing ever do run quite smooth, and out of my misfortune my fortune comes. For it's only a terrible sad thing that be clearing the road for us and leaving nobody in my life to think of but you."

She had assumed somewhat more than her lover at this point, and in a sense, taken the lead.

"Your foster-father?" he said.

"Yes; it's a pretty dark cloud against my happiness, and if it was only for that, I'd be glad to be gone. You can't say yet he don't know me; but you can say he very soon won't. We seem to slip away from him according as he cared for us. He don't know Jane no more at all, and asks her what he can do for her when she comes in the room. But he knows Johnny off and on, and he knows me off and on too. His wife he still knows, and I can see it's life and death to her that he shall go on knowing her; because it will be a great triumph for her if, when he's forgot everybody, he still remembers her."

"I dare say it would be."

"I'd have been jealous as fire that he shouldn't forget me, if it hadn't been for you. But not now. I won't be sorry to leave him now, and just love to remember what he was to me. To think I could ever say that! It's cruel sad, poor old dear."

"There's a bright side, however," he answered. "And though you might say no man could be worse off than to lose his wits, yet for poor old Ben there's one good thing: he'll never know you've gone, or how you've gone."

"I've thought of that; but how can you be sure, if he'd had the mind left to understand, he wouldn't have been glad for me? He liked you."

"You know different, Dinah. He liked me; but he'd never have been glad, given the facts."

She was silent and Lawrence spoke again.

"He's only a shadow of a man now and will grow more and more faint, till he fades away. But you'll have the grateful memory of him."

"Yes; and if ever we get a son, Lawrence, he must be called Benjamin—I will have it so."

He fell silent. Dinah often spoke with delight of children; and it was at those times the man felt the drag on his heart hardest. They had argued much, but her frank puzzlement and even amusement at his problems and doubts began to wear them down. She knew it, but, behind her assumption of certainty, still suspected him a little. He varied and seemed more inclined to listen than to talk. But things were rushing to a conclusion and there could only be one.

It was agreed that they must now hide their friendship and their purpose for the sake of other people. Dinah grew full of plans, and Lawrence listened while she ran on; but she knew that the real plans would be made by him. A sort of vagueness came into their relation and its cause was in his head, not his heart. That, too, she knew. But certain things to-day he told her and certain things, unknown to him, she now determined to do. Impatience must have been created for Dinah this evening, but that she understood his doubts were solely on her account. She believed that nothing but questions of law remained to deter Maynard, and of their utter insignificance she had often assured him.

"I've got the facts," he said, "and I'd like for you to hear them. And, after to-night, we mustn't see each other so often. To make it easier for us when we go, we'd better keep as far apart as need be till then. There's a lot must pass between us and we can't post letters very well—not in the pillar-boxes; but we may want a pillar-box of our own presently."

"What I hate about life," she cried, "is that you've got to pretend such a lot. If this had happened to Jane, she'd love the hiding up and the plotting and turning and twisting, like a hare running away from the hounds. But I hate it. I hate to think the world's full of people, who look at life in such a way that what we're going to do must be wrong."

"They've been brought up with fixed ideas about marriage and think it's got more to do with God than with men and women. The interests of the Church are put high above right and justice for the people. They always were; and them that claim marriage is God's plan, also claim that He would chain wretched, mistaken creatures together for life, quite regardless of their honour and decency and self-respect. It's funny that educated men should write the stuff I read; but the moment you see the word 'God' in a newspaper, you can say good-bye to reason and pity. We're punished—we who make a mistake—for what? Oft for nothing but misreading character, or because truth's withheld from us on purpose. Palk was telling of a man he knew who went courting and was never told his intended's mother was in a mad-house. And he married, and his wife went out of her mind with her first child. Now she's got to be put away and may live for fifty years, and sane, well-meaning people tell the man he must bide a widower for ever-more—at the will of God! God wills he should go alone to his dying day, because his wife's people hid the truth from him."

"But the law—surely the law——?"

"The law's with the Church so far. They hunt in couples. But the law's like to be altered 'tis thought; though no doubt the Church will call down fire from Heaven if any human mercy and common sense and decency is brought to bear on marriage."

"Can't the religious people see that lots quite as good as them, and quite as willing and wishful to do right are being put in the wrong? And can't they see tortured men and women won't be patient for ever?"

"No; they put us in the wrong and they keep us in the wrong, for God's sake—so He shan't be vexed. They don't understand it isn't only adultery that breaks up marriage, but a thousand other things beside. It's human progress and education and understanding; and these pious people only leave one door to escape through. And they don't seem to see that to decent thinking and self-respecting men and women that's a door they won't enter. They say, 'If you want to right your mistake, you must sin.' But if Almighty God made marriage, He never made such filth to be thrust down the throats of them that fail in marriage. Thus, any way, it stands with Minnie Courtier at present—and with me. This is the law and clear enough. A man disappears and blots himself out of life, you may say, and, what's more important, blots himself out of the lives of everybody who knew him, including his wife. And the question is, what can the wife do about it? I've looked into this very close, and I find the issue is like a lot of other things in the law. It often depends on the judge, and how he reads the facts of the case, and whether he's all for the letter of the law, or one of the larger-minded sort, who give the spirit a chance. A man not heard about for seven years may be counted dead in the eyes of the law; but there's no presumption he died at any particular time in the seven years, and it isn't enough to say, 'Seven years are past and I'm in the right to presume somebody dead.' You must have legal permission, and judges differ. You've got to prove that diligent inquiries were made to find the vanished person before you apply to the Court, and a human sort of judge is satisfied as a rule and doesn't torment the public and sets a man or woman free. But if circumstances show that the vanished party wouldn't be heard of, even if he was alive, then many frost-bound judges won't allow he's dead, or grant freedom to a deserted partner even after seven years. So, now, though the seven years are up, even if application was made to assume my death, it rests on the character of the judge whether Mrs. Courtier would be allowed to do so."

"She may not care a button about it one way or the other," said Dinah— "any more than I do."

"Very likely. It's only of late that I've spared a thought to her. There's very little doubt in my mind that she's settled down to being a widow—had enough of men I reckon."

"You don't know, however?"

"I don't know—and it's time I did, I suppose. But how?"

Dinah considered.

"She's a clever woman and she may find herself very well content to keep herself to herself as you say. Or she may not. One thing's sure; she'll never forgive you, and she wouldn't do nothing to help you if she could."

"She can't help, any more than she can hinder."

"'Tis a great thought—that woman. I'd give a lot to know a bit about her," said Dinah. "Suppose, for example——"

Then she broke off, for her mind had suddenly opened a path which must be followed alone, if followed at all. A possibility had occurred to Dinah—a possibility of vague and shadowy outline, but still not quite devoid of substance. She wondered intensely about a certain thing, and since, when she wondered, her spirit never rested until some answer to her wonderment was forthcoming, she felt now that this problem must be approached. Indeed it was no sooner created than it possessed her, to the destruction of every lesser idea. She was on the verge of uttering it to Lawrence, but controlled herself. He might disagree, and she could brook no disagreement, even from him, before this sudden impulse. There was hope in it for them both. She acknowledged to herself that the hope must be small; but it existed.

She changed the subject with suspicious abruptness, but Maynard, following his own thoughts, which led in a different direction, did not observe that after her hiatus and a silence following on it, Dinah resumed about something else. He had also left the facts and drifted to the future.

The suggestion that he himself had raised: to attempt some inquiry concerning his wife, though obvious enough to any third person, did not impress itself upon him as important. He mentioned it and dismissed it. He felt sufficiently certain of her and her present state. The details of his own future presented more attractive and pressing problems. For he was now affirmed to go—either with Dinah, or before her, on an understanding that she would follow. For the present they must certainly part and be associated no more—either by rumour or in reality.

Upon these thoughts she struck, so naturally that it seemed they were unconsciously communicating in their minds.

"We must set up a post office, Lawrence, where the letters won't need stamps; and for the minute I'd be glad if you could give me a few shillings for pocket-money. I've got a hatred now of Bamsey money and the five shillings a week Mrs. Bamsey gives me, because foster-father's past doing it himself. And I've told them that I'm not going to take any of his money in the future. I've told them very clear about that and I mean it."

"I'm glad you have. But they won't agree."

"So they say; but I shall be far ways off, beyond their reach or knowledge, long before then. And Jane knows clearly I won't touch it."

Maynard brought out a little leathern purse and gave Dinah the contents—some thirty shillings.

She thanked him and assured him that would be enough. They parted soon afterwards and arranged to meet once more, on a date a fortnight hence, in late evening, at a certain gate not above a mile from Green Hayes.

"I may have something to tell you by then," she said, "and I'll find a post office. It'll be a year till I see you again."

He took a lingering leave of her and was moved by a last word she spoke at parting.

"We never get no time to love each other," she said, "'tis all hard, hateful talk and plotting. But we'll make up to each other some day."

Then he went his way, leaving her to develop her secret determination.

Conscience smote Dinah that she should enter upon any such adventure without telling him; but the fear that he might forbid her was too great, for she felt very positive the step she designed must be to the good. Certain precious and definite knowledge at least would follow; and the worst that could happen would only leave them where they were.

She meant to go to Barnstaple. When she had broken off her speech, she was about to put it to Maynard whether the woman there might not be in his own position—desirous to marry and perhaps even already seeking the aid of the law to free herself from a vanished spouse. It seemed intensely possible to Dinah; but evidently in the mind of Lawrence no such likelihood existed. That he should not have followed the thought showed how little importance he attached to it—so little that she felt sure he would not have supported her sudden desire to learn more. Therefore she kept the inspiration from him and determined he should know nothing until her quest was accomplished.

And, he, having left her, now endeavoured, as he had endeavoured for many days, to shake his mind clear of cobwebs and traditions and prevenient fears. Even his thoughts for her seemed petty when he was with her. Deeply he longed for Dinah, and the peace that she must bring to his mind, and the contentment inevitable out of a life shared with hers.

Perhaps for the first time he now resolutely banished every doubt, thrust them behind him, and devoted all future thought to their departure from England. He inclined to Australia now from all that he had read and heard about it. There he would take Dinah, and there, as "Lawrence Maynard," he would marry her.

He began to look back upon his doubts as unmanly and mawkish; he began to marvel that, for so many painful months, he had entertained them. He assured himself that the air was clean and cloudless at last, and designed to advance the situation by definite preliminary steps before he met Dinah again.

CHAPTER XXIX
JOE TAKES IT ILL

Melinda Honeysett came to see Mr. Stockman, and it happened that she paid her visit but half an hour after heavy tidings had fallen on his ears.

From the moment of her arrival, she was aware of something unusual in his manner, and presently she learned from him all particulars.

He was in his garden, sitting alone under a little arbour constructed at the side of the house with its eye in the sun; and there he sat with his hands in his pockets, idle, staring before him. Even the customary pipe was absent from his mouth. He was restored to health, as Melinda knew; but she felt at a loss to see him dawdling thus at noon. He looked old and dejected too, nor did he rise to greet her when she entered the garden.

She approached him therefore, and he gazed indifferently and dull-eyed upon her.

"Morning, Joe. They cabbages you gave me be all bolting* I'm sorry to say, and Mr. Ford, my next door neighbour, tells me I can't do nothing."

* "Bolting" —running to seed.

"Ban't the only things that's bolting. Funny as you should be the one to face me after what I've just heard."

"You'm down seemingly?"

"Down and out you might say without straining the truth. It's a blasted world, though the sun do be happening to shine. I've had the hardest blow of my life this morning. I'm still wondering if I ban't in an evil dream."

"Terrible sorry I'm sure. Good and bad luck don't wait for the weather. I be in trouble, too—more or less. Jerry and Jane Bamsey have fallen out and I'm in two minds—sorry for Jerry, and yet not all sorry, for father always said she wasn't any good. Yet I don't know what Jerry will do if it don't come right."

Mr. Stockman seemed totally uninterested at this news. He still looked before him and brooded. Melinda took a cane chair, which stood near his, and mopped her face, for she was hot.

"Only a lovers' quarrel I dare say; but if it was broke off altogether I reckon my brother might live to be thankful. And Orphan Dinah's gone to find work somewhere. I hope she will this time. Jane thinks she's run away to get married."

"Marriage—marriage!" he said. "Perdition take all this bleating about marriage! I'm sick to death of it, as well I may be."

She was astonished.

"I never heard you talk against it for them so inclined. Marriage is a good bit in the air this summer I believe. My sailor brother, Robert, be coming home for a spell pretty soon. And he writes me as he'll wed afore he goes back to sea, if he can find one. And I thought of Dinah. And Mr. Ford, the gardener, next to me—I reckon he means to marry again. He's got a great opinion of the state. Harry Ford's my own age to a day, strange to say. Our birthdays fall together. He had no luck with his wife, but he's going to try again I can see."

"I don't want to hear no more about him, or anybody else," said Mr. Stockman. "'Tis doubtful manners mentioning him to me. If you knew what I know, you'd be dumb with horror."

"Well, I can't be horrified if you won't tell me why I should. Where's Soosie-Toosie?"

She received a shattering answer.

"To hell with Soosie-Toosie!" cried Joe.

"Man alive, what's got into you? Be you ill again, or is it Palk leaving? If that's the trouble, lift your finger and he'll stay. You do that. I lay he meant nothing but good, standing up for Susan. He's a clumsy, ignorant creature; but you're always quick to forgive faults a man can't help. Pardon the chap and let him bide. I've always told you it was going too far to sack him on that. Don't be craking about it no more. It's your fault, after all, that he's going."

He glowered at her.

"You're like cats—the pack of you—never do what a reasonable creature wants, or expects. Put a bowl for 'em and they'll only drink out of a jug. Call 'em to the fire, they'll go to the window. Ope the window for 'em and they'll turn round and make you ope the door. And only a born fool wastes time or thought to please a cat; and be damned if ever I will again."

"Be you talking about Susan, or me?" asked Mrs. Honeysett, with rising colour. She did not know what was disturbing Joe's mind and began to feel angry. He pursued his own dark thoughts a moment longer and then, as she rose to leave him, he broke his news.

"Not an hour ago, when all was peace and I had been able to tell the household I found myself well again, and was turning over an advertisement for a new horseman, they crept before me, hand in hand—like a brace of children."

"Who did?"

"Why, Susan and that blasted sarpent, Palk."

"Palk a sarpent!"

"Do, for God's sake, shut up and listen, and don't keep interrupting. They came afore me. And Palk said that, owing to a wonderful bit of news, he hoped we was going to part friends and not enemies, though he was afraid as he might have to give me another jar. Then I told him to drop my darter's hand that instant moment and not come mountybanking about when he ought to be at work; and then he said that Susan had taken him, and they hoped afore long to be married!"

"Mercy on us, Joe!"

"That's what I heard this morning. And the woman put in her oar when I asked Palk if he was drunk. She said she loved him well and dearly, and hoped that I wouldn't fling no cold water over her great joy, or be any the less a kind father to her. Got it all by heart of course."

"What a world! That's the last thing ever I should have thought to fall out."

"Or any other sane human. It's a wicked outrage in my opinion and done, of course, for revenge, because I cast the man away—cunning devil!"

"Don't you say that. You must take a higher line, Joe. Soosie-Toosie's a good woman, and you always said Thomas was a good man."

"He's not a good man. He's a beast of a man—underhand and sly and scheming. He's got one of them hateful, cast-iron memories, and when I began to talk to them and soon had my daughter dumb, it was Palk, if you please, opened his mouth and withstood me and flung my own words in my face."

"What words?"

"And it shows kind speech to that fashion of man be no better than cheese-cakes to a pig. I told him to think twice before he made himself a laughing-stock to the parish, and then he minded me of the past and a thing spoke when I sacked him, a fortnight ago. I've gone so weak as a mouse over this job I can tell you."

"Take your time. What had you said to him?"

"I'd told him, when he dared to come afore me about my way with my only child, that if there was anything in the world I could do for Susan to make her home a happier place, he might rest assured she would tell me so herself. And the sarpent remembered that and then invited the woman to speak; which she did do, and told me that her life, without this grey-headed son of a gun, wouldn't be worth living no more; and she hoped that I wouldn't pay back all her love and life-long service—'service,' mind you— by making a rumpus about it, or doing or saying anything unkind. And I've got to go down the wind like a dead leaf afore them, because I soon saw that under her mild words, Susan weren't going to be shook."

"She wouldn't be. There's no strength like the strength of a woman who gets her only chance. She knows, poor dear, 'tis Palk or nothing."

"I told 'em to get out of my sight for a pair of cold-blooded, foxy devils— yes, in my anger I said that—and so they have; and soon, no doubt, they'll be gone for good and all. And that's the middle and both ends of it; and the worst and wickedest day's work ever I heard tell about."

"You've dropped below your usual high standards, if I may say so," answered Melinda. "Little blame to you that you should feel vexed, I'm sure; but 'tis more the shock than the reality I believe. I feel the shock likewise, though outside the parties and only a friend to all. 'Tis so unlike anything as you might have expected, that it throws you off your balance. Yet, when you come to turn it over, Joe, you can't help seeing there's rhyme and reason in it."

"You say that! For a woman to fly from the safety and security of her father's home—and such a father—to a man who don't even know what work he's going to do when he leaves me. And a wretch that's proved as deep as the sea. Can't you read his game? He knows that Susan be my only one, and bound to have all some day—or he thinks he knows it. That's at the bottom of this. He looks on and says to himself, 'All will be hers; then all will be mine.'"

"Don't you say that. Keep a fair balance. Remember you held a very high opinion of Palk not two months agone, when he showed by his acts to his dead sister's child that he was a high-minded man."

"I'll thank you to keep my side of this, please," he answered. "I don't much like the line you're taking, Melinda. Just ax yourself this: would any man, young or old, look at Susan as a possible help-mate and think to marry her, if he warn't counting on the jam that would go with the powder? She's my child, and I'm not one to bemoan my fortune as to that, but a woman's a woman, and was the male ever born who could look at Susan as a woman? You know very well there never was."

"You couldn't; but men ain't all so nice as you about looks. And you can't deny that apart from being a bit homely, Susan — —"

"Stop!" he said. "I believe you knew about this all the time and be here as a messenger of peace! And if I thought that — —"

"Don't think nothing of the sort, there's a good man. I'd so soon have expected the sun to go backward as hear any such thing. But 'tis done on your own showing, and you must be so wise as usual about it and not let the natural astonishment upset your character. It's got to be, seemingly. So start from there and see how life looks."

Melinda indeed was also thinking how life looked. Her mind ran on and she had already reached a point to which Mr. Stockman's bruised spirit was yet to bring him. She prepared to go away.

"I won't stop no more now. You'll have a lot to think over in your mind about the future. Thank goodness you be well again—and never looked better I'm sure. What's their plans?"

"Damn their plans—how about my plans?"

"You'll come to your plans gradual. And don't think 'tis the end of the world. You never know. When things turn inside out like this, we be often surprised to find there's a lot to be said for changes after all."

"'Tis mortal easy to be wise about other folk's troubles," he said.

Then Mrs. Honeysett departed and felt Joe's moody eyes upon her back as she went slowly and thoughtfully away. Soosie-Toosie's eyes were also upon her; but that she did not know.

CHAPTER XXX
THE NEST

Joe Stockman, like a stricken animal, hid himself from his fellow men at this season; yet it was not curious that he should conceal his tribulation from fellow men, because he knew that sympathy must be denied. To run about among the people, grumbling because his daughter had found a husband, was a course that Joe's humour told him would win no commiseration. He was much more likely to be congratulated on an unexpected piece of good luck. Even Melinda, with every kindly feeling for him, proved not able to show regret; and if she could not, none might be looked for elsewhere. But he made it evident to those chiefly involved that he little liked the match; he declined to see any redeeming features and went so far as to say that the countryside would be shocked with Susan for leaving her father under such circumstances. To his surprise he could not shake her as at first he had hoped to do. She was meek, and solicitous for his every wish as usual; she failed not to anticipate each desire of his mind; she knew, by long practice, how to read his eyes without a word; but upon this one supreme matter she showed amazing determination.

She did not speak of it; neither did Thomas, and when his master, who had failed for the moment to get a new horseman worthy of Falcon Farm, invited Palk to stop another month, he agreed to do so. But Thomas grumbled to Maynard when they were alone, and at the same time heard something from Lawrence that interested him.

They were hoeing the turnips together and the elder spoke.

"There's no common decency about the man in my opinion," he said. "Goodjer take him! He's like a sulky boy and pretends that facts ban't facts, while every day of the week shows they are. And patience is very well, but it don't make you any younger. Here I've pleased him by promising to stop another month, and when I did that, I had a right to think it would break down his temper and stop the silly rummage he talks about a thankless child and so on. You know how he goes on—chittering at me and Susan, but never to us—just letting out as if he was talking to the fire, or the warming-pan on the wall—of course for us to hear."

"He's took it very hard no doubt. Of course it's a shatterer. He didn't know his luck; and when you suddenly see your luck, for the first time just afore it's going to be taken away from you, it makes you a bit wild," explained Lawrence.

"Let him be wild with himself then, and cuss himself—not us. Look at it—I meet his convenience and go on so mild as Moses, working harder than ever, and all I get be sighs and head-shakings; and you always see his lips saying 'sarpent' to himself every time you catch his eye. It's properly ondacent, because there's duties staring the man in the face and he's trying his damnedest to wriggle out of 'em!"

"What duties?"

"Why, his daughter's wedding, I should think! Surely it's up to him, whatever he feels against it, to give the woman a fatherly send off. Not that I care a cuss, and should be the better pleased if he wasn't there glumping and glowering and letting all men see he hated the job; but Susan be made of womanly feeling, and she reckons he did ought to come to the church and give her away, all nice and suent, same as other parents do. And after that there ought to be a rally of neighbours and some pretty eating and drinking, and good wishes and an old shoe for luck when us goes off to the station man and wife. And why the hell not?"

"I dare say it will work out like that. You must allow for the shock, Tom. He'd got to rely on you and your future wife like his right and left hand; and to have the pair of you snatched away together— — He's a man with a power of looking forward and, of course, he can see, in a way you can't, what he'll feel like when you both vanish off the scene."

"You be always his side."

"No, no—not in this matter, anyway. I know very well what you feel like, and nobody wishes you joy better than me. You've got a grand wife, and I've always thought a lot of you myself as you know. But 'tis just the great good fortune that's fallen to you makes it so much the worse for him. He knows what he's losing, and you can't expect him to be pleased. He'll calm down in a week or two."

"Let the man do the same then and take another. There's a very fine woman waiting for him."

"There is; and he'll take her no doubt; but there again, he knows that you can't have anything for nothing."

"He had his daughter for nothing."

"Yes, and got used to it; but he won't have Melinda Honeysett for nothing. A daughter like Susan gives all and expects no return; a wife like Mrs. Honeysett will want a run for her money. And Joe knows mighty well it will have to be give and take in future."

"Quite right too."

"There's another thing hanging over master. It won't seem much compared with you going. But I'm off before very long myself."

"By gor! You going too!"

"In the fall I reckon."

"When he hears that, he'll throw the house out of windows!"

"Not him. I'm nobody."

"If it's all the same to you, I'd be glad if you didn't break this to Stockman till our job's a thought forwarder," said Thomas. "He can only stand a certain amount. You was more to him than me really. This will very like turn him against human nature in general, and if he gets desperate, he may disgrace himself."

"I shan't speak just yet."

"We was much hoping—Soosie and me—that he'd go bald-headed for Melinda before this—if only to hit back. Because, if he done that, he might cut my future wife out of his will you see. And, in his present spirit of mind, I believe it would comfort him a lot to do so—and tell me he had."

"No, no—he wouldn't lower himself like that. And as for Mrs. Honeysett, I reckon he's to work in that quarter. He can't strike all of a sudden, of course, because the people would say he'd only done it for his own convenience; but he'll be about her before long I expect. He's been saying in a good few places that he must marry now."

"He named her name at Green Hayes to my certain knowledge," said Thomas, "and Mrs. Bamsey heard him do so; and she told Arthur Chaffe, the carpenter; and he told his head man; and he told me. And he said more. He said that Arthur Chaffe had marked that Joe had lost a lot of his old bounce and weren't by no means so charming as he used to be."

"There's no doubt this job has upset him a lot."

"Then where's his religion? He did ought to remember he can't go sailing on and have everything his own way all his life, no more than anybody else."

They hoed together shoulder to shoulder, then reached the end of their rows and turned again.

"There's a religious side no doubt," admitted Maynard. "And we never feel more religious, if we're religious-minded at all, than after a stroke of good fortune; and never less so than after a stroke of bad. And I'm telling you what I know there, because I've been called to go into such things pretty close. There's nothing harder than to break away from what you was taught as a child. 'Tis amazing how a thing gets rooted into a young mind, and how difficult it may be for the man's sense to sweep it away come he grows up."

Mr. Palk, however, was not concerned with such questions.

"I don't want to break away from nothing," he said. "I only want for Stockman to treat me and his daughter in a right spirit. And what I say is, if his religion and church-going, not to name his common sense, can't lead him right, it's a very poor advertisement for his boasted wisdom."

"So it would be; but he'll come round and do right, only give him time," answered Lawrence.

"And what's in your mind?" asked Thomas presently, as he stood up to rest his back. "Have you got another billet in sight?"

"No. I much want to get abroad. It's always been a wish with me to see a foreign country."

"A very fine idea. I'd so soon do the same as not; but I heard a chap say that you find the land pretty near all under machinery if you go foreign. And I shouldn't care to quit hosses at my time of life."

"There's your wife to think on. She'd never like to put the sea between her and her father."

"As to that," answered Palk, "it's going to be largely up to him. If he carries on like what he's doing now, he'll have to pay for it; because the woman's only a human woman and she haven't deserved this conduct. Why, God's light! if she'd stole his money-box and set the house on fire he couldn't take it no worse!"

These things were heard by another pair of ears in the evening of that day, for then Maynard saw Dinah again. But much passed between the lovers before they reached the subject of Susan and Thomas. Maynard had been deeply interested to hear of Dinah's sudden departure, of which she had told him nothing, and he had puzzled ever since learning the fact mentioned by Melinda Honeysett. For he did not guess her purpose, or her destination, and the fact that she had gone away only served to explain her need for money. She let him know, however, before they met, and that without any word; for during her absence, there came a picture postcard to

Lawrence—a coloured picture of Barnstaple parish church; and that told him everything.

He trusted her, but knew her forthright ways and felt very anxious to see her again. The date and place for their next meeting had been fixed between them at their last conversation, and as he had heard that Dinah was returned, he knew that she would keep the appointment. He brooded for hours upon her action and inclined to a shadow of regret that she should have taken it, yet the fact did not astonish him, looking back at their last meeting; for had Dinah asked permission to go, he would not have suffered it in his mood at the time. That she knew; and yet she had gone. He recognised the immense significance of her action and the time seemed interminable until the dusk of that day, when he was free. The night came mild and grey with a soft mist. Their meeting place was a gate in a lane one mile from Green Hayes among the woods ascending to Buckland. There it had been planned they should join each other for the last time before one, or both, disappeared from the Vale.

Maynard felt a curious sense of smallness as he went to the tryst. He seemed to be going to meet somebody stronger, more resolute, more steadfast of spirit than himself. Surely Dinah had done the things that would have better become him to do. And yet he could not blame himself there, for it would have been impossible for him to set foot in the town where, no doubt, his wife still lived. He had wearied himself with futile questions, impossible to answer until Dinah should meet him, and there was nothing left but intense love and worship for her in Maynard's mind when they did meet. If she had any sort of good news, so much the better; but if she had none, he yet had good news for her. He had banished the last doubt during her absence and now told himself that not moral sensibility, but moral cowardice had ever caused him to doubt. He had probed the equivocal thing in him and believed that its causes were deep down in some worthless instinct, independent of reason. She should at least find him as clear and determined as herself at last. He had decided for Australia, and the question of their separate or simultaneous disappearance was also decided. She had to hear to-night that they could not leave England together for her credit's sake. The details of their actions were also defined. He had planned a course that would, he hoped, suit Dinah well enough, though as yet he knew not whether any word of hers might modify it.

She was waiting for him and came into his arms with joy. She guessed that her postcard had revealed her adventure and began by begging for forgiveness. This he granted, but bade her talk first.

"It's made me long to go out in the world," she said. "Just this taste. I've never seemed to understand there was anything beyond Ashburton and Lower Town; but now I've gone afield and seen miles and miles of England, and I've met people that never heard of the Vale. Say you ban't cross again, my dear heart. You know very well why I went. It rose up on me like a flame of fire—to make sure. I told 'em at Green Hayes I had some business up the country and they think I went to be married—Jane's idea that was. She's positive sure I'm married, though I've told her in plain words I'm not. Of course they be curious, but I couldn't tell a lie about it. So I said 'business.'"

"Never mind them. I won't swear I'd have said 'no' if you'd asked me, Dinah—not if I'd thought twice. It was a natural, needful point, and you grasped it quicker than I did, and no doubt made up your mind while I was maundering on about the law. I saw all that after I got your card. But I couldn't have gone myself."

"It was my work and I've done it; and I wish more had come of it. But nothing has. I took a room in a little inn near the station and tramped about and found her shop in the best part of the town. A big place with fine windows—a dairy and creamery and refreshment room. Just 'Courtier' over the windows, in big, gold letters, and a few maidens inside and—tea. I marked her, of course, the minute I saw her. She's in the shop herself— rather grand, but not above lending a hand when they're busy. She's up in the world. They knew about her at the inn where I stopped, and told me the story. They said her husband went mad on the honeymoon and disappeared off the earth. I went to the shop three times and had my tea there, and the second time there was a man at the counter talking to her. But he didn't look much of it. So there it is. She's going on with her life just as you thought, and making money; and what the people see, I saw, and what they don't see, or know, is no matter. But she was quite pleased with herself—a cheerful woman to the eye. You can tell that much.

"She's worn well I should think. She's a pretty woman; but she's hard and her voice is hard. She wouldn't have no mercy on people under her. She drove her maidens in the shop and was down on 'em if they talked much to customers. At my inn she was spoke very well of and thought a bit of a wonder. You was forgot. They said it was thought you killed yourself. And now that the seven years are up, some fancied she might marry again, but others didn't think she ever would, being too independent. A man or two they mentioned; but the opinion I heard most was that she never wanted to change. I couldn't ax too much about her, of course."

So Dinah told her tale.

"I wish it had been different," she went on. "I hoped all sorts of things — that I'd find her married again, or gone, or, perhaps dead. But there she is, so large as life, and I shouldn't think she'd ever marry for love, but she might for money, or for getting a bit more power. I didn't feel to hate her in the least, or anything like that. I felt sorry for her in a way, knowing what she'd missed, and I thought, if it had been different, what a big man you might be by now. But you'll be bigger some day along with me. And so we know where we are, Lawrence."

He asked various questions, which she answered, and he observed how absolutely indifferent Dinah found herself before the facts. She evidently recognised no relationship whatever between the husband and wife. From the adventures at Barnstaple she returned to the present, and he let her talk on, waiting to speak himself till she had finished.

She had been away nine days and returned to find Jane fallen out with Jerry Withycombe. Mr. Bamsey had recognised her on her return and called her by name and made her sit beside him for a long time. But the next morning he had forgotten her again. Faith Bamsey had also thought Dinah must have disappeared to be married, but believed her when she vowed it was not so. John Bamsey was away for the time, doing bailiff's work up the river above Dartmeet.

Then he told her of his determination and greatly rejoiced her, save in one particular.

"We don't go together," he said, "and the details will very soon clear themselves; but there must be no shadow on your memory, here or anywhere, when you're gone. I give Joe notice presently and go to Australia, to get the home ready. You find work and, for a bit, keep that work. Then you leave it for London, or a big town, where ships sail from, and your passage is took and you come along. That leaves them guessing here, and none can ever say a word against you. But so sure as we go together, then Stockman tells everybody that I'm a married man, and the harm's done."

"You do puzzle me!" she answered. "You can't get this bee out of your bonnet, Lawrence — such a clever chap as you, too. What in fortune's name does it matter what Cousin Joe says about you, or what the people believe about me? I know you're not married, and when I wed you I shall be your one and lawful wife. Who else is there — now foster-father be gone? That was the only creature on earth I could hurt, and he's past hurting, poor old dear. I like your plan all through but there. I'm going when you go, and half the joy of my life would be lost if I didn't sail along with you in the ship. That I do bargain for. Oh, I wish it was to-morrow we were running away!"

"I hate to run."

"I love it—yes, I do, now. I wish to God I wasn't going to lose sight of you again. But it won't be for long."

They spoke of the details and he pointed out that her plan must increase the difficulties somewhat, yet she would take no denial.

"What's all this fuss for? False pride," she said. "You've got to think for me the way I want you to think, not the way you want to think. If we know we're right, why should we fret if all the rest of the world thought different? I'm hungry and thirsty to go and be in a new world with you. I want you and I want a new world. And you will be my new world for that matter."

"I know that."

"Together then. 'Twould spoil all any other way. 'Twould be small any other way. 'Twould be cringing to the Vale."

He laughed.

"I can't keep you here in the rain all night. The next thing is our post office—from now on."

"Promise about my going with you."

"That means thinking over all the plans again."

"Think them over again then; and I'll help. And I've found the post office. List!"

They kept silence for half a minute, but Dinah had only heard a night-bird.

"'Tis here!" she said, "twenty yards down the lane. I found it in the spring—a wrennys' nest hid under the ivy on the bank. No better place. 'Tis empty now and snug as need be."

He accompanied her to the spot, lit matches and examined the proposed post office. It was safe enough, for the snug, domed nest lay completely hidden under a shower of ivy, and Dinah had only discovered it by seeing the little birds pop in when they were building.

Lawrence doubted; it seemed a frail receptacle for vital news; but it was dry and as safe as possible.

"I'd thought to put a tobacco tin under a stone somewhere," he said, "but perhaps this couldn't be beat."

He took careful note of it and marked the exact spot as well as he could in the dark. A sapling grew in the hedge opposite and he took his knife and blazed the bark behind, where only he, or Dinah, would find the cut.

"There'll be a letter for you in a few days," she said, "for I know I've forgot a thousand things; and when your new plans be finished, you'll write 'em for me."

"We must go slow and steady," he answered. "I've got to give Joe warning presently, and I don't mean to be out of work longer than I can help. When we know what we're going to do to the day, then I'll speak; and he won't like it none too well. He's terrible under the weather about Susan."

He told her the Falcon Farm news, with details which she had not heard.

"I'm sorry for Cousin Joe, but mighty glad for Susan, and I'm coming up one day to supper to congratulate her—why not?"

"It will be something just to look at you across the table," he said, "but we'd best speak little to each other."

Dinah grew listless as the moment for leave-taking came. Her mood was shadowed.

"I know it's right and wise to keep apart now," she told him. "And I know we can never have none of the old faces round us when we're married, and none of the little pleasures that go with old friends. But I am sorry. It's small, but I am sorry."

"So am I, for your sake," he answered. "And it's not small. It's natural. This is the only home you know, and the only folks you know are in it. And most are kindly and good. It only looks small against the bigger thing of being together for evermore. The time won't be long. 'Twill slip away quicker than you'll like I guess. And there's plenty of new friends waiting for us down under."

"It's cruel of life," she cried. "It's hard and cruel of life to make love like ours so difficult. Open air, daylight creatures, like us, to be called to plot and scheme and hide against the frozen silliness of the world. Just the things I hate most. And now we must trust the house a little bird have made with things that we'd both be proud to shout from the church steeple!"

"I know every bit what you're feeling. I feel it too—I hate it more than you do—knowing what you are. It will soon be over."

"I'll come up and look at you anyhow," said Dinah. "That won't shock the people; and I dare say, now that Susan knows what it is to love a man— but don't you fear. I won't kiss you even with my eyes, Lawrence."

"Susan wouldn't see nothing for that matter," he said. "Love be a dour pastime for her and Palk as things are. They be like us in a way—frightened to look at each other under that roof."

"But firm," she said. "Cousin Joe ain't going to choke Susan off it?"

"Not him. She'll take Thomas, so sure as you take me."

Dinah was cheerful again before he left her.

"When we'm married, I'll always be wanting to kiss you afore the people," she said, "just for the joy of doing it openly."

Then they parted, to meet no more in secret until they should never part again.

He half regretted her determination to sail with him, as he tramped home; yet he felt in no mind to argue the point. In his present spirit, sharing her indignation that his fellow men would thrust him away from Dinah for ever if they could, he cared little more than she for what their world might say and think when they had vanished from it for a larger.

CHAPTER XXXI
JOE'S SUNDAY

Melinda stood at her door and spoke to her neighbour, Mr. Harry Ford, the gardener. He was a red-whiskered man of fifty, and he and Mrs. Honeysett viewed life somewhat similarly.

"You bad creature," she said, "working in your garden o' Sunday!"

This was the sort of remark on which Harry never wasted speech. He went on with his digging.

"I wish the second early potatoes were coming up so well at the Court as they are here in my little patch," he remarked. "But they haven't got the nice bit o' sand in the soil as we have."

He rested a moment.

"How's Jerry going on?" he asked. "Have it come right?"

"No, I'm sorry to say; and yet not sorry neither. She's keeping all this up because he vexed her Easter Monday. They was at Ashburton revel together and she says he took a drop too much and very near ran the trap over Holne Bridge and broke her neck coming home. And he says no such thing. But the real trouble is about the blessed shop Jane wants to start at Ashburton after marriage. She's for a tobacco shop, and Jerry wants for it to be green-grocer's, where he can do his part. My own belief is that Jane Bamsey's getting tired of Jerry. If the wedding had gone through when it was ordained, all might have been well; but owing to Ben Bamsey's illness and sad downfall after, 'twas put off. I never much liked her I may tell you, no more didn't my father."

"He must have been a bit of a wonder—a very clever man they say."

"He was a clever man."

"Did he believe in the ghost in my house, Mrs. Honeysett?"

"He did not—no more than you do."

He paused and looked at her. Melinda appeared more than usually attractive. She was in her Sunday gown—a black one, for she still mourned her parent; but she had brightened it with some mauve satin bows, and she wore her best shoes with steel buckles.

"There is a ghost in the house, however," declared the gardener.

"Never!"

"Yes—the ghost of a thought in my mind," he explained.

"Ideas do grow."

"If they stick, then they grow. Now I'll ax you a question, and you've no call to answer it if you don't want. You might say 'twas a hole in my manners to ax, perhaps."

"I'm sure you wouldn't make a hole in your manners, Mr. Ford."

"I hope not. 'Tis this, then. What might the late Mr. Withycombe have thought of Farmer Stockman up the hill?"

Melinda parried the question.

"Well, you never can say exactly what one man thinks of another, because time and chance changes the opinion. A man will vex you to-day and please you next week. Sometimes what he does and says is contrary to your opinions, and then again, he may do or say something that brings him back to you."

"He liked him and didn't like him—off and on? But he'd made up his mind in a general way about his character?"

"I suppose he had."

"I know he had."

"How should you know?"

"Because I was at the trouble to find out."

"Fancy!"

"Yes. I sounded a man here and there. I went to Chaffe, the carpenter."

"Arthur Chaffe knew father very well and respected him, though he didn't hold with his opinions about religion."

"Religion I never touch—too kicklish a subject. But I spoke to Chaffe, and being friendly disposed to me—and why not?—he said a thing I might be allowed to name to you in confidence."

"Certainly," said Melinda, "if it's nothing against my father."

"Far from it. And I hope you'll take it as 'tis meant."

"I always take everything like that."

"That's right then. Well, Chaffe, knowing me for a pretty quiet man and a hater of gossip, told me the late fox-hunter saw very clear you'd go to Joe Stockman after he was took — —"

"How could he?"

"Well, I don't know how he could. But he did. And though too tender to whisper it in your ear, he told Chaffe that he was sorry!"

"Good Lord, you surprise me!"

"No business of mine, you'll say. And yet I felt somehow that if your father—such a man as him—felt sorry, there was a reason why for he should. And I won't deny but I told Chaffe he ought to mention it to you. He wouldn't, because he said the thing was too far gone."

"What's gone too far?"

"You know best. But people have ears and Stockman's got a tongue."

Mrs. Honeysett showed annoyance, while Harry returned to his potatoes.

"You're telling me what I know, however," she said.

He purposely misunderstood.

"You knew your good father didn't care for Mr. Stockman at bottom?"

"I know he's talking."

"The only thing that matters to know is your own mind, not what's in other people's, or in his."

At this moment a black-coated figure appeared on the high road and, much to Mr. Ford's regret, turned up the lane to the cottages.

"Talk of — —!" he said.

It was Mr. Stockman.

"He's coming here and—and—I hoped something weren't going to happen for the minute," confessed Melinda; "but now I reckon it may be."

"Well, if you're in doubt, nobody else is," said Mr. Ford striking boldly. "Farmer's sounding his victory far and near—not a very witty thing to do when an old man's after a young woman."

Melinda ignored the compliment and viewed the approaching figure with impassive features.

"He's cut the ground from under his own feet as to his age," she answered, "for if you cry out you're old before your time, of course people must believe you."

Orphan Dinah | 253

Mr. Ford could not answer for Stockman was within earshot.

He showed a holiday humour, but reproved Harry.

"Working o' Sunday!" he said.

"There's all sorts o' work, master," replied the gardener. "I dare say now that the better the day the better the deed holds of your job so well as mine."

"You're a sharp one! And how's Melinda?"

"Very well," she said. "You wasn't to church this morning."

"I was not. I meant coming down the hill again this afternoon, to drink a dish of tea with you, if you please; and though twice up and down the hill be naught to me, yet I shirked it."

They went in together.

"Where's Jerry?" he asked.

"Mooning down to Green Hayes on the chance of getting things right."

"Good. He'll fetch her round; though I doubt she's worth it."

"So do I."

"However, I'm not here, as you'll guess, about your brother. The time has come, Melinda."

"You've let 'em name the day then—Susan and Thomas?"

"No such thing; but they'll be naming it themselves pretty soon. They'll be away in a month or two I expect. And I want for the house to be swept and garnished then. I want a lot done. I've suffered a great deal of undeserved trouble in that quarter, and there's wicked words being said about my treatment of my child. The people have short memories."

"There's wicked words being said about a lot of things. It's been said, for instance, up and down the Vale, that you've told a score you be going to marry me, Joe. That's a proper wicked thing, I should think."

He was much concerned.

"Good God! What a nest of echoes we live in! But there it is. When a thing's in the air—whether 'tis fern seed, or a bit of scandal, or a solemn truth, it will settle and stick and grow till the result appears. No doubt the general sense of the folk, knowing how I've felt to you for years, made up this story and reckoned it was one of they things that Providence let out before the event. Marriages be made in Heaven they say, Melinda."

"But they ain't blazed abroad on earth, I believe, afore both parties choose to mention it."

"Most certainly not; but if you move in the public eye, people will be talking."

"Yes, they will, if they be started talking. I met Ann Slocombe to Lower Town three days agone and she congratulated me on my engagement to you."

"Who the devil's Ann Slocombe?"

"She's a woman very much like other women. And I told her it was stuff and nonsense, and far ways from anything that had happened, or was going to happen."

"No need to have said that, I hope. 'Tis the curious case of— —"

"'Tis the curious case of talking before you know," said Melinda tartly. "What would you have thought if I'd told people you'd gone down to Brixham, to offer yourself to a woman there?"

"God's my judge I— —"

Mr. Stockman broke off.

"This is very ill-convenient, Melinda, and quite out of tune with me and the day, and what's in my mind. If I've spoke of you with great affection to one or two tried friends—friends now no more—then I can only ax you to overlook their freedom of speech. I've been in a very awkward position for a long time, and made of justice as you are, you must see it. For look how things fell out. First, just as I was coming to the great deed and going to ax you to be mistress of Falcon Farm, there happened your dear father's grievous illness and his death. Well, I couldn't jump at you with my heart in my hand, while you was crying your eyes out and feeling your fearful loss. And then, just as the clouds were lifting and the way clear, what happened? My misguided girl takes this false step. And that cut two ways. First there was the disaster itself, and then, in a flash, I saw that if I came to you on top of it, enemies—not you, yourself, I well knew that—enemies would be bitter quick to say I was doing it from no honour and respect to you, but to suit my own convenience, because Susan was off. So I held away, because I saw that you'd be put in a false position, with your inclination—so I hope—on one side, and your proper woman's pride on the other. And now I see what a quandary it was, and how I've let you in for these painful adventures—all from too much nice feeling, seemingly."

"You can make a case, of course, but— —"

"Let me finish. I ban't here to argue, Melinda. We've known each other a good long time now and it have been the bright ray in a troublous life, your friendship for me. We looked at things from the same point of view, and took high opinions, and laughed when we ought to laugh, and was serious in due season. And good men are scarce and good women far scarcer. And there never was and never will be a better woman than you. And it would be a second spring to me to have such a one at my right hand. I want you, not for this or that accident of life as have fallen upon me; but I want you just the same as I have wanted you any time these ten years. I couldn't speak till your father was gone, and I couldn't speak after, and in solemn truth, being a man of pretty nice feelings, I couldn't speak an hour before this instant moment. So you must sweep such trifles out of your mind and come to the question with no bias, but just your honest feelings to me and your memory of the past. So there it lies, my dear."

Mrs. Honeysett hesitated a few moments before replying—not because she was in any doubt as to her answer, but from a native sense that all must be done decently and in order.

Joe made the best of the situation and probably, had Melinda's attitude to him remained unchanged, a look back into memory, as he suggested, might have won the day for Mr. Stockman. She was conscious that a year ago she would have pardoned his errors of egotism. She even suspected that, as things were, they did not really lie at the root of the matter. But the root of the matter extended into new ground. Here, however, she could not pursue it. She only told herself that she would never marry Mr. Stockman now; and while sharing his opinion, that her little grievances were really unimportant and not worthy of being offered as a reason for refusal, she only considered how, without them, she might gracefully decline. She let her tongue go and trusted to chance. Then she suddenly saw a way and took it.

"Us have had a very fine friendship indeed, Joe," she admitted, "and, in my humble opinion, it would be a terrible mistake to spoil it this way. For say what you may, friendship ain't love and love ain't friendship; and I do feel, betwixt me and you, it might be a sad pity to lose the substance for the shadow."

"You talk as if love would end friendship, instead of double it, Melinda," he answered; but he was quick-minded and he knew the woman meant to decline him. The thought immeasurably troubled Mr. Stockman, for he had assumed success to be certain. He had, indeed, already proceeded far beyond this point and planned his future with Melinda. He argued now and made a very strenuous effort to prove that there is no friendship like that of married people. He argued, also, that such an understanding as had obtained between him and Melinda since his wife's death was sufficient foundation for a very perfect and distinguished union.

She admitted that it might be so, but declined the experiment. She held that love too often endangered and weakened friendship, even if it did not actually destroy it; and she told him frankly, but with all consideration, that her friendship and admiration for him did not tend in that direction.

"I'm very much addicted to you, Joe, and you've been a big figure in my life for years, and will so continue I hope; but marriage with you don't draw me. You've been like an elder brother to me, and I hope you'll see your way to remain like that. But 'twould spoil all if we went into marriage. And, in a word, I couldn't do it, because my feelings don't respond."

"This is a very painful shock to me," he answered. "Somehow, such was you to me and, as I thought, me to you, that I felt the step could only be a matter of time; and what's more, Melinda, you never did nothing to make me feel otherwise—quite the contrary in fact. I don't say you—however, we'll not go into that side. You know what I mean."

"I do; and we will go into it, Joe, and have done with it. If you think I encouraged you——"

"What do you think?"

"Never—God's my judge! I was very proud of being your friend, and I got plenty of wisdom and good advice from you; and you often took a hint from me also. But nothing tender ever passed between us—never."

"That depends on what you call tenderness. To the seeing eye and feeling heart there may be a world of tenderness in a glance, Melinda, or in a silence, or in a handshake. I did most honestly believe you felt more than friendship for me, just as I have long felt more than friendship for you. And I showed as much, by a lot of touches that a quick woman like you couldn't have mistook. No, no, Melinda, that won't do. You knew."

"I'll take the blame, then, if you think I ought."

"Don't talk of blame. Consider if you ain't making a mistake. You're simply wasted single, and here's a tidy sort of man offering; and all his is yours, from the hour you say 'yes.' Weigh it. I know only too well what I'll lose if you don't come to me. In fairness, then, you did ought to consider if you don't lose pretty heavy too."

"Of course, of course. To lose your friendship would be a very great disaster for me, Joe. It's been a steadfast and lasting thing, and I should feel a cruel lot was gone if that was gone. But if it is to be a choice—— No; leave it as 'tis between us, my dear man. Let's be friends and forget this. I'll get 'e a cup of tea."

"As to friends, you don't quite see what you're doing yet, I'm afraid. You'm acting in an astonishing way that throws down the past, Melinda, and makes you like the rough and tumble of women—them with no fixed views and opinions, as don't know their own mind—if they've got minds to know. I'll be off instanter, Melindy, and leave you in hope that you'll think this thing out and find you're on the edge of a terrible mistake. I never thought I'd misunderstood you like this. Indeed, if I had fancied there was a doubt, I should have probably been too proud to offer at all."

He rose and prepared to depart.

Mrs. Honeysett, glad that he remained calm, was also thankful that he should go.

"I'll never lose sight of you in my mind, or in my prayers," she said.

"I came in full sail," he answered; "now I go off like a ship without a mast, or a rudder. It'll puzzle me to my dying day how you could be so harsh."

He left her in deep dejection, which warmed to anger before he reached home. He convinced himself that Melinda had played him false. For years there had been an implicit understanding in his mind that he had but to put forth his hand to take. And he had been tender and abounded in the little "touches" he mentioned. These Melinda had perfectly comprehended and even appreciated. Nay, she had repaid them in kind. The effect of her refusal was bad. Mr. Stockman saw his stable world reeling about him. He had barely recovered from the shock of Susan's engagement and now, after carefully rebuilding his future environment and allowing himself to dwell philosophically on the bright side of it, he found all in ruins and further necessity for fresh plans.

And that same evening, after supper, when Thomas Palk and Susan had crept out for a walk, Lawrence Maynard came to the master of Falcon Farm and gave notice.

"There's no hurry," he said. "I'm at your service, master, so long as you want me; but I've made up my mind to leave England in the autumn and see a bit of the world before it's too late. I think to go by Michaelmas, or a bit after—to Australia very like—and take up land."

To Maynard's amazement Joe turned upon him with something almost of fury. His cowman knew not of Joe's earlier reverse and all that he had that day been called to endure.

"What—what are you telling me? You going too? You ungrateful devil! You thankless, selfish toad! What have I done—what on God's earth have I done—to be turned down and flouted and tormented at every step of my life in this way? A man whose every act and thought be kindness for other people; and now every man's hand be against me! Persecution I call it; and you—you, who have had to thank me for far more than goes between master and man; you, as I have offered friendship to, and trusted and treated more like a son than a servant! You ought to be shamed to the marrow in your bones to think to leave me—an old, careworn, ill-used wretch with one foot in the grave and all the world turning its back on him."

"Don't—don't!" said Lawrence. "Don't take on like that. There's no hurry for a few months. I've been very proud and grateful for all you've done for me, Mr. Stockman."

"Get out of my sight," answered the other. "There's no honesty, nor honour, nor plain dealing left in man or woman, so far as I can see. It's a hell of a world, and I wish a good few people as I could name, yourself included, had never come into it. My lines have fallen in shameful places, and if I wasn't too old, I'd shake the dust off my shoes against Buckland and everybody in it."

Then Maynard retreated and left Joe panting heavily and staring into the kitchen fire.

He had gone to bed when Susan returned, and she and Tom and Maynard mumbled in low voices for an hour while the latter described his experience. To Stockman's daughter this outburst signified far more than it did to either of the men, for she guessed upon what business her father had been employed that afternoon, and now knew that a terrible disappointment must have overtaken him. She wept half the night on his account and mourned not a little on her own; for Joe's failure must inevitably increase her personal difficulties and double the future problems of Thomas and herself.

CHAPTER XXXII
JANE AND JERRY

Under the first grey of dawn, Maynard posted a letter in the empty wrens' nest and then proceeded down the hill to Lower Town. He was on an errand from Falcon Farm to Mr. Chaffe, and then he would proceed to a farm on the moor, about the purchase of two heifers. For Stockman had long since found that Lawrence knew as much concerning cattle as himself. The present arrangements had been made before the cowman gave notice, and his latest letter to Dinah chronicled the fact that he had done so. He answered also her last note. The letter-box worked well and many communications had been exchanged. Dinah's were full of love and ardour. Her plans amused him. They shared one determination; to take nothing with them. They would sail from Plymouth for Australia presently and they would be married at Sydney as soon as possible after landing. Maynard's money was more than enough and their passages would be state-aided. Preliminaries were complete and there remained only to fix their place of meeting and date of sailing. Then they would simultaneously disappear.

Mr. Chaffe was already in his workshop when Maynard appeared.

"Early birds both!" said he. "I know what you've come about, however. Joe wants me to look into his stables, where the dry rot have got, and see how much must come out and be made good."

"That's right, Mr. Chaffe."

"I've been waiting and expecting it since Palk made the sad discovery. But no doubt your master has his mind pretty full of greater things."

"He has, I'm afraid. And it's making him fall short of his usual sense here and there."

"A man full of sense, however."

"So I've always found him, and full of human kindness also. I've a lot to thank him for—a very good friend to me. But a few days agone I gave notice, because I'm going farther afield before I'm too old, and he took it very bad indeed."

"My! You going too? Where?"

"To Australia. I want to see a bit of life and start fresh."

"And Joe didn't like it?"

"No; but he'll easily find a new cowman. There's nothing to get so savage about that I can see."

"He'd come to look at you as part of his show. No doubt, falling on his other troubles — — But he knows where to look for comfort I should hope. After all, it's but a passing thing. I always say that we who live in a Vale ought to know what a vale means. Life's gone a thought too flowing and easy with Joe. This is all meant to make him think of Beyond."

"Thought of the next world don't make trouble anything less than trouble."

"It ought then."

"Look after this world and the next will look after itself, Mr. Chaffe."

"A very dangerous opinion, Maynard, and I'm sorry you think so. It shows a weakness in you. That ain't the Christian standpoint and you know it."

"Your views are behind the times perhaps."

"Far from it: they're ahead of the times. It's the still, small voice ain't heard in these days. The world knows its noisiest men, not its greatest; and so it don't know its Saviour—not even yet."

"Life's life, Mr. Chaffe, and what you hold runs counter to life. It's no sense preaching earthly misery to humans, because they're built to hate misery and seek happiness."

"I don't preach misery. I only preach that happiness must be looked for in the next world, not this one. It don't belong here and never will."

Maynard shook his head.

"I've thought of these things and I see your Church standing between man and a lot of lawful happiness. Let the Church help to clear up the cruel mess in this world."

"Then join the brotherhood of God and do your share."

"Only the brotherhood of man can do it. Justice ain't the possession of you Church people alone. And while you demand such a lot of injustice, you'll only lose your friends. Take marriage. You won't let marriage be a human thing, nor yet divorce. You let marriage be a trap for people—easy to get in, impossible to get out—then you've got the face to say it's God's will—the God of love and mercy!"

"I'm sorry to hear you talk in this wicked way, and I know where you learnt such bad learning," answered Arthur. "But Enoch Withycombe wouldn't say those things now, Maynard. He's in the Light now, and it would make him a very sad man to hear you."

"I didn't get my opinions from him. I only keep my eyes open and see how life goes; and I know there's hundreds and hundreds of poor people living in misery to-day, because you say God brought 'em together, instead of the Devil."

"We'll talk about this another time. I must try to open your eyes if I can. You stand on very dangerous ground and your little bit o' learning's like a Jack o' Lantern—it'll land you in a bog if you don't watch it. John Bamsey's much the same, only his doubts take him in another direction. The mischief with you young men is that you think your own twopenny-halfpenny opinions matter; and in his case, he lets a small thing like his own experience poison his life and spoil his Christian outlook."

"Your own experience isn't a small thing," argued Lawrence, but the carpenter declared personal experience a very trumpery matter.

"Only the weak mind will let the things that happen to it influence conscience and the knowledge of right and wrong," he said. "Our faith is founded on a Rock, remember, and our bad luck and earthly frets and cares did only ought to make us cling the stouter to that Rock."

They talked but did not convince each other. Then Lawrence went his way, leaving in the mind of Mr. Chaffe considerable uneasiness. In the carpenter's knowledge there were not a few who professed similar opinions, and it greatly saddened him to see the younger generation slipping away from the faith of its fathers. He held that no sound democracy was possible without religion, and to hear young men say that religion had no more to do with democracy than football, was a serious grief to him.

Meantime there had happened behind Lawrence Maynard's back a thing of much import. Though the hour was still early, two people entered the lane through the woods some fifty minutes after he had descended it, and their arrival synchronised at the region of the ivy bank and the wrens' nest. A few seconds more would have seen Jerry Withycombe past the spot, on his way to work in the valley; but chance so willed it that, as he rounded a bend on his way, he saw beneath him, but still far distant, a woman's sun-bonnet, and he recognised its faded blue. She with whom his melancholy thoughts were concerned was evidently approaching, and the fact that she should be out so early, and on the way she knew he must be travelling to his work, created sudden, deep emotion in the woodman. His quarrel with Jane bulked larger in his eyes than in hers. She continued to be obdurate about a trifle, from no opinion that the trifle really mattered, but because it gave her a sense of freedom and a loophole if she so desired. She continued to be really fond of Jerry, and it wanted no great change of mind to bring them together. Indeed she proposed ere long to make it up. And now it seemed as though she were about to do so, and had put herself to trouble and risen early to meet him on his way.

A few moments, however, brought large disappointment for the man. At sight of the sun-bonnet, he had backed and waited to watch. Now he quickly perceived the approaching figure was not Jane's slim shape, but Dinah's ampler proportions. He was cast down from a great hope and scowled at the innocent Dinah. Then a ray of light shot his darkness, for it occurred to him that Dinah might be a messenger of good tidings. At any rate the sun-bonnet was Jane's—picked up haphazard no doubt, when Dinah set forth.

He waited and watched a few moments before proceeding, then marked Dinah stop and do a strange thing. She had not come to seek him it seemed after all; but something she sought and something she found.

In truth the lover of Lawrence was there to leave a letter. She did not expect one and was the more delighted to find the note left an hour before. Jerry saw her peep about, to be sure she was alone, then go to the green bank, insert her hand and bring out a small white object from the ivy. She stood and evidently read a letter. Still he held back, in great wonder at this scene. Dinah next produced something from her own pocket, opened it and appeared to write. She was adding a few words to the note that she had brought. She then put it in the nest and was quickly gone again down the hill.

Jerry waited till Dinah had disappeared; then, having marked the spot where she stood, he shouldered his frail and proceeded. Already he had a suspicion of the truth and presently made cautious search under the ivy-curtain. Nothing rewarded him until he found the old nest and a piece of paper therein. It was folded closely but conveyed no information on the outside. He held it in his hand a few moments and his mind worked in a selfish direction. Here was an item of tremendous interest to one person. He did not doubt that the letter was intended for a man, and felt very sure the fact proved his own sweetheart's assurance: that Dinah was secretly engaged, if not married. His thoughts were with Jane, and it seemed to him that chance had now thrown him an admirable opportunity to win her back. For such a secret as this would be meat and drink to her. Nor need it hurt Dinah. Jerry had not the slightest desire to hurt anybody; but he felt that his information might be well worth Jane's forgiveness; and if Dinah were indeed courting a local man, no harm could befall either her, or him, by the fact of their secret escaping. There might be a good joke in it: that anything to distress and confound the secret lovers could spring from his discovery he did not guess.

To him, then, this post office of Dinah and an unknown appeared a great and delightful find, capable of doing him a very good turn. It meant a triumph for Jane—a sort of triumph she would appreciate; but it also meant a bargain that should recover Jane's friendship before completion.

To find the unknown man would be easy now; indeed Jerry guessed that he had only to open the letter to learn it; but that was not an action possible to him. He restored the folded paper to its place, marked the spot very carefully and was content to leave the rest to Jane. She would have to see him, and that for the moment she declined to do; but he proposed to himself a visit after his day's work and doubted not that, if he pressed it forcibly enough, she might consent. Failing that, he would have to proceed single-handed with his inquiry. He felt sure enough that Jane had all along been right in her conviction that Maynard was the man, and he already anticipated her triumph if this should prove to be so.

That night he called at Green Hayes and it was Dinah who answered his knock. Jerry felt uncomfortable, but salved his conscience and invited her friendship.

She, knowing very well why he was come, left him and returned to the kitchen.

"Jerry wants to see you half a minute, Jane," she said. "He won't keep you, but he's got something to say as you must hear. It's a wonderful thing, he says, and will interest you a lot."

Jane, however, showed no immediate inclination to respond.

"Like his cheek," she said. "Didn't I tell the know-naught fool that when I wanted him I'd let him know?"

"Well, he wants you. And he's bursting with news seemingly. He begged me very earnest to ask you to see him."

"Perhaps his patience is out," said Mrs. Bamsey. "Perhaps he's come to give you up, Jane."

"No," she said. "I ban't feared of that. I only want him to see sense over a little matter here and there. If we are to be married in the autumn, he's got to understand about a few things."

Jane's secrets were secrets no longer. Her dream of a shop at Ashburton was now common knowledge.

"Go to him then. You've kept it up long enough if you really want him," said her mother.

"What should he have to tell me, except he's come round to my views?" asked Jane.

"Perhaps he has," replied Dinah.

Jane rose, dropped a story book and went out. There was a mumble of voices. Then Dinah and Faith heard her go down the garden path with Jerry.

"Thank goodness that's over," said Dinah. "Now you'll have peace, Mrs. Bamsey."

"I don't know," answered the elder. "They're not really well suited. Jane did ought to have taken a town man."

"She'll break him in to bricks and mortar after a bit," prophesied Dinah. "They love each other properly enough."

"If that was so, there'd be no talk of breaking in," said Jane's mother.

Meantime Jerry had spoken.

"It's very kind of you to see me," he said, "and you won't regret it. I've got a great piece of news for you, and it's a triumph for you, Jane, and if you agree to come round and make it up and be same as you was, I'll tell you."

"What's the great news you'd be likely to hear?"

"I didn't hear it: I found it out. And it'll be a lot more to you than me for that matter."

They talked like children.

"Very well then I'll hear it."

"And be friends?"

"I'll be friends, if it's such great news as you say."

"No; that means you'll go back on it after. You must be friends. And we'll regard it still open about the shop. And you needn't fear my news ain't great. 'Tis a triumph for you, and everybody will say so."

Jane's triumphs were few. She considered. She had not the faintest idea of the matter in his mind, yet was glad to be close to him again and hear his voice.

"All right then," she said. "The shop can wait."

"Will you come out for an hour? Then you shall see something, as well as hear tell about it."

She turned, picked up the sun-bonnet that Dinah had donned in the morning, and followed him.

He made her kiss him and then they went up the hill as he told his story in every particular.

"And why for I've fetched you out," he said, "is because you shall see it with your own eyes."

She was deeply interested.

"And 'tis greatly to your credit," declared Jerry, "for you've seen through it from the first, like the clever one you are. 'Tis a feather in your cap, Jane."

"It fits in very suent," she answered, "because Maynard's given warning and be off presently; and if 'tis him, then no doubt they'll be off together. And God knows that won't trouble me."

"Why all this secret business?" asked Jerry. "There's no law against 'em marrying if they want to. What be they shamed of?"

"Can't you see that? The man who's after Dinah must know all about the past and how she served John. He's feared of John. My brother's took this like any proud man would. He's not going to have his name dragged in the dirt and take his wicked wrongs lying down."

Jerry was concerned.

"You don't mean to tell me this is any business of John's? Surely to God he's got sense enough to— —?"

"You can leave John," she said, to calm his anxiety. "I'm not one to make trouble I'm sure. I'm only telling you. The chap after Dinah is afeared of John, and that's why they're keeping it close hid. What other reason can they have?"

"Then I do beg you'll respect their secret plans so far," urged Jerry. "I'm not telling you this for any mischief against anybody. I only wanted for you to have the pleasure of finding yourself in the right; and I thought 'twould be a bit of fun to let everybody know of it, and surprise Dinah and him and have a laugh at 'em—all friendly and well meaning. But if you tell me Johnny still means to be evil disposed to anybody as looks at Dinah, then the case is altered, for that means trouble."

But Jane was not prepared to lose the salt of the adventure for Jerry, or anybody. She kept her intentions secret, however.

"John's not a fool. I didn't mean that he'd do anything. What could he do? I only meant that the man, whoever he is, feels frightened of him. Of course there's no reason why he should be. Only a coward would be. So he's fair game anyway."

"If 'tis to be a laughing matter, I'll go on—not else," vowed Jerry; but she assured him that nothing but laughter would end the incident in any case.

They climbed the hill and he picked up his marks; then bade Jane light matches while he hunted for the nest. It was quickly found; she put her hand in and drew out Dinah's letter deposited that morning.

"He haven't come for it yet," said Jerry. "So us had better be moving, for he might be on his way this minute."

But Jane delayed and held the letter in her hand.

"If he only comes by night, we shall never find out who it is," she answered. "And you've been a very clever chap indeed, Jerry; and the rest you can leave with me. And don't you fear no trouble—of course not."

There was an obvious desire in her mind; but she guessed what Jerry would think of it and so kept it hidden and returned the letter to the nest.

"Well, you're a great wonder to find this out," she said, "and I'll keep my word and be friends. Don't you whisper a word to a soul yet. Leave it to me."

"No, no—this is your bit of fun," he declared. "They'll puzzle like fury to know how it slipped out, and us'll all roar with laughter at 'em I expect."

Indeed, he laughed in anticipation.

"Hush!" she said. "The man may be on his way now. I'll see you Sunday afternoon. And I'll find out for sure who the chap is by then, if I've got to hide and watch for him."

Jerry was overjoyed and embraced her.

"Sunday, then, and thank God we'm all right again, and us must never fall out no more, Jane; and I shall always feel kindly to these people, whether or no, because they've done this good deed for us."

Then they parted, each promising the other to keep a sharp look out on any passer-by. Jerry went his way in the best possible spirits and Jane started to run down the hill. But she did not run far and after her lover was out of the way, she stole back. She had kept his box of matches and now did a thing Jerry had probably forbidden. Not perhaps that his objection might have stopped her, but Jane's mind moved swiftly. Before all else it was desirable to find out the man, and she felt that nobody but a fool would waste time in detective operations while so simple an expedient as opening a letter offered. She had observed that Dinah's missive was merely folded, not sealed, and now she returned to the nest, found it and satisfied herself. Jane's honesty reached a point that amply soothed conscience. She had no intention to read the letter: that she would have held an improper action; but if the first words indicated the recipient, as she doubted not they would, then a great deal of time and trouble might be saved.

Jane opened the letter, having first listened that no approaching footfall broke the silence. Then she struck another match, read the words, "My darling Man," and hesitated. The match went out and she stood with the letter in her hand. Experience told her, from her own occasional communications to Jerry, that one might begin with an endearing but vague term and yet, at some later point in one's communication, mention the loved object by name. Dinah's large, free handwriting was easily seen and Jane considered that it would be possible to skim the letter, without really reading it, on the chance of finding the information she desired. This astute reasoning was rewarded, for, on the second sheet, as her eyes flickered along the lines, the name "Lawrence" very clearly appeared. Then she stopped, dropped her match, folded the letter carefully, restored it to its place and was gone.

"There's only one 'Lawrence' in these parts," thought Jane. Her reflections were now entirely with her brother. She did not echo Jerry's wish, that the matter should end in laughter, and clever though Jane was in some directions, there was a streak of malevolent idiocy about her in others. She now cherished a vague opinion that the man ought to suffer for his secret love-making. She despised him for a coward and rejoiced to think that John might do something drastic in the matter. That Maynard should be called upon to suffer seemed entirely reasonable to Jane; while as far as Dinah was concerned, she panted with delight that her little schemes were now to be made as public as the bird's-nest she had trusted with them. She hated Dinah and had always done so. Anything therefore that could make Dinah miserable must commend itself to Jane.

"And she shall know who she's got to thank, too," reflected the maiden; "there wouldn't be much in it for me if she didn't hear who'd found her out."

Full of these unamiable intentions Jerry's sweetheart returned home and announced that she and her lover were reconciled.

"Thank the Lord for that, then," cried Dinah. "And don't you give him a chance to quarrel again. 'Tis good time lost, Jane."

"You mind your own love affairs," answered the other tartly. "Us all know you've got 'em; but be too shamed of 'em, seemingly, to make 'em public."

With this crushing response Jane retired while Dinah stared after her.

"Don't mind the girl," said Faith Bamsey. "You be such a woman of mystery since you went off about your affairs, that you mustn't quarrel with people if they fling their words at you."

"I don't want to quarrel with anybody, Mrs. Bamsey," answered Dinah.

CHAPTER XXXIII
JOE HEARS THE SECRET

Susan and Thomas were returning from church, where they had sat solemnly together and heard their banns called for the first time of asking. Mr. Stockman, informed that this would happen, declined to go; indeed of late he had worshipped but seldom, permitting personal trials to check his devotions. The betrothed pair discussed Susan's father on the way home and Palk held it an impropriety that Mr. Stockman should not have been present.

"Out of respect to you, he did ought to have been there," he said; "and it's a very oneasy thing; because the next we shall hear may be that he won't come to the wedding neither."

"He's a regular Job for the minute—first one thing took and then another, till I dare say he feels the Lord have turned from him," murmured Susan.

"Not at all. Naught have overtook him that ain't well inside the common lot. Look at the items—firstly, his daughter gets engaged to be married to his hossman—a thing that ought to rejoice him instead of cast him down; secondly, his cowman gives notice—a thing that may happen to any farmer; and thirdly, yonder woman won't take him."

Thomas pointed where, fifty yards ahead of them, Melinda and her brother were walking home from church.

Soosie-Toosie nodded mournfully.

"There's no doubt. And that's a very harsh blow for father anyway. He'd always counted he could fall back on Melinda, like you put by a nest egg for the rainy day. And I'm a good bit disappointed in that quarter— quite as much as father in fact. But you mustn't whisper it, Tom; because of course the world ain't supposed to know father offered and got turned down."

"Other people won't pretend if we do," answered Mr. Palk. "He blew the trumpet about it himself, and everybody well understands that Mrs. Honeysett refused him."

"I'd give a fortune to know why," answered Joe's daughter. "Some day I'll ax her, I shouldn't wonder. Meantime I'd very much like to talk to her on another subject; and that's us."

"We must go on our appointed way. We don't want no outside opinions."

They overtook Melinda, and while Thomas talked with Jerry, the women fell back and Susan spoke of private affairs. She explained her gathering difficulties and Melinda listened with a good deal of sympathy.

"'Tis very undignified of your father, Susan—more like a naughty, disappointed child, than a man with fame for sense. I allow for him, because a good few things have happened to shake him; yet, so far as you and Mr. Palk are concerned, it did ought to be all joy and gladness."

"So it ought; but far from it," answered the other. "Father's got to such a pass now that when I tell him I'm wishful to name the day, he dares me to do so."

"Very wilful and unkind, and something ought to be done about it," declared Mrs. Honeysett. "I've been thinking a good deal on Joe lately, as I dare say you can guess; and no doubt you know very well why he came to see me a fortnight agone, Soosie. But I don't forget the past and I don't want to lose his friendship, nor yet yours. And I've thought a lot about you and him."

They lagged and mumbled together for some time; but it was clear that Melinda's views commended themselves much to Susan, and when they joined Jerry and Thomas at the turn to Mrs. Honeysett's house, Joe Stockman's daughter thanked her friend gratefully for some inspiring suggestions.

She talked without ceasing to Tom all the way home, and he listened and nodded and declared there might be a good deal in it.

"'Tis a great thought," he said, "and if you feel kind to it, then I might. Us'll see—'tis a rod to hold over the man, because it be full time for your father to find out where he stands."

"'Tis a sort of bargain of course," admitted Susan; "but you wouldn't call it a one-sided bargain."

"Not at all. It lets him out so as he can save his face before the folk. And it shows him what good-tempered creatures you and me are."

Thomas thought it might be possible to speak at the end of that day.

"I'll ax him to have a spot out of my bottle to-night," he said, "and if he condescends so far as to do so, then I'll open on him—not otherwise."

Mr. Palk was disappointed, however, for during the evening there came in John Bamsey to supper.

He appeared to be in a good temper and hid the object of his visit until after the meal was ended. He spoke chiefly of his own work on the river, and then of his father. Mr. Bamsey had sunk to be the mere husk of a man and his son frankly hoped that he might soon pass away.

"To know he was dead wouldn't be half so wisht as to see him alive like this," he said.

John was tactful with regard to Susan and Thomas. Indeed, he congratulated them out of earshot of Cousin Joe, and hoped it would be all right. To Maynard he was civil and no more.

Then, when opportunity came to do so, unheard by anybody else, he asked Mr. Stockman to walk out and smoke a pipe as he had something private to tell him. Joe was bored, for no affairs but his own interested him at this moment; but he obliged the younger, and through a warm, thundery night they strolled upon the Beacon. For a time the elder uttered general grievances and when he mentioned Lawrence Maynard, John struck in.

"That's why I wanted to get you away from them. There's a bit of news about Maynard; but perhaps you know it. And when it's out, he's got to reckon with me."

"Maynard's a very disappointing chap," declared the farmer. "Never did I like a man better, and never did I treat a man better, and I'm quite reasonable in that quarter when I say this is no ordinary case of a hand giving notice. He's outside his right to do any such thing with me; for I've been as good as a father to him for very near two years, and he well knew I never counted upon his going, and he's got no justice or honesty in him to do so."

"No, there's not much honesty or justice in him. And I dare say you wondered why he was going."

"I wondered certainly."

"I'll tell you. He's going to be married, and he couldn't dare to be married here, because he knew that he'd got me to reckon with. So he's planned it on the quiet, and he'll disappear presently no doubt; and then somebody else will disappear too. And that's Dinah Waycott."

Mr. Stockman was much agitated.

"Good powers! D'you know what you're saying, John?" he asked.

"Very well indeed. And I'll tell you how it was; but I don't want Maynard to know his dirty job be found out, and I'll beg you to keep dumb about it till things are a bit forwarder. I can get forty shillings or a month out of him, and give him a damned good hiding and disgrace him for his underhand, blackguard conduct—stealing another man's girl—but I want to do a bit more than that if it's in my power. And so long as you're not on his side no more, you'll be the best one to help me. I'd do a lot to break this off and punish Dinah, same as she punished me; and why not? She deserves it quite so well as him."

"Begin at the beginning," said Joe. "Tell me what you know. I'm your side without a doubt in this matter. There's a lot hid here you don't understand, and, for the credit of human nature, I hope you're wrong. This may be something that you've given ear to, out of ill feeling against Orphan Dinah. You must be terrible sure of your ground, for there's very good reasons why you ought to be mistaken. But if you're right, then you be the tool of Providence and it's well you came to me."

Johnny, who had learned everything from Jane, told the story with only one addition contrary to facts. Jane lied in a minor particular and concealed the incident of looking into Dinah's letter. Instead she declared that she had hidden herself, and watched, and seen Maynard come for the letter and leave another on the following evening in late dusk. The conclusion amounted to the same thing.

Joe was deeply impressed.

"I always held him a bit sly," he said, "and I've lived to find him ungrateful and hard-hearted where I'd every right to expect something very different. He struck me at the very moment when a decent man would have scorned to do so, with all my own troubles thick upon me. But this is something a lot deeper than his conduct to me, and even a lot worse."

"I'm glad you think so," answered John. "I'm very glad you see he's a secret, cowardly sort of one. He kindiddled Dinah away from me no doubt; and very like it is Providence, as you say; and if you don't think he ought to marry her, then I hope you'll help me to prevent it."

Johnny felt exalted. He had not expected much from his visit to his kinsman; he had even feared that Joe might already know the facts and attach no importance to them; but it seemed that Mr. Stockman was quite of John's opinion. Indeed he declared so.

"I certainly think they ought not to marry," he answered. "And I think a great deal more than that. Keep your mouth shut close for the present. There's plenty of time—unless."

"When's the man going?"

"No date be fixed."

"My mother was put out when Dinah went off a bit ago. She got the idea from Jane that Dinah had gone to be married then. But when they taxed her, she swore she had not."

"She couldn't tell a lie if she was paid to," declared Mr. Stockman, "and Maynard certainly weren't in that, because he was here and I saw him every day about his business. We must rest the blame on the right pair of shoulders. And it'll break 'em without a doubt. But we'd best to go careful. Don't you take a step alone. How many know?"

"Only Jane and Jerry and me."

"Maynard don't suspect?"

"Neither of 'em—they couldn't."

"Then tell your sister and Withycombe to keep dumb as mice for the minute; and so will I. This is a very serious thing indeed—and a great shock to me. To think he was that sort!"

John was pleased but mystified. He failed to see why this event should make so tremendous an impression on Mr. Stockman.

"I'm very glad you think it is so bad," he said. "I was in a bit of doubt if you'd take my side."

"As to sides," answered Joe, "I'm going to take the side of right, which is no more than to say I'll do my duty. And that looks pretty clear. I dare say you are a bit astonished, but understand me. I'm not making your quarrel mine, and I don't hold at all with your talk about forty shillings or a month out of Lawrence Maynard. This goes a very great deal deeper than forty shillings or a month, I may tell you. I'll say no more for the minute; but I shan't do naught till I've seen you again. Only keep this in mind: Maynard ain't planning this hookem snivey job and doing it all in secret, because he's afraid of you, but because he's afraid of me."

Johnny became more and more puzzled. It was clear, however, that he had won a powerful friend and might now hope to strike a harder stroke than any with his fist.

"So long as you be going to queer the man's pitch, and punish him, and get Dinah away from him, I don't care a damn," he said. "If Dinah finds out; but perhaps he's made her think— —"

"Yes; he's made her think a lot, and he's told her a great many dark and devilish falsehoods—that's very clear indeed," answered Joe.

"And if her eyes be opened, she may come back to sense yet!" cried the sanguine youth. "Shame will show her the truth perhaps."

Mr. Stockman did not answer. He was occupied with his own reflections.

"This shakes me to the vitals," he declared presently. "I thought I knew pretty well all there was to that man; and I knew less than naught. If anybody had said he was a wicked scoundrel, I'd have denied and defied it; but— —"

They had descended from the Beacon and were walking on the Buckland road. Then Joe stopped.

"You go your way now," he said, "and leave me to put this together. You do naught and I'll do naught for the minute. But there may not be any too much time. He was going at Michaelmas. 'Tis certain now that's a blind. He'll take French leave presently and we've got to be before him. Come to supper o' Wednesday, John. Then us'll see how it looks. That poor woman—as honest a creature as ever stepped."

"If he's up to any tricks— —"

"He is, by God! Now I'll leave you. And be so silent as the grave till you see me again."

Deeply wondering and greatly rejoicing at his success, John Bamsey went down the hill, while Mr. Stockman turned and slowly ascended. His excitement gave way to listlessness presently, for this discovery and the subsequent sensation could not advance Joe's own problems. He considered for a moment whether any course existed by which advantage could accrue to himself out of Maynard's position; but he saw none.

A trap from Ashburton descended, flashing its lights through the leafy darkness of the road; and when the ray illuminated Mr. Stockman, he heard a woman's voice bid the driver pull up. It was Mrs. Honeysett who spoke, and she seized an opportunity to relieve the existing painful conditions. For she had not seen Joe since she declined him; but here was an excuse and she took it.

"You'll be wondering what I'm doing at this time of night," she said, "but I can't pass you."

Then she alighted and a man alighted with her.

"Just been to Ashburton to meet my brother, Robert," she explained. "You remember him. He's home for a bit at last."

A huge figure towered in the gloom over Joe and a heavy hand grasped his own.

"I remember you," said the farmer, "but I forgot you were such a whacker. Sailed all the Seven Seas, I suppose, since you was last to Buckland?"

"He's two inches taller than what dear father was," declared Melinda, relieved to find Mr. Stockman in a humour apparently amiable. "Robert's going to take a nice rest along with me. In fact he doubts sometimes if he'll go back to sea at all."

"No, no—I don't doubt that," answered the sailor. "But I be going to give work a rest."

"And find a wife, if he can," continued Melinda. "Us must help him, Joe."

"I always swore as I'd marry a maiden from the Vale," said Robert Withycombe.

"The puzzle will be to find one, I tell him," laughed Melinda "I know a likely girl all the same, and so does Mr. Stockman, Bob."

Joe guessed to whom she referred, and it showed him that Melinda knew nothing of the threatened tragedy.

"I reckon you mean Orphan Dinah," he said. "Well and why not? A very sensible young woman. The man that gets her will be lucky."

"They'd be a proper pair and I hope Bob will think well of her. But he must be warned that she's already changed her mind in one quarter."

"That's not against her," replied Joe. "That shows strength of character and she had every right to do so. I only hope I know another woman who'll be wise enough to change her mind."

Before this veiled attack, Melinda was silent and Robert spoke.

"My girl, when she comes along, won't have no time to change her mind. She've got to marry me and be quick about it. Then us must find a little house to Southampton, or else Plymouth."

Stockman, with certain ideas moving in his head, issued an invitation.

"Perhaps you'll be in luck—who knows? I'd pleasure you for your sister's sake, because she and me are very good friends, and I hope always will be. You come to supper o' Wednesday, Robert, and bring Jerry along with you. I don't ax you, Melinda—not this time. I want to have a tell with your brothers; mind you make 'em come."

"Come and welcome," promised Robert, while his sister wondered what might be behind this invitation. They parted; the trap with the sailor and his kit-bag rolled down the hill and Joe proceeded home. He was gloomy and his thoughts concerned themselves with Melinda, but not hopefully. All had changed with her refusal. Even if she did, indeed, find herself in a mood to accept him on another invitation, it would never be the same to Mr. Stockman. He did not care for her enough to let any future 'yes' make him forget the grave rebuff already suffered. Indeed he did not very much want her now. Like a skeleton between them must ever persist the recollection of her refusal. He only realised the attractive features of the old arrangement at the moment when it was about to end, and he still smouldered with intense heat when he reflected on his daughter's marriage. In the light of this evening's revelation he was disposed to add another sin to those upon the head of Lawrence Maynard. It occurred to him that the cowman might have had a hand in Susan's romance and urged Thomas forward upon his hateful course. He began to be convinced that Lawrence had inspired Thomas, possibly for private ends hidden from Joe. He suspected that these men had made a cat'spaw of him, and since Thomas was certainly not equal to any such task single-handed, to the subtler Maynard might chief blame be assigned.

He found himself hating Maynard and taking grim satisfaction in the thought Lawrence had over-reached himself. Here, at any rate, was an outlet for Mr. Stockman's pent-up indignation. One man should have justice at his hands, and if the downfall of Maynard indirectly smote Palk, or even changed his determination, so much the better. Joe indeed always hoped that something might happen even at the last moment to upset the marriage of Susan, and he would have stuck at no reasonable means of doing so. He had assured himself long ago that, for her own sake, such a step must be taken if the least opportunity occurred.

CHAPTER XXXIV
AN OFFER

Now force was ranged against force, and while Dinah and Lawrence Maynard matured the final details of their exodus, half a dozen men had become aware of their secret enterprise and were concerned to upset it in the name of right. Only the manner of doing so offered material for argument. The situation was reached on the Wednesday night of Joe's supper party, for when John Bamsey duly arrived to learn the secret, he was surprised to find Jerry Withycombe and his brother, Robert, also of the company. Mr. Stockman had so far accepted the inevitable that his friends might discuss Susan's approaching wedding in his presence, and to-night Robert Withycombe chaffed Mr. Palk and Susan while he ate. Presently, indeed, he drank to their united bliss and challenged the rest of the company to do so. Thomas was gratified and Susan felt much moved to see her father humbly drink the toast with the rest. Then the diplomatic Joe asked Robert if he had called at Green Hayes, and what he thought of Jerry's future wife.

Robert praised Jane very heartily.

"She's a bowerly piece," he said, "and clever as they make 'em. What the devil she finds in this chap I can't guess; but love's blind no doubt. I shall see 'em hitched up afore I go."

"And yourself, too, by all accounts," said Mr. Palk.

"'Tis odds he won't find nobody good enough," declared Jerry. "He fancies himself something cruel, because he's sailed pretty near round the world."

"There's one good enough for any living man at Green Hayes," asserted Mr. Stockman. "Have you seen Orphan Dinah, Robert?"

"I have, and I ain't wishful to talk on that subject in public—not yet," answered the sailor guardedly.

"He's hit—he's hit!" cried Joe. Then he remembered that Johnny was present and turned with a great show of innocence to Maynard, who took his supper with the rest.

"Here's a man that knows Dinah Waycott, and have took a walk or two with her for that matter. And a very clever man too, and I'm terrible sorry he's going to leave me. What would you say of Orphan Dinah, Lawrence?"

Maynard was unruffled.

"Lucky the man who gets her," he answered; "she's one in a thousand."

The talk ranged and John grew more and more impatient to know when vital matters would be reached; but he perceived that Mr. Stockman could not speak before the company. After supper Maynard disappeared and then, when his daughter had cleared away, Joe beckoned John and took him outside.

"I don't trust my family circle in this matter," he said, "and so we'll light our pipes and go out. 'Tis a moony night and to walk a mile after supper is a very good rule, thought I don't practise it. Call them two men. They've got to know so well as you."

In ten minutes Thomas and Susan had Falcon Farm to themselves, while Joe, with John and the Withycombe brothers, strolled through a still and moonlit night.

Then he told them that Lawrence was married, and had run away from his wife.

"That's how we stand, neighbours. Maynard's a secret sort of man in most of his dealings, but when he came here, he found me not lacking in friendship, and he told me that much about himself. And I thought the better of him for it; because it's often the wisest and properest thing that parties can do, to put a few leagues between self and partner, if marriage be poisoning 'em both. He weren't to blame for that, so far as I can tell; indeed, I upheld the man in his action; but now the case is altered, and we may be pretty sure the fault was his and some innocent creature have already suffered at his hands. And there's no reason why another should.

"It's all clear enough now. He remembered, no doubt, that he'd told me his secret, and so he's running this job on the quiet and have doubtless forged good reasons for Dinah's ear why they should bolt presently, instead of proclaiming the thing like decent people would. It's because Maynard be married that he's doing this; and now good chance puts the secret into the hands of honest men and we must act according. I always leave a rogue to Providence myself, and never yet found I could do anything better than what Providence done; but in this case there's a victim, and the victim can be saved, thank God."

They talked and poured their indignation into the moonlight. Johnny abounded in drastic suggestions. He desired, above all, to face Maynard with Dinah, then let her hear the truth and beat the cowman before her. But one, who as yet knew the least of Dinah, raised a question.

"How if he's told her and she's willing to chance it and don't care?" asked Robert.

Mr. Stockman protested.

"You little understand the sort she is. She'd die rather than sink to such a deed. No; he's caught her with a parcel of lies, and he merits a pretty good punishment no doubt. You might say the loss of her will be punishment enough; but there's more to it than that I dare say."

"By God, yes!" vowed Johnny.

"If he's catched and headed off in time, the law can't touch him," said Robert.

"Then 'tis for us to take the law in our own hands," added Johnny, "and we will."

Joe warned him.

"All in good time," he answered. "It's life or death for Dinah, and therefore we be called to act; but what we shall do and how we shall both save her and be evens with this rogue will take some planning. Rough justice must be done I grant. He must have rope enough to hang himself with, and he must get the surprise of his life presently; but we must be clever, else we'll spoil all. I've got ideas, but he's a downy chap and nobody must do anything to make him smell a rat."

They abounded in suggestions and Johnny pointed a danger.

"While we're talking and planning," he said, "they may give us the slip any night and be out of reach and vanished off the earth so far as we're concerned. And I say this: 'tis time we knowed what was in their letters. They be keeping apart very clever indeed, so as nobody should link up their names, though my sister always swore they was up to something; but they write, and Jane has watched Dinah go up for a letter more'n half a dozen times; and now it's time we know what's doing, else we'll get left."

"To look into a knave's letters to frustrate his tricks be no crime, I reckon," admitted Robert Withycombe. "What d'you say, Mr. Stockman?"

They all agreed that to read the secret correspondence was permissible, for Dinah's sake. Indeed Joe held that this had become a duty.

Robert expressed sorrow for her; but he knew the situation with respect to John Bamsey and did not, therefore, say much. His own emotions to Dinah, if any had been yet awakened, cooled rapidly. He had no mind to seek a maiden so much involved.

They parted presently; but John was going to tell Jane the truth that night, and impose upon her the task of reading letters when she could, to gather what definite information of Maynard's plans they might contain.

"I hate for Jane to do anything so mean," declared Jerry, "but I see it did ought to be done."

"It ain't mean, my son; it's for the sake of justice, and to come between Dinah and living death," explained Joe.

Then the younger men went their way to Buckland, and John, leaving the brothers there, started for home. He passed Maynard on the way and guessed that he had left, or brought, a letter. Much he longed to challenge him, and fully he intended to play an active part in the future proceedings; but he hid his secret knowledge, and said 'Good night' and passed down the hill, while the unsuspecting cowman, who had just posted a letter to Dinah, responded with friendly voice.

But Maynard did not overtake his master, and hearing Tom's slow voice droning in the kitchen with thin interjections from Soosie-Toosie, he retired on returning home.

Indeed matters of some moment for Joe awaited him, for the time brought his thoughts sharply back to himself. Susan hastened to pour out his evening drink when he came back, and Thomas, who always rose to his feet when his master entered the kitchen, now asked if he might be permitted to say a few words.

He spoke and Susan fluttered about in the background, while Joe listened and sipped from a glass of spirits and water.

"You see things be risen to a crisis," began Tom, "and I feel very much that the time's ripe for an understanding. It's mournful to keep on like this, and to-day, by the post, there came a very fine offer of work for me to a gentleman's farm nigh Exeter. Everything done regardless, and good money and a cottage. So now's the appointed time to speak, and Susan and me feel very wishful to pleasure you, and we've come by an idea."

"Go on then. It don't much matter putting your ideas before me, as I'm not axed to influence them. You'll do as you want to do."

"No," said Thomas; "in reason we want to do your will if it can be done. You've been very harsh of late, master, and, of course, I can well understand your feelings about losing Susan. But I never shall see why you was so cruel rude about it. You may treat people like dirt, if you do it kindly, and they won't mind; but if you call 'em dirt, then they get a bit restive; and restive I've got, and so have she. But here it is—an offer in a very friendly spirit; and we haven't come to it without a lot of thinking and balancing the bright side against the dark. And, on the whole, for Susan and me it's a bright thought, and we hope you may think so too."

"But there's one little thing, father," began Susan, and Mr. Palk stopped her.

"Leave all to me," he said, "I'll set it out. There's several little things for that matter, and if the master don't see his way, so be it. First, there's what we be offering, and next there's the conditions to set against it. And we offer to stop after we'm married and to go on just as usual. As a son-in-law I know you've got no use for me; but as a hossman, you've been suited. And as a hossman I'll willingly bide and do all I know regular and steadfast for the same money as I'm getting now. And I pray God, if that happened, you'd come to find me a good son-in-law likewise. And that means your darter bides at your right hand so long as you want her there. And I'll go farther than that. I'll say if at any time in the next five years you take a wife and want us away, we'll go."

"I wish it too, with all my heart, father," declared Susan. "I'd be lost away from you, and worriting all the time to know whose hands you were got in. And marrying Thomas won't make no difference, except there'll be two to think about you instead of one."

Mr. Stockman puffed his pipe and showed by no expression that he appreciated the proposal.

"I'll give you this credit," he said, "I dare say you mean well."

"No two people ever meant better, father."

"And now for the powder. I expect that, even if I was to see my way, you've got a barrelful of ugly things you'll demand. And I tell you at once that it just hangs on a razor-edge whether the idea be good enough as it stands, without any conditions to it at all. I should have conditions also, and one of them would be that you undertook to stop and not change your minds after a year, or bolt off and leave me at your own will."

"Never," answered Susan. "It's understood we don't go unless you wish it."

"And now your conditions, Palk, if you please."

"There ain't no powder about 'em, but only right and reason," said Thomas, "and be it as 'twill, there's only three of 'em. Firstly, that we have a proper, human wedding, all joyous and cheerful, with you smiling and a few neighbours to the spread after, and a nice send off; secondly, that we be allowed ten clear days for a honeymoon round about somewhere; and thirdly, and lastly, that Susan, when she comes home, be allowed a virgin girl under her, to help the labour of the house. Just a maid-of-all-work, as any other married woman would have for her dignity. That's all we ask, master, and I do hope you may be brought to see there's nothing to it but will make for your comfort and satisfaction. Susan you know, and you've often said she was the light of the house, and she wants so to continue; and I do believe, when you get to know me better and see how I go on and how I treat Susan, that you'll come to feel a kinder feeling for me also."

"Don't say 'no' without thinking over it and giving us the benefit of your wisdom, dear father," pleaded Soosie-Toosie, her large eyes fixed upon him.

"I never say 'no' to anything, without thinking it over, Susan. 'Tis all the other way, and I'm prone to give people the benefit of the doubt too often. I'll turn this over. You've put the case very clear. We shall see. I'm one for the long view, as you know. I'll look all round it."

CHAPTER XXXV
FOR RIGHT AND JUSTICE

Joe Stockman decided that he must submit to the propositions of Thomas and his daughter. He declared that the decision was marked solely by affection for Susan, and a determination that his son-in-law should have every opportunity to show his worth under the new conditions. He also let it be known how this arrangement was his own idea and, indeed, mentioned it in several quarters as a fact, before he informed the lovers that he was agreeable. This matter settled, Joe, who was really much gratified and relieved, modified his gloom, and to the surprise of those most concerned, proceeded with his part of the contract in a spirit not unamiable. He planned a substantial entertainment for the wedding-day, permitted Susan to secure a maid, and decreed that the honeymoon might last a fortnight.

All progressed smoothly; the farmer became affable to everybody, including Mr. Palk, and made no opposition to the minor details of housekeeping and general control that the marriage would involve.

"I've drawed the sting of the trouble," he confessed to himself.

And then, two days before the wedding, he received certain secret information concerning the matter of Lawrence Maynard. He expected it, for during the same week Maynard had specified a date for leaving.

Then came the vital news from Jane, who dipped into the secret letter-box from time to time and skimmed the lover's letters to glean facts. These she had now learned, and they embraced the time of departure and details concerning it.

Thus Jane and John, with the Withycombe brothers and Mr. Stockman, heard what was planned, and the younger conspirators now waited for Joe to determine what actions should be taken. For him zest had already dwindled out of the adventure. He had secured a new cowman and the maid-of-all-work was skilled in the dairy; therefore Joe felt satisfied, so far as his own comfort and welfare were concerned. But there remained Dinah to be saved, and various courses of action offered themselves, the simplest being to make all publicly known at once.

Joe, however, decided to take another party into the secret before any final action, and he was inspired to do so by the visit of Arthur Chaffe, who arrived at this time, to look into the matter of the dry rot in the stables.

They met and conversed on various subjects, beginning, English fashion, with the weather; but the weather was not a topic that Arthur ever permitted to waste his time.

"An early autumn," said Joe. "The leaves be falling in the topmost trees a'ready."

"I wish one old leaf would fall," answered the carpenter. "It's among the saddest things I've known that Ben Bamsey lives on—a poor spectrum and shadow of his former self. A very harrowing thing for all concerned, and I've prayed on my knees daily, for a month now, that it may please God to take him. What a man prays for will show you the measure of his wits, Joe, and the nature of his character; and for my part I've always made it a habit to pray for others more than for myself, and found it a very good rule."

"No doubt, no doubt, Arthur. But most people have looked upon Ben as dead ever since last spring. There's only the outer case of the man left: the works be gone. And a good thing here and there. He's took from some shocks and surprises. Run your eye over this job and see what's to be done, then I'll have a tell with you about something else that calls for a lot of brain power. Right must be done in a certain quarter; but the question is how best to do it."

Chaffe proceeded, and when he had settled the matter of the dry rot, he spoke of the approaching wedding and declared his immense satisfaction that Soosie-Toosie would stop with her father.

"It's like your good sense, and there's no doubt at all you've done a wise thing. And Thomas Palk's mind be opening out very well I find. He's a very good man and, in your hands, though old for a learner, can't fail to enlarge. In fact I'm very glad about it, and so's everybody. You'd have missed her, of course, and she'd have felt a lost creature away from you."

"So I believe, and so I acted," answered Joe; "and now list to me, Arthur, and face a very critical affair. 'Tis understood you don't mention it again to a living soul for the minute; but I'll ask you to give it your full attention. I'll tell you now, and after a bit of dinner, which you'll take with me, please, you can say what you think about it."

Mr. Chaffe protested at stopping for dinner. He was desperately busy and begged to be allowed to return home; but Joe would not suffer it.

"No," he said, "a soul be in the balance, Arthur, and I never yet heard you put your work before the welfare of a soul."

"If a soul's the matter, you must speak and I must hear," answered the old man; and then he listened to the story, from the moment of Maynard's arrival at Falcon Farm up to the present and the secret flight, planned to take place within ten days.

"Maynard goes from me," concluded Joe, "and the next morning he meets Orphan Dinah at Shepherd's Cross, on Holne Moor. From there they get down to the in-country, take train for Plymouth, at Brent I expect, and sail that night, or the next day, to Australia. A very simple and easy plan if it wasn't interfered with; but of course it ain't going to happen, and the question is how best to stop it in a righteous and seemly fashion."

Mr. Chaffe was much concerned.

"Who can say he's ever fathomed man or woman?" he asked. "This throws a light into darkness, Joe, and shows me many things that have troubled me. Not about Dinah, for she's above board and a good Christian by nature and upbringing; but about Maynard. He's foxed her into this dark and dangerous deed, and I'll be bold to say the blame's on his shoulders only, though nothing ought to have made her agree to run away unbeknownst from her friends. That shows a lightness; but no doubt the man have made her love him, and love blinds the best. There's a lot to thank God for, however. You can see Providence looking far ahead as usual. For if Maynard hadn't confided the truth to you years ago, we should never have known, and he'd have brazened it out and committed bigamy in our midst no doubt."

"He would—the rascal; and I feel his crime did ought to be punished, whether it succeeds or not. He's tried to do a blackguard act, and it is for us just men to make him feel his proper reward and chasten the wretch—if only for his future salvation. But seeing that I've fallen out with him already in a manner of speaking, when he gave notice, I'm in the position where it wouldn't become me to smite him, because people would say it was revenge. And so I put it to you, who stand for nothing but the cause of religion and justice."

Mr. Chaffe nodded.

"A very proper line to take. And I might, of course, go in my turn to higher ones. You see it's a matter for State and Church both, Joe. This man be out to break the law and ruin an innocent and trusting woman; and he's also flouting righteousness and planning a great sin. We must rise to the proper answer; and my feeling would be to take a line on our own, if I can think of the right one. And if I can't, then we must hand it over to the lawful authorities."

"No," said Mr. Stockman. "In my view that would be paltry. We've got to keep the man and woman apart and read him a sharp and bitter lesson. That's well in our power without going to the police. They couldn't lock him up if he hadn't done the crime, so it's for us to make justice on the spot and fall on the man like the trump of doom, just when he thinks he's triumphed. That's how I see it. And we don't give him no long drawn out punishment, but just crush him, like you'd crush a long-cripple,* and leave him to his bad conscience. And as for Dinah, when she finds out the size of her danger and sees the brink she was standing on, she'll soon forget her troubles, in thankfulness to God for her great escape."

* "Long-cripple" — viper.

"It calls for a fine touch," declared Arthur. "There's no doubt our duty stands before us, Joe, and, at a first glance, I'm minded to see with you, that this feat is within our power and we needn't call for no outside aid. The thing is to know just how to strike. Your idea of falling on the man like the crack of doom be good on the whole. But we mustn't overdo it, or forget we're sinful creatures ourselves. He's got a fearful punishment afore him in any case, apart from what we may do, because he loses Dinah just at the very moment when he thinks he's got her safe for evermore. And that's enough to go on with for him. But the right thought will certainly come to my mind, since we be acting in the name of religion."

"I'm all for mercy as a rule," answered Stockman; "but not in this case. Mercy's barred out, because of Maynard's wickedness."

"There don't seem no very loud call for mercy certainly, when you think of the far-reaching thing he's led the poor girl into. No; we may stop at justice I reckon. I'll brood upon it, Joe. I see the line, I believe; but I'll take it afore my Maker. We want a bit of physical force—we may even have to handle him, as I see it."

"D'you think so?"

"Yes. For the sake of argument, would John Bamsey and the Withycombe brothers be strong enough to withstand him?"

Joe believed they might be.

"If they surprised the man, they would. Robert Withycombe's a huge, strong chap. What be in your mind?"

"Wait till it takes a clearer shape. Put by the thought till after the wedding. That must be all happiness and joy; and when that's well over and the happy pair are away, we'll turn to Maynard. We must come to it with clean hands, Joe, as humble, willing tools of Providence. Us mustn't allow ourselves no evil hate, or anything like that, but just feel but for the grace of God us might have been tempted and fallen into the pit ourselves. There's a bright side, even for him, and I hope in time he'll live to see what we saved him from."

"We must have a masterpiece of cleverness, and I'll think too," added Mr. Stockman. "Don't squeak, Arthur; don't tell a living soul about it. We must just teel a trap for the beggar and catch him alive. And we must spare Dinah all we can."

"As to Dinah," answered Mr. Chaffe, "if what I see rising up in my mind be the right course, we may have to give Dinah a pinch also. I quite agree she must be spared all shame if possible; but I always go the way I'm led by the still small voice, Joe; and if the ideas creeping in me blaze out and command to be followed, then very like Dinah may have to be in it—for her own good. You must remember that Dinah's only a part of human nature, and we can read her feelings very clear when this bursts upon her."

"How can we?" asked Joe. "I never can read any woman's feelings very clear at any time. They never feel about anything same as we do, and their very eyes ban't built to look at the shape and colour of things as ours be. They're a different creation in fact, and 'tis folly to pretend they ain't."

"A different creation, no," answered Arthur. "They feel and suffer same as us, and Dinah Waycott, afore this great downfall, will take the ordinary course of human nature. Her Christianity will help her to keep a tight hand on herself; but, being a woman, she'll want to give Lawrence Maynard a bit of her mind, and he'll deserve it and didn't ought to be spared it."

Mr. Stockman was rather impressed.

"By God, that's true," he said. "And I'm rather glad you thought of it and not me, Arthur. For if I'd hit on that, people would without doubt have said 'twas the poison of revenge working in me. But coming from you, of course it can be no more than justice. It's just a thing a bachelor might have hit upon. The average married man would have felt a twinge of mercy, and only your high sense of justice would screw you up to such a pitch."

"Nothing be done yet," answered Mr. Chaffe. "And if my thoughts look too harsh in your eyes presently, I'll willingly tone 'em down where possible. But often the surgeon as ban't feared to cut deep be the best to trust. We've got to save the man's soul alive, and seeing the size of the wound upon it and the danger in which he stands, we should be weak to botch our work for the sake of sparing him, or ourselves pain. For that's what mercy to the wicked often comes to, Joe. We forgive and forget for our own comfort far too often, and let a sinner off his medicine, only because we don't like to see the ugly face he makes over it."

"In fact, mercy would be weakness and false kindness," admitted Joe. "And if we want a couple more strong men presently, I know the proper ones. We must all be ministers of right in this matter, and I'm glad of your clear head and high opinions. For now I know we shall come through with credit to ourselves and the respect of the people."

"There again, we must take care our feet don't slip," answered Mr. Chaffe. "It may hap that this ain't a case for the people. As a lesson and warning it may have to be told about, for the sake of the young; but, against that, we may find, for Dinah's sake, that it might not be convenient to make it a public affair. And now we'll put this away for the Lord to work on, Joe. Be sure it won't slumber nor sleep, but take the shape He wills in our hands. We'll talk of the wedding now for ten minutes afore I be off. How would you like a triumphant arch over the lichgate to church? It can very easy be done."

"No," said Mr. Stockman. "I'm going through with it as a father should, Arthur, and we're to have a very fine meal, with a pastry-cook from Ashburton to prepare it and serve it. I'm doing my part, and I'm giving Susan away in church, and I've asked all the neighbours, including five outlying friends of Palk's. But, between you and me and without unkindness, I feel no temptation to lose my head about what's going to happen. I don't hunger for large diversions, nor yet triumphant arches over the lichgate, nor anywhere else. I want for it to be over and them back home, so as I may see how it's going on and what measure of peace and comfort I can count upon in the future. The time for triumphant arches be when a pair have stood each other ten years, and can still go on with it."

"Keep your nerve and give 'em every fair chance and trust God," said Mr. Chaffe.

"Be sure of that," answered Joe. "I only wish I felt so sure that, hunting in a couple, they'll do their duty to me so well as I shall do mine to them."

CHAPTER XXXVI
THE WEDDING DAY

A kindly spirit might have been moved somewhat to observe Soosie-Toosie's wonder and delight when wedding presents began to appear before her marriage. She could hardly remember being the recipient of any gift in her life, and she felt amazed, almost prostrate, under the sense of obligation awakened by a tea-set from Green Hayes, a metal teapot and milk jug from Melinda, a "History of Palestine," with coloured pictures from Mr. Chaffe, and other presents only less handsome. Thomas, too, was remembered by former friends, and the kinsmen of the Stockmans, who dwelt at Barnstaple, sent Susan an eider-down quilt of fiery scarlet and green, which she secretly determined should comfort the couch of her father when winter returned. This gift inspired Mr. Palk.

They had not yet decided where the fortnight's holiday should be spent, and he suggested that Barnstaple would serve the purpose.

"Then I could be introduced to your relations," he said.

"And so could I," added Susan, "because I've never seen 'em in my life, and father haven't seen 'em for twenty years—have you, father?"

Joe admitted that he had not, but the eider-down quilt impressed him and he held it desirable that the families might be better acquainted. He was not in the least proud of Mr. Palk; yet, upon the whole, he thought it well that his daughter should come within reach of her relatives. The honeymoon was therefore fixed for Barnstaple.

Lawrence Maynard's gift took a practical form. He did not design to carry anything from England but his money and a few clothes. The remainder of his property, including a small chest of good tools, a tin trunk, and a pair of leggings, some old clothes and some boots, he gave to Thomas, who accepted them gladly.

"Us wish you very well, though Joe do not," said Mr. Palk, "and I hope some day, when you've got time, you'll write to me and tell about Australia—especially how hosses be out there."

The wedding was well attended and Melinda, who came over in the morning to help Soosie-Toosie with her new dress, declared that the bride, in a steel-blue gown and a large white hat with a white feather in it, had never looked so well. Mr. Palk was also clad in blue, of another shade. His wedding garment was of ultramarine shot with a yellow thread, and he wore a yellow tie with a green shamrock sprigged upon it. The best man came from Newton Abbot. He was older by many years than the bridegroom, but he had merry eyes and a merry face and declared a score of times that he had known Mr. Palk from childhood, and that an honester man didn't walk.

From Buckland Court came Susan's bridal bouquet of orchids and white roses, which Mr. Ford carried up the evening before and himself immersed in a jug of water for the night. A pair of distinguished candlesticks and a clock came from the Court also, greatly to the gratification of Mr. Stockman; while his landlord sent Susan a cheque for ten pounds.

At the wedding were the family of Withycombes (the sailor had given Susan two amazing shells from the other end of the world); while from Green Hayes came John and Jane Bamsey and their mother. Dinah was with them at church, but did not attend the wedding breakfast, asking rather to return to her foster-father at home. Those who understood were not surprised to learn her wish to do so. Mr. Chaffe was present and also enjoyed the banquet. No less than fifteen sat down, and they openly declared in each other's ears that Joe had "spread himself" in a very handsome manner.

One speech only was made, and Arthur proposed the health of bride and bridegroom in an oration which made Soosie-Toosie shed a few tears despite herself. Then Thomas was held back, as he rose with the rest to drink his own everlasting happiness; and his wife cut the cake, declaring it was a terrible pity to spoil such a pretty thing.

They drove off in their blue attire presently, and the last seen of them was Mr. Palk waving his new grey wide-awake from one window of the wedding chariot and Susan fluttering a handkerchief from the other.

Many curious eyes rested on Maynard during the course of the meal, but he was innocent of the fact and preserved a cheerful demeanour. Those who watched him mused, according to the measure of their intelligence, as to what was proceeding in his mind; but none guessed; all the conspirators rather found in his brown face and dark eyes evidences of a devious and lawless spirit hiding itself for its own purposes. He was in reality considering how far different would his own doubtful nuptials be in a strange land amid strange faces.

When the entertainment was at an end and most of the wedding guests had gone, with expressions of their gratitude, certain men, by arrangement, drifted away together. Maynard, in the farmyard milking the cows, saw Mr. Stockman with Mr. Chaffe and a few others saunter over the autumnal moor and sit presently together upon a flat ledge of rocks under the Beacon.

And there it was that Arthur learned the last news concerning Maynard, the date of his departure and the hour at which, upon the day following, he would meet Dinah at their last tryst. He himself had come primed with an inspiration as to what should be done.

"Jane's thankful to God she haven't got to do no more hateful spying," said Jerry Withycombe. "But there it is. He meets her at Shepherd's Cross somewhere after six o'clock on the morning after he goes off from here."

"And at the cross the man must face his outraged fellow creatures," declared Mr. Chaffe. "And when Dinah comes, she shall see and hear the bitter truth. All be clear in my mind's eye now and I see a very high and solemn deed, which must be done in the spirit of justice only—else it will fail. We be the instruments, and if any man have any hate or ill will towards the evil doer rather than the evil deed, then he'd better stand down and let another take his place. For Maynard have got to be handled, and when he fights against us, as he will, with the whole force of his baffled wickedness, we must act without passion and feel no more rage in our hearts than the Saviour did when he cast the devil out of a poor, suffering creature. We must be patient under Maynard's wrath."

"'Tis a young man's job," said Joe, after Arthur had described his dramatic purpose, "and we can very well leave it to them. Us older blades needn't be called to be there at all, I reckon."

"I wouldn't say there was any cause for you to be," answered Arthur, "but I shall certainly be there. It's my duty; I be the voice that will reach his heart and his conscience, I hope, when the rough work's done and the blow has fallen. And there's the woman to be thought upon also. One has to consider this matter from every point of view. I shall take Orphan Dinah back to her home, when all is over, and she understands how the Lord has looked after her."

"'Tis a matter of the man's fighting powers," said Robert Withycombe. "No doubt I could manage him with Jerry's help; but I reckon we don't want a scrap and a lot of blood about, or broken heads. Be we three men—Jerry and John and me—strong enough to make him yield without a dust up?"

"And why not a dust up?" asked Johnny; but Arthur admonished him.

"If you feel like that, you'd best not to come, Bamsey," he said. "I tell you again that all's spoiled if we don't carry this thing out in a proper manner. Robert be perfectly right. The man had far better feel he is up against a force beyond his strength to oppose. We don't want no painful scene to spoil the dignity. And if you three ban't equal to it, we must get in somebody else. But not police; I'm very wishful to keep professional people out of this."

"All depends on him," said Mr. Stockman. "If he was to put up a fight, then there'd be temper and hard knocks and fur flying, no doubt. You want to drop on the man like a flap of lightning; but if it's going to be a rough and tumble first, and him perhaps escaping after all, then I say get another pair of hands, so as he will see it's no good opposing you, even if he wants to. He must be faced with such force as will make him throw up the sponge at once and take what you mean to give him. He must feel 'tis just as vain to make a fuss about it as a man feels when he makes up and knows he's going to be hanged inside the hour."

"I wish we was going to hang him," whispered John to Jerry.

They decided that it would be wise to add a powerful member to their number, in order that Maynard would be prevented from making any unseemly effort to evade his punishment.

"Abel Callicott will do very nice," said John. "He's a prize-fighter and he's to Ashburton now. If I tell him we're out to punish a rogue, and Robert here tells him too, he'll understand there's no cowardice meant, or nothing like that, and he'll help. The man wouldn't waste his time trying to fight or trying to run away then."

"They prize-fighters are generally good-tempered creatures and often religious," admitted Mr. Chaffe. "If he'll come in the right frame of mind, well and good. But don't let there be no mistake. We must all be on the spot and out of sight before they arrive. In fact, to be safe, us will do wisely to get up over the night before. I pray it may be fine weather, else it will be as painful to our bodies as our minds. We'll foregather at Shepherd's Cross and we must leave a good margin of time for fear of accidents."

They talked thoughtfully and seriously. Arthur Chaffe lifted the minds of them to the high issue involved and the gravity of what they purposed. They worked objectively with the facts and had no subjective glimmering of the reasons that lay behind the facts in the lives of those about to commit this deed. Here was a married man deceiving a single woman—a frank situation, that left no place in the argument for any extenuations. Dinah they knew, and they believed their knowledge precluded the possibility of such a character consenting to live in sin under any possible circumstances. The man they did not know; but it was enough that he had planned this wickedness. One who could plot thus had put himself beyond the pale.

Their attitude was entirely to be commended, and each felt worthy of the occasion. Joe Stockman and John Bamsey alone might have been accused of mixed motives, and certainly the master of Falcon Farm would not have admitted them. As for John, in the atmosphere of the conference, even he abated something of his fire—at least openly. In secret he trusted that Maynard would fight, and that it might be his privilege to administer a quietus. But, indeed, no great possibility in this direction offered, since there must be four men to one in any case. Johnny abandoned much thought of the man, therefore, and centred on the future of the woman.

For the rest, Robert and Jerry merely proposed to do what now appeared a duty; while as for Mr. Chaffe, no more placable spirit ever planned how to chasten a sinner for his own good. He was much pleased with what he had arranged, yet desired no credit afterwards.

"We must be silent, neighbours, when all is done," he said. "Each man will take his part, and when it is over, we will keep our mouths shut and put it behind us. 'Unto God be the praise'; we don't want none."

CHAPTER XXXVII
SHEPHERD'S CROSS

The new cowman came on the day before Maynard left Falcon Farm and Mr. Stockman was satisfied with his ability and intelligence. And then came the moment when Joe shook hands and bade Lawrence farewell. All animosity had died, for the elder was not vindictive. He pictured the experiences that awaited his old servant and found it in his heart to be sorry for him. Only thought of the enormity of the deed he had so deliberately planned steeled Mr. Stockman.

"I shall hear tell of you, no doubt," were the last words that he said at parting.

To Holne went Maynard, put up with an acquaintance for that night, and, at five o'clock on the following morning, set out to meet Dinah at Shepherd's Cross, a mediæval monument that marked a forgotten monkish way of old. There Dinah, whose departure was designed to be secret, would meet him, and together they would descend to Brent, where neither was known, and so reach Plymouth, whence their steamer sailed that night.

The morning dawned fine and touched with frost. The wind blew gently from the east. There was no sting in it, but it created an inevitable haze, and distance quickly faded under its blue-grey mantle, while at hand all shone clear and bright in the sunrise fires. The heavy dew of a cloudless night was not yet dried off the herbage, and the grass, nibbled to a close and springy velvet by sheep and rabbits, spread emerald green between the masses of heather and furze, where the lover climbed Dene Moor. Still the autumn heath shone with passages of colour; but into the rich pink of a month earlier had crept a russet warmth, where innumerable heather bells passed to death with a redness that drowned the purple. As yet this new colour was genial in tone, shone in the sunlight and glowed along the reaches of the fading fern; but a time approached when from ruddy to sere the countless blossoms must sink. Then the light would fade and the flowers wither, till winter winds tinkled in their grey inflorescence and sang the song of another dying year. Now only the splendour of their passing and the pale gold, where brake died in patches amid the standing fern, prophesied changes to come.

A few raddled sheep browsed their morning meal and made harmony with the bright colours of the dawn, while Maynard, stooping, picked up the wing feather of a carrion crow and reflected that this was the last black plume he would ever find to clean his pipe on Dartmoor. He was sorry to leave it, but had found no time for regret until this moment. Life had passed so swiftly and demanded so much thought and contrivance of late, that only now he spared a few minutes to consider all that he was leaving, and how much had been good and precious to him. He had formed a hazy and nebulous picture of his future environment, but knew that it could in no way resemble this. He guessed that he must often look back, and doubted whether his future scene of life would entirely take the place of the one he was about to leave. But he remembered Dinah's attitude and her expressed joy that the Vale should be left behind them and all things become new.

Now he centred upon her and again thin shadows crept through his mind. For good or evil they had listened to their own hearts alone; but he still found questions asking themselves and doubts limning deep in his soul when he thought of her; he still felt a smoulder of indignation in himself that this cup should be forced upon them. There was an ingredient of bitterness, a dumb question why fate should have called him and Dinah to do a thing against which he rebelled, and the doing of which was an outrage upon her love of truth and directness. She might make light of the burden, but he resented the fact that she was called to bear it. Such is the force of inherited conviction and tradition that he could not, as she had done, discredit and dismiss his past as an empty dream. She honestly so regarded Maynard's story; otherwise he knew she would never have come to him; but it was only for his sake that she made the sacrifice, and he felt it a cruel fact that any sacrifice should be called for from her. His past was real enough, and the shadow must fall on her and the children to be born of her. That the world would never see the shadow, or know of its existence, did not matter. For him and his wife it could never vanish. Even yet he did not perceive that no shadow whatever existed for Dinah. The thing that still haunted him like a fog, like the robe of the east wind hanging on the skirts of the moor, must, he felt, be appreciated by her also, and might, indeed, grow more solid and real for her in the future. Regret for the inevitable thus found a place in his mind despite his reason, because it sprang from foundations other than his reason.

Swinging forward with an ash sapling in his right hand and a leathern portmanteau in his left, Lawrence presently saw his goal ahead. Sunshine played over the blue hazes and touched the grey summit of Shepherd's Cross, where the ancient stone stood erect and solitary on the heath. It reared not far distant from rough, broken ground, where Tudor miners had streamed the hillside for tin in Elizabethan days. The relic glimmered with lichens, black and gold and ash colour. Upon its shaft stuck red hairs, where roaming cattle had rubbed themselves. It stood the height of a tall man above the water worn trough at its foot, and the cross was still perfect, with its short, squat arms unbroken, though weathered in all its chamfering by centuries of storm.

Here he sat down, knit his brows to scan the northern slope of the hill, whereon Dinah must presently appear, and wondered how far she might have already tramped upon her way. He had found his own climb from Holne shorter than he imagined and was at their place of meeting before the time.

Then, suddenly, behind him he heard feet shuffling and turned to see five men spring up from their hiding-places at hand. They were familiar faces that he saw, and for a moment no suspicion that they were here upon his account entered the mind of Maynard. It occurred to him that Shepherd's Cross might be a meeting-place for hounds at this early hour. Yet he did not know that cub-hunting was yet begun. And then he marked behind the four now beside him, the tall, thin figure of Arthur Chaffe—one who would certainly attend no meet of hounds.

He was not left long in doubt. The men brought ropes. They closed round him, as he rose to confront them, caught his arms, dragged him to the cross and, with the celerity of executioners, quickly had him fast bound by ankles and wrists against the granite—crucified thereto with his arms extended upon the arms of the cross and a dozen coils of rope about his shoulders, trunk and legs. John Bamsey handled one wrist and saw that his cords bit.

Here was Mr. Chaffe's inspiration; that the erring man should be lifted on the Christian emblem of salvation, for his heart to be taken by storm, and for Dinah to behold the great event. He apprehended a wondrous purification in Maynard as the result of this punishment and he hoped thai he himself might have time to say the necessary words and utter a trumpet note in the sinner's ear before his victim reached Shepherd's Cross.

The men had come by night and hidden as near the tryst as possible. Now they completed their work and stood off, some grinning, some scowling, at the prisoner. His hat had fallen and his ash sapling and his leather bag lay together where he had sat. The light of day shone upon his bare head and he stared at the faces round him, still dazed and silent before the terrific surprise of their attack. But though he said nothing, others spoke freely enough and some chaffed and some derided.

"You didn't think you was going to get chained up this morning, you dirty, runaway dog!" said John Bamsey, while Robert Withycombe laughed.

"You ban't the first thief as have found yourself on a cross—eh, my bold hero? Not but what a cross be almost too holy a sign to rope such a scamp upon."

"You—you that thought you could fox an honest woman and turn her away from an honest man! You wicked lying trash, as ought to have the skin tanned off your bones!" roared John.

But the thunder did not make Maynard shrink. He turned his head to the veteran and spoke.

"What does this mean, Mr. Chaffe?" he asked.

Jerry Withycombe began to answer him, but John took the words out of his mouth. Jerry was too mild for this occasion.

"It means that I happened to find the wrens' nest, and I told about it, and John's sister found 'twas you plotting against Orphan Dinah and——"

"It means that all the world knows you're a married man, you blasted wretch," stormed Johnny. "It means you kindiddled the woman away from me with lies and cunning and thought to get her out of England and ruin her, and then, no doubt, fling her off, like you flung off your lawful wife. It means you're found out for what you are—the scum of the earth. And she's going to know it, and see you where you stand, and hear where your filthy plots and wickedness was going to land her. And if she don't sclow down your face for you when she knows and tear your damned eyes out, she ought to!"

Maynard looked at the furious man, but did not answer. Then Mr. Chaffe intervened.

"That'll do, John Bamsey," he said. "Us have carried out our work in a high spirit so far and we don't want no crooked language."

"Crooked language be the right sort for crooked deeds I reckon," declared Mr. Callicott, the prize-fighter—a sturdy and snake-headed youth who had assisted the others. "If it's true this bloke's married and was going to run away and do bigamy with an innocent girl, then you can't talk too coarse to him, I reckon."

"You're right to be angered, but righteous wrath must keep its temper, Callicott," explained Arthur. "Now hear me talk to the man and show him how it is with him. He be dazed, as you see, and stares through us and looks beyond, as if we was ghosts."

"He knows very well we ban't ghosts," said Jerry.

"You see him," continued Mr. Chaffe, as though he were lecturing on a specimen—"you see him in the first flush of his surprise—gazing out at the risen sun and too much knocked over even to make a case."

"What sort of case should he make—a man that meant to seduce another chap's sweetheart?" asked John Bamsey.

"If he haven't already," suggested Mr. Callicott.

"Hear me, and let him hear me," answered Arthur; and then he turned to Maynard.

"You ask why we have laid in wait for you and done this," he said. "But you know why we have done it only too well, you bad man, and the true wonder in your mind is to guess how we found out. For well you knew that when honest God-fearers were led by Providence to discover what you was up to, they'd stop it in the name of the Lord. Don't stare into the sky, nor yet over the hill for that poor woman, as you meant to destroy body and soul. Just you turn your wits to me, Lawrence Maynard, and listen; and then tell me before God, if you've got any just quarrel with any man among us. And this is what you done—you knowing you was married and had a wife you'd thrown over. You come here and make a woman care for you; but since your watchful Maker has already opened your mouth, so that your master heard you was married, you know you couldn't pretend to wed her honest before men, but must hatch lies for her and make a plot. And her love was quick, no doubt, to think nothing you could do or say was wrong, so she consented to follow you to foreign parts, where her shame might be hid and where she'd be in your power—to cherish or to desert according as your fancy took you. For well you understood that she could never be no more than your leman and at your mercy. That's what you planned, poor man; but God in His might chose different, and willed to give you up to your fellow creatures and led this young Jerry Withycombe to find your secret, so we learned what you was going to do. And it is my work and ordinance that you stand here now tied to the Cross of your Redeemer, Lawrence Maynard. And may the cross enter into your heart and save your soul alive yet. And then you'll see we five Christians be the willing instruments of Heaven, and have put ourselves to this hard task for love of humanity and in the spirit of our Master. We be here, not only to save Dinah, but to save you; and you can say 'Amen' to that, and I hope your Father in Heaven will touch your hard heart to bend and see what we've saved you from."

"In fact you're getting out of it a damned sight softer than you deserve, and a damned sight softer than you would if I had my way," growled Bamsey; but the sailor stopped him.

"Shut up, John, and let Mr. Chaffe talk," he said. "What he tells be very fine, and us must follow his lead and take a high hand with the man."

"We're all sinners," continued Arthur, "and nobody more so than you, John Bamsey, so I'll beg you hold in and let me do my part."

Then he droned on to the roped cowman.

"Evils must come, but woe be to them that bring them, and you've shown me in the past that you're a thinking creature with all your intellects, and now you see where your doubtful thoughts and lawless opinions have brought you. And I hope it will be a case of 'Go and sin no more,' in the words of the Saviour of us all, Maynard. All things go round and round, you must know. The worm gnaws the nettle that the butterfly may rise up into the sunshine; and the butterfly rises up into the sunshine that the worm may gnaw the nettle; but we, as have immortal souls, be called to deny and defy nature, and lead captivity captive, and trample on the adder and the basilisk. All which things you knew very well, yet set your face to add to the evil of the world to please your own base passions. And you didn't care that a young and harmless woman, who was God's business quite as much as you yourself—you didn't care where you dragged her down, so long as you got what you wanted, and defied principalities and powers, and lied to your own better nature just the same as you lied to her."

"The woman be coming," said Robert Withycombe. His sailor's eyes had seen Dinah still far distant. She was clad in a brick-red gown—her best—and carried a basket of yellow, woven cane that made a bright spot on the heath.

"Yes," said Arthur Chaffe. "Like a lamb to the slaughter the virgin cometh, Lawrence Maynard; and I hope 'tis your voice she will hear, telling how God hath watched over her, and how right and religion have won another victory on this glad morning."

But the prisoner preserved an obstinate silence. He seemed to be rapt away out of sight or sound of Mr. Chaffe and the rest. His eyes rested on Dinah; his ears appeared to be sealed for any attention he paid to his captors. Arthur drew his wind and the others spoke.

"He's waiting for her to come," said Mr. Callicott. "He be going to say his say afore the woman and don't care a damn for you, master."

"He'm in a dream," murmured Jerry. "I don't believe he's hearing what Mr. Chaffe be pouring at him."

Then Dinah, who had long seen the group, made haste and dropped her basket and hastened to Maynard, ignoring the rest.

Her face was scarlet and she could hardly speak for the throbbing of her heart.

"Lawrence—Lawrence—what's this?" she asked. "What have they done?"

She had left her home before dawn, unknowing that another was awaking also at Green Hayes and had heard her go. Her last act was to slip into Benjamin Bamsey's room, where he slept alone, and kiss the unconscious old man upon his temple. Then she had gone; and Jane had heard her do so and seen the vague shadow of her descend the garden path and vanish into the farm yard. Mrs. Bamsey was kept in ignorance of Dinah's plans, but when morning came and they sat at breakfast, her daughter informed her of all that had happened and told her that she might expect to see her father's foster-daughter return with Mr. Chaffe in an hour or two. Faith Bamsey took the revelation calmly enough and showed no great emotion; while Jane roamed restlessly through the morning and desired to see Jerry and hear of what had happened on the moor.

Now, in answer to Dinah, Maynard, who was suffering physical pain from his position and his bonds, answered very quietly, while the men round the pair listened to him.

"They have done what they thought was right, Dinah. They found out that we were going to leave England together, and they heard from Mr. Stockman that I was married. And they took a natural view and thought I was deceiving you as to that. So they laid in wait and tied me here, until you heard the truth."

"I know the truth," she said. "I know a deeper truth than any they can know. I know that in God's sight——"

"Stop!" cried Arthur Chaffe. "Listen to me, Orphan Dinah, and thank Heaven on your knees that your fellow creatures have saved you from the evil to come."

She looked at all of them with a flaming indignation.

"Did you set 'em to this dirty task—old as you are? Did you think so badly of this man that you supposed he would try to do me harm? Did you think there was no other side? Did you plot behind his back, when you'd found out our simple secrets? Did you plan this cruel insult and disgrace for one that never harmed you or anybody?"

"He harmed us all, Dinah, and I beg you'll keep your temper," answered Arthur. "You're talking far ways short of sense and you don't know what we saved you from."

"Be you shadows, or real people, you grinning men?" she asked, turning upon the others. "Do you know what you've done in your clumsy, brutal strength? Do you know you've wronged and tortured a man whose boots you ain't worthy to black?"

"Hear the truth and don't be an idiot!" answered John Bamsey.

"'Truth'! What do you know of the truth? You—shallow, know-naught creatures, that go by spoken words and make words stand for truth? It's a lie to say he's wedded. Is every man wedded that's married? Have none of you ever seen married people that never felt or knew the meaning of marriage? 'Tis for pity to the likes of you, beyond the power of understanding, that we took these pains; and now we shan't run away behind your backs, but go before your faces—a parcel of zanies, that think because a thing be said it must be true."

"Let the man speak," said Mr. Chaffe. "I command that you speak, Lawrence Maynard. The woman's beside herself and dead to reason. 'Tis your bounden duty to speak for yourself."

"Loose him then and he'll speak fast enough," cried Dinah. "Who be you—a cowardly, hulking pack of ignorant clods to lay fingers on him! If you had sense and decency and any proper Christianity in you, you'd have gone to work very different and spared me this wicked outrage, and him too. You'd have come to us and bid us speak. What do you make us? Loose him, I tell you—ban't one among you man enough to understand that I know all there is to know about this—that it's my work we're going, my work—me that loves him and worships him, and knows the big-hearted, patient, honourable chap he is. God! If you could see yourselves as I see you—meddling, nasty-minded bullies, you'd sink in the earth. Loose him and then listen to him. You're not worth the second thought of a man like him."

Lawrence spoke quietly to Robert Withycombe.

"You see how it is. Don't keep me trussed here no longer. I'm in pain and no good can come of it. If you care to listen, then I'll speak. I'm very glad to let you know how things are, for you've got a credit for sense; so has Mr. Chaffe."

"It's a free country," said Mr. Callicott, "You chaps seem as if you'd made trouble where there isn't none. Pity you didn't look into this first and play your games after."

He opened a knife to sever the ropes that held Maynard. None attempted to stop him save John, and then the sailor came between.

"Cut him loose, Callicott."

Mr. Chaffe was deeply dismayed and made an effort to save the position.

"Orphan Dinah," he said, "for the love of your Saviour, and your foster-father, and right and religion, come home with me this minute. I can't believe what you say, for you know not what you say. Does the man deny he's married? That's all I want to know; and if he is, then do you mean to tell me you're going to live with him? There it is in brutal words and ——"

"The brutal words are yours, because you're bound up in words and know naught about the truth of what this means, Arthur Chaffe," answered Maynard, who now stood free. "Do you think two people who have set out to share their lives for evermore, didn't count the cost every way? Believe me, we did, so understand that what seems wicked to you, ban't wicked to us. I don't count, but Dinah does. She knows every single word of the truth, and may I die on this stone if she doesn't."

"Come," said Dinah. "We're not called to lay our hearts bare for these men. Let 'em know there's as good and honourable and Christian people in the world as themselves; and if I, knowing far, far deeper than they know, am content and proud to be your wife in God's sight for ever and ever, who else matters, and who else shall judge? You be no more than the buzzing of gnats to us, and there's no power in one of you to sting this man, or me."

"Think, think what you're doing, Dinah," pleaded Mr. Chaffe.

"And haven't I thought, and don't I know a million times more than you can, or ever will? Understand before we go. This man was never false to any woman—never—never. He don't know the meaning of falseness. He never looked at me, John Bamsey, till I'd left you, and I never thought of him till long, long after I was free. And when I loved him, he told me he could not marry me—and why—and I saw that it was moonshine and only a pair of weak, worthless creatures would be frightened and part for that— only cowards feared of their neighbour and the laws—laws that selfish Christians bleat about and want kept, because to torture other people won't hurt their comfort, or cloud their homes. What do you know of marriage— one of you? What do you know of the dark, deadly things that may come between people and separate 'em far as heaven from hell, while parsons and lawyers and old bachelors and old women want 'em chained together to rot—for Christ's sake! Look deeper—look deeper!"

While the men stood silent, Maynard picked up his stick and bag and Dinah's basket.

Mr. Chaffe had sunk upon a stone and was wiping his eyes with a red pocket handkerchief.

"You!" he said. "You brought up in a Christian home by God-fearing people, Dinah!"

"And fear God I always shall; but not man," she answered scornfully. "Did these chaps do this because they feared God? Ask them!"

She took her package from Maynard and he spoke.

"Have no fear that any harm be done to righteousness," he said. "No woman knows her duty to her Maker better than this woman, or her duty to her neighbour. If ever I was in doubt, and I have been, my doubts be cleared afore what you men have done to-day, and I thank you for that. You've shown how paltry it was to doubt, I reckon, and I doubt no more. I be the better and stronger for seeing your minds, you well-meaning chaps! My life and thought and worship belong to Dinah; and where no secrets are hid, there's no blame counted against us, and never will be, I hope."

They turned their backs upon the listeners and went away side by side; they moved among the stones and bushes until they sank out of sight and vanished for ever from that company.

"To hell with them!" said John, "and curse all women for the sake of that blasted woman!"

But the rest did not share his passion. Only Mr. Chaffe mourned; the others were impressed at what they had heard and the prize-fighter was amused.

"A pretty parcel we look," said Callicott, "bested by that calm man and quick-tongued woman. And be damned if I ban't their side. We don't know naught about it, and if we did very like we'd praise 'em for a bit of pluck. Anyway she knows what she's doing all right."

"If the Lord can read their hearts, it evidently don't much matter to them that we can't," declared Robert Withycombe; "and be it as it will, if he was a Turk, or Indian, the man could have two wives and no harm done. And if there's only one Almighty, Mr. Chaffe, why for should He hold it a parlous crime for us to do what a chap across the water can do every day of the week?"

But Arthur Chaffe was too stricken to argue. He stared in great grief after the vanished man and woman.

"My God, why hast Thou forsaken them?" he moaned.

They parted presently and went their different ways, leaving Shepherd's Cross with the sunlight on its face and the severed ropes about its foot.

CHAPTER XXXVIII
RETURN FROM THE HONEYMOON

Though, before the event, Mr. Chaffe had enjoined secrecy in the matter of Lawrence Maynard, yet, since the affair fell out so contrary, none obeyed him. It made a good story, and though many who heard it shared Arthur's concern, none sank into such a deep dejection as he over this trial and failure of faith. Jane Bamsey shared John's indignation that both parties had won their way; while her mother mourned with Mr. Chaffe over Dinah's downfall. For the rest Robert Withycombe and Callicott, the boxer, related their experience in many ears, and more laughed than frowned who heard them.

The attitude of Joe Stockman was defined in a conversation held a week later with Melinda.

She came to Falcon Farm in a condition somewhat nervous, for she had great news for Joe and felt doubtful how he would take it. She had accepted the hand of Harry Ford in marriage and acknowledged to herself that propriety demanded Mr. Stockman should be the first to know her decision.

She brought a bouquet for Susan, who was returning that evening with her husband.

"Everybody's beginning a new life seemingly," said Mrs. Honeysett. "And I was wishful to know your view touching Orphan Dinah, because as you think in that matter, so shall I."

But this diplomacy was wasted.

"No, no—you don't think like what I do—let's have no pretences, Melinda. And as to my late cowman, if the new one ain't so clever with women, he's quite so clever with cows. Chaffe have been up here wringing his hands, and your brother, the sailor, have told me the tale also; and on the whole I dare say it will be all right for Dinah. She come out very clear, so Robert says. They was both in deadly earnest and now they are gone beyond reach of prayers or cusses alike, and I don't wish 'em no harm. If the time had to come again, I'd keep my mouth shut about it. Anyway they'll be married as far as words can marry 'em, when they get to Australia; and if the world thinks you're married, that's all that matters."

"So Mr. Ford says. He's took a pretty large-minded view. In fact nobody don't wish 'em any harm, except Jane Bamsey and her brother."

"And you be going to marry the gardener, Melinda?"

She started.

"I thought you was to be the first, after my family, to hear it, Joe."

"So I was. Robert told me last night."

"I do hope you'll feel kindly to us."

"Red to red—eh? Fire to fire when a red woman marries a red man; because it's well known when red loves red—however, I'm not one to cry danger afore it's in sight. Live and let live is my motto, and never more than now, when my own days be running out so fast."

"Don't say that, Joe."

Mr. Stockman's age had in fact leapt up by a decade since Melinda's refusal to marry him. He now spoke of himself as a man of seventy-five and intended to behave as such, save in the matter of his own small pleasures. He was not really regretful of the situation as it had developed, and knew exceedingly well that he would be more comfortable with Soosie-Toosie than he could have been with a wife. But he intended to get something— indeed, a good deal—out of pending changes, and designed a programme for his son-in-law that embraced more work and larger responsibility. That Thomas would be equal to the coming demands he also felt assured.

Joe spoke of him now.

"We must be reasonable to age. Justice the married pair will be prepared to do me; but damn it, when you be in sight of seventy-five and feel older, along of trial and disappointments, you've a right to a bit more than justice from the rising generation; and I mean to have it."

"Of course you will."

"As to you, I'll be your friend as before, Melinda, and Ford must understand I am so. There's something in me that holds out the hand of friendship again and again until seventy-times seven; and in your case, though it's turning the other cheek to the smiter, still I do it."

"A proper living Christian, as we all know," declared Mrs. Honeysett, much relieved. She talked for some time and presently left, filled with admiration for Joe's sentiments.

Then came home Susan and her husband in the best of spirits, to be gratified in their turn by the amiability of their welcome. They had often debated what form it would take, and forgot that Mr. Stockman had suffered the unexampled experience of being without his daughter for a fortnight.

Both were deeply interested in the story of Lawrence and Dinah; but while Soosie-Toosie ventured to hope that the right thing had happened, Thomas took a contrary opinion.

"Two wrongs don't make a right," he said, "nor yet two hundred. I speak as a man who now knows the dignity of the married state, and I think they've done a very wicked deed and will be punished for it. She's a lost creature in my opinion."

"Why for, Thomas?" asked Mr. Stockman.

"Because marriage be the work of the Lord upon two human hearts," said Mr. Palk; "and when they have clove together by the plan of their Maker, they be one and can no more be set apart by any human contrivance than the growing grain from the young corn. Be God likely to make a mistake and bring two people together unless He knew they was made for each other? 'Tis only our wicked craving for novelty makes us think there's misfits."

"If us all waited till your age, no doubt there wouldn't be so many," admitted Joe, "and so long as the law don't make love a part of marriage, so long there'll be failures. But we must be merciful to circumstances so far as we can. Many marry each other as was never intended to do so by their Creator, and when such wants to part, it may often be that He'd like to see 'em allowed to do so afore the man cuts the woman's throat, or she puts poison in his tea."

"But if marriage wears like ours will, then give God the credit," suggested Mrs. Palk.

"'Tis a magnificent state in my opinion," declared Thomas, "and there'll be no shadow of turning with me and Susan. We be wonderful addicted to each other a'ready."

"Take that woman to Barnstaple," added his wife. "There was a case, father. Her husband left her more'n seven years ago and was thought to have lost his reason and killed himself, which no doubt he did do. She tried her bestest to find the man high and low, but couldn't, and a bit after the seven years were over, Mrs. Courtier called upon the law to say she was free. And the law done so. And she married a publican while we was there, and Mr. and Mrs. Alfred Stockman went to the wedding, for everybody was well content about it. 'Twas a great affair."

"Charity covers a multitude of sins, no doubt," said Thomas, "and charity may cover him and her; but it won't cover their children—not if the Church and the Law can help it."

"The law can't act unless you set it in motion," explained Joe, "and so far as we know, the man's real wife will never hear what he's done."

"And if Mrs. Courtier, why not Maynard?" continued Soosie-Toosie. "And if I'd known of these adventures, I'd have sent the paper to Lawrence—to cheer him up; because he was a good man in his way and wouldn't have done evil to Orphan Dinah, or anybody."